THE ANGRY LAND

LOOK FOR THESE EXCITING WESTERN SERIES FROM
BESTSELLING AUTHORS WILLIAM W. JOHNSTONE AND
J.A. JOHNSTONE

The Mountain Man
Luke Jensen: Bounty Hunter
Brannigan's Land
The Jensen Brand
Smoke Jensen: The Early Years
Preacher and MacCallister
Fort Misery
The Fighting O'Neils
Perley Gates
MacCoole and Boone
Guns of the Vigilantes
Shotgun Johnny
The Chuckwagon Trail
The Jackals
The Slash and Pecos Westerns
The Texas Moonshiners
Stoneface Finnegan Westerns
Ben Savage: Saloon Ranger
The Buck Trammel Westerns
The Death and Texas Westerns
The Hunter Buchanon Westerns
Will Tanner, U.S. Deputy Marshal
Old Cowboys Never Die
Go West, Young Man

Published by Kensington Publishing Corp.

WILLIAM W. JOHNSTONE
AND J.A. JOHNSTONE

THE ANGRY LAND

A SMOKE JENSEN NOVEL
OF THE WEST

PINNACLE BOOKS
Kensington Publishing Corp.
www.kensingtonbooks.com

PINNACLE BOOKS are published by

Kensington Publishing Corp.
900 Third Avenue
New York, NY 10022

PUBLISHER'S NOTE: Following the death of William W. Johnstone, the Johnstone family is working with a carefully selected writer to organize and complete Mr. Johnstone's outlines and many unfinished manuscripts to create additional novels in all of his series like The Last Gunfighter, Mountain Man, and Eagles, among others. This novel was inspired by Mr. Johnstone's superb storytelling.

All Kensington titles, imprints, and distributed lines are available at special quantity discounts for bulk purchases for sales promotion, premiums, fundraising, and educational or institutional use.

Special book excerpts or customized printings can also be created to fit specific needs. For details, write or phone the office of the Kensington Sales Manager: Kensington Publishing Corp., 900 Third Avenue, New York, NY 10022. Attn. Sales Department. Phone: 1-800-221-2647.

PINNACLE BOOKS, the Pinnacle logo, and the WWJ steer head logo Reg U.S. Pat. & TM Off.

First Kensington Books hardcover printing: May 2024
First Pinnacle Books mass market printing: July 2024

ISBN-13: 978-0-7860-5069-7
ISBN-13: 978-0-7860-5070-3 (eBook)

10 9 8 7 6 5 4 3 2 1

Printed in the United States of America

Chapter 1

"Mark my words, that varmint's a killer. You'd better not go anywhere near him."

Sally Jensen smiled in response to the dire warning Pearlie Fontaine, the Sugarloaf Ranch's foreman, had just given her. She tried not to sound condescending as she said, "I've been riding for quite a while, Pearlie. I think I can stick on this bronc, as you or Smoke might say."

"Yeah, if Smoke was here . . ." Pearlie's voice trailed off in an incomprehensible mutter.

"What was that?" Sally asked.

"Nothin', nothin' at all," Pearlie said, shaking his head.

Sally's eyes narrowed as she looked at him. She put a hand on one of the corral poles and said, "Good. I thought I heard something about how if Smoke was here, he'd put me over his knee and tan my bottom, but I was sure you wouldn't say such a thing."

"No, ma'am." Pearlie cleared his throat. "Not at all."

Sally decided she had given him enough trouble. After

all, she was just having some fun with him and didn't want to embarrass him too much. Pearlie was one of the best friends she and Smoke had, and they never would have built the Sugarloaf into the beginnings of a very successful ranch without his help.

Besides, that gray mustang was waiting inside the corral for her, and she was looking forward to taking him down a notch.

One of the other hands had saddled the horse and tied him to the snubbing post. He was green broke and had been ridden several times, including by Pearlie. About to climb over the fence, Sally paused and looked back at the foreman.

"I was watching when you rode him. He didn't give you too much trouble, did he?"

Pearlie snorted. "He knew better'n to do that. But I swear, Miss Sally, I could see the look in his eye. If I'd given him half a chance, he'd have tried to buck me clear to Timbuktu."

"Well, you didn't give him a chance, and neither will I." Sally tried to seem confident and wished she felt as certain as she sounded.

Without waiting for her nerves to get any tighter, she hauled herself up and threw a leg over the fence.

Always a perfect lady in public, today she wore boots, canvas trousers, a man's flannel shirt, and had a broad-brimmed hat pushed down on her dark hair and held in place by a taut chin strap. She and Smoke had started the Sugarloaf by themselves a few years earlier, and from the first day, she had always done her share of riding the range.

Not only that, but it was also part of Sally's nature not to shy away from any challenge. Riding that gray mustang was something she could be proud of. And Smoke would be impressed when he got back from the nearby town of Big Rock, where he was meeting today with the other cattlemen from the valley.

Dust puffed up around Sally's boots when she jumped down from the fence and landed inside the corral. She walked toward the mustang. He turned his head to watch her approach, but didn't seem skittish or upset.

Pearlie pulled himself up the corral fence and perched on the top rail with a worried look on his face.

The cowboy who had saddled the gray, Tom Baxter, said, "Are you sure about this, Miss Sally?"

"Of course. Wait until I get in the saddle, Tom, and then turn him loose."

Baxter hesitated before responding. Sally was the boss's wife, and all the crew respected her for that, as well as for never being afraid of hard work. But Sally saw the glance Baxter threw toward Pearlie and knew that if the foreman said no, he wouldn't obey her orders.

Pearlie gave the cowboy a curt nod, though, indicating that he should let Sally go ahead with what she wanted to do. Baxter said, "Yes, ma'am."

The mustang continued standing there placidly as Sally grasped the saddle horn in both hands, put her left foot in the stirrup, and swung up onto his back. The horse shifted slightly under her weight, but showed no signs of bucking.

"Good boy," Sally said as she settled herself. She lightly stroked the mustang's shoulder.

She took a deep breath and nodded to Baxter. He untied the reins holding the mustang to the snubbing post and handed them to Sally, then backed off toward the fence. She tightened her grip and lifted the reins. She was about to nudge her boot heels against the mustang's flanks when she cast a last glance toward Pearlie on the fence.

She just had time to register the sudden look of alarm on his face before the mustang exploded underneath her.

Smoke Jensen looked around the town hall in Big Rock where the meeting was taking place. More than a dozen ranchers had come to town today to discuss an idea Smoke had come up with.

Sheriff Monte Carson was on hand, as well, but only as an interested observer and friend of Smoke, since he wasn't in the cattle business.

"I want to thank you boys for showing up today," Smoke began. "I know it meant a ride into town and chores you had to postpone, but I hope you'll think the time was well spent."

"I'm always interested in whatever you have to say, Smoke," Wallace Dixon said. "Without you, this valley might not even be settled yet, and Big Rock sure as shootin' wouldn't be here!"

"That's the truth," Carl Featherstone added. "All of us who came along later owe you a mighty big debt."

Smoke shook his head. "Nobody owes me anything. We're all in this together, and we all had a hand in settling the valley and founding Big Rock."

Smoke wasn't the sort of hombre to waste time standing around listening to others sing his praises. But in point of fact, the Sugarloaf had indeed become the first spread in the valley when he and Sally rode in here a few years earlier, not long after their marriage.

A lot had changed since then. A man named Tilden Franklin started a town called Fontana, but the gunmen and outlaws who worked for him ran roughshod over the honest citizens who moved in. There had come a point when the decent folks moved out and started their own town, which they called Big Rock. Eventually, Franklin's crooked, brutal tactics started a war . . . and Smoke ended that conflict with his guns, along with a lot of help from assorted friends and allies.

Those allies included Monte and Pearlie, both of whom had been hired guns working for Franklin before seeing the light and coming over to the side of law and order. Now they were two of the staunchest friends Smoke had.

With Tilden Franklin and his hired killers gone, Fontana had dried up and blown away. More ranchers had moved in, taking advantage of the valley's lush meadows and ample water. The railroad had arrived in Big Rock a year or so earlier . . . and that was why Smoke had called this meeting today.

"Those of you who have been around here for a while remember when we had to drive our herds all the way to Abilene to ship them back east to market," Smoke went on. "That wasn't as long or as rough a drive as ranchers down in Texas had to make to reach the railhead, but it was still a big chore."

Ben Harper, who'd had an outfit in Texas before moving north and west to Colorado, nodded and said, "I made several of those drives up the Chisholm Trail. Wouldn't want to do it again. We always lost men and cattle."

"Since the railroad reached Big Rock, we haven't had to worry about that. We can just drive our cattle to town and ship them right here, and that's what we've been doing. The freight rates are high, though, and can cut pretty deeply into a ranch's profit."

Nods and mutters of agreement came from those gathered in the town hall.

"But that got me to thinking," continued Smoke. "We've all been making deals individually with the railroad to ship our beef. I've heard that spreads in Texas sometimes pool their herds to make the drive to the railhead together. Isn't that right, Ben?"

"It sure is," said Harper. "Those are big herds, but every ranch throws in some men for the crew so there are plenty of cowboys to handle the critters."

"If all of us here in the valley"—Smoke made a surrounding motion with his hands—"gathered our herds together into one big bunch, we might be able to convince the railroad to drop their price per head. The railroad would get a bigger payday all at once, but all of us would wind up with a few extra dollars in our pockets, too."

Featherstone said, "If that worked, the savings could add up to considerable money over time."

"They wouldn't want to risk losing all of our business, so they're bound to go along with the idea," Wallace Dixon said. He slapped his thigh with enthusiasm. "I'll bet a hat they'd agree to the deal!"

"Careful there, Wallace," called one of the other men. "The way you're goin' bald on top, you can't afford to risk losin' your hat!"

That brought laughter from the rest of the group. The middle-aged Dixon grinned, took off his hat, and ran his hand over his thinning hair and shiny dome.

Smoke chuckled, too, and then said, "We wouldn't need a big crew. Each rancher could drive the cows he wants to ship to the holding pens just outside town like they do in Abilene. Once they're loaded onto the cattle cars and headed east, they'd be the railroad's responsibility."

"Well, that's true, but I'm not sure I'd feel comfortable just turnin' my stock over to the railroad with nobody to keep an eye on it until the critters were bought and paid for in Abilene."

Several men spoke up in agreement with Dixon's point.

"I know what you mean," said Smoke. "That's why I figured that if we were to do this, we'd need to appoint somebody trustworthy to represent all of us and just keep an eye on things, as Wallace said, until everything is squared away."

"Now that sounds like a deal," Ben Harper said. "And I know just the man to go along with the cattle and oversee everything. He's standin' up there at the front of the room!"

"Smoke's the man for the job," Carl Featherstone agreed.

Shouts of agreement came from the men.

Monte Carson sidled up next to Smoke and said, "I told you they'd want to put you in charge. That's what you get for coming up with bright ideas."

"I halfway expected as much," Smoke admitted. "I'd be fine with it if somebody else wanted the job, but at the same time, it was my idea, so I guess I ought to take responsibility for it and make sure everything goes like it's supposed to."

The discussion continued for a while longer. Roundup season was already upon them, so each rancher had a good start on gathering a herd suitable for shipping to market. They agreed they could finish their roundups, pool the herds in Big Rock, and have them ready to go within a week.

The small holding pens that already existed would need to be expanded. Some men from each crew could devote themselves to that task while the cattle were being gathered and then driven to town.

In the meantime, Smoke would meet with the railroad officials and negotiate a better price for the cattlemen. Wallace Dixon was selected to give him a hand with this.

"The station manager will likely have to burn up the telegraph wires communicatin' with the district manager back east," Dixon commented. "The fella here in town ain't high enough in the peckin' order to decide that his own self. We ought to have time to get it settled, though, before we have to load those beeves."

Several men suggested shipping rates that would be agreeable to them. Smoke made note of the suggestions and promised that he and Dixon would negotiate the best rate they possibly could. If the plan worked out and the ranchers were able to proceed in this fashion in the future, it would make their spreads more profitable and successful, which would be good for everybody in the valley.

The meeting broke up with handshakes and back slaps all around. Obvious feelings of excitement and anticipation gripped the men as they left the town hall.

Smoke and Monte remained behind. Monte thumbed back his hat and said, "As happy as those fellas are now, they'll be just that mad at you if this doesn't work out, Smoke. You're taking on a big job."

"Won't be the first time," said Smoke. "And I have to admit, the whole thing kind of goes against the grain for me. Except for Preacher and Sally, and then you and Pearlie and Louis, I've been pretty much a loner for most of my life. Even with you boys, we're just good friends. We're not in business together."

"It was your idea," Monte reminded him.

"I know. But I was trying to think of what's best for everybody in the valley."

"You can't look out for everybody else. Those men are

going into this with their eyes wide open. If things don't go to suit them, they won't have any right to blame you, because you'll have done your best to make it pay off."

"That's true." Smoke smiled. "And maybe I'm getting ahead of myself with the worrying. Could be it'll be a smooth-running, profitable operation all around."

"Sure," Monte said as he clapped a hand on Smoke's shoulder. "What could possibly go wrong?"

Chapter 2

The gray mustang bowed its back and went straight up in the air. Sally cried out in surprise, but she clamped her legs around the horse and grabbed the saddle horn with her free hand. The mustang swapped ends in midair, which would have thrown a lot of cowboys, but Sally clung to the saddle like a tick.

The horse came down straight-legged with such force that the impact jarred all the way up Sally's spine and felt like it was going to shake her teeth out by the roots. That didn't happen, of course. She bent forward in the saddle and held tightly to the horn as the mustang arched its back and crow-hopped around the corral.

When that didn't work, the mustang went to straight bucking, again and again and again. Sally's head was thrown back and forth so violently it felt as if it were about to fly right off her shoulders.

She hung on for dear life.

She was barely aware that Pearlie was in the corral

now, along with Tom Baxter. The two cowboys dashed and darted around as they tried to get close enough to grab the gray's harness and bring him under control. They were risking life and limb to do so, but were forced back by the mustang's flashing hooves.

Sally managed to stay on the horse for what seemed like an hour . . . an awful, bone-jarring, stomach-clenching hour. In reality, the ride was almost certainly less than a minute. Not even thirty seconds, actually, Pearlie would inform her later. That mustang packed a whole heap of bucking into a short period of time.

Then it came to an abrupt end as the horse leaped into the air and changed ends again. Sally tried to hang on, but her grip had run out of strength. Although half-stunned by the mustang's frenzy, she still had the presence of mind to kick her feet free of the stirrups as she felt her rear end part company with the saddle leather.

She suddenly found herself in midair, a heart-stopping flight that saw her rise seemingly in slow motion and then slam to the earth with incredible speed. The hard landing knocked all the breath out of her body. Her mind was stunned. She wasn't sure her heart was beating. She wasn't even sure she was still alive.

Then strong hands clamped on her shoulders and pulled her up into a sitting position. She gasped for air. The world spun crazily around her, the corral fence going so fast it was just a blur. The hands gently shook her as a familiar voice said, "Miss Sally. Miss Sally!"

The spinning slowed and the corral fence finally stopped moving. Pearlie's face loomed large in front of her. Eventually, Sally figured out that he was kneeling there, holding her shoulders and staring at her with a mixture of fear and anger on his rugged features.

As her eyes focused on his and he realized she was aware of where and who he was, he burst out, "What the hell!"

It was a measure of how upset he was that he would speak to her like that. Like most western men, he was always courteous, even chivalrous, around women, and doubly so with her since she was his best friend's wife.

She struggled to make her voice work and finally said, "I . . . I'm all right . . . Pearlie. . . ."

"You scared the britches off me, gal!" Clearly, he hadn't regained his composure yet. "I figured you'd break your neck, the way that damn mustang flung you off, and then he acted like he was gonna trample the stuffin' right outta you. . . ."

Pearlie had to stop and take a deep breath. He sounded a little calmer when he went on, "If Tom hadn't grabbed that varmint's reins when he did, you might'a been a goner. I told you that blasted horse was a killer, Miss Sally. I told you!"

She nodded shakily. "You did," she admitted. "I . . . I'm sorry."

"Well, as long as you're all right, I reckon it don't matter." Again he drew in a breath. "And I'm sorry for flyin' off the handle like that. The way I was talkin' to you sure ain't proper."

She summoned up a smile. "It's all right. I'm not insulted. Not even a little bit. You were just worried about me, that's all. And I . . . I should have listened to you and heeded your warning."

It was very difficult for Sally to admit when she was wrong. She just wasn't built that way. But in a situation such as this, the truth was clear as day.

Pearlie must have realized he was still holding her shoulders, because he let go of her like she was a hot stove lid. He straightened and stepped back. His hand went to the butt of the gun holstered on his hip.

"I'm gonna put a bullet through that outlaw hoss's head," he muttered.

"No, don't!" cried Sally. "You can't kill him just because he threw me."

"Seems like a good enough reason to me."

"It's not," Sally insisted. "Especially since you told me not to ride him. Let me ask you this, Pearlie. . . . Can you make a good mount out of him?"

"Well, he's got plenty of sand, that's for sure. A good bronc buster could maybe work the rough edges off him. I ain't sayin' I'd want the job, mind you, but some of the boys might like the challenge."

"Then please, don't shoot him. That would be wasteful." She looked across the corral to where Tom Baxter was standing and holding the mustang's reins. The gray looked utterly peaceful and friendly again. "Besides, I feel like this is somehow my fault. I must have done something to set him off."

"No, ma'am, some critters are just loco part of the time, and you never know when they'll show it." Pearlie took his hand away from his gun. "But I'll do like you say, especially since you don't seem to be badly hurt. We'll give him another chance . . . for now."

"Thank you." Sally smiled. "Now, if you'll help me up . . ."

"You ain't gonna try to ride him again, are you?"

"No, I think I've learned my lesson about that."

Pearlie extended a hand and clasped wrists with her. With very little effort, he pulled her to her feet and then let go of her.

And promptly, Sally screamed and collapsed back to the ground.

During the ride back to the Sugarloaf from Big Rock, Smoke thought about what had happened at the meeting and went over the plan again in his head. Although the chance that something would go wrong always existed, he believed the idea of the ranchers in the valley combining their herds for shipping to Abilene was a solid one that would pay off.

He had discussed it thoroughly with Sally before sending messages to the other cattlemen and asking them to meet with him. As always, she'd been a good sounding board. She was smart and levelheaded and above all honest, so he could count on her to point out any flaws in the plan that he hadn't seen.

She was an enthusiastic supporter of the idea, so he knew it was a good one.

When he came in sight of the ranch house, he spotted someone standing on the porch. Smoke wouldn't have been surprised to see Sally waiting for him, but he could tell the person on the porch wasn't her. As he came closer, he recognized Pearlie.

That put a frown on Smoke's face. Normally at this time of day, Pearlie would be in the barn or out on the range or at least in the bunkhouse. The fact that he stood on the ranch house porch in an obvious attitude of waiting was a good indication something was wrong.

Smoke nudged his horse into a faster gait. He wanted to find out what had happened.

"Howdy, Smoke," Pearlie called as his boss and friend drew rein in front of the porch. He lifted a hand in greeting, and Smoke tried to tell himself that was a good sign. Pearlie wouldn't have wasted time on such a gesture if there was a bad problem.

"What is it?" Smoke asked without returning the greeting.

"Miss Sally's hurt—"

Smoke stiffened in the saddle as his heart slugged hard in his chest. A few years earlier, his first wife, Nicole, and their infant son, Arthur, had been murdered by some of Smoke's enemies. He wasn't sure if he could stand another such shocking loss.

"But she's gonna be all right," Pearlie hurried on, evidently seeing how his words had shaken Smoke. "She twisted her knee pretty bad and can't walk, but nothin's broke and Doc Spaulding says she'll heal up just fine."

Smoke swung down from the saddle and looped his horse's reins around the ring on the hitching post he had positioned near the front steps.

"You say Dr. Spaulding's been here?"

"That's right."

"I didn't run into him on the way out from town."

"Well, you see, that was a stroke of luck," Pearlie explained as Smoke came up onto the porch. "I sent one of the boys to Big Rock to fetch him, but he hadn't gone a mile 'fore he ran right into the doc headin' in this direction. It seems that Doc was called out to the Haskell place to tend to some of Miz Haskell's, uh, female complaints, and he was on his way there already. Pinky Ford, the fella I sent to fetch him, brought him straight back here to tend to Miss Sally. The doc said it sounded like her problem was more urgent than Miz Haskell's. And then when he was done, he just went on about the business he'd had to start with."

That somewhat long-winded explanation made sense,

Smoke decided, but it didn't answer the most important question.

"What happened to Sally? You say her knee's hurt?"

Pearlie cleared his throat. "Yeah, she, uh, she took it in her head to ride that gray mustang, and he bucked her off."

Smoke stared at the foreman for a second before he said, "That mustang's still green broke. He's raw as can be. Sally had no business being on him."

Pearlie slipped his hands into his back pockets and stood a little straighter. He looked Smoke straight in the eye and said, "I told her the same thing. Didn't pussyfoot around about it, neither. But she was bound and determined to do it."

"And you didn't feel like you could stop her?"

"Reckon I'd have had to hog-tie her to do that. Wasn't sure how you'd feel about it if I did. And I ain't totally convinced she wouldn't have shot me if I tried."

For one crazy moment, Smoke wasn't sure whether he was mad or wanted to laugh. Sally wouldn't have shot Pearlie if he'd physically restrained her, of course . . . but he could see how Pearlie might have some doubts about the matter.

A little calmer now, he went on, "Was anything else hurt when she got thrown?"

"Nope. She got the wind knocked out of her when she landed and she was a mite addlepated for a minute, but I thought she was all right. So did she, until I helped her stand up. Then she let out a howl and her right knee went out from under her, and right back down she went. It all happened so fast and there was so much dust in the air, I never got a good look at how she lit down when the gray throwed her. Doc said she must've landed so that knee twisted under her. Could've happened that way, all right."

Smoke took off his hat, raked his fingers through his

short, ash-blond hair. As he put the hat back on, he said, "I'm not happy about this, but I can see how she put you in a bad spot. She gets ideas in her head sometimes, and there's no talking her out of them. But next time she wants to ride a horse she's got no business being on, go ahead and hog-tie her if you have to."

"You best make sure she understands that, too," Pearlie responded dryly.

Smoke laughed. He couldn't help it. He said, "I reckon I'd better go in and visit with her. She'll have heard my horse and figure I'm back."

Sally was sitting up in bed with pillows propped behind her when he reached their room on the second floor. She wore a cotton nightdress, but it was pulled up on the right side to reveal that leg with bandages wrapped thickly around the knee.

"Oh, Smoke," she said as she sat up straighter and acted like she was going to swing her legs out of bed. "I thought I heard you ride up, and then you were talking to Pearlie outside."

He held out a hand to stop her and said sternly, "Just stay where you are. You're hurt."

Sally settled back against the pillows. "It's not that bad. I just twisted my knee. Well, Colton said that I sprained it, but whatever you call it, I'm fine."

Smoke shook his head. "That's not the way I heard it. Pearlie said you let out a pretty good yell when you tried to stand on it. It must've hurt for you to do that."

"It did feel a little like someone had stuck a knife in there and was poking around with it," she admitted. "A red-hot knife, at that. But I got over it and it feels fine now."

Smoke saw her eyelids drooping a little and asked, "Did the doctor happen to give you something to help with the pain?"

"Yesss," Sally said slowly, "and he said it might make me a little drowsy. . . ."

"That's why it doesn't hurt now." Smoke sat down on the bed's edge. "I've known cowboys who were thrown from horses and injured their knees, and they never really got over it. They hobbled around the rest of their days, especially when they tried to rush things."

"This is nothing like that," Sally insisted. "The doctor just said for me to rest and stay off it as much as possible for the next few weeks. I think he's just being overly cautious, though. As long as I use crutches, I ought to be up and around in a day or two—"

"No, you won't. We're going to do exactly what Dr. Spaulding says." Smoke smiled. "I'm not taking any chances on you not being able to dance with me at all the town socials from now on." He grew more serious. "What in the world made you think you ought to ride that loco gray mustang?"

"He's such a pretty horse. I thought maybe I could make him one of my regular saddle mounts. I knew from watching the men work with him that he's high-spirited—"

"Crazy is more like it," Smoke said.

"I think you're all being too hard on him. With time and patience, I believe he'll be a fine horse."

Smoke wasn't going to waste his breath arguing with her. He put his hand on her shoulder, leaned closer, and kissed her for a moment.

"Don't worry about it," he told her. "We can see about all of that later. For now, you just do like the doctor said and rest, so that you can get back to normal as soon as possible. I'll be right here to take care of you."

"Oh, Smoke, you don't have to do that. I know you have other things to do. . . ."

She was having trouble now keeping her eyes open, he

could tell. He shifted his position, slipped an arm around her shoulders, and let her lean against him.

"Just rest," he said again. "I'm not going anywhere."

And as she snuggled against his side, he thought about what he had just promised and what it meant.

He wasn't going to be able to take that herd to Abilene after all.

Chapter 3

"Don't you worry about a thing, Smoke," said Wallace Dixon. "I'll get those beeves to Abilene and get a good price for them."

Dixon and Smoke were in Smoke's office on the ranch house's first floor. It was late afternoon. Smoke had sent Pinky Ford over to Dixon's ranch with a note asking the cattleman to pay a visit to the Sugarloaf.

Knowing Smoke wouldn't have made that request without a good reason, Dixon had saddled up immediately and returned with Pinky.

Now the two ranchers sat with cups of strong coffee, Smoke behind the desk and Dixon in the comfortable leather chair in front of it. Smoke had explained about Sally's injury and informed Dixon that he wouldn't be able to take charge of the combined herd and deliver it to Abilene.

"Of course, it could be that I'm gettin' a mite ahead of myself," Dixon went on after taking a sip of the potent black brew in his cup. "Maybe you didn't figure on askin' me to take over. If that's the case, I'd be plumb happy to suggest one of the other fellas—"

Smoke held up a hand to stop him. "I'd trust any of the men who were at that meeting, Wallace, but there are none of them I'd trust more than you. We were already going to work together on negotiating with the railroad. I know you can do that and deal with the buyers once the cattle are in Abilene."

"I appreciate the faith you're showin' in me. We haven't known each other that awful long."

"I like to think I'm a pretty good judge of character," Smoke said with a smile.

"If it's all right with you, after I've talked things over with the railroad, I'll ride out here and let you know where things stand before I make a final deal with them."

"That's fine if that's what you want to do, Wallace, but you don't have to. I'm dumping this in your lap, after all. I won't have any right to complain about any decisions you make."

"I'm just glad I can help out. You say Mrs. Jensen is gonna be all right?"

"That's what the doctor thinks, and Colton Spaulding is pretty smart." Smoke chuckled. "She's upstairs resting right now. The doctor gave her something to help her sleep. But I'm sure when she wakes up, she'll feel like she's fine and ought to be up and around again. That's why I don't want to leave her for the next couple of weeks. My wife can be a mite . . . stubborn, let's say. Even headstrong."

"Persistent," said Dixon. "That's a good quality, I reckon."

"Yes, but only when appropriate. I think the world and all of Pearlie. He'd charge hell with a bucket of water if I asked him to. But I'm not sure he's really equipped to handle Sally. He's too much of a gentleman."

"But you, bein' married to her, can lay down the law if you need to. Is that what you're thinkin'?"

"Well . . . within reason," Smoke allowed.

Both men laughed and then finished their coffee. Dixon leaned forward, set his empty cup on the desk, and said, "I'll need to take a couple of fellas along with me on the train to help me keep up with that livestock. How about a member of my crew and one of your boys from the Sugarloaf? That way we'll have two spreads represented."

"That's a good idea," agreed Smoke. "And I know just who it should be from my crew. Pinky Ford, the cowboy I sent to fetch you, has been itching for more responsibility, and he's shown me enough that I think he can handle it. How about taking him along with you?"

"If you vouch for him, that's plenty good enough for me, Smoke."

Both men rose to their feet and reached across the desk to shake hands. Dixon said, "Give my best to Mrs. Jensen. I hope she feels a whole heap better soon."

Then he left the Sugarloaf to head back to his ranch. Smoke watched him ride away and felt confident that he had made the right decision about how to handle this troublesome situation.

Gangling, sandy-haired Pinky Ford's actual front handle was Hobart, a name he disliked intensely. He'd been called Hobie growing up, but when he'd signed on to ride for the Sugarloaf, the first time he'd gone out on the range he'd been wearing a faded red bandanna around his neck, a token of the affections of a gal he'd courted over in Kansas. Without hesitation, the other boys had dubbed him Pinky, and the name had stuck.

Over the next week, he became Smoke's liaison to the

effort of pooling the valley's herds. He rode around to the various ranches to check on how their roundups were going, he carried news from Wallace Dixon about the negotiations with the railroad, and he checked on the progress of expanding the holding pens on the outskirts of Big Rock. The pens were just east of the settlement, so the eastbound train that would carry the cattle could make its regular stop at the depot in town, then travel on a short distance and stop again so the livestock could be loaded.

Meanwhile, on the Sugarloaf, Sally lived up to Smoke's prediction and tried to say she was fine to get up and walk around the next day after the gray mustang had thrown her. Smoke could tell from the look in her eyes that her knee still hurt, but she was too stubborn to give in to that or even admit it. She insisted that it didn't hurt at all.

A part of him wanted to let her get up and try to walk, just so she could see how wrong she was. But he wasn't going to take a chance on her injuring herself even more, so he didn't back down.

He knew better than to forbid her to get up, though. That would just prod her to do it out of sheer stubbornness. He knew he couldn't tie her to the bed, either, because she would never forgive him for that.

Instead he asked her, for his benefit, to follow the doctor's orders and not try to rush her recovery. He talked about how lost he was without her being up and around and how he needed her to get well so she could take care of him as she usually did.

He knew she was smart enough to realize that was just a ploy to get her to cooperate. She even said, "I have to give you credit for that helpless act, Smoke. You're just about the most unhelpless man I've ever met."

"I don't know what you're talking about," he said, shaking his head. "All I know is that the place sure doesn't run as well without you being up and around. Why, if you were to damage that knee even more and couldn't get up for a month, I'm not sure the Sugarloaf could survive!"

"I don't know whether to laugh or throw something at you . . . so I guess I might as well laugh." She did so as she leaned back against the pillows propped behind her. "All right, when I have to get up, I'll use crutches, but I'll rest as much as possible until Dr. Spaulding says my knee is healed . . . but not one second longer, understand?"

"Fine by me," said Smoke, smiling.

Sally wasn't always that cooperative in the days that passed, but for the most part, she kept her word and didn't try to get up any more than was absolutely necessary. When she did, he made sure she used the crutches he made for her, and he stayed close to her in case she needed help, too. Smoke only had to admonish her a few times about pushing herself too hard.

Of course, he had to leave her alone some of the time, so he couldn't be certain she was being careful, but she seemed to be getting better, so he figured she was behaving herself most of the time.

Pinky reported that several of the spreads in the valley were moving their herds toward Big Rock. The holding pens were filling up, including the new ones. Wallace Dixon had struck a bargain with the railroad that would save the ranchers quite a bit, especially over time. Smoke enthusiastically agreed with the proposal when Pinky relayed the details from Dixon.

"Have you ever been to Abilene, Pinky?" Smoke asked the youngster.

"No, sir, I haven't. I reckon Big Rock is the biggest town I ever set foot in." Pinky grinned. "I hear that Abilene's a pretty rip-roarin' place, though."

"You'd best be careful over there," Smoke warned him. "I don't know who the marshal is now that Bill Hickok's moved on, but Abilene has a reputation for lawmen who don't put up with a lot of shenanigans. All those Texas cowboys coming up the trail have toughened them up, I suppose."

"I don't reckon Mr. Dixon will let me get into too much trouble. He's takin' along an old hand of his, Bill Caldwell, and Bill's a pretty solid fella, not the sort to roust around much. I'm sure he'll keep me in line, too."

Smoke nodded. "I know Caldwell. Good man. You just keep your eyes open on this trip, Pinky. You can learn a lot from the men you'll be traveling with."

"Maybe," Pinky allowed. "I figure I've already learned a lot just workin' on the Sugarloaf with you and Pearlie and the rest of the boys, Mr. Jensen."

When Smoke took Sally's breakfast tray up to the bedroom on the morning the cattle were scheduled to be loaded on the train and shipped east, she said, "Don't you want to be there to see them off and make sure everything goes smoothly?"

"I wouldn't have minded," he admitted, "but it's more important that I stay here and take care of you. Besides, Pearlie ramrodded the drive to town and will be there to keep an eye on things, so I'm sure it'll all go just fine."

"I have an idea how you can go. Take me with you."

Smoke raised an eyebrow in surprise and opened his mouth to tell her that wouldn't be a good idea, but before he could say anything, she went on, "Hear me out, Smoke. You don't want me walking, right?"

"That's right. The doctor said you were to stay off that leg as much as possible for another week."

"Then I won't walk. It's as simple as that. You can fix up a place for me in the wagon and then carry me downstairs. Unless you think I'd be too much of a burden . . ."

"Not hardly." Smoke's shoulders were unusually broad, a good indicator of how much strength he packed into his body. He'd never had any trouble picking up Sally when he needed to . . . or when he just wanted to.

"I wouldn't mind being on hand for the departure myself," she went on. "The Sugarloaf is my ranch, too, you know, and if this new way of doing things works out, it could be important to the ranch's future."

"That makes sense," Smoke said. "I could fix things up in the back of the wagon so you'd have a good place to sit, and if we packed in plenty of pillows around you, seems like your leg would be just as safe and stable as it is here in bed."

"That's what I thought. Now, why don't you leave that tray and go get ready for the trip?"

He grinned. Sally was going to get her way . . . but there was nothing new or unusual about that.

The eastbound train was due at midmorning. Smoke and Sally reached Big Rock well before that. Smoke had prepared the back of the wagon by placing a mattress, some boxes, and a lot of pillows and blankets in there, arranging them so that Sally was able to sit with her legs stretched out comfortably in front of her. After placing her gently in the makeshift nest, he climbed to the seat and took up the reins. The wagon rolled at a gentle, easy pace toward the settlement.

Quite a crowd had gathered near the holding pens to observe what folks in the valley hoped would prove to be a momentous occasion, the start of something that would make the cattle business even more successful.

Once Smoke had brought the wagon to a stop far enough away from the tracks that Sally wouldn't have to worry about cinders, Monte Carson and Louis Longmont came over to say hello. Like Monte, Louis had once been a hired gun as well as a gambler, but he had put that part of his life behind him. He was now the owner of Longmont's, a combination saloon and restaurant that was the nicest place in Big Rock. He still enjoyed a friendly game of cards—and a more serious, high stakes contest from time to time—but his days of hiring out his Colt were over.

"Morning, Sally," Monte said as he pinched his hat brim and nodded to her. "I was mighty sorry to hear that you'd been hurt."

"As was I," said Louis, removing his hat completely. "I trust you're well on the road to recovery?"

"I think so, but Smoke's still treating me like a porcelain doll."

"You're prettier than any doll I ever saw," Smoke said.

"I'm not sure flattery has any medicinal value," she told him, "but I don't suppose it hurts to try."

Monte gestured toward the holding pens, which were packed full of cattle, and said, "Mighty big day today, eh? That's a lot of beef on the hoof."

"A big gamble on the part of all the ranchers in the valley, you mean," said Louis. "Some of them have committed just about all the cows they plan to market this year to the effort. If anything were to go wrong, it would be a terrible blow to the whole area."

"Nothing's going to go wrong," Smoke said. "Wallace Dixon is in charge. He's a good man and will take care of everything."

Louis nodded and said, "He's a good man, I agree about that. I might have sent Pearlie, if it were me."

"Don't think I didn't consider it. But it seemed like one of the owners ought to go along with the cows, and Dixon's well-liked and respected by everybody in these parts."

"Yes, of course. I'm sure he'll do fine."

Smoke felt unease stirring inside him. Louis hadn't

meant anything by his comment; Smoke knew that. It was just starting to bother him a little that he wasn't going along himself. It had been his idea, after all.

He wasn't the brooding type, though, and he didn't have time for that, anyway, because at that moment the train's whistle sounded shrilly in the distance. The east-bound was approaching Big Rock. In less than a half hour, it would be stopped next to the holding pens and cows would be driven through the loading chutes into the cars.

Pearlie rode over and grinned as he reined in. "You ready to get these critters on their way, Smoke?" he asked.

"More than ready," Smoke replied.

A short time later, the massive locomotive with its diamond-shaped stack rolled slowly along the steel rails, passing the holding pens and easing to a stop so that the first of the long line of cattle cars was next to the loading chute. A railroad worker hopped down from the grab bars he'd been hanging on to and rolled the big door on the side of the car open.

Loading cattle into boxcars was loud, dusty, dangerous work, but all the cowboys here today had done it before and knew what they were doing. They worked hard, whether they were on horseback or afoot, whether they were slapping coiled lassos on cows' rumps or wielding the long poles used by some of the men to prod the beasts through the loading chutes. Some folks had started calling the men who did that particular job cowpokes.

Noise and dust haze hung over the pens and the train as the task continued for several hours. Most of the crowd drifted away, bored after a fairly short time. Smoke offered to take Sally home, but she tied a scarf around her nose and mouth to help with the smell and the dust and shook her head.

"I'm fine," she said. "We'll stay until it's done. This is part of ranch work, and—"

"The Sugarloaf is your ranch, too," Smoke finished for her.

She glared at him for a second, then laughed. "That's right."

Finally, all the cattle were loaded. Wallace Dixon, Bill Caldwell, and Pinky Ford rode over to the wagon. The men pinched their hat brims and greeted Sally with polite nods, then Dixon said, "That's it, Smoke. We're ready to roll, I reckon. Ought to be in Abilene by tomorrow morning." He shook his head. "Sure a lot faster than driving those hardheaded critters on horseback all that way."

"The railroad has changed the cattle business, all right," Smoke agreed. From the wagon seat, he extended his hand. "Thanks again for taking over this job, Wallace."

"My pleasure," said the older man as he clasped Smoke's hand. "We'll take good care of 'em."

"I know you will." Smoke shook hands with Caldwell and Pinky, too, and wished them luck. He added to Pinky, "Be careful in Abilene."

"Don't worry, Mr. Jensen," Caldwell said. "I'll look after the sprout."

Pinky just grinned.

As Smoke watched the three men ride off, Sally said, "You wish you were going with those cattle, don't you?"

Smoke didn't really answer the question. He said, "I'm sure Wallace and those two fellas will do just fine."

Chapter 4

Bill Caldwell was a solidly built man of medium height, with dark hair and a permanent nut-brown tan on his face from working outside all his life. Pinky enjoyed talking to him. Caldwell had ridden for quite a few different spreads in various parts of the country. He had some good stories to tell, although he was taciturn by nature and Pinky had to work to draw those yarns out of him as they sat facing each other on hard wooden benches in one of the passenger cars. Wallace Dixon sat across the aisle, smoking cigars and reading a book he had brought along with him.

It was late afternoon, not long until sunset, when Caldwell, in the forward-facing seat, nodded toward the window and said, "Looks like we've done crossed the state line. We're in Kansas now."

"How in the world can you tell that?" Pinky wanted to know. He leaned forward and stared out the window at the flat, grassy plains rolling by. "It all looks the same to me, and has for miles and miles!"

"When you've traipsed around the frontier as much as I have, you get a feelin' for where you are," Caldwell explained. "The landscape here in Kansas is just a tad bit flatter than it is farther west over the Colorado line."

Pinky had a feeling that Caldwell might be making that up, but he didn't challenge the older cowboy's word. He'd been raised to respect his elders and learn everything from them that he could. He wanted this journey to be educational.

Across the aisle, Dixon closed his book. "Reckon I'll walk on back and make sure those cows are doin' all right."

"They're fine, boss," Caldwell said. "Shut up in those cattle cars like that, there ain't nowhere they can go. And you know the cars are still there, because nobody could cut 'em loose without us knowin'."

"I suppose you're right about that, Bill," Dixon admitted, "but I think I'll stretch my legs anyway."

"Back where you can take a look at the first cattle car in the string?"

"Maybe," Dixon said with a grin. He set the book aside, stood up, and ambled toward the door at the rear of the car.

"Should we go with him?" asked Pinky.

"He didn't invite us along for our company, did he?"

"No, I reckon not."

"Here's another thing you ought to take note of," said Caldwell. "When the boss wants to do somethin', you don't argue overmuch with him."

"That makes sense. I don't ever argue with Mr. Jensen."

"Unless," Caldwell went on, "you got a mighty good reason to object. I'll let you in on something, kid. Even the smartest man makes a mistake ever' now and then. If you see your boss about to do somethin' you know is gonna backfire and cause harm to him, it's your duty as somebody who rides for the brand to speak up. It might not work. It might even backfire on *you*. But you'll know you done everything you could to help, no matter how it turns out."

"That makes sense," Pinky said. "I'll remember that, Bill. But at the same time, I hope I'm never put in a position where I have to tell my boss he's makin' a mistake."

"Ridin' for Smoke Jensen, there's at least a chance of that, kid. Probably a good chance."

Caldwell sat back, took the makin's from his pocket, and began rolling a quirley. Pinky, who didn't have nearly as much experience at that task, pulled out his own tobacco pouch and packet of papers and followed suit. He tried to watch what Caldwell did and imitate him without being obvious about it. He hoped that someday he would be as good a cowboy as the older man.

Outside, the Kansas plains continued to roll past, awash in reddish-gold light now as the sun sank in the west, somewhere beyond the point where the steel rails dwindled and disappeared.

In the locomotive's cab, Lee Griffith, the engineer, and Andy Powers, the fireman, went about their tasks with the easy efficiency of long experience. Both men had worked for the railroad for quite a while, and they had been teamed on this particular run for almost a year. Their homes were in Abilene, where a new crew would take over when the train reached that point early the next morning. Griffith was married, with a couple of half-grown kids. Powers was an old bachelor, too set in his ways to ever get hitched.

A locomotive cab was no place for idle chitchat. Between the roaring flames in the firebox, the engine's rumble, and the clatter of wheels on steel rails, the racket was loud enough that a man could hardly hear himself think, let alone carry on a conversation other than the necessary communication between engineer and fireman. So it was a good thing the two men were old friends and didn't really need to talk to be comfortable with each other.

Powers had been leaning out the window on the cab's left side, watching the scenery in the gathering dusk since the fire didn't need stoking at the moment. He leaned out a little farther and frowned as something up ahead caught his eye. Then he stepped across the cab to Griffith's side and tapped the engineer, who was checking the locomotive's gauges, on the shoulder.

"I think I saw something up ahead on the tracks," Powers said, raising his voice so Griffith could hear him over the normal clamor.

"What?"

"I think I saw something—"

"I heard that part. What is it?"

"Don't know. Couldn't tell. But something."

Griffith frowned, too, and leaned out the window on his side to study the tracks in front of them.

"You're right," he said. "Can't tell what it is, just something dark blocking the tracks."

He reached for the throttle to slow the train while Powers went back to the other side and hung his head out again. Powers yelped in surprise as a crimson flower suddenly bloomed in the gathering darkness.

"Whatever it is, it's burnin'!" he yelled to Griffith.

Grimacing, Griffith hauled back harder on the throttle and then grabbed the lever for the emergency brake, throwing it on as well. The entire train lurched violently as it began to slow. Sparks flew out in glittering showers from the wheels as the brakes clamped on the rails.

Wallace Dixon stood on the platform at the rear of the last passenger car. A few yards away, across the coupling, was the front end of the first cattle car. The long line of them jolted over the joints in the rails, causing the familiar *bump-bump-bump* that could lull a man into sleep if he let it.

Dixon wasn't drowsy at the moment. He was still too excited about this trip. He didn't want to let his friends and neighbors down. Like Smoke, Dixon hadn't shipped all the cattle from his ranch that were ready for market. This was more of a trial run for him. But some of the smaller spreads had thrown everything they had into the effort and were counting on a good return for their continued survival.

Taking a cigar from his shirt pocket, Dixon clamped the cheroot between his teeth and fished out a match. He snapped the lucifer to life with his thumbnail and held the flame to the cigar's tip. He had just puffed the cheroot alight when the platform jerked wildly under his feet with no warning.

That jolt threw him hard against the door behind him. The cigar fell from his mouth, bounced, and rolled off the platform. Dixon rebounded from the impact, stumbled, lost his balance, and had to grab the railing around the platform's outer edge to keep from falling. When he got his feet solidly underneath him again, he continued to grip the railing as he leaned over it and peered toward the front of the train.

Smoke and cinders from the locomotive's stack streamed alongside the train and stung Dixon's eyes. He squinted and caught a glimpse of something burning up ahead. Was the fire blocking the tracks? It had to be, judging by the way the train was slowing down so abruptly.

There was only one reason somebody would start a fire on the tracks. They were trying to stop the train.

And that meant a holdup.

Dixon jerked the door open and ran into the passenger car, figuring he'd better rejoin the two cowboys.

They were going to have some outlaws to fight off.

"You should keep going!" Powers yelled at Griffith up in the cab. "Bust through whatever that is burnin'!"

"Can't!" Griffith shouted back at the fireman. "It might derail us!"

"There's nothin' big enough out here on the prairie to derail us! It's gotta be brush!"

Griffith stared at him for a second, then burst out, "By Godfrey, you're right!"

He lunged for the levers, disengaging the brake and throwing the throttle open again.

The train had already slowed quite a bit and would need some time to build up speed again. Even so, it still had enough momentum for the cowcatcher on the front of the locomotive to smash through any barrier not made of heavy logs. And as Powers had pointed out, no trees big enough to provide such logs grew out here in this region.

Neither man had ever had to deal with a train robbery before, so Griffith's impulse to slow down had been based on instinct, not experience. He was glad Powers had pointed out his mistake. They still had a chance to thwart the plans of the would-be robbers.

That chance disappeared abruptly as a man on a galloping horse suddenly appeared beside the cab. Running flat out, the horse was able to match the train's diminished speed. The rider left the saddle in a daring leap that carried him to the edge of the cab's floor. He caught the side of the opening and yanked himself inside.

Powers yelled a warning and lifted his shovel as the intruder palmed a gun from its holster. The man attacked swiftly and savagely, crashing the barrel down on Griffith's head. The engineer's cap blunted the blow's force somewhat, but it was enough to drive Griffith to his knees.

Powers struck with the shovel at the gunman, who twisted aside at the last second and took the hit on his left shoulder. He had avoided the shovel's full impact, but it knocked him back a step anyway.

Before Powers could try to strike him again, the man lifted the gun and fired. In the cab's close confines, the tongue of flame that licked from the revolver's muzzle reached out and scorched the front of Powers's work shirt and overalls.

The heavy slug smashed into the fireman's chest and drove him backward. His eyes went wide with pain and shock. He dropped the shovel and it landed on the floor with a clang. As Powers reeled back, he reached the edge of the floor and toppled out of the cab, with barely time for a yell before he was gone.

The gunman swung the Colt around to cover the stunned engineer. Displaying some familiarity with the train's controls, the man used his other hand to close the throttle and throw the brake on again.

Then as the train once more began jerking and shuddering to a halt, he said to Griffith, "Don't do anything stupid, mister, and maybe you won't die like your friend."

The first jolt had almost thrown Pinky Ford off the bench seat onto the floor. He caught himself and said, "What the hell!"

"Somethin' wrong with the train," said Bill Caldwell. He had jerked forward and kept himself from falling by grabbing the bench where Pinky sat. He came to his feet and stood with his boots well-braced and far enough apart to compensate for the swaying that gripped the train.

Pinky was up, too, looking around wildly. "Are we gonna crash?"

"Damned if I know, kid."

Chaos filled the car as men shouted curses and questions, women screamed, and children sobbed in fear. The train continued to rock along, but Pinky could tell it was slowing down.

"Train robbers!" he said as the thought occurred to him. "I'll bet you anything, Bill. Outlaws are fixin' to rob the train!"

Caldwell reached down to the Colt revolver on his hip and wrapped his right hand around the gun's plain walnut grips. "They're liable to get more than they bargained for if they do."

"We got to find Mr. Dixon."

Caldwell nodded. "Yeah, come on. We'll head back toward them cattle cars."

Yelling men clogged the aisle. Pinky and Caldwell shoved through the press toward the rear of the car. The train continued to slow, then without warning, it jerked heavily again and Pinky would have sworn it started picking up speed.

What in the blazes was going on?

They hadn't quite reached the door at the rear of the car when Wallace Dixon flung it back and charged through the opening.

"Robbers are tryin' to stop the train!" he shouted, the same conclusion that Pinky and Caldwell had come to already.

"What do we do, boss?" asked Caldwell.

"They'll probably try to take over the engine." Dixon drew his gun. "Let's get up there and ventilate the skunks!"

Caldwell pulled his iron as well. With Dixon in the lead, the three men began pushing their way forward along the crowded aisle. Since Dixon and Caldwell both had guns in their hands, folks were quicker to get out of their way this time.

As Pinky brought up the rear, he hoped that nobody took *them* for train robbers and tried to shoot them. The way his two companions were waving guns around, that could happen.

He wished, too, that Smoke was here. He admired both Dixon and Caldwell, but Smoke Jensen was on a whole other level when it came to handling gun trouble.

They had reached the forward platform of this car when Pinky felt the train slowing down again. Somebody up there in the cab couldn't make up his mind.

Then, over the screech of steel on steel, a swift rata-plan of hoofbeats sounded somewhere close by. Half a dozen men on horseback swept up on the right side of the train, and as they drew alongside the platform where Pinky, Dixon, and Caldwell had paused in surprise, the riders opened fire.

Gun thunder crashed as a line of muzzle flashes split the evening shadows. Bullets swarmed around the three men on the platform. The whining buzz reminded Pinky of the time he had blundered into a hornet's nest when he was a kid. These slugs packed a much deadlier sting than those angry hornets, though.

He dropped to a knee and yanked his gun from its holster, fumbling a little but managing not to drop it. The revolver was a single-action .45. Pinky thumbed the hammer back as he raised the weapon. He tried not to pay attention to how badly his hand was shaking. He pointed the gun at the riders racing alongside the train and pulled the trigger.

The gun roared and bucked against his palm, then the next instant, what felt like a giant hand punched him in the chest. He lost his balance, went backward, and sat down hard. The gun he clutched in his fist suddenly seemed a lot heavier. Gritting his teeth with the effort, he brought it up anyway and got the hammer eared back again. As Pinky fired his second shot, Bill Caldwell crumpled to the platform beside him. The front of Caldwell's shirt was dark with blood.

So was the white shirt Wallace Dixon wore under his suit coat. Dixon leaned against the railing and clung to it with his left hand as he fired at the outlaws. Pinky could tell the older man was hit hard, but Dixon stubbornly continued to fight.

Until a bullet struck him in the head and dropped him like a stone. Dixon didn't move again.

That just left Pinky. He braced his left hand against the platform's planking to keep himself from collapsing and thrust out the gun in his right hand. Yelling incoherently, he triggered one more round, never knowing if any of his bullets found their targets.

Then he felt another terrific impact, this time against the side of his head. He was aware of the gun slipping from his fingers, but that was the last thing he knew before darkness took him.

The burning barrier on the tracks had indeed been constructed of brush, just as Andy Powers suggested. The train was still going fast enough that the cowcatcher on the front of the engine smashed through it easily, scattering burning brands for several yards on both sides of the tracks.

The engine traveled another hundred yards before finally shuddering to a halt.

Lee Griffith's head was spinning from the wallop he'd gotten. The outlaw who had killed Andy Powers and stopped the train was still in the cab, keeping Griffith covered. He didn't make a move to interfere, though, as the engineer pulled himself up from the floor and peered fuzzily along the tracks.

What seemed like dozens of riders swarmed around the train. Griffith expected them to blast their way into the express car, but instead, they concentrated their activities around the cattle cars.

It was hard for Griffith to believe what he was seeing. Some outlaws dismounted, got a ramp from somewhere, put it in place at the first cattle car, rolled the door back, and hazed the animals out. Men on horseback were ready to drive them away from the tracks, and as that operation was repeated over and over, they formed up a herd.

Meanwhile, other outlaws wearing bandanna masks over the lower halves of their faces took over the passenger cars, kept everybody under control, and collected whatever valuables the passengers had.

Even though Griffith had never been through a robbery before, he had heard a number of his fellow railroaders talking about them. Train robbers were usually after express shipments and loot from the passengers. They never bothered with livestock! True, this was a particularly large shipment of cattle and would be worth quite a bit if the thieves had a ready market, but it still seemed loco to Griffith.

As night fell, however, it became obvious that rustling was exactly what they were doing and even seemed to be their main objective, although they weren't going to pass up any other loot they could get their hands on.

The outlaw in the cab must have gotten some sort of signal Griffith didn't see. He said, "You've still got some steam up, mister. You can get out of here now. Go on to Abilene."

"But . . . but Andy . . ."

"Was that your fireman's name? Don't waste time worrying about him. He's done for. Didn't give me any choice but to drill him, the stubborn little fool. Anyway, once he walloped me with that shovel, I wasn't gonna let him get away with that." The outlaw moved to the edge of the cab and motioned with his gun barrel. "Get to the controls and move on out, I said. Or I can kill you, too, and tie the throttle down before I hop out of here."

That would lead to a runaway and an eventual crash, more than likely. Griffith couldn't allow that to happen. He still had a responsibility to the passengers. Groggily, he moved to the controls, disengaged the brake, and slowly opened the throttle. With a slight jolt, the train lurched into motion.

When Griffith glanced over his shoulder, he saw that the outlaw was gone. The masked man must have jumped out and disappeared into the night. He was probably on a horse by now, joining his friends as they drove their stolen herd away into the darkness.

Griffith swallowed hard and wondered if they had killed anybody else besides Andy Powers.

Chapter 5

Sally had tried to persuade Smoke that she could get around all right with the help of a cane, but he had insisted on waiting until Dr. Colton Spaulding made one of his regular visits to the ranch to check on her so he could get the doctor's opinion. Spaulding had been by the Sugarloaf this morning, driving up bright and early in his buggy, and Sally had asked him about a cane as soon as he came into the bedroom.

"We already have a good cane," she had said. "Smoke used it a few years ago when he hurt his leg."

She didn't mention the injury to Smoke's leg had involved getting shot. The doctor probably remembered that occasion.

"It's all right if you want to give it a try," Spaulding had said. "Let me see how you do with it."

After Sally had demonstrated that she could get around all right with the cane, Spaulding gave his approval.

"Just don't try to do too much at a time," he had cautioned her. "That knee will get tired very easily, and you still need more rest than anything else. I don't think you still have to be confined to that bed all the time, though."

She had given Smoke a smile of triumph.

Sally was still smiling as Smoke helped her down the stairs and out onto the front porch at midday. She had the cane in her left hand and her right arm was looped in his left arm. Supported on both sides that way, she had little trouble reaching one of the rocking chairs. She sighed as Smoke helped her sink carefully into it.

"My goodness, I've missed the fresh air," she said.

"You had fresh air every day," said Smoke. "I made sure one of the bedroom windows was open."

"That's not the same as being outside and being able to feel the sun and take a deep breath." She did exactly that and then sighed again in satisfaction.

Despite his caution, Smoke was glad to see the smile on her face and realized he probably had been a mite overprotective. Sally could be stubborn at times, but she was no fool. She wasn't going to do anything that was likely to reinjure her leg. Accidents could never be ruled out, but Smoke knew now that in all likelihood, she would be back to her old self in just a few more days.

He propped a hip against the porch railing close by. She said, "When do you expect Mr. Dixon to get back from Abilene?"

"That depends on how long it takes him to get the price the cattlemen's association wants. He and Pinky and Caldwell might be back tomorrow, but more likely the day after, I think."

"So there's an actual cattlemen's association now?"

"Well, for practical purposes you could call it that," Smoke allowed. "I figure we'll take a vote and make it official once Wallace and the others get back."

"Why don't you go do some work, Smoke?" Sally suggested as she placed the cane across her lap. "I'm sure there are jobs that need to be done, and you must be eager to get back to them."

Smoke shook his head. "Nope, Pearlie's got everything under control. That's what's nice about having a top hand for a foreman. I can count on him to take care of running the ranch so I can concentrate on more important things . . . like you."

"I'm a thing, am I?"

"Well, that's not the way I meant it—"

Smoke stopped in midsentence, straightened from his casual stance, and peered off into the distance, toward the road that led to Big Rock.

"What is it?" asked Sally.

"Rider coming," Smoke said. "Moving along at a pretty fast clip, too. That usually means news of some sort."

"It could be good news, couldn't it?"

"Might be," Smoke agreed, but he didn't sound particularly sincere in voicing that opinion.

Smoke's keen eyes had spotted the rider when he was barely in sight, but as he came closer, Sally could see him, too, along with the cloud of dust the horse's hooves kicked up.

"Isn't that Ernie from the telegraph office?" she asked.

"Yep. And the way he's got that horse in a lather, he must have an important message to deliver."

The Western Union office was located inside the train station in Big Rock. The telegraph line had arrived in the settlement not long after the railroad, making Big Rock fully connected with the outside world.

The young man named Ernie was an assistant telegrapher, but he spent most of his time delivering messages. He pulled his horse to a stop in front of the ranch house a few minutes later, threw a leg over the saddle, and dropped quickly to the ground.

"Telegram for you, Mr. Jensen," he announced. He was a little breathless because of the hard ride out from town.

Smoke went down the steps to take the envelope Ernie held toward him. "Must be mighty important," he said. "You just about ran that horse into the ground, and you look pretty played out yourself."

Ernie shook his head and said, "I don't know what's in it, sir, but the boss told me not to waste any time getting out here and giving it to you."

Smoke opened the envelope and took out a folded piece of paper. As he read the letters printed on it in semi-block style, he used his other hand to pull a silver dollar from his pocket.

"You don't have to do that—" Ernie began. Then he stopped short as he saw the expression that came over Smoke's face. He took an involuntary step back.

Grim lines settled over Smoke's rugged features. His jaw was a taut, angry line. His eyes glittered coldly.

Most men who had seen Smoke Jensen looking like that had died shortly afterward, amidst the crashing of guns and swirling clouds of powder smoke.

Sally had noted the way her husband's back stiffened and leaned forward as she said, "Smoke, what is it?"

Smoke gave a little shake of his head as his fingers clenched on the telegram and crumpled it. He drew in a deep breath and was in control of his emotions again. He shoved the rage he felt into the back of his mind.

Noting how the young man standing in front of him looked frightened, he tried to force a reassuring smile but couldn't quite do it. His voice was calm and steady, though, as he said, "Sorry, Ernie. Didn't mean to look like I was about to shoot you."

Ernie swallowed hard. "That's, uh, that's all right, Mr. Jensen. I thought at first you were mad at me, but then I realized whatever's in that wire caused it. I'm sorry I had to bring you bad news."

"Don't shoot the messenger, as the old saying goes, I reckon."

"And it's a mighty good saying," replied Ernie, bobbing his head.

"Go ahead and take the dollar. You earned it, making such a fast ride out here."

"Thanks." Ernie took the coin. "If there's anything else I can do . . . any message I can take back to town . . ."

"No, just head on back to Big Rock. I'll be in directly to talk to some folks. And take it easy on that horse. He's run enough today. Let him get a drink before you go."

"Yes, sir."

Ernie led his mount toward the pump and watering trough near the barn. Smoke turned and came back up the steps. Sally still had the cane across her lap, but she gripped it in both hands now and her knuckles were white with tension.

"What is it?" she said.

"Wallace Dixon is dead. So is Bill Caldwell. Pinky's shot up and may not pull through."

Sally let go of the cane with her right hand and pressed that hand to her mouth in shock. After a moment she said, "What happened? Was there some sort of fight in Abilene?"

Smoke shook his head. "Before they ever got there. Yesterday evening, outlaws stopped the train not long after it crossed over into Kansas from Colorado. They set a fire on the tracks, took over the locomotive cab and killed the fireman, riddled the passenger cars with gunfire, looted everything of value from the passengers and express car, and stole all the cattle the valley's ranchers were shipping to Abilene. Wallace and Caldwell were killed in the attack and Pinky was wounded."

"Oh, Smoke . . . those poor men."

"They weren't the only ones killed," said Smoke. "There were a dozen other fatalities, including some women and children. The outlaws rode alongside the train on horseback and emptied their guns through the windows in the passenger cars. That created enough chaos that nobody got around to putting up much of a fight. Pinky told the marshal in Abilene that he and Wallace and Caldwell got off a few shots, but he didn't figure they did much damage."

"So Pinky was able to tell the marshal what happened?"

Smoke nodded. "Yeah, and the rest of the story came from the engineer, the conductor, and others who survived the holdup. I don't know how many folks were wounded in the shooting. The telegram from the marshal doesn't go into that much detail."

"I'm sure Pinky is the one who told him to wire the news to you."

"I expect so." Smoke's expression became even bleaker. "I'll have to get all the other fellas together and let them know what happened."

"Have them come here," Sally suggested.

Smoke shook his head. "You're hurt. We don't need a bunch of upset men stomping around the house. You should have peace and quiet."

"Nonsense," she said crisply. "It would take a lot more than that to bother me. Those men are our friends, and they have every right to be upset and angry. Send Pearlie to round them up, and I'll make some lemonade. I can do most of that sitting down."

Rather than argue with her, Smoke nodded. "All right.

I'll ride out and find Pearlie. I have a pretty good idea where he's working today. Then I'll come back here and help you get ready."

"Give me a hand getting into the kitchen before you go."

Smoke took her arm and helped her stand. Once she was on her feet, she looked up into his eyes and said, "You're going to do something about this, aren't you?"

"Reckon I have to."

"And you're not going to let me hold you back." This time it wasn't a question, but rather a declaration on her part.

The men gathered on the porch since there was more room there. They were angry, as Smoke had known they would be when he broke the news to them, and some of them were frightened, too.

They had every right to feel that way. Men, women, and children had been slaughtered, gunned down in brutal and wanton fashion in the course of the robbery. The rustling of their cattle threatened the livelihoods of most of these men. The ranches on which they and their families depended might not survive the loss.

Smoke was in better shape financially than most of them; he had other resources on the ranch, including a vein of gold that only a few people knew about. He could tap that vein if he needed to. Losing that many cattle would be a blow to the Sugarloaf, but the spread would pull through.

That didn't mean Smoke was any less angry about what had happened. A friend had been murdered along with one of the man's top hands, and a young fella who rode for the Sugarloaf had been gunned down as well and

might not live. Along with the deaths of the other inno-
cents, that amounted to an outrage that could not be allowed to stand.

The men milled around talking for a few minutes before Smoke raised his voice again and said, "I want to
thank all of you fellas for coming here today. I sure wish
we were getting together under better circumstances."

"Smoke, what are we gonna do?" Carl Featherstone
asked. "This is gonna ruin us!"

Several others spoke up in angry agreement.

"Nobody's going to be ruined," Smoke said, cutting
through the clamor. "Those killers will be brought to justice."

"How can you know that?" a man asked. "Do you trust
those Kansas lawmen to find them?"

"I'll trust them until they give me a reason not to,"
Smoke said, "but I'm not relying on them. I'm going after
the men responsible for this myself."

That brought a moment of silence as all the ranchers
gathered on the porch looked intently at him. Then Ben
Harper said, "Your wife's hurt. That's why you didn't go
with the cows in the first place."

The sound of Sally's cane thumping on the planks
made all the men look around as she emerged from the
house. "I'm fine," she said, "and I'm certainly not going
to stop Smoke from tracking down those outlaws and seeing to it that they get what's coming to them. If anyone
can recover that stolen herd, it's him."

"Nobody's gonna argue with that," Harper said. "Didn't
mean to imply otherwise. Some of us can go with you if
you want, Smoke."

Smoke shook his head and said, "No, you men are
going to have your hands full keeping things going on

your spreads. I'll need to move pretty fast, and I can do that better by myself."

"Yeah, the trail's getting colder with every minute that goes by, I reckon," said Featherstone. "But that's a big gang, Smoke. Mighty heavy odds against you, even if you do manage to locate them."

Smoke smiled. "I'll figure out a way to handle the odds, don't worry about that."

None of the men appeared to doubt it. They had all heard the stories about Smoke, how he had ridden alone into an outlaw town and killed nineteen hardened gun-wolves in one epic battle, how he had faced up to over-whelming odds again and again and always emerged triumphant.

Sally spoke up again, saying, "I tried to tell him he should take Pearlie with him, anyway."

"Pearlie's too important to the Sugarloaf," said Smoke. "I'll rest a lot easier at night knowing he's here taking care of things."

"Let's say you're able to recover those cattle," one of the men said. "How will you get them to Abilene?"

"There are always plenty of cowboys around over there. They come up with the herds from Texas and don't want to head home yet, or they're figuring on getting a job somewhere else. It shouldn't be hard to round up a crew that can help me handle the herd."

Ben Harper, who had come from the Lone Star State himself, said, "Most of those Texas boys are pretty gun-handy, too, if you need help dealin' with the skunks who held up that train." He stuck out his hand. "And there's nobody I'd rather count on to see that justice is done. Good luck to you, Smoke."

Smoke was moved as each man in turn stepped up to clasp his hand and wish him well. It had been his plan they had agreed to in the first place, risking everything they had to do so. He owed it to each and every one of them to recover those rustled cattle if he could. He would do everything in his power to accomplish that.

And if it took getting a hand from some tough, fast-shooting Texas hombres . . . well, that was all right, too.

Chapter 6

The two riders jogging their horses northward across the Kansas prairie were a study in contrasts.

The one in the black, high-crowned hat was tall and lean, with a sun-browned face, a hawk-like nose, and a thick black mustache that drooped over his wide, good-humored mouth. He wore a cowhide vest, a white shirt, and denim trousers with the legs stuck down inside high-topped black boots. The man carried a heavy, ivory-handled Colt in a black holster on his right hip.

He rode a muscular Appaloosa. A man who was experienced in judging horseflesh would be able to tell just by looking at the animal that it possessed plenty of speed and stamina.

The other rider was much shorter and stockier, which was evident even though both of them were on horseback. This second man had a thatch of bright, curly red hair under a thumbed-back brown Stetson. He wore a buckskin shirt and whipcord trousers and packed a Colt with a plain walnut grip. His squarish face was open and friendly, with a scattering of freckles across his nose and cheeks.

The dun underneath him was barrel-chested and powerful, not as flashy as the Appaloosa but a sturdy, dependable mount.

The two riders had a couple of things in common. Each carried a Winchester in a saddle sheath, and their gazes were alert and intelligent as they looked around the countryside through which they rode.

"Ought to be gettin' to Abilene pretty soon, Sam," the stocky redhead commented.

His lean, hawk-faced companion nodded. "You're right about that, Walt," he said. "And I'm plumb ready to get off this trail, too. We've been followin' it long enough."

"I think I see some chimney smoke up yonder," Walt said with a note of excitement in his voice. He pointed, then went on, "But you already spotted it, didn't you?"

"About half a mile back," the man called Sam admitted.

Walt shook his head. "I don't know why I even try. There's no beatin' those eagle eyes of yours. I don't reckon I can match up to any of your senses."

"Maybe not, but you're a heap better cook than I am."

"Glad to know I'm good for something."

Sam chuckled. "Don't get a burr under your saddle. You know there's nobody I'd rather have for a trail pard than you, old son."

"Well, you're tolerable yourself . . . most of the time."

After trading those gibes, the two fell silent for a while, the easy quiet of long, companionable friendship. They had ridden plenty of trails together, some darker than others, and intended to continue doing so for as long as they possibly could.

A short time later, they reined their horses to a halt atop a shallow, rolling rise. As flat as the landscape was overall, a man didn't need much elevation in order to see a considerable distance. As these two pilgrims leaned forward in their saddles to ease weary muscles, they peered across the plains at a large cluster of buildings a couple of miles away.

Abilene was a good-sized settlement and would only continue to grow. Originally a squalid hamlet that served as the center of the buffalo hunting business, the arrival of the railroad had turned it into an actual town. For a few years it had been hell-with-the-hide-off, but it had settled down some when the railhead moved on farther west. Several two-fisted, fast-shooting lawmen, including Wild Bill Hickok, had helped put the place on the road to being civilized.

Not that Abilene was fully tamed. It was still the closest point where the railroad could be reached from some of the ranches in Texas, so quite a few herds still came up the trail and passed through the holding pens and loading chutes on the outskirts of town.

That meant plenty of Texas cowboys spent time in Abilene, which meant booming business for the saloons, gambling dens, and houses of ill repute.

In addition, a number of cattle ranches had been established in the area, to the north and west, so their herds and cowboys were a common sight in town, too. To the south and east of Abilene, farmers had moved in and were producing excellent crops in the rich soil.

All that indicated a promising future for Abilene. Sam and Walt likely wouldn't be around to see it, though, because the two of them never stayed in one place for too long if they could help it.

Right now, as they nudged their horses into motion and set a slightly faster pace toward the settlement, they were thinking about their first destination once they reached town: the Alamo Saloon.

Quite a few horses and wagons were in the main street

as Sam and Walt rode in. Pedestrians thronged the board-walks. Most were men, but quite a few women were in evidence, too, as well as a number of kids darting here and there.

"Quite a crowd, and this ain't even Saturday," Walt commented as he and Sam drew rein in front of the Alamo Saloon.

"Busy place, all right," agreed Sam. They swung down from their saddles and tied the horses' reins to a hitch rack.

The Alamo was an impressive enterprise. The saloon's front took up an entire block, with entrances at both corners. Big windows sparkled. Sam and Walt went to the doors on the west end and walked into the saloon.

A gleaming hardwood bar was on their left. It ran along the side wall and then made a right angle along the rear wall, forming an Lshape that ended midway across the saloon's width. Tables where men sat drinking filled the space inside the L. Beyond them were gambling tables covered by green felt, along with roulette wheels and faro and keno layouts. A stage where musicians played and scantily clad dancers sometimes cavorted was in the far back corner, with an open space in front of it where customers could dance with the working gals in their low-cut, spangled dresses. A smaller entrance was at the front corner on that end of the saloon.

Sam let out a low whistle of admiration as he and Walt stood there looking around. He nodded toward the cut-glass chandeliers hanging from the ceiling, the shelves full of gleaming bottles behind the long bars, and the big paintings of abundantly endowed nude ladies that hung on the walls.

"Mighty fancy place, all right," Sam said.

Walt grinned. "I don't know much about art, but I know what I like," he said. "And those cherub fellas hangin' around those ladies in their all-together make those pictures art, right?"

"I reckon you can call it whatever you want."

"I call it mighty inspirin'."

"Well, all that trail dust we've been swallowin' has inspired me to get a drink," said Sam. "Come on."

"Now you're talkin'. Some good cold beer would sure cut the dust nice, right about now."

Most of the tables were occupied, and men were lined up at the bar. There were some open spaces, however, so Sam and Walt made their way toward one. They had to wind their way around several of the tables to reach their destination, and as they were passing one of them, Sam's elbow brushed against the hat of a man sitting there.

The contact was slight, but it was enough to tip the man's hat forward so it fell off his head. As it landed on the table, it knocked over a bottle of whiskey sitting in front of the man. The bottle fell toward one of the other drinkers. Amber liquid glugged out and formed a stream that trickled into the second man's lap.

He leaped to his feet and yelled, "What the hell!"

The man whose hat Sam had dislodged bolted up as well. "Watch where you're going, you damn cow nurse!"

There was a lot of racket in the saloon, but not so much that Sam and Walt didn't hear the angry exclamations. They stopped and Sam looked back over his shoulder. He asked in a mild voice, "Are you talkin' to me, friend?"

"Damn right I'm talking to you!" The man snatched his fallen hat off the table and shook it at the two newcomers. "You knocked my hat off!"

"Oh. Well, I'm mighty sorry about that, but it don't look like no harm was done."

"No harm?" said the second man. He motioned toward the wet spot on his trousers where the whiskey had spilled. "What do you call this?"

Walt grinned. "Not being fast enough to get to the outhouse?"

"Now, that ain't a very tactful thing to say," Sam admonished him. "Fella can't help it if he's got a little problem with his plumbin'."

The second man's face flushed with fury as he glared at the two drifters. "That . . . that's whiskey!"

"Reckon it's like beer," drawled Sam. "They say you don't buy it, you just rent it."

The man whose hat he'd knocked off clapped the headgear back on. The hat was a cream-colored Stetson, expensive and obviously almost new. He was well-dressed in a brown tweed suit and a darker brown vest. His companion was in a gray suit with a black hat. Stickpins glittered in both men's cravats. Their garb, their relatively untanned features, and their uncallused hands marked them as gamblers, more than likely.

"You two cowboys can't waltz in here with manure on your boots, cause trouble, insult my friend and me, and then just walk away," the first man declared. "We demand apologies!"

Walt hooked his thumbs in his old, scarred gun belt and snapped back, "Or what?"

"Or . . . or you'll regret it," the man blustered.

"Sorry, I reckon," Sam said without sounding the least bit sincere about it.

Even so, Walt turned to him and said, "Don't apologize to these two. If they're such delicate little flowers as to get their feelin's hurt so easy, they hadn't ought to be drinkin' in a man's saloon." He smirked at the two men. "Maybe there's a ladies' tearoom here in Abilene. You ought to go look for it." He jerked his head toward the bar. "Come on, Sam, let's get that drink. My gizzard's got at least an inch o' trail dust in it!"

The two well-dressed men clenched their fists and

looked like they wanted to tear into Sam and Walt, but they didn't advance on the drifters. Sam made a scornful noise in his throat and turned to follow Walt toward the bar.

They bellied up to the hardwood and each propped a booted foot on the brass rail along the front of it, near the floor. A bartender with slicked-down hair, wearing a white shirt, red vest, and sleeve garters, sidled up and asked, "What'll it be, gents?"

"Is your beer cold?" asked Walt.

"The coldest you'll find this side of Denver."

"Then we'll have two mugs of it to start, and I hope you've got plenty back there!"

"It's not likely we'll run out," the bartender said with a smile as he took two mugs from a shelf and started filling them from a tap.

While the apron was doing that, Sam watched the mirror along the backbar. He kept an eye on the two men he and Walt had had the run-in with. He saw them talking to a couple of other men, the second pair more roughly dressed. Something changed hands. A few folded bills, Sam assumed.

"Here you go, fellas," the bartender said as he placed the full mugs in front of Sam and Walt. Foam overflowed the tops and puddled on the hardwood around the mugs.

Walt grabbed his mug and drank thirstily, swallowing several times.

"By grab, that's good!" he said as he lowered the mug but didn't set it on the bar.

Sam was being a lot more deliberate in his actions as he picked up his mug. In the mirror, he saw the two well-dressed men and the two allies they had recruited approaching the bar. On the other side of the hardwood, the slick-haired barkeep's eyes widened in alarm.

Sam whirled as one of the rough-looking men suddenly rushed at him. He had the mug's handle in his left hand. With a flick of his wrist, he sent the foamy contents into the attacker's face. Taken by surprise, the man skidded to a stop, gulped, gasped, and tried to paw away the suds that had momentarily blinded his eyes.

Sam hit him in the face, driving a straight, powerful right to the man's left cheekbone that sent him reeling back to crash onto a nearby table. The men sitting there leaped up, yelling angrily.

Walt hadn't been paying as close attention to the situation as Sam and therefore had less warning. He realized he was under attack and tried to spin around in time to meet the second tough's charge, but he was too late. The man's fist hooked into his belly and sank deep. Walt doubled over and dropped the mug he was holding. The beer that was still in it splashed around his feet.

The man who had walloped Walt clasped both hands together and raised them above his head, poised to bring them down in a devastating blow to the back of the bent-over redhead's neck.

Sam struck first, heaving the now empty mug he held so that it bounced hard off the second tough's head. That staggered the man, and with his arms still raised that way, he wasn't able to defend himself as Sam drove in quickly and hammered a left to his jaw.

That left Sam open for the attack launched by the man whose hat he had knocked off. That hombre might have been dressed like a dude, but there was nothing weak about the punch he whipped in at Sam. The fist crashed into the side of Sam's head and knocked him against the bar. The hardwood's edge dug painfully into his ribs as he fell against it.

Sam tried to straighten, but the second well-dressed man rammed a shoulder into him and drove him against the bar again. Sam gasped in pain. He brought his left arm up and caught the man under the chin with his elbow. That knocked the man away from him.

Everybody had lost their hats by now. The first two men to attack had recovered somewhat and plunged back into the fracas. Outnumbered two to one, Sam and Walt put their backs against the bar and started slugging as their four opponents crowded around them. Fists flew in a wild knot of flailing and punching in front of the bar.

Drinks forgotten for the moment, the Alamo's other patrons crowded around to watch the battle and shout encouragement and the occasional jeer at the combatants. A fight such as this often turned into a general brawl that engulfed the whole place, but at least for the moment the other customers seemed content to be spectators.

Sam blocked a punch, hooked a right into the belly of one of the toughs, and caught the man with a left to the jaw as he bent forward. That jerked the fella's head to the side and caused his eyes to roll up in their sockets. His knees buckled and he collapsed on the sawdust-littered floor.

Walt bored in on the other tough, his shorter stature allowing him to pepper the larger man's midsection with a flurry of hard punches. The man was starting to look a little green from that punishment, but he didn't have time to get sick because Walt seized an opening and brought up a haymaker from the floor. It landed on the man's chin, clicked his teeth together loudly, and rocked his head back until it looked like it might topple right off his shoulders.

That man fell, too, senseless from the terrific blow Walt had landed. The redhead might not be very big, but he packed a lot of strength in his compact body.

Walt took a step back and leaned against the bar beside Sam. Both drifters had bloody scrapes and bruises forming on their faces, but they lifted their fists and waited for the two well-dressed men to rush them again.

It looked like that wasn't going to happen. The man in the gray suit, breathing hard, said, "Forget it. I . . . I've had enough." The area around his left eye was darkening and swelling where a fist had landed on it.

The man in the brown tweed exclaimed, "What! You're going to let these two saddle tramps get away with what they've done?"

"I'm a lover, not a fighter," the man said. "You know that, Carmody."

The man called Carmody snorted in disgust. "I can't take on both of them by myself!"

"One of us'd be happy to step aside and even things up, mister," said Sam. "You can even take your pick."

Carmody sneered at them, but he hesitated and finally muttered, "The hell with it." He looked around, picked up the cream-colored Stetson, and groaned. "My hat!"

"Yeah, it got stomped pretty good, what with us dancin' around like that," Sam told him. "Reckon maybe you should've just let things go, instead of gettin' a burr under your saddle."

Carmody was trying to knock the sawdust and dirt off his hat and punch it back into shape. He looked up with a snarl and said, "This isn't over yet, cowboy." He put on the no longer pristine Stetson and added to his friend, "Come on, Gene."

As the two men headed for the door, Walt called jeeringly after them, "What about your pards here?" He waved a hand toward the toughs he and Sam had knocked out.

Carmody and Gene ignored him and pushed on out of the Alamo, but as they left, Carmody called back to Sam, "I'll see you again, mister!"

"Any time you're ready," Sam responded to the implicit threat.

The bartender motioned to some of the bystanders and told them to drag the unconscious men out of the saloon.

"What'll we do with them, Pete?" a man asked.

"Leave them in the alley, I guess," the bartender replied. "I just don't want them waking up in here and starting trouble all over again." He summoned up a weak smile for Sam and Walt. "Sorry about that, boys. You want beers to replace the ones you lost? On the house."

"On the house?" repeated Walt. "Shoot, that's worth a little ruckus!"

The barkeep filled two more mugs and placed them in front of Sam and Walt while several men hauled the senseless brawlers out of the saloon.

Sam took a swallow of his beer and then asked, "Who were them fancy dans who got their backs up?"

"I heard them call each other by name just like you did, but that's really all I know about them," the bartender replied with a shake of his head. "They showed up in town a couple of days ago, as far as I know. They've been in here a few times, played some cards, drank a little. Kept to themselves and haven't caused any trouble. They look like professional gamblers. Maybe they're trying to set up a high stakes game and don't have it all arranged yet."

"What about the hombres who threw in with 'em?"

"Those two?" The apron blew out a disdainful breath. "Ollie Hopgood and Seth Craig. Just a couple of bums. They came up the trail with a herd from Texas about six months ago. Pushing cattle was too much hard work for them, I suppose. They haven't been in any hurry to get back to it. They've been hanging around ever since, doing a few odd jobs when they need money. I think I saw them playing cards with those other two, but I don't think they're friends or anything. They were willing to pitch in against you, though, as long as they got paid for it."

Sam nodded slowly. "Yeah, I saw Carmody slip 'em some dinero. Obliged to you for the information."

"And the beer," added Walt.

"You fellas plan to stay around Abilene for a while, or are you looking for riding jobs?"

"Well, that sort'a depends on what we run into, I reckon," Sam said.

The bartender glanced past him, and a concerned expression appeared again on the man's face.

"You may not have much to say on the matter," he advised in a low voice. "Marshal McCormick just came in. He must've heard about that fight . . . and he doesn't like troublemakers."

Chapter 7

Sam set his mug on the bar and turned slowly toward the Alamo's entrance. A man big enough to block the light stood there, tall, broad-shouldered, and barrel-chested. He had a round face, shaggy blond hair, and a mustache of the same shade. A broad-brimmed brown hat was pushed back on his head. Pinned to the buckskin shirt stretched across the broad chest was a marshal's star.

The lawman held a sawed-off shotgun in big, ham-like hands. The muzzles looked a little like the mouths of cannons as they pointed in the general direction of Sam and Walt.

"We didn't start that ruckus," Walt protested over his shoulder to the bartender.

"Maybe not, but you're still here and the other fellas aren't."

On legs like the trunks of trees, the marshal came toward the bar. He let the twin barrels of the sawed-off sag a little, but he could still bring it into play in a hurry if he needed to. He came to a stop in front of Sam and Walt and jerked his big head in a curt nod.

"Howdy, boys," he rumbled. "New in town, aren't you?"

"That's right," Sam said. "Just rode in a little while ago." He paused, then added, "Nice town you got here."

"And I intend to keep it that way. That's my job. I'm Marshal Ben McCormick." The lawman paused for effect, too. "Big Ben, some call me."

"It suits you," said Walt.

"You have the advantage of me," McCormick said.

"My pard is Walt Smith," Sam said with a nod toward the redhead. "I'm Jones. Front handle Sam."

"Smith and Jones, eh? I wouldn't find other names matching your descriptions if I went through the reward posters in my office, would I?"

"There ain't no Kansas dodgers on us," Sam declared. "That's a fact."

He didn't elaborate on the question of whether there might be wanted notices issued on them from other states or territories.

If McCormick noticed that omission, he didn't mention it. Instead he said, "I got reports of a big fight in here a little while ago, and a couple of men matching your descriptions were involved."

"Is there some ordinance in this town that says a fella can't defend himself if he's attacked?" asked Sam.

"Self-defense? That's all right. But according to what I heard, you men provoked this fight."

"We never did!" Walt said, sounding offended.

"You didn't knock a fella's hat off?"

"I reckon I did," Sam admitted, "but it was an accident. He didn't have no call to get so all-fired het up about it."

Walt added, "Sam even went so far as to apologize to the gent, even though I told him he hadn't ought to."

"But there was a fight anyway, because of something you did." McCormick held the shotgun in his right hand and tapped the sawed-off barrels in the palm of his left hand. "I don't like fighting in Abilene." He looked at the bartender. "Any damages, Pete?"

"Not really, Marshal. Some beer got spilled, that's about it. Weren't even any mugs broken."

"You don't want to collect from these fellas?"

"Nope. I even gave them beers on the house to replace the ones they lost."

The lawman frowned. "I don't like it. I don't like it one little bit." But he sighed and went on, "I reckon if Pete here doesn't want to press charges against you, there's nothing I can do about it. But I'm going to keep my eyes on you two while you're in Abilene, I can promise you that." He squinted at the drifters. "I'm still convinced I've seen you both before . . . and the only place I could've done that was on wanted posters. I'll be checking as soon as I get back to my office."

"You do that, Marshal," Sam told him. "You won't find us."

"We'll just see about that. If there's one thing I have a good memory for, it's owlhoots."

With that, McCormick turned and stomped out of the saloon, his back stiff with anger.

"Fella seems a mite proddy," Sam commented as he swung back around to face the bar.

"Maybe a little," the bartender conceded. "But imagine you're a star packer and have to follow in the footsteps of Bear River Tom Smith and Wild Bill Hickok. Those men cast a mighty big shadow."

Walt shuddered. "I don't reckon I want to imagine I'm a lawman," he said. "That's a plumb horrifyin' thought."

He and Sam nursed their beers for a while longer. Then Sam said, "Carmody was still pretty mad when he and Gene left. You reckon he's the sort who might try to even the score with some back-shootin'?"

The bartender shook his head and said, "I honestly don't know, friend. But if I was you, I think I'd keep an eye out behind me."

"We always do," said Sam. "It's sort of a habit."

"How do you think we've lived this long?" Walt added with a smile.

Since the bartender had stood them to a round, it was only fair that they buy another beer, Sam decided, even though Walt groused that would deplete their already scanty funds.

"We've got enough money left for a little grub and a room for the night," Sam said. "We'll worry about tomorrow when it gets here. Something'll turn up, more than likely. It usually does."

They asked the bartender about inexpensive places to eat and stay. "You're lucky Abilene isn't the boomtown it once was," he told them. "Nothing was inexpensive here during the years when so many herds were coming up the trail from Texas. But prices have settled down along with everything else. You can get a pretty good supper at One Lung's place."

"One Lung?" repeated Walt. "That don't sound very appetizin'."

"The café actually belongs to a Chinaman named Wan Long," the bartender explained with a chuckle, "but everybody calls him One Lung. He's a mighty fine cook, too. Not just that Chinese stuff, either. He fries up a tasty steak."

"We'll give it a try," said Sam. "What about a place to stay?"

"The Empire Hotel isn't fancy, but it's clean enough for the price and you won't have to share your bed with a bunch of bugs. Tell the fella at the desk I sent you, and he might give you a little better deal, depending on how drunk he is."

"We're obliged to you," Sam told him with a nod.

"Just be careful, especially if you're out and about after dark. Abilene may have tamed down some, but there are still plenty of dark alleys where trouble can hide."

"Trouble in the form of a couple of fancy pants dudes?"

"Just take the advice for what it's worth."

Sam and Walt left the Alamo Saloon and reclaimed their horses. They led the Appaloosa and dun down the street toward a livery stable and wagon yard that Sam spotted. The proprietor, a stocky man with a rust-colored beard, was happy to take the two horses for the night and quoted a very reasonable price.

"I'm thinkin' you could get more than that in a place like Abilene."

The liveryman shrugged and said, "I like taking care of horses and working on wagons and buggies. A fella can get rich on other things besides money."

"That's a mighty fine way of lookin' at life," Sam agreed. "Take good care of these old boys."

"They'll be here waiting for you, in good shape, when you need them."

"Nice hombre," Walt commented as they walked away with their warbags over their shoulders. They carried their Winchesters, as well.

"There are still plenty of good folks in the world," Sam said. "Just happens we don't run into 'em that often."

The liveryman had told them where to find the Empire Hotel. It was on a side street, half a block off the main business district. A two-story frame building, it appeared to be well-kept, although plain and strictly functional. The slender, high-strung gent at the desk signed them in and gave them the key to a room on the second floor. As the bartender at the Alamo had promised, the price was sensible.

Sam and Walt left their warbags and rifles in the hotel room and went in search of Wan Long's café.

That establishment lived up to its billing, as well. It was in a small building with a dozen tables and a counter with stools along it. Most of the tables were occupied, so the drifters counted themselves lucky they were able to grab one.

From the looks of it, Wan Long's family worked with him. A handsome, middle-aged Chinese woman was behind the counter, and two pretty teenage girls who resembled her waited on tables. When the swinging door behind the counter was opened, Sam caught glimpses of a middle-aged man working at a big stove and oven in the kitchen, moving quickly among several frying pans and large, steaming pots.

Still following the bartender's advice, they both ordered steaks with all the trimmings. The food was as good as advertised, especially when washed down with several cups of strong black coffee and followed by bowls of deep-dish apple pie with cream.

When they were finished, Walt leaned back in his chair and patted his slightly swollen belly above his belt buckle.

"Everybody's been so nice, I reckon I could just live here," he declared. "Ain't we been fiddle-footed long enough, Sam?"

Sam cocked a bushy eyebrow and said, "You forget why we rode this way in the first place."

"I know, I know. We got things to do."

"And you didn't appear to think Abilene was such a nice place a few hours ago when those fellas were whalin' away at us."

"I'm just sayin' that if a fella had to settle down, this wouldn't be a bad place to do it." Walt sighed. "But that probably ain't in the cards for the likes of us, is it?"

"Not any time soon, I reckon."

One of the pretty Chinese gals brought the coffeepot and refilled their cups. Sam and Walt lingered a while longer, enjoying the peaceful, friendly atmosphere in the café. When they left, Sam made sure there was a silver dollar on the table for the girl who'd waited on them.

Night had settled down over Abilene when they came out onto the street. They stopped and stood there for a moment, enjoying the cool breeze that had sprung up after the warmth of the day. It was a pleasant evening. The sounds of music and laughter floated from the saloons on that breeze.

A few wagons still rolled along the street, and men on horseback moved here and there. Most of the stores were still open, although they would be closing soon. The saloons would continue operating until midnight, possibly later, but the lamps in the houses along the side streets would be blown out one by one as the regular citizens turned in for the night.

Walt said, "I think I'll take a *pasear* back down to the livery stable and check on our horses. I know that fella seemed mighty capable, but I like to see for myself that they're bein' took good care of."

"Sounds like a fine idea," agreed Sam. "I'll mosey on toward the Alamo and see you there after a spell."

"Remember to keep your eyes open."

"I ain't likely to forget," Sam said.

He stayed where he was for a moment, standing in an

easy slouch and watching as Walt walked off into the shadows. When he couldn't see his redheaded partner anymore, he turned and strolled the other way toward Abilene's biggest saloon.

He could see the Alamo ahead of him, light spilling out through its many large windows. That glow didn't reach as far as where Sam walked slowly along the street. The businesses he was passing were already closed, so the shadows were thick here.

He was just passing the mouth of one of those alleys the bartender had warned them about when Colt flame suddenly bloomed like a crimson flower in the darkness. Sam ducked instinctively as he heard and felt the wind-rip of a bullet's passage near his head. His hand flashed down to the ivory-handled revolver on his hip.

A second shot blasted from the alley, this one from a different position since there were two bushwhackers hidden in those stygian shadows. Sam jerked his gun up and triggered two swift shots in return. Then a bound carried him onto the boardwalk on the same side of the street as the alley, in front of a darkened store that was currently empty and had a FOR RENT sign in the window. He dived for the alcove where the store's front door was set as another slug screamed past him.

Sam pressed into the small space for a moment, then wheeled to the side and fired twice around the alcove's corner. One of the gunmen burst out into the open and ran diagonally across the broad street, firing as he made his dash. None of the wild shots found Sam, but one of them shattered the building's front window.

Sam sent a bullet whistling after him, but it kicked up dust several feet behind the running man. The bushwhacker threw himself behind a watering trough.

That gave him good cover and a commanding position.

He could fire directly across the street toward Sam now. Sam reached back with his free left hand, found the doorknob, and twisted it as he rammed his shoulder hard against the panel around the door's outer edge.

With a splintering sound the lock tore free and the door flew open. Sam half-dived, half-fell through the entrance. As he sprawled on the floor just inside the doorway, more bullets whipped through the air above him.

Some of those slugs were coming a mite too close for comfort. He rolled to his left and came up on one knee next to the bullet-shattered window. He made a face as a piece of broken glass cut his trouser leg and poked into his flesh. *There are worse things than a little scratch*, he told himself. He reached into his pocket, brought out a handful of fresh cartridges, and started plugging them into the revolver's cylinder.

Meanwhile the gunfire from outside continued. The man across the street was keeping him pinned down.

The other bushwhacker, who was on the same side of the street as the building where Sam had sought refuge, could reach the rear door by way of the back alley behind the businesses. Sam finished reloading his gun and was ready when the door crashed open behind him.

He turned, stretched out on his belly, angled the gun up, and fired. Four shots blasted out so close together that they formed a continuous peal of gun thunder. Gouts of muzzle flame lit up the empty, dusty chamber for an instant.

Sam felt as much as heard the thud of a body hitting the floor, and then as the echoes rolled away, a man groaned somewhere in the darkness.

At the same time, rapid footsteps sounded outside. The man who'd been behind the water trough was charging toward the building while it seemed like Sam was busy with the threat from the rear. Sam twisted around, caught sight of the running figure, and fired through the open window.

The second bushwhacker stumbled abruptly. The gun in his hand went off, but the bullet plowed into the dirt in front of him. Momentum carried him forward for several more steps, all the way to the boardwalk in front of the store.

The shape he was in, he couldn't manage the step up. He pitched forward and landed facedown on the planks. The gun slipped from his fingers and clattered away.

Sam pushed upright, stepped into the doorway, and swung back and forth to cover both fallen gunmen. Neither bushwhacker moved or made a sound.

By now some of the more daring citizens were running in his direction to find out what all the shooting was about. By the time Sam had fumbled a lucifer from his shirt pocket, several men had reached the boardwalk in front of the building.

"You boys better stay back," Sam advised them as he used his left thumbnail to snap the match into life. The sudden glare washed over the body sprawled on the boardwalk. Even though the man lay face down, the gray suit and the black hat that had fallen from his head identified him as the man called Gene, one of the two who had clashed with Sam and Walt in the Alamo.

Sam turned and held the match so that its light fell on the man inside the abandoned store. The brown tweed suit and cream-colored Stetson were instantly recognizable. One of the townsmen peering through the broken window exclaimed, "Hey, it's that gambler Carmody!" Mutters of agreement came from others in the crowd.

A deep voice boomed from somewhere close by, "Step aside! Out of the way, blast it!"

The townsmen moved hurriedly to clear a path. Marshal Ben McCormick, still carrying the sawed-off shotgun, stomped up in his usual aggressive manner. In the light from the match Sam held, he saw the bodies of Carmody and Gene and reacted by swinging the scattergun up and pointing it at Sam.

"Drop that gun, you murdering owlhoot," he ordered, "or I'll blow your head right off your shoulders!"

Chapter 8

Sam stiffened. He didn't drop the gun as Marshal McCormick had commanded, but he was careful to keep it pointed toward the planks at his feet so as not to give the big lawman any excuse to stroke that shotgun's triggers. He wanted to make sure the townsmen knew he wasn't trying to provoke any more shooting.

"Hold on a minute, Marshal," he said. "I didn't murder nobody. These two varmints bushwhacked *me*. You said self-defense is legal in this town."

"You got any proof those men attacked you?" demanded McCormick. "Any witnesses to back up your story?"

"Well, I don't know—"

McCormick bellowed at the bystanders, "Anybody here actually see this gunfight?"

No one answered, other than a couple of the men clearing their throats and shuffling their feet. It was clear that nobody was going to speak up to corroborate Sam's claim of self-defense.

"Looks like nobody's on your side," said McCormick, sneering and sounding pleased with himself. "Now, I'm not going to tell you again. Put that gun down and kick it over here to me."

By this time the match had burned down and Sam had dropped it before the flame could scorch his fingers. He bent, placed the ivory-handled revolver on the planks, and then carefully pushed it toward McCormick with his foot.

"One of you boys pick that gun up and hand it to me," the marshal ordered. A townsman gingerly retrieved the gun and gave it to McCormick, who shoved it one-handed behind his belt. "Now somebody fetch a lantern."

That took a few minutes. When a man brought a lantern that cast a yellow glow over the boardwalk and the alcove, McCormick had the man shine the light on Gene's body. Two other men rolled him onto his back, revealing the large, bloody stain on the front of his shirt.

"Let's take a look at the other one," snapped McCormick. He used the sawed-off shotgun to motion Sam out of the doorway.

The lantern's harsh glare spilled over Carmody's motionless form. McCormick ordered him turned onto his back, too. The front of his shirt was even more sodden with blood than Gene's.

"That's enough," McCormick said. "I just wanted to make sure they were both dead. No need to stand around gawking at them. Take that lantern, and the rest of you go on about your business."

"Shouldn't somebody go get the undertaker, Marshal?" a man asked.

"He'll be here soon enough. He'll have heard that shooting. Now move on, like I said."

The crowd started to disperse, but one stubborn hanger-on pointed at Sam and said, "What are you gonna do with him?"

"What the hell do you think? I'm going to lock him up." The lawman leveled the shotgun and moved closer to Sam. "You're under arrest for murder."

"Murder! Blast it, Marshal, I told you those men bush-whacked me—"

McCormick moved in, his actions fast and smooth for such a big man. He rammed the sawed-off's twin barrels into Sam's midsection with such brutal force that Sam doubled over and staggered, catching himself against the wall of the alcove.

"I've had enough backtalk from you, you dirty Texas owlhoot! That's right, I know who you are. I found that wanted poster with your picture on it, just like I told you I would. Now move on down to the jail or I'll bend this scattergun over your head and not worry if it stoves in your skull. I can drag you behind bars, dead or alive."

Sam put a hand against the wall to brace himself as he straightened. He stayed a little hunched over as he pressed his left arm against his belly where the marshal had hit him. Looking up with his haggard face twisted in angry lines, he said, "I ain't gonna forget that, Marshal. One of these days you're gonna be sorry you and me crossed trails."

"I'm always sorry when trash like you rides into Abilene. Get going, damn your mangy hide!"

Sam pushed away from the wall and stumbled along the boardwalk. McCormick followed him. The crowd had broken up, but several men still stood nearby, watching with avid, somewhat morbid interest as Sam made his unsteady way toward the marshal's office and jail. McCormick told him which way to go.

Sam's eyes darted toward the boardwalk on the other

side of the street. He spotted a familiar figure. Walt stood there looking back at him. The eyes of the two men met for a second. Sam shook his head, and Walt faded back into the shadows.

Anyone observing that brief glance would have thought that Sam was warning his friend and trail partner not to try anything. If Walt attempted to interfere with what Marshal McCormick was doing, he'd just wind up behind bars, too. That wouldn't do Sam or anybody else any good.

Knowing what the lawman's reaction would be, Sam said, "I tell you, I didn't have any choice, Marshal. I had to shoot those two tinhorns, or else they would have killed me."

"That'll be up to a judge and jury to decide," McCormick declared loudly and pompously. "If you're telling the truth, you won't have anything to worry about. If you're not"—the lawman laughed—"I reckon I'll have the pleasure of watching you hang, saddle tramp!"

Walt stayed where he was until Sam and McCormick had disappeared down the street toward the sturdy stone building that housed the marshal's office and jail. Walt and Sam had taken note of the place when they rode in earlier that day. It was always a good idea to know where the local law was likely to be found.

Standing with his back pressed against the front wall of an apothecary that was closed for the night, Walt took off his hat, ran a hand over his head, and sighed as he thought about his next move.

A wagon with a closed back pulled up in front of the abandoned store where the shooting had occurred. A man in a dark suit and a couple of burly helpers climbed down from the seat. That would be the local undertaker and his assistants, Walt knew. Quickly, with a minimum of fuss, they loaded the two bodies in the back of the wagon. One of the assistants took up the reins, turned the team of horses, and drove back up the street toward the undertaking parlor.

Walt and Sam had taken note of *that* business's location, too.

The broken window and a dark, irregular stain on the boardwalk in front of the door alcove were the only remaining signs of the violence that had taken place. There would be a stain on the floor inside, too, where Carmody had fallen.

Once the undertaker was gone, Walt headed for the Alamo. He had visited the livery stable earlier, as he had told Sam he was going to, and found that the horses were doing fine and were well cared for, just as expected. From there, he and Sam had said that they would meet at the saloon.

Sam wasn't going there after all, but that didn't mean Walt couldn't.

Right about now, he could use another beer. He was feeling the strain of being on his own for a change.

He felt eyes on him as he entered the place. The buzz of conversation slackened for a moment as men turned their heads to look at him. Then they resumed talking to their friends as Walt moved doggedly toward the bar.

The shoot-out down the street was probably the main topic of conversation in here tonight, thought Walt. There had been a time when more than a dozen shots being fired and two men being killed wouldn't have caused much of a stir in Abilene. Those wilder days were several years in the past. Now a corpse-and-cartridge session like that was big news in the town.

Several bartenders were on duty tonight, including the one who had been present during the trouble earlier. He had been friendly, so Walt wedged himself into a small open space along the bar where the man was working.

"Say, there you are," the bartender greeted Walt. A solemn look replaced the habitual professional smile he'd worn at first. With a sympathetic shake of his head, he went on, "I heard about what happened to your friend. I'm really sorry. Can I get you a drink?"

"Yeah, whiskey this time," said Walt.

The apron poured the shot, slid it across the hardwood. "I warned you boys about dark alleys."

Walt threw back the fiery liquor and set the empty glass back on the bar. "Could've been worse, I reckon," he said.

"Oh?"

"Damn right. What's the old sayin'? Better to be judged by twelve than carried by six?"

"So you think a jury will find him innocent because he acted in self-defense?"

Walt leaned forward and lowered his voice. "It doesn't matter. I don't reckon Sam will be judged by a jury."

The bartender frowned. "What do you mean by that?"

Walt glanced in both directions along the bar, then over his shoulder, and then said just loud enough for the man to hear him over the hubbub in the saloon, "I don't intend to let him stay in jail and stand trial."

The bartender leaned back and looked alarmed. "You don't want to be talking like that, friend," he said. "You can get in real trouble bucking the law. Big Ben McCormick wouldn't take kindly to that at all."

"McCormick's the reason I'm not gonna let Sam rot behind bars. That so-called lawman has got it in for us. I'm surprised he didn't gun Sam down like a dog on the way to jail and claim he was trying to escape. I don't trust that big ox any farther than I could throw him."

"Maybe not, but if you try to bust your friend out, you'll wind up behind bars yourself . . . or worse."

Walt pushed the empty glass across the bar. "Gimme another."

When he had downed the second shot of whiskey, he dragged the back of his left hand across his mouth and then sighed. "That jail looks pretty sturdy," he admitted. "I reckon I'd have a hard time gettin' Sam out of it by myself."

"Now you're showing some sense," the bartender said with a nod.

"But I remember one time," Walt went on, his voice rising a little as the whiskey appeared to take effect, "down in Texas in our old stompin' grounds around Comanche, Sam got throwed in jail once over some cattle a fella claimed he stole. Well, those cattle did go missin', but there was no proof that Sam and me had anything to do with it. Didn't stop Sheriff Strickland from arrestin' him anyway. There's a big ol' oak tree growin' there in the town square, they call it the hangin' tree, and some folks started yellin' about how they were gonna take Sam outta jail and string him up to it, like they strung up other owl-hoots from time to time. I couldn't let that happen, so I had to get him out."

Some of the other men along the bar had turned to listen to the story as Walt went on. One of them said, "How'd you manage that? I reckon you must've got him away, or else you boys wouldn't be here in Kansas."

"Damn right I got him out," said Walt. He picked up the glass, which the bartender had filled for a third time without asking. He swallowed the whiskey and banged the empty back down on the bar. "I, uh, borrowed a team of mules from a wagon that was tied up there on the square and led 'em down to the jail, which is a couple of blocks away. This was at night, you understand, when there was nobody around. I hitched those jugheads to the bars in the window of the cell where Sam was locked up and yanked 'em right out. The deputies made it a mite hot for us, but I had a couple of fast horses waitin' and we were out of Comanche County before anybody could stop us."

"I'm not sure you should be telling stories like that, friend," the bartender said. "They could land you in some trouble."

Walt laughed, sounding drunk now. "Ol' Sam and I did worse'n that down there in Texas, but like he tried to tell that fat marshal, we ain't wanted in Kansas. Leastways . . . I don't think we are."

One of the men at the bar said, "Breakin' your pard out of jail down in some two-bit Texas town is one thing, but the jail here in Abilene is different. I don't reckon you can get him out of it."

"Not by myself, I can't." Walt sounded desolate as he said that. He held out his hand and went on to the bartender, "Gimme the bottle, why don't you?"

"I'll have to charge you. . . ."

Walt dug out a five-dollar gold piece and dropped it on the hardwood. The bartender nodded and pushed the half-empty bottle over to him.

Walt took hold of the neck and carried the bottle and his glass to an empty table in a corner. He sat down, poured a shot into the glass, and sat there nursing it, looking like his best friend had died . . . which apparently was a possibility as long as Sam was locked up. He looked so miserable that none of the men who had been talking to him at the bar wanted to intrude on his gloom.

He had been there about a quarter of an hour when a man in a frock coat and flat-crowned black hat pulled back the chair on the other side of the table and asked, "Mind if I join you, friend?"

Walt looked up into a lean face with a narrow mustache and a neat goatee. Even more than Carmody and Gene, this man looked like a professional gambler. The long, slender, nimble fingers reinforced that impression.

"I don't reckon you and I know each other, mister," Walt said, slurring the words just slightly. "I wouldn't call us friends."

"Perhaps that will change when you've heard what I have to say." The stranger gestured toward the empty chair. "May I?"

Walt waved at the chair, too. "Help yourself."

The man took off his hat, revealing neatly combed and pomaded dark hair. "My name is Yancey," he introduced himself, not elaborating as to whether that was his first or last name.

"Walt Smith."

"So I've heard. And your partner, who, unfortunately, is behind bars at the moment, is Sam Jones. I've also heard that those names grace any number of wanted posters in Texas and elsewhere."

"We ain't wanted in Kansas," Walt said stubbornly.

"The past is of no real concern to me," said Yancey. "I'm more interested in the future. I believe we can be of assistance to each other, Walt."

"How do you figure that?" Walt asked with a bleary frown.

"You want your friend Sam out of jail, correct? You don't want him to go to trial for shooting those two men?"

"I don't trust no Kansas judge nor jury!" Walt poured himself another drink, then belatedly added, "I don't have another glass."

"It doesn't matter, I assure you. I'm interested in more

than whiskey right now." Yancey leaned forward. "What would you say if I told you that I can arrange for your friend to be freed from his confinement?"

"You mean, like, hire him a lawyer or somethin'?"

"Nothing quite so formal."

Walt laughed. "No offense, mister, but you don't look like the sort of fella who could bust a man out of jail."

"Not me personally, perhaps . . . but I have friends. Friends who are quite capable of performing difficult tasks. Even violent tasks."

"You mean you're in with a bunch of outlaws."

"I wouldn't phrase it quite so crudely."

"Are you the boss of the gang?"

Yancey looked like the question irritated him, but he controlled the reaction and said, "I belong to an organization, but I'm not the head of it. You would have to speak to the person who is before an arrangement could be made. I assure you, however, that if your conversation is satisfactory, your friend Sam will be out of jail before morning."

Walt hadn't downed the last drink he poured himself. He pushed the glass away and rested both hands flat on the table. "That's puttin' it pretty plain," he said. "Who is this boss of yours?"

Yancey shook his head. "You don't need to know that. You simply have to convince him that if we give you and your friend a hand, then you and Sam will be willing to work with us."

"I don't get it. You say I've got to talk to him. If I do that, I'll know who he is, won't I?"

Yancey just smiled and didn't say anything.

Seconds ticked past, became a minute. Walt said, "Lemme get this straight. . . . If I agree that Sam and I will throw in with your bunch, then you'll bust him out of jail?"

"Not me personally—" Yancey began again, but Walt cut him off with a slashing motion of his hand.

"I know that part of it. If that's the deal, we'll take it."

"You're confident that you can speak for your friend?"

Walt let out a snort. "Believe me, if it means he'll get out of jail, Sam'll be willin' to do whatever it is you and your bunch want."

"If the stories I've heard are correct, it won't be anything you and Sam haven't done before."

Walt leered. "Well, that covers quite a bit of ground." He pushed himself to his feet and stood there swaying just slightly, like a man would who had consumed as much whiskey as he had. "Let's go see this mysterious boss of yours."

Chapter 9

Walt left the Alamo Saloon with Yancey. By that time, not many of the other patrons were paying much attention to Walt anymore, so only a few of them watched the two men go. As they stepped out onto the street, Walt drew in several deep breaths of the cool night air, as if he were trying to chase the cobwebs out of his head.

"Are you all right?" asked Yancey.

"I'm fine," Walt replied. "I had a mite to drink, but whiskey don't muddle me none."

"Come along, then."

Yancey led the way for a couple of blocks along the boardwalk before he turned a corner and went into a wooden, false-fronted building on a side street. The door was open, and Walt heard a familiar clicking sound coming from inside the place.

It was a pool hall with half a dozen tables. Only a couple of them were being used. The balls were racked and

ready on the other tables. To the left was a short bar with
kegs of beer behind it. In the back of the room were four
regular square tables with dominoes scattered on them.

Only one domino table had a man sitting at it. He toyed
with the dominoes in front of him, turning them face
down, then face up. The room was dimly lit by a couple of
lanterns up front. The feeble glow from them barely
reached back to where the domino tables sat, so Walt
couldn't get a good look at the man as he and Yancey approached.

It wouldn't have mattered how bright the place was,
Walt realized with a shock as he saw that the man wore a
black cloth hood under his dark hat. It had eyeholes in it,
but other than that it completely concealed his face. He
wore a long, heavy coat as well, so Walt couldn't tell anything about his other clothing.

"Is this the man?" the hooded stranger asked in a low,
harsh tone as he turned the dominoes face down again.
Walt could tell that he was deliberately disguising his
voice, and the hood muffled it some, as well.

"This is him," replied Yancey. "Walt Smith from
Texas."

"Sit down, Walt Smith," the hooded man invited. "Play
a hand with me."

"What the hell is this?" Walt burst out, unable to contain himself. "This is like somethin' out of a dime novel!"

"You mean because my identity is hidden?" The hooded
man chuckled. "Those cheap entertainments you speak of
are composed by desperate men with lurid imaginations,
often fueled by alcohol or other perversions, but occasionally they hit upon something useful, purely by accident, I assume. I prefer to keep my face and name to
myself. But I assure you, my intentions are sincere and
my plans profitable to those who take part in them." He

shuffled the dominoes and then pushed them into the center of the table. "Now, if you would help your friend . . . and yourself . . . sit down and play a hand."

Walt glanced around. Yancey stood not far behind him, right hand hovering so that he could reach easily under the frock coat. Walt knew there had to be a gun under there, and those nimble fingers could snatch it out in less than the blink of an eye.

The men who had been playing pool had paused in their games and stood leaning on their cue sticks, their attitudes tense and watchful. They were all armed and looked like they knew how to use the guns.

The situation was plain as day, thought Walt. *If I refuse to cooperate with the loco hombre in the hood, I will never walk out of here alive.*

"Sure," he said, forcing a smile onto his face as he pulled back the chair opposite the hooded man. "I've always enjoyed a good game of dominoes."

He drew nine dominoes and set them up facing him. The hooded man drew as well and pushed the boneyard to the side. Walt said, "Since you shuffled, I reckon I get to down."

The hooded man nodded.

"Got double-five anyway," said Walt as he placed the domino in the center of the table. "That's ten . . . if we're keeping score."

The hooded man played the five-blank. "And ten for me."

"And ten more," said Walt, pushing the double-blank into position.

"I'm sure Yancey explained our proposition." The blank-three went down.

"Not in detail. He said you'd get Sam out of jail if he and I agreed to go along with whatever you asked us to do." Walt played the five-two going the other way from the double. "Another nickel for me."

"I'm told you have experience with cattle that don't necessarily belong to you."

"Plenty of it," Walt declared. "I don't see no reason to beat around the bush. We're top hands, and nobody's better with a runnin' iron than me. That ain't braggin'."

"No, you sound like a man who's just stating a fact. You can speak for your friend?"

"I asked him that," Yancey put in. "He says he can."

"Damn right I can. Hell, when Sam and I drifted into these parts, this is just the sort of setup we were lookin' for. You get him out of jail and Sam will be fine with whatever you say."

Play had continued as they talked. The hooded man laid down the double-six. With a four at the other end of the line, Walt grinned and nudged the five-four up to the spinner.

"I do believe that's twenty."

The hooded man cut off the double-six with the six-two and recouped ten of those points. "You had a good hand," he commented. "Don't forget who rattled those bones."

That comment made Walt glance at the hooded man's hands. He noticed some white stains on the fingers and knew the man was a pool player, too. Those stains came from chalking a cue.

"I won't forget," Walt said. "What do I call you, anyway?"

"You won't have to call me anything." A chilly edge came into the hooded man's voice as he spoke. "In all likelihood, you won't be speaking to me again after tonight. You'll be dealing with someone else."

Walt inclined his head toward the gambler. "Yancey?"

"Yancey works here in town. You're getting too curious, Smith. Just go along with what you're told, and everything will become apparent to you."

"Yes, sir." Walt figured the note of respect was a good idea.

"So we have a deal?"

"Yes, sir, we sure do."

The tense feeling in the air eased somewhat. After a moment, the clicking of balls behind him told Walt that play had resumed on the pool tables.

He frowned as he studied the lone domino he had left in front of him. "Dadgum it. I was all set to domino, but now I can't play."

"I suppose you'll have to visit the boneyard."

Walt drew one of the extra dominoes to him, set it up, and sighed. He reached for another. He had to repeat that five more times before he finally drew one that would play.

The hooded man turned his sole remaining domino face up and sent it into the center of the table with a flick of a chalk-stained finger.

"I'm out."

Walt smiled and shook his head ruefully as he turned the dominoes in front of him face up. "You've got, let's see . . . fifteen . . . twenty . . . thirty points coming to you. Looks like you win after all."

"I always do," said the hooded man. "And you'd do well to remember that."

Yancey put a hand on Walt's shoulder and told him to come along. They left the hooded man sitting at the domino table and went out to the street.

"Now what happens?" asked Walt.

"Your horses are at the livery stable?"

"That's right."

"Get them," Yancey said. "Saddle them and have them ready to ride. Be behind the jail with them in an hour."

"That's it?"

"You can leave the rest to the boss," Yancey assured him.

"I sure hope this works," Walt muttered.

"That man hasn't steered us wrong so far. All of his plans have worked perfectly."

"Say," Walt added as if the idea had just occurred to him, "do you know who he really is?"

"I have enough sense not to worry about that," Yancey replied sharply. "All I care about is that my association with him has been lucrative so far. If I did have an idea as to his true identity . . . and I'm not saying that I do . . . I wouldn't be foolish enough to go around speculating about it where word might get back to him."

"I suppose that's the smart way to look at it."

"It's the safest way, that's certain. Now see about getting those horses, and be ready to ride hard when the time comes."

Sam lay on the bunk inside the jail cell with his arm across his face, shielding his eyes from the light. He wasn't asleep. He was listening intently. He knew Walt would be working to get him out of here, but he had no way of knowing how long it would take to set that up. The breakout might come tonight, or it might take a day or two.

Sam hoped that he wouldn't have to spend too long behind bars. Jails generally weren't meant to be comfortable, and the one in Abilene certainly wasn't. The bunk was just a steel frame bolted to the wall with a thin mattress and an even thinner blanket on it. Even if Sam wasn't trying to stay alert, it was unlikely he would have dozed off.

After a while, Sam swung his legs off the bunk and sat up. From where he was, he could see through the open door between the cell block and the marshal's office. Big Ben McCormick was out there; Sam could smell the foul smoke from the marshal's cheap cigar. McCormick had sent his deputies home for the night, telling them that he would remain on duty and guard the prisoner. *He made it sound as serious as if he had Jesse James locked up in here*, Sam thought.

Despite his best intentions, Sam got drowsy. He snapped fully awake, though, when somebody pounded on the front door of the marshal's office.

"Marshal McCormick! Marshal!" a man shouted from outside. "Please help! There's trouble down at the depot!"

"What in blazes?" McCormick muttered loud enough for Sam to hear him. Sam could see part of the front door from where he was. McCormick's large, bulky form moved into view and the lawman called, "Mr. Durham? Is that you?"

"Oh, thank goodness! Marshal, I think some men down at the depot are waiting to rob the westbound train when it comes through at ten o'clock!"

McCormick turned his head, cast a dubious glance toward the cell block as if trying to figure out what he should do, which responsibility he should make his priority. Then he lifted the bar that held the door shut from its brackets and swung the door inward.

Half a dozen men boiled in after it.

McCormick yelled and grabbed for the gun on his hip, but two of the intruders had hold of a prisoner, a medium-sized, balding man in a well-worn suit. They practically threw their captive at the marshal, using him as a battering ram of sorts. The hapless-looking gent clutched at McCormick, their legs tangled, and both men went down hard.

Sam was on his feet now, gripping the iron bars in the cell door and watching the struggle anxiously. All the intruders had their hats pulled low, and bandannas covered the lower halves of their faces. One of them stepped forward quickly, and as McCormick finally succeeded in pulling his gun from its holster, that man kicked it out of the lawman's hand.

Then several of the men pointed guns at the two squirming on the floor, and the one who had disarmed McCormick growled, "Settle down, Marshal, or we'll fill you and Durham full of holes."

Sam had no idea who Durham was, other than someone the outlaws had taken prisoner. The man grabbed McCormick's arm and cried, "Please, Marshal, don't let them hurt me! They . . . they kidnapped me and forced me to say those things to you—"

Angrily, McCormick shoved the townsman away. He let out a stream of profanity, then concluded by demanding, "What do you dirty coyotes want?"

"You've got a man locked up back there," replied the man who seemed to be the spokesman for the gang. "He's one of ours, and we want him."

McCormick jerked his head around to glare through the open cell block door at Sam. "Damn you!" he raged. "I knew you were an outlaw! Got your own gang, do you?"

Even though he couldn't see their faces, Sam was confident he had never laid eyes on these hombres before. But he just smiled and said, "Looks like you're about to lose a prisoner, Marshal."

"Get up and unlock that cell," the boss outlaw ordered McCormick.

The marshal looked like he wanted to argue, but it was hard to do that while staring down the barrels of half a dozen revolvers. He glanced at the frightened townsman, who had scooted over until he was sitting with his back against the desk, looking terrified. McCormick shook his head in disgust.

"Better move," said the spokesman, "or we'll start by blowing this little pipsqueak's brains out."

The townie's eyes widened. He started trembling and turned even paler than he already was.

"Take it easy, Durham," muttered McCormick. "I won't let 'em kill you." He looked up at the outlaws surrounding him. "If you want that blasted Texan, you can have him. The keys are right there."

He nodded toward a ring of keys hanging on a nail in the wall behind the desk.

One of the masked men stepped around the desk, grabbed the keys, and went into the cell block. He stopped in front of Sam's cell and looked through the bars at him. He sounded like he was grinning as he said, "Ready to rattle your hocks out of there, cowboy?"

"I've been ready ever since that badge-totin' tub of lard slammed the door behind me," said Sam.

The outlaw unlocked the door and swung it open. Sam stepped out into the narrow aisle between the rows of cells. The others were all empty tonight.

"Your pard's waiting behind the jail with your horses," said the man who had freed him. "We'll go out the back."

"One more thing first," Sam said. His long legs carried him to the office door.

The masked man who had been giving orders gestured to Marshal McCormick with his gun. "On your feet, Big Ben," the outlaw grated. "We've got one more thing to do."

McCormick glared defiantly as he pushed himself up. The outlaw's gun started rising to line up on his chest.

Before the man could fire, Sam stepped in front of McCormick and said, "I've been wantin' to do this ever since I laid eyes on you, Marshal."

Sam's knobby-knuckled fist came up in a blur of speed and smashed into McCormick's jaw with all the force of the former prisoner's rangy body behind it. The lawman's head snapped back hard and his knees buckled. He collapsed in a heap at Sam's feet.

"That'll pay you back some for roughin' me up," Sam said.

The boss outlaw said, "I don't blame you. Now step aside and I'll take care of— "

"This whole deal's been pretty quiet so far," Sam interrupted him. "The rest of the town don't know what's goin' on. But you start shootin' and they will."

The masked man stiffened as if he didn't like Sam interfering with his plans. But after a second he jerked his head in a nod and said, "You're right. It's better if we put some distance behind us before anybody knows you're gone." He glanced at Durham, who was still sitting on the floor looking scared. "We need to shut this little mouse up, too."

Durham cringed back against the desk and held his hands up. "No, please!" he cried. "You . . . you can put me in one of the cells and gag me so that I can't yell. Just please don't hurt me!"

The boss outlaw made a disgusted sound, but nodded to two of his men. "Do like he says."

In a matter of minutes, Durham was tied, gagged, and locked in the same cell Sam had occupied. The masked men dragged the unconscious Marshal McCormick into another cell, pulled his arms behind him and snapped handcuffs around his wrists, and stuffed a rag in his mouth to keep him quiet when he came to. It might be hours before anyone found them.

Sam had also retrieved his hat and gun belt and holstered Colt. It felt good to have the iron's weight on his hip again.

The outlaw with the keys unlocked the rear door and removed the bar from it. When it opened, Sam heard horses moving around outside. With the masked men around him, he went out into the alley behind the jail. Enough light spilled through the doorway for him to see Walt standing there holding the reins not only of his dun and Sam's Appaloosa but also half a dozen more horses. Then the door closed and thick shadows cloaked the alley again.

"Let's go," the boss said quietly.

Walt handed over the reins to each of the masked men. He and Sam swung up into their saddles.

"Take it slow and easy on the way out of town," the boss ordered. "Don't run the horses until we're far enough away that nobody will hear them."

That made for a nervous ten minutes as the group of riders moved slowly out of town, heading west. They didn't pick up the pace until the lights of Abilene had fallen well behind them.

Then, obeying a hissed command, they nudged their mounts ahead and picked up speed. The group, which had stayed in a compact bunch, spread out a little. Sam and

Walt rode side by side, with masked outlaws ahead of them and also behind.

But none of the others were close enough to overhear as the man who had called himself Walt Smith said, "It was mighty good to see you comin' out of that jail, Stovepipe. I wasn't sure what was goin' on in there."

"Don't worry, Wilbur," said Stovepipe Stewart. "It all worked like a charm."

Chapter 10

Austin, Texas, two weeks earlier

Stovepipe Stewart and Wilbur Coleman walked into the brick office building on Congress Avenue, a few blocks south of the state capital. A brass plaque beside the entrance read CATTLEMEN'S PROTECTIVE ASSOCIATION.

A male secretary showed Stovepipe and Wilbur right into the office of the association's head man, a tall, spare gent with a mostly bald dome and a neatly trimmed white mustache. Everybody who worked for him just called him the Colonel.

"Sit down, boys," he said as he waved a gnarled hand at the pair of red leather chairs in front of the big desk. The office was simply furnished—desk, chairs, a couple of filing cabinets—and the wood-paneled walls were covered with an assortment of maps depicting various areas of the western United States. "I got your report on that job you just finished up over in New Mexico Territory. Fine work, as usual."

Stovepipe took off his hat, crossed his legs, and hung the broad-brimmed black Stetson on his knee. "Thanks, boss. Things got a mite dicey there for a spell, but we were able to sort 'em out."

"That's putting it mildly," the Colonel said in a dry voice. "Half a dozen rustlers behind bars and no telling how many more sent across the divide in that big battle."

Wilbur said, "That was a bad bunch, Colonel. If they'd all been wiped out, it would've been fine with me."

Stovepipe chuckled. "Now, Wilbur, don't go givin' in to them bloodthirsty tendencies of yours. We're lawmen, of a sort, but that don't make us judge, jury, and executioners."

The Colonel picked up some papers from his desk, tapped them to straighten them, and then handed them across to Stovepipe. "I know you just got back, but there's more work for you. Have a look at those reports, and then pass them over to Wilbur."

Stovepipe scanned the reports quickly. His keen brain soaked up everything that was in them and sorted through what he read almost instantly. As he handed the documents to Wilbur, he said, "Sounds like an organized gang of train robbers and rustlers operatin' along the railroad up in Kansas. Do they only hold up trains carrying good-sized herds bound for market?"

"Four so far," confirmed the Colonel. "They've all been herds pooled from several spreads. Most of the owners affected are members of the association. You saw that I've received more than a dozen letters asking me if there's anything we can do." The Colonel cleared his throat. "Up until now, there really wasn't, because you boys were tied up on that other case. But now that you're back . . ."

The Colonel's voice was vehement as he leaned forward and continued, "I want you to go to Kansas, find out who's behind this ring, and break it up! It's bad enough that our members sometimes have to contend with rustling on their home range. They shouldn't have to worry once they've put their cows on the train and shipped them off to market!"

Wilbur, who didn't read quite as fast as Stovepipe, had finished the reports and correspondence. He placed the stack of papers on the desk and said, "The one thing these wide-looping jobs have in common is the railroad."

"I was thinkin' the same thing, Wilbur," said Stovepipe. He nodded slowly and deliberately, the same way he did most things . . . unless swift action was called for. "It would be easy for somebody who worked for the railroad and had access to the shippin' information to tip off the gang about which trains to hold up."

"You reckon we ought to try to work our way in on the railroad? Get jobs as brakemen or something?"

Stovepipe rasped a thumbnail along the line of his beard-stubbled jaw. "We might be able to do that, but it'd be pure luck if we were on the right train at the right time. We wouldn't know when the gang was primed to pull another holdup."

"How do you think we ought to tackle the job, then?"

Stovepipe smiled and said, "We'd know what the gang was plannin' if we joined up with it."

"You mean become rustlers?"

"You know the old sayin' . . . It takes an owlhoot to catch an owlhoot."

"Nobody ever said that," declared Wilbur.

"I just did."

"And you are pretty old," Wilbur gibed back at his partner. "Older than me, anyhow. How do you figure we'd find the gang to join up with them? Think maybe they've put up a sign sayin' they're hirin' experienced rustlers?"

"No, we'd have to fix things so that they'd recruit us," mused Stovepipe. "We could make ourselves look like just the sort of badmen they'd hanker to have ridin' with them."

The Colonel said, "I think you might be on to something, Stovepipe."

During the next half hour, the three men worked out the details of the plan. Stovepipe and Wilbur would have to have help from a couple of other agents working for the association, and they would need the cooperation—and discretion—of the local law in Abilene, too.

"Don't worry about that," the Colonel said when Stovepipe brought up that subject. "The man wearing the marshal's star in Abilene right now is Ben McCormick. Big Ben, everybody called him when we were in the same company during the Late Unpleasantness. He'll help us, and I'd trust him with my life, not just the ability to keep a secret."

"That's good, Colonel, because our lives will likely be ridin' on him bein' able to keep a secret," Stovepipe said.

The next day, he and Wilbur started north to Abilene. Two other association detectives, Phil Carmody and Gene Billings, headed in the same direction. The two pairs of men traveled separately, however, just to make sure that no one saw them together who might spot them later in Abilene and realize there was a connection between them. The plan they had worked out hinged on everyone believing that Carmody and Billings were strangers to Stovepipe and Wilbur.

The previous afternoon, the Colonel had traded several wires with Marshal Ben McCormick in Abilene, arranging for the lawman's part in the plan. As the Colonel had predicted, McCormick was happy to help them and pledged that not only would he keep the secret of what they were doing, he would also insure the telegrapher's discretion.

That was the angle that worried Stovepipe the most. If

the Colonel said Ben McCormick was trustworthy, that was good enough for Stovepipe. But the telegrapher was an unknown quantity, and they could only hope that McCormick was able to convince the man to keep his mouth shut.

As far as Stovepipe could tell, the plan had gone off without a hitch. The "trouble" he and Wilbur had with Carmody and Billings, the ambush and shoot-out, the "killings" of the other two operatives, and then Stovepipe being locked up, all of it fell into place. Wilbur had spread stories about their lawbreaking past in Texas, dangling that like bait . . . and the mysterious hooded mastermind and his gang had swallowed it, hook, line, and proverbial sinker.

The only thing that had come close to going wrong was the leader of the group breaking Stovepipe out of jail had gotten it into his head to shoot Marshal McCormick. Stovepipe had had to think and act quickly to prevent that and still preserve his masquerade as Texas outlaw Sam Jones.

The Colonel would never forgive Stovepipe if he allowed his old friend and comrade-in-arms to be gunned down like that!

So now Stovepipe and Wilbur were on their way . . . somewhere . . . surrounded by some of the very men they had come here to bring to justice. It was a mighty tense situation in which the two range detectives found themselves, so it was lucky that both of them were icy-nerved hombres.

They rode all night, stopping only occasionally to allow the horses to rest. Not much talking went on during those halts. The outlaws had been willing to run the risk of breaking Stovepipe and Wilbur out of jail, but they weren't welcoming the two men into the gang with open arms. It would take some time for them to be accepted, Stovepipe knew.

By the time the sun came up behind them, the men and horses were all tired and ready to be at their destination. Fortunately, it was almost in sight, although Stovepipe and Wilbur didn't know that as the riders approached a low bluff that cut across the landscape from north to south in front of them.

The outlaws had long since lowered the bandannas that masked their faces. The fact that Stovepipe and Wilbur could see what they looked like in the growing light ratcheted up the tension that much more. They really had to pull off their deception now. If they didn't, it was a surefire death sentence.

The leader, a rangy man with rusty red hair sticking out from under his hat, hipped around in the saddle and said to Stovepipe and Wilbur, "We'll be at the hideout pretty soon. You boys ready for some breakfast?"

"Durned sure am," replied Stovepipe. "And after ridin' all night, some shut-eye would be welcome, too."

"You might've wound up with your eyes shut permanent-like if we hadn't gotten you out of that jail. You'd do well to remember that, Jones."

"I ain't likely to forget it. I've already said that I'm much obliged to you fellas, but I don't mind sayin' it again."

The leader waved that off. "You'll earn your keep, if things work out. If they don't . . ." He shrugged. "Well, none of us will have to worry about that, will we?"

Stovepipe and Wilbur exchanged a glance. They knew what the outlaw meant. If things didn't work out, both of them would be dead.

The redheaded owlhoot led the group straight toward what appeared to be the unbroken face of the bluff, which rose about twenty feet above the endless prairie behind them. When they got closer, Stovepipe spotted what at first appeared to be a notch that soon turned into the opening of a narrow passage cutting through the terrain as if a giant knife had been pressed down into it.

The trail didn't run as straight as a knife edge, though. It had a few kinks, as Stovepipe and Wilbur discovered as they rode through it. The passage was wide enough for two men to ride abreast. The redhead and another member of the gang went first, followed by the two range detectives, then the other four owlhoots stretched out single file behind them.

The walls of the cut were sheer, offering no way out. Of course, Stovepipe and Wilbur didn't want out. They had come all this way to discover what was waiting at the end of the hidden trail.

After several minutes of riding, the bluff fell away on both sides and the trail emerged into a small, narrow valley bounded all around by hills. Several soddies were built into the side of one of those hills. Thin curls of pale smoke rose from tin pipes shoved through the earthen roofs of those soddies. Faint, tantalizing smells of coffee and bacon drifted through the air on dawn breezes.

Stovepipe spotted a number of horses grazing on sparse grass inside a rope corral about fifty yards away from the primitive dwellings. He had thought that when they reached the hideout, the stolen cattle might be secreted there, but he saw now that wasn't the case. The saddle mounts were the only animals in sight. The valley was too small to hold even a single shipping herd, let alone the several that were missing.

Men began to emerge from the soddies. They must have heard the hoofbeats of the approaching horses. All of them wore holstered revolvers. Some were two-gun men. A few carried rifles as well as packing handguns.

All were roughly dressed, with hard-planed faces—an intimidating bunch of gun-wolves if Stovepipe had ever seen one.

A man strode out to meet them. He wore canvas trousers stuck down in high-topped, fringed boots. Suspenders draped over a homespun shirt that had been white once before being darkened by grime and sweat. The curved brim, dark brown hat on his head had an eagle feather stuck in the band. A black mustache drooped over his lips and a pointed goatee jutted out from his chin.

He came to a stop and didn't look happy as he stood there with a Winchester held at a slant across his chest. He demanded, "Who the hell are these strangers, Clete? I expected you to come back from Abilene with supplies and maybe a little news, not two ugly galoots like this."

Wilbur frowned and leaned forward in the saddle as if he wanted to take issue with that "ugly" assessment. Stovepipe caught his friend's eye and gave a tiny shake of his head, urging Wilbur to let the comment ride.

He could understand Wilbur's annoyance, though, since the fella calling them ugly was no prize in the looks department himself.

"It wasn't my idea to bring them along, Jester," the redheaded outlaw called Clete replied. "It was orders."

Jester frowned. "From him?"

"That's right." Clete turned a little and waved his left hand at Stovepipe and Wilbur. "Meet Sam Jones and Walt Smith from Texas. Jones is the tall, skinny one. We broke him out of Big Ben McCormick's jail."

"What was he locked up for?"

"A shooting scrape that left a couple of tinhorn gamblers dead. But they were already on the dodge from rustling charges down in Texas. Yancey talked to the little one, then to the boss, and he decided they might be of some use to us. The boss decided, that is."

"I knew Yancey wouldn't make a decision like that," snapped Jester. His hostile stance eased some as he lowered the Winchester and held it at his side in his right hand. He moved closer and looked up at Stovepipe and Wilbur. "You two headed north when it got a mite hot for you down in Texas, eh?"

"Never said that, exactly," Stovepipe answered stiffly.

"Oh, hell, don't worry about admitting it. Everybody here is in the same boat. The law's after us somewhere. My name's Jester McMillan. You've probably heard of me."

Stovepipe hadn't, but he knew the outlaw probably wouldn't want to hear that. So he said slowly, "McMillan . . . Yeah."

"I'm the ramrod of this outfit. Go ahead and light down from those horses. My woman just about has mornin' grub ready, and she always makes plenty. You boys can join us."

"We appreciate that. Like your friend told you, my handle's Jones—"

"And your partner's name is Smith," McMillan cut in. "Yeah, that's fine for now. We don't stand much on formality around here." His voice hardened as Stovepipe and Wilbur swung down from their saddles. "Don't get the wrong idea, though. You're here because the fella I work with thinks it's a good idea. But if I don't agree, it'll be too bad for you gents."

"Are you sayin' we'd have to leave? Feet first, maybe?"

McMillan laughed. "Hell, no. You won't be leaving at all if I decide you can't be trusted."

"Well, that's puttin' it plain, anyway."

McMillan turned and motioned. Two outlaws walked up. McMillan said, "Give your horses to these boys. They'll see to it that they're taken care of. We'll go get that breakfast, and then you might want to rest up for a spell after riding all the way out here from Abilene."

"Hospitable of you," drawled Stovepipe. "We're obliged."

"No need to be inhospitable . . . until the time comes, if it does." Jester McMillan jerked his head toward the soddy from which he had emerged a few minutes earlier. He led the way with Stovepipe and Wilbur following him. Here in the hideout, he obviously wasn't worried about turning his back on them. He knew that if they tried anything, they would be shot full of holes a couple of seconds later.

Clete and the rest of the men who had busted Stovepipe out of jail headed for the corral to put their horses away before scattering to other parts of the camp.

As they neared the soddy, McMillan called, "Lena! We've got company."

Stovepipe wasn't sure what to expect, but as a woman stepped out of the primitive structure, wiping her hands on a cloth, he was pretty sure this wasn't it.

Because she was one of the downright prettiest gals he had seen in a long time.

Chapter 11

The woman who had come out of the soddy had thick, dark hair that tumbled in waves around her face, across her shoulders, and halfway down her back. Her olive-skinned face was, perhaps, not classically beautiful, but Stovepipe found it very attractive, especially the compelling brown eyes.

She wore a low-necked white blouse that showed off her lush figure. A long brown skirt hugged her wide, richly curved hips.

A gun belt was strapped around those hips with a Colt revolver riding in the attached holster. In a camp full of hardened outlaws, it wasn't really surprising that a beautiful woman would go armed.

She lowered the cloth she had been using to wipe her hands and held it at her left side. Her right hand hung near the Colt. The look she gave Stovepipe was challenging. Her gaze darted over to Wilbur for a second and then came back to the taller range detective.

"Who are these men, Jester?" she asked in a husky voice.

"Smith and Jones, if you can believe that," McMillan answered.

The woman let out a skeptical snort, clearly not caring if such a sound wasn't ladylike. "I can't," she said, "but I don't suppose it matters what their real names are, does it?"

"Not so's you'd notice." McMillan nodded at them. "Jones is the tall drink of water."

"Mr. Smith. Mr. Jones. What brings you here?"

Stovepipe took off his hat before he answered her. "I figured the surroundings would be healthier, ma'am, seein' as the last place I spent any time was a jail cell."

"And I wasn't behind bars," Wilbur said, "but I go where Sam goes."

McMillan said, "Yancey came up with the idea of breaking Jones out of jail and figured we might be able to use them. The boss agreed, or at least that's what Clete says."

"Clete is smart enough not to lie about orders from the boss," the woman said. She was still looking at Stovepipe. "So you're new recruits, so to speak."

"Yes'm, I reckon you could say that."

She smiled slightly. "And polite, too. You take off your hat and say 'ma'am' and everything." She glanced at McMillan. "Maybe some of the other men around here could learn something from you."

McMillan scowled. "I know everything I need to know," he snapped. "Like I'm hungry and breakfast is ready."

"So it is," the woman agreed. "Go on in. You too," she told Stovepipe and Wilbur. "Since Jester isn't going to introduce us, I'll tell you that my name is Lena."

Stovepipe had heard the outlaw address her by that

name, but he nodded and said, "It's an honor and a pleasure to meet you, Miss Lena."

"Likewise, ma'am," Wilbur added as he took off his hat, too.

She glanced at McMillan as if to say *See?*, but he just scowled some more and headed into the soddy, saying, "C'mon," over his shoulder.

Stovepipe gestured for Lena to go ahead, then he and Wilbur followed her into the soddy.

These earthen dwellings were made for shelter, not comfort. Slabs of sod were cut out and piled up to form walls on three sides; the hillside itself was the rear wall of the single room inside. An interlocking framework of branches tied together with twine supported thinner slabs of sod that formed the roof. The floor was dirt, as well.

Furniture consisted of a rough-hewn table with four equally crude chairs around it, a potbellied stove in one corner, a Dutch oven, and a narrow bunk with a corn shuck mattress placed atop woven rope webbing. A tangle of dirty blankets lay on the mattress.

Surrounded by dirt like this, the air in the room had a damp, oppressive feel to it. The smells of coffee, bacon, and fresh biscuits coming from the stove helped alleviate that a little.

"Sit down," Lena told the men. "And take your hats off. This may feel like a barn, but that doesn't mean you're going to act like animals."

The men doffed their hats as they sat down. McMillan said, "Damn it, now you've got her thinkin' she ought to be treated like a lady."

"Nothin' wrong with that," said Stovepipe.

"Huh. Why don't you tell 'em where you came from and the job you were doing there when you took up with me, Lena?"

"You just hush up, Jester McMillan," she said without turning from the stove. "There's at least a chance I've changed, but you're still the same jackass you always were."

The sudden flare of anger in McMillan's eyes told Stovepipe the words weren't just the affectionate banter they might have been. It appeared that McMillan and Lena didn't actually like each other all that much, although Stovepipe had no doubt she was the outlaw's woman.

None of which had anything to do with why he and Wilbur were here, so he warned himself to rein in his naturally chivalrous nature. Stirring up trouble between McMillan and Lena wouldn't do their cause any good. She was a grown woman and could look after her own interests.

She brought over a coffeepot and three tin cups, filled the cups with the strong, black, steaming brew. She followed that with tin plates heaped with bacon and thick biscuits.

"It's not what you'd call fancy," she said, "but it'll fill your bellies."

"Fancy enough for me, ma'am," Wilbur assured her. "When you've made many a meal on jerky and creek water on a cold, dark night, sittin' down to a table and a meal like this is mighty welcome."

"Ridden some lonely trails, have you, cowboy?"

"Yes, ma'am. Mighty lonely. The sort of trails where the owls hoot sort of mournful-like."

"That's enough," McMillan said. "Let a man eat in peace, why don't you?"

Lena sniffed and turned away. Stovepipe started to ask her if she wasn't going to join them, then he remembered his resolution of only a few minutes earlier. He stuffed another bite into his mouth and didn't say anything.

The rest of the meal passed in silence except for when McMillan demanded more coffee. As Stovepipe used his last piece of biscuit to wipe up the final smears of bacon grease, he ventured, "What is it you fellas do? You must have somethin' profitable in mind to have gathered up a bunch like this. Bank job, maybe?"

"Bank job, hell," said McMillan. "When you rob a bank, you have to ride into a town and risk getting shot at by a bunch of storekeepers and hayseeds to get your hands on any money. And unless you have inside information, you never know for sure how much loot's going to be in one of those vaults." He downed the last of his coffee, leaned back, and sighed. "We have a better setup, one that's bound to pay off big in the end, and not nearly as much risk as raiding a town and having to fight your way out."

"Is that so? I'm all ears. And so's Wilbur. See the way his stick out?"

"Hey," Wilbur began.

"Don't get so damn nosey," McMillan cut in. "You'll know what you need to know when you need to know it." He chuckled suddenly, the first sign of anything approaching good humor he had displayed. "You were talking about ears, and I said not to get so damn nosey. Haw!"

Behind his back, Lena rolled her eyes. Stovepipe saw that and had to make an effort not to laugh. He thought she saw the amusement in his eyes, though.

McMillan grew more serious as he went on, "Just keep your mouths shut, don't go prying into our business, and wait until the time is right. Otherwise you're liable to get on my nerves, and you don't want that."

"No, sir, we sure don't," Stovepipe agreed. "We'll just sort of lie low, won't we, Walt?"

"Yeah. That's fine with us, McMillan."

Stovepipe finished his coffee and said, "That fella Clete said we might be able to get a little shut-eye."

McMillan nodded and pushed to his feet. "Yeah, come on. I'll show you where you can sleep. You can borrow some bunks in one of the other soddies."

Stovepipe and Wilbur stood up. Stovepipe couldn't stop himself from saying, "We're mighty obliged to you for the breakfast, ma'am."

"It sure was good," added Wilbur.

"Thank you," Lena said. "It's always nice to know your efforts are appreciated."

McMillan grunted and motioned curtly for them to follow him.

He took them to the soddy closest to the makeshift corral. Two men sat on kegs in front of the blanket that hung over the doorway. One of them was whittling while the other smoked a pipe.

"Tom Church and Jonas Page," McMillan said with a nod toward them. He jerked a thumb at his two companions. "Sam Jones and Walt Smith."

Church was the whittler, Page the pipe-smoker. They said their howdies, and McMillan went on, "These two Texans are gonna borrow your bunks."

"Don't have no ticks, do you?" asked Church. "I've heard about you Texas boys bringin' tick fever up the trail with you."

"No nasty little varmints crawlin' around on us as far as I know," said Stovepipe.

Page grinned, nudged Church with an elbow, and said, "They might not be able to claim that after they've spent a while in them bunks, ain't that right, Tom?"

"Ignore these two jokers," McMillan said. "Later I'll introduce you to the rest of the bunch."

Wilbur said, "How long do you think it'll be before we see some action?"

McMillan scowled at him. "There you go, getting nosey again. We had a talk about that, didn't we?"

"Sorry, boss. Reckon I forgot."

Being called boss seemed to mollify McMillan. He gave them a curt nod and headed back toward his soddy.

Wilbur frowned and said to Church and Page, "Say, you boys really were jokin' about there bein' vermin in those bunks, weren't you?"

"Sleep a spell in 'em and find out," Church said. Then he grinned and reached up to slowly and deliberately scratch under his arm.

Abilene

Smoke was already on the passenger car's front platform with his carpetbag in his left hand as the train slowed its speed and rolled into the Abilene depot. He swung down to the station platform before the train even stopped moving.

He had brought a couple of good saddle mounts with him from the Sugarloaf, so the first thing he did was to make arrangements for the horses to be unloaded and taken to a nearby livery stable. Then he headed for the marshal's office.

A big, broad-shouldered, barrel-chested man sat at the desk in the office. He looked up when Smoke walked in. Smoke immediately noticed two things: the badge pinned to the man's shirt, and the bruised, swollen lump on his jaw. It looked like somebody had walloped him with a two-by-four.

"Something I can do for you, mister?" asked the lawman. The puffy jaw made his voice a little thick.

"You're Marshal McCormick?"

"That's right."

"I'm Smoke Jensen, from Big Rock, Colorado. You sent me a telegram a couple of days ago."

Recognition flared in McCormick's eyes. He might not have ever seen Smoke before, but he knew the name, sure enough. He got to his feet and extended a brawny arm across the desk to shake hands.

"Mighty pleased to meet you, Jensen. I've heard plenty about you. Sorry we're not crossing trails under better circumstances."

"So am I," Smoke agreed. "Before we discuss anything else, I want to know about my man Hobart Ford."

"Hobart? He said his name was Pinky."

"That's what his friends call him. Is he still alive?"

McCormick nodded. "As a matter of fact, he is. I went by the doc's house this morning to check on him. As bad as those outlaws shot him up, I didn't figure he'd pull through. The doc says he's stubborn, though, and stronger than he looks."

Smoke allowed himself a slight smile at that. "I believe it," he said. "I'll want to see him for myself, and make sure the doctor knows to spare no expense in taking care of him."

"Don't worry about that. Doc Metzger wouldn't let anybody die because of money, not even a stray dog. The man's just a natural-born healer."

"I'm glad to hear it," said Smoke. "Now, your telegram gave me the basics of what happened, but if you know any more details, I'd like to hear them."

"Sure." McCormick nodded Smoke into the leather chair in front of the desk. Gingerly, he touched the purple lump on his jaw and went on, "You must be wondering if I ran smack-dab into a mule kick."

"Couldn't help but notice that somebody fetched you a good clout," Smoke said as he sat down.

The marshal grunted. "Had a prisoner escape last night. I locked him up for shooting and killing a couple of other fellas. I didn't realize he had a gang in town with him that would break him out."

"I don't suppose that has anything to do with the raid on the train?" Smoke asked.

McCormick frowned. "I don't hardly see how it could have. The gent I locked up didn't ride into town until a couple of days after that. He and the fella he was with came from the south, too." The big lawman shrugged. "Of course, they could've circled around from the west, I suppose. Can't rule that out. If I ever see the varmint again, I'll ask him. And after that sucker punch he gave me, I'd sure like to see him again, you can bet a hat on that."

Giving in to momentary curiosity, Smoke asked, "How did they get the drop on you?"

"They grabbed the station manager from down at the depot, a gent named Clark Durham, and forced him at gunpoint to feed me a phony story about somebody getting ready to rob the westbound when it came through." McCormick shook his head. "I should've known better than to open the door, but by the time I figured that out, it was too late."

"Sorry you lost a prisoner, Marshal. But about that train holdup . . ."

For the quarter hour, Smoke and McCormick discussed what had happened. Smoke didn't learn any more than he already knew, however, except the exact location of the incident. The story as conveyed by Pinky, the train crew, and the other survivors, and then passed on to him in the tersely worded telegram, had been pretty much complete.

McCormick leaned back in his chair, which squealed a little under his weight, and clasped his hands together on his ample belly. "If you don't mind me asking, what is it you intend to do, Mr. Jensen? Did you come to get your wounded man and take him home? If you did, I think it's gonna be a spell before he'll be up to traveling."

"No, I'm happy to leave him in the care of your Dr. Metzger," Smoke said. "I plan on finding those stolen cattle."

McCormick's bushy eyebrows rose in surprise. "Did you bring a posse with you from Colorado?"

"No, just me."

The marshal looked a little like he thought Smoke was loco. He said, "If you want to pick up the trail of that rustled herd, you've come too far. They stopped the train a long way west of here."

"I know that. And I considered making a straight tracking job out of it. But then I thought I might take a different approach and try to find out who was behind the holdup." Smoke paused. "I believe he might be here in Abilene."

McCormick sat up straight with a look of keen interest on his face. "You know who the ramrod of that gang is?"

Smoke shook his head. "No, but I have an idea he's somewhere in town."

"You're gonna have to explain that. I don't follow at all."

"The outlaws knew there was going to be a big herd on that train, big enough to make it worthwhile to stop it. This was the first time all the spreads in the valley where my ranch is located have pooled their herds to ship them to market. It wasn't exactly a secret on our end, but there was no reason for anyone here in Abilene to know about it except folks who work for the railroad."

"And you think one of them tipped off the rustlers and planned the holdup?"

"Seems like the possibility is worth checking out," said Smoke.

McCormick looked dubious. "Sounds like a long shot to me. But if you want to poke around the railroad, I don't reckon there's any law against it. Red Winters may not take kindly to it, though."

"Red Winters?" Smoke repeated.

"Local superintendent for the railroad."

"I thought you said a fella named Durham was the manager."

McCormick chuckled. "Clark Durham runs the station. Red Winters runs the *railroad.* He's Durham's boss, and the boss of everybody else who works for the line. Seems to think the whole shebang is his own personal possession, too . . . the station, the tracks, the rolling stock, the people who work for him. The railroad is Red's baby, and he doesn't like it when anybody messes with his baby."

"He ought to be pretty upset about that holdup, then," Smoke said.

"Yeah, I'd say so. But he won't like it if you come around acting like somebody who works for him might be behind it."

"I reckon he'll just have to get over it," Smoke said. "But the next thing I want to do is go see my rider, if you don't mind telling me where to find Dr. Metzger's practice."

"Sure." McCormick gave Smoke directions, then shook hands with him again as both men stood up. "If there's anything else I can do for you, Jensen, just let me know. Of course, my jurisdiction extends only to the town. But as long as you're in Abilene, I'll be glad to help."

"Thanks, Marshal," Smoke said, keeping his true reaction to himself. He wasn't overly impressed with Marshal Ben McCormick; the lawman didn't seem all that bright.

Chapter 12

Smoke found Dr. Allan Metzger's practice on one of Abilene's side streets. The neat frame house behind a picket fence and flower bed contained both Metzger's office and his living quarters, according to Marshal McCormick. Smoke opened the gate in the fence and went up a short walk to the porch.

An attractive woman in her thirties answered his knock. "Yes? Can I help you?"

Smoke took off his hat and said, "I'd like to see one of your patients. Hobart Ford. He works for me. I'm Smoke Jensen."

The smile that appeared on the woman's face made her even more attractive. "We've heard a great deal about you, Mr. Jensen," she said. "Pinky has told us all about you and your ranch."

"You call him Pinky, too?"

"He insisted." The woman stepped back and ushered Smoke inside. "I'll show you to Pinky's room and let the doctor know you're here."

She led him past what would have normally been a parlor but was set up as an office and waiting room. She opened a door in a hallway and said, "You have a visitor, Pinky."

"Smoke!" the young cowboy exclaimed as Smoke stepped through the doorway with a smile on his face. "It's mighty good to see you!"

"Likewise," Smoke said as he moved alongside the bed where Pinky was sitting up, propped on an abundance of pillows. Bandages swathed the youngster's torso, but his color was good and he seemed surprisingly alert considering that the doctor probably was giving him medication for the pain of his wounds.

Pinky raised his arm and shook hands, then his smile went away and he looked solemn as he said, "I sure am sorry about losin' that herd, Smoke. Mr. Dixon and Bill Caldwell and I did everything we could to stop those train robbers, but there were just too many of 'em. And they didn't show no mercy." Pinky swallowed hard. "They killed so many people it just makes me sick, and hurt so many others."

"Including yourself," Smoke pointed out. "Don't worry, Pinky, I know you put up a good fight."

"I hope I ventilated some of the sons o'—"

He stopped short as the nurse appeared in the doorway again, this time accompanied by a short, spare man with gray hair.

"Mr. Jensen? I'm Dr. Allan Metzger."

Smoke shook hands with him and said, "Doctor, I sure do appreciate you taking such good care of Pinky here."

Metzger wore a pair of wire-framed spectacles. His face remained impassive, but his eyes were friendly as he said, "Most of the credit goes to young Mr. Ford himself. The lad has an iron constitution. I simply took steps to prevent his wounds from becoming infected. He's done the rest of the work himself." Metzger paused, then added, "Whoever feeds him has been doing a good job of keeping him healthy."

"That would be my wife, Sally. I'll pass that along to her when I get home."

The doctor frowned slightly. "I hope you're not planning on taking my patient back to Colorado right away, Mr. Jensen. I'm afraid he still needs a lot of rest and recuperation before he'll be strong enough for such a trip, even on the train."

"No, sir, I'm perfectly happy to leave him in the care of yourself and this lady for now."

Metzger nodded toward the woman and said, "I'm sorry, I should have introduced you. This is my nurse, Miss Theresa Harrell."

"Pleasure to know you, ma'am. And thank you for everything you've done for Pinky, too."

"He's a good patient," she said. "Very cooperative."

"Aw, shucks . . ." muttered Pinky. Smoke saw that he was blushing. Even under the circumstances, he probably enjoyed the attention of an attractive, somewhat older woman.

Smoke went on, "Doctor, I'd like to settle up with you for what you've done so far and see to it that you're paid some in advance for the rest of Pinky's recuperation. And any time you need more, if I'm not around town you can always wire Mrs. Sally Jensen at the Sugarloaf Ranch, care of the Western Union office in Big Rock, Colorado."

"I appreciate that, Mr. Jensen, but if I intended to worry very much about money, I never would have become a doctor. We'll work everything out."

Pinky said, "Smoke, you're not plannin' to stay here in Abilene until I'm ready to go home, are you?"

Smoke shook his head. "No, I'm afraid I can't do that. I have another job I have to tend to."

"Trackin' down those rustlers and gettin' that stolen herd back?" Pinky asked eagerly.

"That's the idea. I'm going to give it my best shot."

Pinky sighed and said, "I wish I was well enough to come with you."

"So do I, but in the meantime, tell me all you can remember about what happened."

Dr. Metzger said, "We'll leave you two to talk. Just don't tire out this young man too much, Mr. Jensen."

"I'll only stay as long as Pinky is up to it," Smoke promised.

The doctor and nurse left the room. Smoke pulled a ladderback chair beside the bed and sat down. He and Pinky talked for a while. The young cowboy recounted the events of the train robbery as well as he remembered them.

"I'm sorry there's not more I can tell you, Smoke," he concluded. "Honestly, when I got shot, just before I passed out I figured I was a goner. Nobody was more surprised than me when I woke up."

"Well, I'm glad you did. Do you recall anything about the men who held up the train? Anything unusual about the way they looked?"

Pinky shook his head. "They were wearin' masks and had their hats pulled down low. I never saw the faces of any of 'em. It bein' nighttime like it was, I probably wouldn't have been able to tell much about 'em, even if I had."

Smoke reached over and patted Pinky's leg under the sheet that was drawn up to his waist. "Don't worry about that. From here on out, all you have to do is rest and get better."

"Mr. Jensen . . . Smoke . . ." Pinky's face was serious.

"What is it?"

"If you could settle the score for Mr. Dixon and Bill Caldwell, I sure would appreciate it."

"You can count on that, Pinky," vowed Smoke. "One way or another, I'll see that justice is done."

On his way back to the railroad station, Smoke stopped by the livery stable to make sure his horses were being cared for. Satisfied that they were, he headed on toward the large, redbrick depot.

At some point he'd have to see about getting a hotel room, he supposed, but right now he was still more interested in the job that had brought him to Abilene.

He stopped at the ticket window and told the clerk on the other side of the wicket, "I'm looking for Red Winters."

"Mr. Rudolph Winters's office is over there on the other side of the lobby," the clerk said as he pointed to a door. "Do you have an appointment?"

"Nope."

"I don't know if Mr. Winters will see you, then."

"He'll see me," Smoke said, adding, "Much obliged," as he turned to cross the lobby. He didn't look back to see what the clerk's reaction was.

A small sign on the door read RUDOLPH WINTERS, SUPERINTENDENT. On another door a few yards away was a sign reading CLARK DURHAM, STATION MANAGER. Smoke wondered for a second if he ought to speak to Durham first, then discarded the idea. He believed in going straight to the top and not wasting time.

He turned the knob and went into a small anteroom with a desk in it. A young man in a cheap suit sat there. He looked up and said, "Yes?"

"I'm guessing you're not Mr. Winters."

"No, I'm his secretary. How can I help you?"

"I need to talk to Winters." Smoke stepped toward another door on the far side of the anteroom.

The secretary was on his feet instantly, holding out a hand. "Excuse me, sir, you can't—"

"No offense, son, but I reckon I can."

Ignoring the secretary's protest, Smoke opened the door and stepped into Winters's office.

Two men were in the office, standing in front of a large map on the left-hand wall. Also on that wall was a large blackboard with a grid marked on it, along with times written across the top and names of towns down the left-hand side. Some of the squares in the grid had check marks in them. It was a schedule board, Smoke realized, where Winters could keep track of all the trains running through his section.

An open door in the right-hand wall led into another office. Smoke figured the connecting office probably belonged to Clark Durham, the station manager. It made sense that Winters and Durham would work closely together.

And they had to be the two men in front of the map who turned to face him in surprise. "Excuse me," the smaller man said. "We told Chester we weren't to be disturbed—"

"Don't get mad at the young fella," said Smoke. "He tried to stop me. Well, he didn't try all that hard . . . but I didn't give him a chance to, either."

"Who the hell are you?" demanded the larger man.

They might both be railroad executives, but that was where the similarities ended. The big man was brawny, with a shock of white hair and a rugged face with a deep, permanent tan from long years working outside. Despite the white hair, he was probably still in his forties. An air of strength and vitality came from him, and even though he wore a suit, shoes, a white shirt, and a cravat with a fancy stickpin in it, he looked like he would be just as much at home in work boots, canvas trousers, and a flannel shirt.

The other man was smaller, balding, and pale, obviously someone who had spent most or all of his working years in an office. He was probably in his late thirties, Smoke guessed.

"You're Winters," Smoke said, nodding to the white-haired man but not answering his question, "and you're Durham." He gave a second nod to the other man.

"That's right," Winters said as he took a step toward Smoke. "And I don't like folks having the advantage on me. I asked you who the hell you are, mister. I'll add, what the hell are you doing here?"

"My name is Smoke Jensen. I came to talk to you about a herd of cattle stolen from one of your trains a few days ago by a bunch of owlhoots and killers."

For a second, Winters glanced over his shoulder at the map on the wall behind him. Smoke looked at the map, too, and recognized it as a map of the country's midsection, stretching from Missouri on the east to Colorado on the west. A line going across the middle of Kansas had to be the railroad.

Smoke took that in instantly, in the heartbeat that Winters glanced back, and he noted as well that several pins were stuck in the map, right along that line.

Winters faced him again and asked, "What business is that of yours?"

"Some of them were my cows. The rest belonged to my friends and neighbors. And I was the one who came up with the idea of shipping them all at the same time, so I sort of feel responsible for what happened."

"Those outlaws are responsible, nobody else," snapped Winters.

Smoke nodded. "That's true, of course. But I feel like I'm duty-bound to try to set things right."

"That's the railroad's job, and the law's job, as well." Winters regarded Smoke with a frown. "I recognize your name, Jensen. You have a reputation for taking the law into your own hands, don't you?"

"I just try to do what's right," Smoke said. "I don't want to see the other ranchers suffer a bad loss because of some idea I came up with."

"Well, the railroad's not going to make up the loss, if that's what you're getting at. The contract your representative signed with us makes it clear the railroad isn't to blame for any loss outside our control . . . and getting held up by a bunch of bloodthirsty owlhoots sure as hell wasn't in our control!"

Winters's face was starting to flush angrily. Smoke wondered fleetingly if that was how the man had gotten his nickname or if his hair had been red before it turned white.

Winters took a deep breath and reined in his temper with a visible effort. "I lost a fireman and a good friend in that holdup," he went on, "and passengers who trusted our line to carry them to their destinations were killed, too. I want that bunch brought to justice just as much as you do, Jensen. More, I'd wager."

Smoke didn't waste time arguing about who wanted justice more. He said, "Have you made any progress toward finding out who was responsible for what happened?"

Clark Durham spoke up for the first time. "The sheriff in the county where the holdup took place got together a posse and tried to follow the thieves. They lost the trail after several miles."

"Seems hard to believe anybody could push a herd that size without leaving plenty of sign," Smoke said.

"There's a lot of rugged country out there in that part of the state," said Winters. "It's not like around here. Drive a herd over a wide enough rocky stretch and you can give pursuers the slip."

Smoke considered that. He had spent some time in western Kansas, not a lot but enough to know that Winters was telling the truth about the terrain. Folks tended to think of Kansas as being all lushly grassed farm and ranch country, but that wasn't the case everywhere.

Of course, he wasn't convinced that he would have lost the trail, and he knew some old mountain men he was sure wouldn't have, but for now he felt like he had a better chance of tracking down the outlaws by starting here in Abilene.

"What about the boss of the outfit?" he asked.

Winters looked puzzled. "The boss of those rustlers? He's with the rest of the gang, I suppose."

"I don't think so," Smoke said. "I think he's a lot closer than you might realize."

It took a moment for Winters to realize what Smoke was implying, but once he did, that flush began to creep over his face again.

"Are you saying you think *I* had something to do with that holdup?"

"Maybe not you, necessarily," Smoke replied coolly, "but they didn't hit that train just at random. They knew there was a big herd on it. And since the deal was arranged here in Abilene, this is the most likely place they could have found out about it."

"That's impossible," Clark Durham said. "All of the railroad's employees are trustworthy. We only hire dependable people—"

Winters stepped in front of Durham and motioned curtly for him to be quiet. "I'll handle this, Clark. I'm the superintendent of the line in this section, so the responsibility begins and ends with me." He glared at Smoke. "I won't have you going around town spreading dirty lies like that, Jensen."

"And I don't cotton to being called a liar," Smoke said.

Winters was only a couple of feet away now, right up in Smoke's face, with his jaw thrust out belligerently. He said, "If you don't like it, then watch what comes out of your mouth."

Smoke smiled faintly, but his eyes were cold and hard with anger of his own. "The way you're acting, Winters, some folks might wonder if you're feeling guilty."

That was enough to push Winters over the edge. With a snarled curse, he swung a punch at Smoke's head.

Chapter 13

Smoke hadn't come here to fight. He'd been after information, and he had also thought that maybe he and Winters could work together to root out whoever was in league with the rustlers . . . assuming, of course, that Smoke's theory was correct.

But Winters's proddy attitude had rubbed him the wrong way, and when you got right down to it, he had no way of knowing whether the railroad superintendent might just be the man he was after.

Regardless of that, no way in Hades was he going to stand there and let anybody attack him without fighting back, so he ducked under the blow, stepped in, and hooked a hard right to Winters's midsection.

The impact knocked Winters back a step. Smoke could tell that middle age had softened his belly a little, but underneath that was a slab-like layer of muscle. Smoke would have bet that Winters had spent some time swinging a sledgehammer and driving spikes as a younger man. He just had that look about him.

Winters caught his balance and drove forward again, ignoring Durham's cry of "Rudolph, stop this!" He launched a left at Smoke, who moved to block it before he realized that the punch was actually a cunning feint. He hadn't given Winters enough credit for being a smart fighter, not just a brawler.

The next instant, the railroad man's right fist crashed against Smoke's jaw, and Smoke gave him plenty of credit for packing a powerful punch. The blow twisted Smoke halfway around and gave Winters the opening he needed to tackle Smoke, wrap strong arms around him, and bull him backward until both of them slammed into the wall between the office and the anteroom.

Smoke took the brunt of that impact. It knocked the breath out of him and stunned him, but only for a second.

Winters rammed a shoulder against his chest to pin him to the wall, then began a flurry of punches to Smoke's body. Smoke absorbed the punishment and hammered a fist against the side of Winters's head. That stunned Winters long enough for Smoke to plant a hand in the middle of his chest and give him a hard shove.

Winters stumbled backward. Smoke went after him, landing a left hook on his jaw and then driving a straight right into his face. Winters fell onto the desk, scattering the papers that had been on it. An inkwell overturned and spread a dark pool across the blotter.

Landing on the desk like that put Winters in position to jerk up both legs and straighten them in a double kick to Smoke's chest that threw Smoke back the other way, out of control.

The door to the anteroom had just opened, and the startled clerk, anxious to find out the cause of all the commotion in the superintendent's office, appeared in the doorway just in time for Smoke to crash into him. Somehow the young man stayed on his feet as he caught Smoke under the arms and kept him from falling. That was more of an accident than anything else.

Smoke would take that stroke of luck, however. He got his feet planted under him and straightened as Winters rolled off the desk and squared up to continue the battle.

The two men surged together and traded punches while Durham and the secretary looked on in horror. Passengers who had been waiting in the station lobby were drawn by the ruckus, too, and clustered around the door to try to catch a glimpse of the fighting.

The big shape of Marshal Ben McCormick parted that crowd forcibly. McCormick shouldered his way through and stomped into the office. Without hesitating, he grabbed Smoke from behind, wrapping his arms around Smoke's chest and jerking him away from Winters.

"Hang on to him for me, Big Ben!" yelled Winters. "I'm gonna teach him a lesson!"

"Back off, Red!" McCormick bellowed. "This fight's over!"

Smoke could have broken free from McCormick's grip, but he figured it might be better to let the marshal break up the fight. That would allow Winters to save face. Smoke didn't like or trust the railroad superintendent, but he didn't want to make a permanent enemy of the man until he knew for sure it was necessary. If Winters was innocent of any wrongdoing, Smoke might wind up needing his help later on.

McCormick turned and pushed Smoke away from him, which opened up a big enough gap between Smoke and Winters for the lawman to step between them. McCormick held out a hand toward each man and said, "That's it, fight's over. Understand?"

"I want this man arrested, Marshal," Winters raged. "He came in here spouting all sorts of crazy accusations, and then he attacked me!"

"You threw the first punch, Winters," Smoke said.

"Damn right I did! You had it coming. You said I was working with those rustlers!"

"I never said that. I said somebody connected to the railroad might be working with them. You're the one who took that as a personal attack and came after me."

McCormick looked at Durham and asked, "What do you say, Clark? What actually happened here?"

"Well . . ." Durham looked very uncomfortable at the prospect of going against his boss. "I don't suppose Mr. Jensen actually accused Rudolph of anything. . . ."

"But you acted like a guilty man would," Smoke snapped at Winters, who balled his fists, growled, and started to step forward again.

McCormick lifted a big hand to stop Winters's advance, then said, "You're following the wrong trail, Jensen. The railroad runs through Red Winters's veins just like his blood. He'd never do anything to hurt it."

"Maybe not," Smoke allowed, "but he still took a swing at me."

"Not sure I blame him, if you said those things. Might be a good idea for you to get your hat and leave."

The young secretary took that as his cue to bend down and pick up Smoke's hat from the floor where it had fallen during the fracas. He handed it to Smoke, who knocked it into shape against his thigh and then put it on his head.

"I'm leaving the depot, but I'm not leaving Abilene," he said. "I'm still convinced the answers to my questions are here in town, and you'll find that I'm mighty stubborn when I go looking for the truth, Marshal."

"Just don't start fights with our citizens while you're doing it," McCormick said.

Smoke gave him a curt nod and left the office. He felt

Winters's hostile gaze boring into his back when he went out.

That was all right. He hadn't come to Abilene to make friends. And Winters had acted more than a little guilty, although Smoke was inclined to believe McCormick's claim that the superintendent wouldn't do anything to harm the railroad.

The people in the station lobby were buzzing as Smoke strode toward the entrance. It was good that they were talking about him, he told himself. He knew how towns like this operated; gossip about the fight would spread like wildfire from one end of the settlement to the other. By nightfall, at least half the folks in Abilene would know that he was bound and determined to root out anybody who might be connected to the rustlers.

If he was right—if the train robbery had had its origins here in town—then the man or men he was after might decide to strike first.

This wouldn't be the first time Smoke had painted a target right on his back. That was one way of drawing out his quarry.

"Hold on, Jensen," Marshal McCormick called from behind him as Smoke walked out into the street.

Smoke stopped and turned around. "What is it, Marshal?"

"Where are you headed next?"

"Why do you want to know?" Smoke asked coolly.

McCormick's beefy shoulders rose and fell in a shrug. "I thought I'd head that direction so I'd already be on hand when the next fight breaks out."

"You got to this one mighty quick."

"I just happened to be nearby when somebody ran out of the depot yelling about a brawl inside."

"Well, as a matter of fact, I figured I'd head for the

hotel next and get a room," said Smoke. "I wouldn't mind washing up after that tussle."

"Not going to accuse the hotel clerk of being the ring-leader of a gang of rustlers and killers?"

Smoke didn't want to, but he had to chuckle at that. "Not unless he looks particularly shady." Smoke paused, then went on, "When you put it that way, I reckon maybe I shouldn't be surprised Winters got a burr under his saddle."

"He took what you said as an attack against the rail-road, and that railroad's his baby."

"I'll keep that in mind."

"Probably a good idea." McCormick sighed. "Of course, the best idea would be for you to go home and let the proper authorities handle this."

"The problem with that is that I don't see anybody doing anything about it."

"Well," said McCormick, "there could be things going on that neither of us can see right now."

Late that afternoon, Stovepipe and Wilbur strolled around the camp, apparently aimlessly.

In reality, they were taking note of everything they could see and filing away the information in their minds. They knew how many men and horses there were at the hideout, and they had a pretty good idea which men went with which soddy. They knew about the small spring at the far end of the valley that formed a little pool provid-ing water.

They had also learned that apparently Lena was the only woman in camp. At least, they hadn't laid eyes on any other females. Stovepipe couldn't help but wonder if that created any tension in camp, what with Jester McMillan having a woman to take care of his needs but the rest of the men being forced to do without.

McMillan seemed to run things with a pretty firm hand. There might be some resentments, but Stovepipe was willing to bet that McMillan kept a lid on them.

He and Wilbur had slept a good chunk of the day away and awakened without feeling anything crawling on them. They were thankful for that. They had slept through the midday meal, which was too bad, according to Church and Page. They would just have to wait until supper.

"There's usually a big pot of stew simmerin'," Church had explained, "but you don't want to go samplin' it early. Blind Ezra don't take kindly to that."

"Who's Blind Ezra?" Stovepipe had asked.

"The old fella who does most of the cookin' around here. He used to drive a chuck wagon with the trail drives that came up from Texas, and between drives he worked as a biscuit-shooter on one spread or another. But he'd been a long rider when he was younger, and I think he got a hankerin' for that kind of life again. Anyway, when his eyes started to go bad on him a while back, he throwed in with us and does the cookin', looks after the remuda, things like that."

"He ain't completely blind, mind you," added Page. "He can still see well enough to know what he's puttin' in the stew pot. If the day comes when he can't . . ."

Church made a *sssskk* sound and drew his finger across his throat in a meaningful gesture.

"But Miss Lena does the cookin' for the boss, right?" Wilbur had asked.

"Lena Cooley does all kinds of things for Jester," Page had replied. "One of these days he'll shoot her, or he'll wake up some mornin' with *his* throat cut, but until then, they're a pair, I reckon."

Now as they walked around, Wilbur said quietly enough

that only Stovepipe could hear, "I was hopin' that when we found the hideout, we'd find those rustled cows, too."

"Ain't near enough water or grass here for that," said Stovepipe under his breath. "They've either already disposed of the herds they stole earlier, or else they've got all those critters bunched up and hid somewhere."

Wilbur gave his companion a startled look. "That'd be a mighty big herd," he said.

"Yeah, but if you had a market for 'em, that would make for a mighty big payoff, too."

"Where could they get rid of that many cows at one time?"

"Let me think on that," Stovepipe said.

Since they were nearing the edge of the camp and didn't want to arouse suspicion, they turned and started ambling back toward the center of the valley. They hadn't gone very far when a pained yelp came from one of the soddies just ahead of them.

A dog burst past the blanket hanging over the entrance. A big, rangy cur, mostly black but with some brown, tan, and white on his face and chest. A man slapped the blanket aside and charged out after the dog.

"Damn thievin' varmint!" the man yelled. He jerked the gun on his hip from its holster and raised the weapon to draw a bead on the fleeing animal, limping slightly as he ran.

Stovepipe took a swift, long-legged step and swung his arm up and out. He caught the outlaw's gun arm and knocked it up just as the revolver exploded. The bullet whistled high and harmless into the sky.

The man whirled toward Stovepipe. His face above the heavy beard stubble was dark with fury. "What the hell do you think you're doin'?" he demanded.

"Keepin' you from murderin' a defenseless dog," Stovepipe replied. He glanced toward the spot where the rangy cur had disappeared on the other side of camp. The dog seemed to be out of danger for the moment, anyway.

"Defenseless?" the outlaw repeated. "The dirty varmint stole some of my grub and then threatened me when I went to chase him out."

"And what did you do then?" asked Stovepipe sharply. "Kick him? I saw the way he was limpin'. I'm not sure he ever threatened you. Looked to me like he was just tryin' to get away."

"He had a good swift kick comin'," the man snapped. "And as for you callin' me a liar, I don't cotton to that, mister."

"Maybe you ain't lyin'. Maybe you were just mistaken. I reckon that dog could've just been scared of you, and you took that for him snarlin'."

The words appeared to mollify the outlaw slightly.

Not so the next statement out of Stovepipe's mouth. "Or," the tall range detective drawled, "maybe you're just the sort of cowardly, no-good, sorry son of a gun who'd enjoy kickin' a poor hungry dog."

Chapter 14

Abilene

The Merchants Hotel was a two-story, whitewashed frame building with a large sign announcing the name perched at the roof's edge above the windows of the second-floor rooms. A tall chimney stuck up at each end of the roof's peak. It was an impressive structure and, according to Marshal Ben McCormick, the best hotel in Abilene.

Smoke rented a room there and dropped off his carpetbag before heading back out onto the street. He had been to Abilene before, but it had been a while. Nothing much had changed about the town except that there were more women on the boardwalks and fewer cowboys.

That was a sure sign a place was settling down and becoming a real city, not just a wild cow town.

He was trying to figure out his next move when he spotted a familiar figure coming along the boardwalk on the same side of the street. Smoke drew back in an alcove for a moment so the man wouldn't notice him as he came closer.

Just as the man passed him, Smoke stepped forward and said, "Mr. Durham, could I talk to you for a minute?"

Clark Durham, who now wore a gray, soft felt hat, stopped with a startled jerk. His eyes turned toward Smoke and he said, "Mr. Jensen. Please, I don't want any more trouble."

Smoke shook his head. "No, sir, neither do I. I promise I'm not looking for any."

Durham composed himself, cleared his throat, and said, "That's not exactly true, is it? You're looking for the men who held up the train, killed those people, and stole those cattle. Aren't you?"

"Somebody needs to see that they get what's coming to them," Smoke replied. He couldn't keep a steely edge from creeping into his voice as he spoke.

"Well, that's certainly true," allowed Durham. He looked down at the boardwalk for a second, then lifted his gaze and went on, "If I was the sort of man to, ah, go after them myself, I have to admit I'd enjoy seeing them get their come-uppance."

"Well, then, give me a hand," Smoke suggested. "Because I don't intend to stop until I've corralled the whole bunch."

Durham frowned in thought.

During their previous meeting, Smoke had been focused on Rudolph "Red" Winters, so while he had noticed a few bruises and scrapes on Durham's face, he hadn't really considered the implications of those marks. Then the fight had broken out and he hadn't had time to think about it.

Now he said, "You look like you've tangled with some trouble recently, so maybe you're more the sort of hombre to go after rustlers than you think you are."

"This?" Durham motioned toward his face. "I assure you, Mr. Jensen, I didn't seek out this trouble. I was part of a jailbreak last night, through no choice of my own."

"What happened?" asked Smoke, curious how somebody like Durham had gotten mixed up in a thing like that.

The station manager explained how he had been forced at gunpoint to act as a decoy by the masked men who had broken a prisoner out of Marshal McCormick's jail.

"It was terrifying," Durham said with a wide-eyed look that told Smoke some of the leftover fear was still percolating around inside him. "They roughed me up, but I suppose it wasn't really all that bad. But for a moment I thought one of the outlaws was going to murder Marshal McCormick right in front of me! He was about to shoot the marshal when the man they were helping to escape struck him instead. Struck the marshal, I mean. He knocked the poor man senseless, but I suppose that's much better than being shot."

"Much better," Smoke agreed.

"At any rate," Durham continued, "they left after locking Marshal McCormick and me in the cells. We were tied and gagged, so we couldn't raise the alarm. No one knew what had happened until one of the marshal's deputies happened to come by the jail around midnight, and by that time all the outlaws were long gone, of course."

Smoke thought about it and asked, "Do you think what happened last night might've had any connection to those train robberies?"

"What?" Durham looked confused. He shook his head and said, "No, I don't see how it could have. The man who was rescued from custody didn't arrive in Abilene until well after the most recent holdup, and I believe he was a stranger. The gossip around town is that he was an outlaw from Texas, and he must have brought his entire gang with him."

"Could be, I reckon," Smoke said. "I'm sorry you got roughed up."

"It could have been much worse." Durham drew in a deep breath. "Like those poor people on the train who were slaughtered during the holdup."

"I can tell you'd like to see justice done for them. Why don't we go somewhere and talk it over? Your boss doesn't have to know about it."

"Well, I suppose we could go back to my office at the station. That's where I was headed."

Smoke chuckled. "Winters might not want to see me again this soon."

"Rudolph? You don't have to worry about him. He told me he was going home for the rest of the day. I believe that the, ah, tussle the two of you had shook him up more than he wanted to admit."

"He's a pretty good scrapper, I'll give him that."

"He came up in the railroad business the hard way, you know. He laid track back east and was a construction boss when the transcontinental railroad was being built several years ago. This district superintendent job is the most important position he's had, and I suppose that's why he's rather defensive about it."

"I didn't mean to rub him the wrong way, but I'm convinced there's some sort of tie-up between the railroad and those holdups, besides the fact that your trains are being targeted."

Durham rubbed his chin and frowned some more. "I really do hate to think that might be the case, Mr. Jensen, but if it is, I'd like to see whoever is behind it ferreted out. Let's go back to the station, and I'll answer any questions you may have."

Smoke nodded. "I appreciate that."

He fell in alongside Durham as they walked toward the train station. "I'd just been down at the apothecary picking up a bottle of nerve tonic," Durham said. "Dr. Metzger believes it will help me."

Smoke knew that such patent medicines tended to be mostly alcohol with some flavorings and maybe a few things that actually were good for a person thrown in, but if Durham believed the stuff would make him feel better, it probably would. The alcohol content would dull any aches and pains, at least for a while, and do the same to ease the troubles of the mind. Problem was, those effects wore off pretty quickly and left a fella hanging his head and moaning.

But that was none of Smoke's business, so he just said, "I hope you get to feeling better."

"Thank you for your concern, Mr. Jensen. I'm sure I'll be fine."

As Durham had said, there was no sign of Winters around the depot. He led Smoke into the office next door to the superintendent's office. It was as spartanly furnished as Winters's chamber and also had maps and a schedule blackboard on the walls.

"Let me check with the telegrapher to make sure everything is on time and I'll be right back," said Durham. "Please, have a seat."

Smoke sat down in front of the desk. Durham went back into the lobby and returned a couple of minutes later. He wrote some times and made a couple of check marks in the grid on the blackboard, then went into the adjoining office.

"I keep both schedules updated," he said as he came back into the office and took a seat behind the desk. "Rudolph is more concerned with the big picture, I suppose you could say, but he likes to know that everything is running on time."

"And while he's doing that, you're the man who takes care of the details."

Durham looked pleased at Smoke's assessment. "Well, I try," he said. "I like to think that between the two of us, we do a good job of keeping everything working properly."

Smoke got down to business. "Who negotiated the deal with my friend Wallace Dixon over the price of that herd being shipped?"

"That was Rudolph. I was aware that he was discussing the matter with Mr. Dixon, but such things don't really fall under the purview of my job. I'm more concerned with the day-to-day operation of this depot."

"But you knew about the shipment?"

"Of course."

"Who else here did?"

"There are several clerks who work in our freight department," Durham said. "One of them, Asa Tuttle, maintains the records of all the livestock shipped on the railroad. For accounting purposes, animals are considered as freight. So he was aware of the particulars, certainly."

"What about the other clerks?"

Durham shrugged. "The men all work together in the same office. It's entirely possible that Asa could have mentioned the shipment to one or all of the others. There was nothing secret about it."

Smoke shook his head and said, "No, I reckon there wasn't." He tugged at his earlobe and frowned in thought. "You mind if I ask how long those men have worked here?"

"Not at all. They've been here for several years. . . ." Durham's voice trailed off. He frowned, too, as he went on, "Wait a moment. One of them did start more recently than the others. His name is George Hoffman. He's been working here for the past five or six months. I'd have to look up his record to be sure. . . ."

Once again, Durham's words faded away. A look of alarm appeared on his face, as if he had just remembered or thought of something disturbing.

Smoke thought back to what he had seen on his earlier visit. He recalled those pins on the map in Winters's office, and the rapidly turning wheels of his brain latched onto an idea.

"That holdup wasn't the first one where a bunch of cattle were rustled right out of the livestock cars, was it?" he said. "It's happened four or five times before, all of them since this fella Hoffman went to work here."

Durham leaned forward in his chair and made a face like he had just bitten into something rotten. "I hate to think that anyone who works for the railroad could do such a thing," he said. "We've always tried to hire dependable, trustworthy people."

"What about that fella Tuttle and the other clerks who work with the freight? What sort of men are they?"

"They're all family men. Middle-aged and well-established."

"Any of them like to take a drink or two too many? Maybe sit in on a high-stakes game of cards or visit houses of ill repute?"

"Good heavens," said Durham, his eyes wide. "I can't imagine any of them doing such things."

"It's hard to know everything about a man's personal life when you just work with him," Smoke said. "Sometimes he'll do things you might never expect of him. And that could open him up to somebody else being able to bring pressure to bear on him."

Durham shook his head. "No," he said flatly. "I just don't believe that's possible with Asa or the other men."

"Except for Hoffman."

Durham sighed and said, "He's younger. And he's a single man, which means he's more likely to frequent saloons, gambling dens, and, ah, places with unsavory reputations. I'm not saying that he actually does that, mind you, but I have to admit that it seems more like something he would do rather than any of the others."

"And since he works with Tuttle, he might know about the livestock shipments."

"Yes." Durham nodded slowly. "Yes, that's certainly possible." He drew in a deep breath. "Should I call him in here so that we can question him?"

"No, I don't reckon that would be a good idea," Smoke answered without hesitation. "That would tip him off that we suspect him, if he does have anything to do with the holdups. There's an old saying about how you can give a man enough rope to see if he'll hang himself."

"If he's part of that gang, hanging is what he deserves," Durham said with unexpected vehemence. "They've wantonly slaughtered more people than I care to think about."

"And a couple of them were friends of mine," said Smoke, nodding. "If Hoffman's guilty, we'll see to it that justice is done. And we'll start by me keeping an eye on him for a while. Tell me what he looks like."

"He's a medium-sized young fellow. Twenty-five years old, perhaps. He has dark curly hair and side whiskers, but other than that he's clean-shaven."

"You know where he lives?"

"A boardinghouse." Durham told Smoke where the place was located. "You say you're going to follow him?"

"I'd like to find out what his habits are, what businesses he visits. That's a place to start, anyway."

"I wish you luck, Mr. Jensen." Again Durham looked as if something had just occurred to him. "You had better be careful."

"Why do you say that?"

"Because if someone sees you following him and he *is* part of the gang, won't that put you in danger? They'll realize that you're suspicious of him, and they'll want to put a stop to your investigation."

Smoke smiled and said, "That wouldn't be the first time I've had somebody gunning for me, Mr. Durham. I suppose I'll just have to take my chances, and if that leads me to whoever's behind those holdups, I'm willing to run the risk."

Chapter 15

At Stovepipe's angry words, the outlaw's eyes widened until they seemed as if they were about to pop right out of their sockets. A few feet away, Wilbur wore a worried expression. He didn't seem particularly surprised, though, that his partner would talk like that to a rustler and cold-blooded killer who already had a gun in his hand.

Stovepipe was always calm and deliberate and the type to avoid trouble if possible.

Until he wasn't.

And this was one of those times.

Vile curses suddenly spewed from the outlaw's mouth. His gun started to come up again. Stovepipe drove the edge of his left hand against the man's gun wrist, knocking that arm to the side before the weapon came level.

At the same time, Stovepipe's right fist shot out and crashed into the middle of the outlaw's face. The man was approximately the same height, so that made it easy for Stovepipe to aim the punch. He probably outweighed the range detective by thirty pounds, but Stovepipe struck so swiftly and with such power that the outlaw went over backward in a hurry and slammed down onto his back. He lost his hold on the gun, and Wilbur kicked it away almost before it hit the ground.

Surprise had been on Stovepipe's side, but the outlaw recovered quickly and bounced back up. Even though Stovepipe was armed and he now wasn't, the rage he felt drove him to charge forward anyway, swinging wild punches.

Stovepipe darted aside quickly, but he wasn't quite fast enough to avoid the entire flurry of blows that came flying at him. A hard fist clipped him on the side of the head, knocking his hat off and throwing him off balance for a second.

As Stovepipe staggered, that was enough of an opening for the outlaw to tackle him. They both went down hard, but Stovepipe was on the bottom and the man's weight forced the air out of his lungs. His head bounced off the ground. The world spun crazily around him and bright red stars exploded behind his eyes.

The outlaw rammed a knee into Stovepipe's belly and fumbled at his throat, trying to get his fingers locked around it. Stovepipe hooked a solid right into his left side. The outlaw gasped in pain. Stovepipe's eyesight was still a little blurred from all those exploding stars, so he aimed at the sound and lifted his left fist in a short blow that caught the outlaw's chin and rocked his head back. Stovepipe's back arched as he threw the man off to the side. He rolled the other way to put some distance between them.

Stovepipe got his hands under him and pushed up to one knee. By now the other outlaws in the camp had realized that a fight was going on. The shot had attracted their attention in the first place, and then the sight of Stovepipe and the other man slugging away at each other made them gather hurriedly to watch. Stovepipe glanced at them and saw the looks of eager anticipation on their faces. Anything that broke up the monotony of camp life was welcome.

"Get him, Butler!" yelled one of the watchers. Evidently, that was the name of the man who had tried to shoot the dog.

Butler climbed to his feet while Stovepipe was doing the same. Butler clenched his fists and advanced slowly. His nose was swollen twice its normal size and more than likely was broken. The blood that had leaked from it was smeared across the lower half of his face.

"I'm gonna rip you to pieces, you meddler. You damn piece of Texas trash!"

Stovepipe saw Lena push through the crowd of spectators and plant herself in their front rank. He didn't spot Jester McMillan in the bunch, but he knew the boss outlaw had to be aware of what was going on by now.

"We can take this as far as you want, mister," he said to Butler. "If you're waitin' for me to holler calf rope, you can go to Hades."

Butler roared more curses and lunged at him. Stovepipe knew what to expect this time. Butler was faster than many men his size. Stovepipe allowed for that and stepped forward at an angle to his left. He dipped his right shoulder so that Butler's right fist went over it. Twisting at the waist, Stovepipe hammered his left fist against the outlaw's right ear.

At the same time, Stovepipe stuck his right foot between Butler's calves and jerked the man's right leg out from under him. That, coupled with the blow to his head, sent Butler crashing to the ground again.

Grunting with the effort, Butler tried to get up again. Stovepipe Stewart, range detective, would never kick a man while he was down, but "Sam Jones," outlaw, rustler, and most likely a killer, wouldn't be bound by such a code of honor.

The toe of Stovepipe's left boot thudded heavily into Butler's shoulder, flipping him over and sending him rolling.

"Hey, that ain't fair!" shouted one of the watching outlaws.

Lena happened to be next to him. "Shut up!" she snapped at him. "If Butler ever got Jones down, he'd stomp the life out of him, and you know it."

Stovepipe knew that, too, which was why he hadn't allowed Butler to keep him pinned on the ground for very long.

No matter what role he was playing, he wasn't going to stomp and kick Butler to death. But as Butler tried to get up again, swaying groggily now, Stovepipe didn't let him clamber all the way to his feet. Instead, he stepped in and swung a roundhouse right with all the power he could muster.

His knobby-knuckled fist struck Butler's jaw with a sound like an ax thudding into a solid chunk of wood. Butler's head slewed far to the side on impact. His eyes rolled up in their sockets and he buckled forward. His bloody face hit the ground hard, but he didn't feel it. He was already out cold.

The men who'd been yelling in excitement or calling out encouragement to Butler suddenly fell silent. They all seemed a little stunned to see him defeated. After a moment, one man whistled in amazement, and another said, "Lord have mercy. I never thought I'd see ol' Battlin' Butler get whipped like that."

"Battlin' Butler?" Wilbur said.

"Yeah," replied the man who had spoken. "He used to fight bare-knuckles bouts for money in those river towns up and down the Mississipp'." He stared at Stovepipe in disbelief. "And he didn't hardly lay a finger on this long, skinny drink of water!"

"Aw, I was just lucky he didn't tag me more'n he did," Stovepipe said. He didn't want to get too far on the bad side of any friends Butler had here. Although he knew from experience that owlhoots such as these rarely formed close friendships. They joined gangs for the money they hoped to make, not out of any sense of camaraderie.

Lena stepped forward from the crowd and said, "Your head's bleeding."

"It is?" Stovepipe reached up and carefully touched his fingertips to the side of his head where Butler had hit him. They came away red. "It sure enough is. Well, what do you know about that?"

"Come with me," Lena ordered. "I'll clean that up."

Wilbur gestured toward the unconscious Butler and asked, "What about him?"

"I'll throw some water on him," one of the gang offered.

The crowd began to break up. Stovepipe picked up his hat and carried it. He and Wilbur walked toward Jester McMillan's soddy with Lena between them.

"Where's the boss?" Stovepipe asked.

"Jester's around somewhere," replied Lena. "Like that bad penny, he's never far off."

She took them into the soddy and had Stovepipe sit at the table. After dipping a rag in the water bucket, she used it to swab away the blood, then parted Stovepipe's hair with her fingers and examined the wound.

"Oh, it's not bad at all," she announced. "Not much more than a scratch."

"Head wounds always bleed a lot," Stovepipe said. "Mine do, anyway."

"That's because his head's so swoled up with how wonderful he is," put in Wilbur. "Ain't hardly room for all the blood, too."

Lena laughed. It was a good sound, thought Stovepipe. "Do you get hit in the head a lot, Sam?" she asked him.

"Well . . . more than I'd like, if I had my druthers, I reckon."

Lena took the other end of the rag she had used to wipe away the blood and poured some whiskey from a bottle on it. "This will sting," she warned.

"Yes, ma'am, I know. But it's best to go ahead and clean it good."

Stovepipe winced at the whiskey's fiery bite, maybe acting like it hurt a little more than it actually did.

"I think that will be all right," Lena said as she stepped back. "You don't even need a bandage, and you can wear your hat without it rubbing against the wound, if you don't pull it down too tight."

"Yes'm, I'll be careful about that." Stovepipe looked up at her and went on, "I'm mighty obliged to you. I can pay you for your doctorin' services—"

"Don't try to flatter me, cowboy. I'm no doctor. Just a tired old whore."

The blunt statement made Stovepipe frown. Even though he had had a pretty good idea about Lena's background from the things McMillan had said, hearing her talk about herself like that bothered his chivalrous nature.

But again, he told himself to put that aside. He and Wilbur needed to fit in here if they hoped to do their job . . . and stay alive.

Stovepipe was sitting at one end of the table. Lena sat down to his left and went on, "What in the world made you pick a fight with Roy Butler, anyway?"

"I didn't exactly pick a fight with him. I just stopped him from shootin' a dog."

Lena frowned. "That big black and brown cur that's been hanging around the camp?"

"That's right. Butler chased it out of his tent, and I've got a pretty good idea that he kicked the critter. Then he pulled his gun and was fixin' to shoot it."

"And you stopped him."

Wilbur said, "Sam's got a soft spot for dogs and horses."

"Yeah, I suppose I do," Stovepipe allowed. "All innocent critters, actually. I don't like to see 'em bein' treated mean. After I knocked Butler's gun arm up in the air, though, I would've been happy to let that be the end of it."

Wilbur laughed. "Don't you believe it, Miss Lena," he said. "Once Sam realized that Butler had kicked that dog, the fella was in for a beatin'. He just didn't know it yet."

"Well, I have to admire you for taking up for that dog," said Lena. "Although he *is* a pest at times. He'll steal food if you turn your back on him, and when he wants attention, he'll sit and whine until you give it to him. He's kind of sweet-natured, though, I can't deny that."

"Does he belong to one of the fellas?" asked Wilbur.

Lena shook her head. "No, he just showed up one day. No telling where he came from. He was skinny enough you could tell he'd been on his own for a while. I guess the whole camp just sort of adopted him. He ranges around all over the place."

"I hope he's smart enough to stay out of Butler's line of sight for a while," Stovepipe said. "I might not be around to protect him next time."

"He's good at surviving. I'm sure he'll be all right."

"And I will be, too, thanks to your kind attention, ma'am." Stovepipe picked up his hat from the table and got to his feet. "Reckon Walt and I should be movin' on—"

Jester McMillan appeared in the doorway and said, "Sit back down, Jones. I need to talk to you two."

The outlaw chief didn't look happy. Stovepipe sank onto the chair and said, "Sure thing, boss."

McMillan stalked into the soddy and said, "What the hell were you thinking? You attack one of my men for no reason? I thought you wanted to join this gang, Jones. And this after we busted you out of jail!"

Before Stovepipe could say anything, Lena responded, "He had a reason, Jester. That brute Butler was about to kill the dog that's been hanging around camp."

McMillan stared at her. "What? This was about a damn *dog*? Butler's still out, so he couldn't tell me what started the fight, and none of the other boys knew for sure. Now you tell me it was about a dog?"

"Sorry, boss," said Stovepipe. "I just can't stand by and see a helpless critter bein' mistreated."

McMillan turned to him and said, "You know some of Butler's friends want me to shoot you."

"I wouldn't be happy about that."

"If you need to run us off to settle things down—" Wilbur began.

"Nobody's getting run off." Under the drooping mustache, McMillan's lips twisted in a snarl. "You two know where this place is now. Nobody leaves here unless he's one of us."

McMillan's hand wasn't far from his gun. Neither was Stovepipe's. The dank air inside the soddy seemed to thicken even more. Stovepipe watched the outlaw's eyes, not his hand. He knew that was where he would see the decision first.

After a few seconds that seemed longer, McMillan drew a deep breath and said, "I never was going to trust you two until you'd proven yourselves. You've just dug yourselves a deeper hole to climb out of. Now you not only have to win my trust, you'll have to convince the rest of the gang that you deserve to be here, too."

"How do we go about doin' that?" asked Stovepipe in a cool voice.

Slowly, McMillan shook his head. "I don't know yet. But I'll figure something out, you can count on that." He pointed a finger at Stovepipe. "Until then, you'd better not stir up any more trouble, Jones. If somebody wants to kill a dog, you damn well let him kill it. And steer clear of Roy Butler."

"That's what I figured on doin'," Stovepipe said. He was talking about staying away from Butler; he wasn't making any promises about dogs.

McMillan switched his angry gaze to Lena. "What're these two doing in here with you?"

She nodded toward Stovepipe and said, "His head was bleeding where Butler walloped him. I had just finished cleaning the wound when you came in." She put her fists on her hips. "I've patched up the men before, Jester. I thought that was part of my job."

"Well, don't let it go to your head," snapped McMillan. He jerked a hand at Stovepipe and Wilbur. "Go on and get out of here. And stay out of trouble!"

"You got it, boss," Wilbur said as Stovepipe stood up and they headed for the entrance.

Once they were outside, they turned in the opposite direction from where Butler's soddy lay. As they walked toward the dwelling shared by Church and Page where they had gotten some sleep earlier, they felt the gazes of the other gang members following them. Some of those looks were hostile, some merely curious.

"Sorry I got us into this mess," Stovepipe muttered under his breath.

"Shoot, I wouldn't expect anything less of you, pard. We've ridden together long enough that I know how you are." Wilbur grinned. "A mite touched in the head about some things, I mean. But I like you that way."

"Yeah, I reckon. Still, it wasn't a very smart thing to do."

"Not everything you do in life has to be smart. Sometimes what's right ain't all that wise."

Stovepipe chuckled. "You can be downright profound when you want to, you know."

"Well, don't go around talkin' about it, for Pete's sake."

They were nearing the corral now. A couple of outlaws moved toward them, angling to intercept them. McMillan must have given orders to keep them away from the horses, just in case they had in mind trying to escape from the hideout.

Stovepipe summoned up a friendly grin, nodded to the pair of outlaws, and said quietly to Wilbur, "We'd best head on back. We don't want these hombres thinkin' we're about to make a break for it."

"Not yet, anyway," Wilbur agreed.

They turned to go back the way they had come from, and as they did, the dog that had provoked the ruckus emerged from a nearby clump of brush and trotted toward them, his long tail wagging enthusiastically.

Stovepipe stopped and went to one knee. The dog bounded up to him and licked his face as he scratched its ears. "You don't know how close you came to disaster, do you, you big varmint?" he asked. The dog just continued wagging its tail.

Wilbur chuckled and said, "Well, we've made one friend here, anyway."

"Yeah." Stovepipe glanced toward the soddy that Lena Cooley shared with Jester McMillan and added quietly,

"At least one . . . but I don't reckon we can count on any more than that."

"And if you think we can count on that other one . . . Well, that might not be wise."

Stovepipe knew his partner was right.

But for now, he continued rubbing and scratching the dog's ears and said, "We ought to give you a name. Miss Lena says you range all over the place. How's about we call you Ranger?"

Chapter 16

Smoke made it a point to be near the train station at six o'clock that evening. Clark Durham had told him that George Hoffman's work shift ended at that time. With the description he had of the young freight clerk, Smoke figured he could spot him without much trouble.

Sure enough, as Smoke lingered in an alcove half a block away, he saw the medium-sized, curly-haired young man emerge from the depot and start up the opposite side of the street. Smoke half-turned and eased along the boardwalk as if he were looking in the store window beside him.

Actually, from the corner of his eye, he was tracking Hoffman's progress along the street.

The late afternoon light was fading toward evening, but it was bright enough that Smoke could tell that Hoffman wore gray tweed trousers, a white shirt with a black vest over it, and a black string tie. A dark brown derby was on his head. He was a dapper young man. The clothes appeared to be of good quality. Smoke didn't know how much a freight clerk earned, but Hoffman was a little better dressed than he would have expected.

Maybe Hoffman spent some of his cut from those hold-ups on the duds, Smoke thought.

Or maybe he was getting ahead of himself. A fella was innocent until proven guilty. The law said so.

Smoke ambled along the street until Hoffman turned a corner. Then he crossed to the other side in time to see the clerk going into a house a block away on the side street. That would be the boardinghouse where Hoffman lived, Smoke knew.

More than likely, the young man would have supper and then might stay in the rest of the evening. After all, he had to get up and go to work the next morning. But Smoke would wait for a while, just to make sure, before he went in search of his own supper.

A few cottonwood trees grew along this side street. Smoke drifted into the shadows underneath one of them and waited there with a shoulder propped casually against the tree's trunk. He didn't think he looked too suspicious.

The light faded more. The shadows around Smoke thickened. A slightly cool, refreshing breeze sprang up, carrying with it the scent of sage. The heat of summer was still a ways off, but the days were warm enough at this time of year that the moving air felt good on Smoke's face.

He figured on allowing George Hoffman an hour. If the young man hadn't come out of the boardinghouse by then, he was probably in for the night. Smoke possessed a keen sense of time and wouldn't need to haul out his turnip watch to check on how long he'd been keeping this vigil. He would know when the moment was right.

He estimated he had been standing under the tree for a little more than forty-five minutes when the boardinghouse's front door opened and a man came out. It was almost full night now, with only the faintest orange glow along the western horizon. Enough light came through the open door, though, for Smoke to recognize George Hoffman.

The clerk had donned the coat that went with his trousers. He had the derby on his head again. As he came down the steps from the porch and went out the walk to the gate in the front fence, he whistled a jaunty tune that came clearly to Smoke's keen ears. He continued whistling as he closed the gate behind him, stuck his hands in his pockets, and headed toward Abilene's business district.

George Hoffman looked for all the world like a young man out for an evening's entertainment.

Smoke meant to make sure that was all Hoffman was up to.

He remained in the shadows until Hoffman reached the corner. Then he strode quickly after the clerk and reached the main street in time to see Hoffman go into a saloon. It wasn't the Alamo or one of the larger, well-known saloons, but rather a smaller establishment called the Fandango. Even from a distance, Smoke could read the name painted on the front windows on either side of the batwinged entrance.

Not getting in any hurry now, Smoke approached the saloon and looked through one of the windows, again trying to appear casual in his actions. He stood there as if he were just trying to see what was going on inside.

George Hoffman stood at the bar with a mug of beer in front of him, talking to the bartender. A saloon girl in a spangled dress came up on his right side and spoke to him. Hoffman turned his head to smile at her. She put a hand on his arm and moved it up and down. He said something to her and she threw her head back and laughed. Smoke couldn't tell if the reaction was a professional one or genuine.

The girl nodded toward the stairs in one of the back corners of the saloon. Smoke knew she was inviting Hoffman to her room on the second floor. Hoffman smiled again and shook his head. The girl pouted, but he was adamant in his refusal of her offer. She turned away with a little flounce. Hoffman patted her rear end in farewell, then drank the rest of his beer and got a fresh mug from the bartender.

Carrying the beer, he strolled over to a table where a poker game was in progress and watched a couple of hands before one of the players threw in his cards, shook his head disgustedly, and stood up. Hoffman slipped smoothly into his place as he vacated his chair.

So far, Hoffman's actions were interesting, but not necessarily suspicious. He liked to drink, he liked flirting with a pretty girl, and now as the poker game resumed, he seemed to be enjoying playing cards. Any young, unmarried fellow with a steady job and not many expenses or responsibilities might do such things.

None of what Smoke had seen meant that Hoffman was working with the outlaws. But none of it cleared him, either, Smoke reminded himself. He would have to keep watching for a while and see if Hoffman did anything incriminating.

He couldn't stand here peering through the window all evening, though. That could draw unwanted attention. Turning away from the saloon, he stepped down into the street and walked back across it. The dark mouth of an alley provided a good vantage point from which he could continue to observe the Fandango.

Time dragged past. The street emptied out more as businesses closed for the night and folks headed home.

Eventually only the saloons were still open. Smoke's patience wore thin, and he crossed the street again to look through the saloon window once more.

A hand was ending at the poker table when he got there. George Hoffman shook his head as he threw in his cards. He didn't have any money in front of him, so Smoke wasn't surprised when the young man pushed his chair back and stood.

The man across the table, whose frock coat, fancy vest and cravat, and snowy white shirt made him look like a professional gambler, said something to Hoffman, who shrugged and shook his head again. He turned away from the table. Instead of going back to the bar, he headed for the entrance.

Smoke drew back, but as he did, he caught a glimpse of the same saloon girl approaching Hoffman. The clerk gave her a rueful smile and shook his head. It was obvious Hoffman was broke. The girl scowled at him. He spread his hands and walked past her.

Smoke stepped off the boardwalk into the dark, narrow passage between the Fandango and the building next to it. He heard the batwings slap back and forth as Hoffman came out of the saloon. Then the young man's footsteps approached along the planks. Smoke drew back into deeper shadows. He watched as Hoffman's silhouette passed between him and the glow from lights farther along the street.

Tracking the young man from the sound of his steps, Smoke waited until Hoffman had put a little distance between himself and the saloon. Smoke was confident that Hoffman was on his way back to the boardinghouse, no longer able to afford any entertainment, but since he'd already invested this much time in watching the clerk, he figured it wouldn't hurt anything to follow Hoffman all the way to his destination.

Hoffman was far enough ahead that he wasn't likely to

notice Smoke trailing him. Smoke moved out of the alley and looked to his left, the direction Hoffman had gone, as he stepped up onto the boardwalk.

From the corner of his right eye, he saw a stray beam of light reflect from something in the alleyway on the far side of the street. That glint gave him only a fraction of a second's warning, but that was enough as Smoke's razor-sharp reflexes took over.

He threw himself forward as a rifle cracked in the alley across the street. What felt like a puff of hot breath caressed the back of his neck. That sensation was actually the wind-rip of the rifle slug as it came within a bare inch of hitting him.

Smoke's Colt was already in his hand by the time he sprawled belly down on the boardwalk. He thrust the gun toward the alley where the bushwhacker lurked and tripped the hammer twice on a pair of swift shots.

From somewhere behind him, back beyond the Fandango, another gun roared. A bullet slapped one of the planks close beside him, chewing splinters from the wood and spraying them against his cheek.

So there were two ambushers out to claim his life, maybe more. Smoke rolled to his right, toward the street. More shots ripped apart the fabric of the night. He didn't know how close they came, but they didn't hit him, and that was all that mattered right now.

He reached the edge of the boardwalk and dropped a foot or so to the ground. That gave him a little cover from the gunman coming up behind him. He was still an easy target for the man across the street, though. Smoke got his hands and knees under him, surged up, and ran for a wagon parked next to the boardwalk about twenty feet ahead of him.

A bullet whistled past his left ear. Another kicked up dust near his feet as muzzle flame spouted once more from the rifle in the alley. Smoke fired twice more in that direction as he ran, just to keep the hidden rifleman occupied.

Then he left his feet in a dive that carried him behind the wagon. He rolled underneath it.

He twisted around on the ground as he heard rapid footsteps on the boardwalk on his side of the street. The man who had been behind him was charging toward him now. Smoke tipped the Colt up and fired a shot that made the attacker dive to one side into an alcove.

Smoke's revolver was empty now. In earlier years, he had carried two guns as a matter of course, but in recent times he had gotten out of the habit of it. He wasn't sure why; it was just one of those gradual changes that happen in a person's life.

Maybe he ought to go back to packing two irons, he thought now as he plucked fresh cartridges from the loops on his shell belt and thumbed them through the Colt's loading gate. For a while he had thought the frontier might start to get civilized, but clearly that wasn't the case just yet.

With a full wheel now, he stretched out in the impenetrable shadow underneath the wagon. The men who were trying to kill him might not be able to see him, but they knew where he was, and while the wagon wheels offered a little protection, there was still plenty of open space where bullets could come through. He couldn't stay there.

He waited until the man in the alley opened fire again. That was a pretty good sign that the man on this side of the street was trying another advance. Smoke ignored the bullets thudding into the wagon wheels or tearing through the air above him and peered toward the spot where the other gunman had taken cover.

Spotting a flicker of movement, a dark, fast-moving shape crossing between him and distant lights, Smoke let his instincts guide the shot and squeezed the trigger. The Colt roared and bucked in his hand. A man let out a thin, high-pitched squall of pain, then Smoke heard a heavy impact that he figured was a falling body hitting the boardwalk. He twisted the other way, stuck the gun barrel between two spokes of a wagon wheel, and blasted three rounds into the shadows of the alley across the street.

It stayed dark over there. No muzzle flashes of return fire showed.

That didn't mean the bushwhacker was dead or out of action or even hit. He could be lying low, hoping to draw Smoke out into the open again.

As the echoing gun thunder began to die away, Smoke heard a dragging sound, followed by a gasp and some unsteady steps. The man on this side of the street, the one he'd wounded, was trying to get away. Smoke didn't want that. He wanted to get his hands on the varmint so he could question him.

Clark Durham had warned him that if he watched George Hoffman, he might be painting a target on his back. That was what had happened, and as far as Smoke was concerned, this attempt on his life confirmed that the young clerk was tied in with the outlaws.

But he didn't believe that Hoffman was the mastermind. For one thing, Smoke was convinced Hoffman hadn't noticed that he was being trailed. That meant he hadn't ordered the attack on Smoke. Somebody else who worked for the gang had been keeping an eye on Hoffman, making sure that suspicion didn't fall on him. Whoever that person was had seen what Smoke was doing and decided to get rid of him.

Those thoughts flashed through Smoke's mind in the time that it took for him to slide out from under the wagon. He saw an unsteady figure stumble along the boardwalk half a block ahead of him. He was about to call out for the man to stop when another shot ripped from the alley across the street. The man ahead of Smoke jerked and went down hard.

Smoke pivoted, crouched, and slammed a shot at the alley mouth. He had known that the hidden rifleman might still be lurking over there, but he'd expected the man to make another try for him, not his own partner in attempted murder.

Looked like maybe the fella had decided it was more important to tie up that loose end and keep Smoke from getting any answers to his questions.

No more shots came from the alley. Instead, a moment later Smoke heard the swift rataplan of hoofbeats from somewhere behind the buildings on the other side of the street. He still didn't know if any of his shots had hit the bushwhacker, but evidently, even if they had, the man wasn't hurt badly enough to keep him from getting away.

Keeping his gun trained on the fallen figure, Smoke went forward until he reached the man. He kicked one of the fella's feet and didn't get any response. He didn't hear any breathing coming from the man, either. Deciding it would be worthwhile to risk a light, Smoke used his left hand to fish a lucifer from his shirt pocket and snapped it to life with his thumbnail.

The flickering glow from the match revealed that the man wouldn't be answering any questions, that was for sure. The rifle shot had struck him in the head and blown away a good-sized chunk of his skull, allowing blood and brain matter to ooze out onto the boardwalk next to his shattered head.

Not surprisingly, the street had cleared in a hurry when the shooting started. Now that the guns had fallen silent and seemed to be staying that way, folks' curiosity began to get the better of them and they emerged here and there, easing from the buildings and other places where they had taken cover. Nobody wanted to get in too big a hurry to venture out, though, just in case hell started popping again.

A tall, broad figure appeared, striding decisively down the center of the street. Nobody could accuse Marshal Ben McCormick of being timid. He carried his shotgun at the ready. Smoke didn't want to give McCormick any excuse to get trigger-happy, so he slid his Colt back into its holster.

The lucifer hadn't burned down all the way yet, so it still cast its feeble glow over the scene on the boardwalk as McCormick came up.

"Jensen?" the lawman boomed. "Is that you?"

"That's right, Marshal," Smoke replied.

"Who in blazes is that?"

"I don't know, but he ambushed me and tried to kill me."

"So you blew his head off?"

"His partner took care of that," said Smoke.

"What the hell are you talking about?"

"There was another bushwhacker," Smoke explained. "When it looked like I might capture this one, the other man shot him to keep him from talking."

"That's kind of jumping to a conclusion, isn't it?"

"I don't know how else you'd explain it."

McCormick grunted and said, "Let's see if we can figure out who he is." He turned his head and called to the crowd of interested bystanders that had drawn steadily closer. "Somebody fetch a lantern! Move, blast it!"

A man scurried off to return no more than a couple of minutes later with a lantern. Smoke didn't know where he had gotten it and supposed it didn't matter. The man handed it to McCormick, who passed it on to Smoke.

"Light that up," the marshal ordered.

Smoke had tossed the burned-out match into the dirt just beyond the boardwalk. He lit another and held the flame to the lantern's wick. When it caught, he closed the door and held the lantern up by its bail.

The circle of light illuminated the dead man. The grisly sight caused considerable muttering among the on-lookers. McCormick hooked a boot toe under the man's left shoulder and rolled him onto his back.

"Hard to say with part of his head gone, but I reckon I've seen him around town before," McCormick said after studying the corpse for a moment. "I think his name's Carter, Carpenter, something like that. Typical hard case, spent most of his time in the saloons and the whore-houses."

"He and his partner must have figured on gunning me down and robbing me," Smoke said, although he was con-vinced the motive for the attack on him wasn't robbery at all. This man, whatever his name was, had been part of the gang holding up trains and rustling herds right out of the cattle cars.

"Maybe you're right," McCormick said slowly, "but you seem to have a habit of showing up wherever there's trouble, Jensen."

"My wife tells me the same thing."

"Smart woman. Why don't you go home and see her?"

"I will," Smoke said, "as soon as I finish my business here."

Chapter 17

Stovepipe and Wilbur managed to avoid Roy Butler for the rest of that day, which was a good thing because the dog Stovepipe had dubbed Ranger didn't want to leave his side. Ranger seemed to understand that Stovepipe had saved his life, and now he was devoted to the tall, lanky range detective.

"I know this ain't the first critter that's latched on to you," Wilbur commented. "The way they act, you'd think you spoke the same language as them."

"Close enough, I reckon," Stovepipe said as he scratched Ranger's ears for the hundredth time, or what seemed like it, anyway. Any time Stovepipe tried to do anything else, Ranger stuck his nose under his arm and prodded him for attention. "He seems to understand what I'm sayin', and he ain't shy about lettin' me know what he wants."

They found some empty crates and sat outside the soddy with Tom Church and Jonas Page. The four men watched as Blind Ezra, a short, thick-set man with a head that was bald except for tufts of white hair sticking out above his ears, dumped various ingredients into the stew pot simmering over a fire. The smells that drifted through the late afternoon air were tantalizing.

"Once you get a bowl of stew, you'd best not turn your back on it," Church advised Stovepipe. "Happen you do, that mongrel will steal it from you, sure as sunrise."

"Him?" said Stovepipe, grinning. "Why, he's plumb innocent. He'd never do that."

Page snorted.

Lena walked up and asked, "How's your head, Jones?"

Stovepipe had his hat thumbed well back on his head, nowhere near the cut Lena had cleaned earlier in the day. He said, "It's fine, ma'am. The ache that wallop left behind has just about gone away."

"Roy Butler probably wishes he could say the same thing. His jaw is so swollen up that he probably won't be able to eat solid food for several days. He'll have to make do on the broth from Ezra's stew." Lena looked at Ranger sitting next to Stovepipe and made the same comment Wilbur had earlier. "I see you've made a friend."

"Yes'm, he seems right fond of me."

"Both of you better keep away from Butler. If there's any more trouble, Jester won't cut you any slack. Butler's proven he's a valuable man. You two haven't."

"Maybe we'll get the chance to prove we're handy to have around," said Wilbur. "Sam and me, we've ridden a heap of hard trails."

Lena nodded, said, "Mm-hmm," and went on, "Just remember what I said about being careful."

She walked off.

Church watched her go and said quietly, "That there is a mighty handsome woman."

"Don't go gettin' ideas, Tom," Page advised him. "Jester'll shoot you if you look too interested in Lena. Just be patient, man. He'll get tired of her sooner or later, and then one of us other fellas might have a chance of takin' up with her."

Church scowled. "I ain't fond of the idea of gettin' another hombre's leavin's."

Page laughed and said, "Hell, any woman willin' to consort with a dirty owlhoot like you will likely be some other hombre's leavin's, less'n you want to give up this life, move into a town somewhere, and start goin' to the church socials." He dropped a wink toward Stovepipe and Wilbur. "And you might be surprised what some o' them prim an' proper church gals have gotten up to when they figured nobody was lookin'."

Blind Ezra banged the long-handled spoon he used to stir the stew on the side of the pot and bellowed, "Come an' get it, you no-account rannies, 'fore I throw it all to the hogs!"

Church grinned and said to the two newcomers, "There ain't no hogs around here. Ezra just says that 'cause he used to be a chuckwagon cook, and that's what they all yell."

The stew tasted as good as it smelled, especially with fresh-baked bread and strong coffee to go with it. Some chuckwagon cooks dished up fare that was barely palatable, but others were good at whipping up grub that a hungry man could dig into with gusto.

One case Stovepipe and Wilbur had worked for the association had found them on a cattle drive where a young fella named Mackenzie handled the cooking. Mac, as folks called him, was as much gunfighter as cook, but when he turned his attention to food, he was as handy with a Dutch oven as he was with a revolver. As Stovepipe shoveled stew into his mouth now, he thought that Blind Ezra was pretty near in the same league as ol' Mac.

Seeing the way Ranger was eyeing him hungrily, Stovepipe fished a chunk of beef out of the stew and tossed it to the big cur. Ranger plucked it out of the air with a snap of his powerful jaws. Stovepipe tossed a piece of potato next. Ranger caught it equally deftly.

"That big galoot'll never stop beggin' now," Wilbur pointed out.

"That's all right," said Stovepipe. "He's had a hard life, I reckon."

Wilbur grunted. "Haven't we all."

Since there were no bunks in the camp not spoken for, the two of them would have to find some place to spread their soogans for the night. Luckily, the weather was mild and no storms threatened. Stovepipe and Wilbur had spent plenty of nights under the stars in worse conditions than this, so neither of them minded the arrangement.

When darkness had settled down over the prairie, the two men got their blankets from their gear in the pile of saddles and saddlebags near the corral, conscious of the fact that they were still being watched closely. As they were looking for a good spot, Jester McMillan approached them and said, "You two come with me."

"What's up, boss?" asked Stovepipe.

"You can put your bedrolls over there next to my soddy," McMillan said. "It's level enough, and there aren't any rocks or roots to bother you."

And it was close enough that if they started moving around during the night, McMillan might hear them, thought Stovepipe. He understood the real reason McMillan had made the offer, but he said, "Why, we're obliged to you, Jester. Mighty nice and accommodatin' of you."

McMillan grunted. "It was Lena's idea," he said.

Stovepipe didn't believe that for a second. But on the other hand, if McMillan actually was telling the truth, that was a bit intriguing.

McMillan walked off, leaving the two men to follow him when they were ready. Wilbur said quietly to his partner, "I know what you're thinkin'. Don't let it go to your head. And don't start thinkin' you can trust that woman. She's always gonna do what she figures will work out best for her, just like every other gal in the world."

Stovepipe chuckled. "Why, you sound downright cynical, pard."

"I got eyes and ears and I wasn't born yesterday, that's all," Wilbur said.

They pitched their bedrolls where McMillan had suggested—although it had been more of an order than a suggestion. As they stretched out on the blankets, Ranger lay down next to Stovepipe. As he reached over to scratch the cur's ears, Ranger gave him a discouraging look, as if saying that was enough affection for the time being; it was time to sleep. Stovepipe chuckled and said, "All right, old son, whatever you want."

He heard Lena and McMillan talking inside the soddy. The thick, earthen walls muffled the voices enough that he couldn't make out the words. They weren't arguing, exactly, but the voices had a certain snappish tone to them.

Church and Page had made it sound as if McMillan had had women out here before and eventually had grown tired of all of them. Stovepipe hated to think about what might happen to Lena if McMillan abandoned her and she was no longer under his protection.

Maybe this job would be over and done with before that had a chance to happen. It would be wrapped up if he and Wilbur had anything to say about it.

And if they had any luck to speak of.

* * *

Sometime during the night, the sound of hoofbeats woke Stovepipe. He slept lightly to start with, and even more so when he was surrounded by enemies.

When he heard the horse coming into camp, he was awake instantly. Even though he had no reason to believe that he and Wilbur were in danger at the moment, his hand moved instinctively closer to the butt of the gun he had placed beside him after wrapping the shell belt around the holster.

"Rider comin' in," Wilbur said in little more than a whisper.

"Yeah." Stovepipe sat up. Beside him, Ranger lifted his head. A faint growl came from deep in the big dog's throat. "Take it easy, boy. Probably nothin' to do with us."

The hoofbeats stopped. A low-pitched exchange of voices came from the edge of camp. Even though this hideout seemed to be well-hidden, Stovepipe was sure McMillan posted guards at night. One of them had just stopped the new arrival.

But then the horse came on at a walk. The sentry had passed whoever it was.

From where Stovepipe and Wilbur were on the ground, the horse and rider loomed enormous against the sky, blotting out some of the stars. Stovepipe looked at those stars and reckoned it was an hour or so after midnight. When the newcomer reined to a halt in front of the soddy and swung down from the saddle, Stovepipe saw that he wasn't as big as he had first appeared. He was fairly tall but on the lean side.

"Jester," the man called into the crude dwelling. He acted like he hadn't seen Stovepipe and Wilbur on their bedrolls, and it was possible that was true.

McMillan shoved the blanket over the doorway aside

and stepped out with a Colt in his hand. "Who in blazes—Oh, it's you, Yancey."

Wilbur leaned closer to Stovepipe and whispered, "I thought I recognized that voice. It's Yancey, the gambler who offered me the gang's help in bustin' you out last night. I wonder what he's doin' all the way out here."

"He ain't the boss of the whole gang, though, right?" Stovepipe whispered back.

"No. He took me to see some other fella who wore a hood. I never got even a glimpse of his face, but he was the one makin' the decisions and givin' the orders, no doubt about that."

It had to be something important to bring Yancey all the way out here, so Stovepipe wasn't surprised when the gambler said, "The boss sent me to talk to you."

McMillan sniffed, wiped the back of his free hand across his nose, and cleared his throat. He sounded as if he'd been asleep before Yancey called out to him as he said, "Come on in. This had better be important, though. I don't like surprise visitors in the middle of the night."

"I don't like long rides in the middle of the night, either," Yancey responded. The two men brushed the blanket aside and went into the soddy.

"I'd sure like to hear what they're talkin' about in there," breathed Stovepipe.

"Reckon we can risk it?"

"No reason for both of us to put our necks on the line."

"Shoot, that's what we do for a livin', ain't it?"

Wilbur was right, but Stovepipe said, "Stay here. I'll see if I can slip up close enough to the door to hear what they're sayin'."

He stood up and in his stocking feet eased along the front wall of the soddy. As he came close to the opening, he heard McMillan say, "Any coffee left in that pot?"

"A little," Lena replied sleepily.

"Stir up the fire and heat it up, then," McMillan snapped.

Yancey said, "I have a flask of something that will warm us up even more."

"Not that fancy coin-yak you drink, is it?"

"No, it's rye whiskey, not cognac," said Yancey. "I know you have simple tastes, Jester."

"Don't go making fun of me."

"I wouldn't dream of it."

Stovepipe made a face in the darkness. He wished they would quit jabbering and get down to business.

But then Wilbur said, "Hsst!" When Stovepipe looked around, he saw his partner gesturing urgently. He knew Wilbur meant that someone was coming. He faded back along the wall and then dropped back down onto his bedroll.

A moment later, a tall figure strode past and went to the door of the soddy. "Jester, you need anything?"

Stovepipe recognized the voice of Clete, the outlaw who had ramrodded the jail breakout the previous night.

McMillan raised his voice enough for Stovepipe to make out the words. "Yancey's brought word of trouble from town. Come on in, Clete. You can sit in on this. Lena, get another coffee cup for Clete."

"I'm not sure there's enough left in the pot," she said.

"Then boil up some more, damn it! Do I have to tell you everything to do, woman?"

Even though Stovepipe couldn't see it, he could imagine the look Lena was giving McMillan, especially if the outlaw chief had his back to her.

After almost being caught once, Stovepipe didn't figure it would be wise to try to eavesdrop again. The voices faded to where he couldn't understand what the men were saying anymore.

He and Wilbur would find out soon enough, he told himself. Whatever news Yancey had brought from Abilene, it was unlikely that McMillan wouldn't share it with the other members of the gang.

Time passed, and eventually Clete left, taking Yancey with him. The two men disappeared into the night, leading Yancey's horse and heading off toward the other dwellings. Evidently Clete was going to share his lodging with the visitor and Yancey wouldn't return to Abilene until the morning.

It was quiet now inside the soddy. As Stovepipe sat listening intently, a frown creased his forehead. Had McMillan and Lena gone back to sleep in there? It was possible, he supposed. Whatever news Yancey had brought, clearly it wasn't urgent enough to act on tonight. McMillan was going to let it wait.

Wilbur had reached the same conclusion. "Hadn't we better get some more shut-eye?" he suggested.

"You're a sleepy son of a gun, aren't you? But I don't reckon I can blame you. Yeah, let's turn in again." Stovepipe looked over at Ranger, who hadn't budged except to lift his head. "You've got the right idea, don't you, fella? You don't get upset about things you can't do anything about."

Ranger thumped his tail against the ground and then sighed. Stovepipe stretched out, rolled up in his blankets, and with the frontiersman's ability to snatch sleep whenever he could, dozed off almost immediately.

The camp was quiet until about an hour before dawn, when Blind Ezra began rustling around preparing breakfast. He whistled an off-key tune to himself as he did so. The sound woke Stovepipe and Wilbur, but evidently the others were all accustomed to it because the camp continued to slumber.

The outlaws came stumbling out of their soddies in the dawn light, however, roused by the smells of coffee and bacon and biscuits. Stovepipe sat up, stretched, and yawned, then frowned in surprise as he realized the dog no longer lay beside him. He supposed Ranger had slipped off to hunt rabbits or prairie hens or some other critters that were up and moving around in the early morning hours.

Stovepipe and Wilbur went to the spring, dunked their heads in the cold water as some of the other men were doing, and were fairly wide awake when they returned to McMillan's soddy. They found the boss outlaw waiting for them.

"I got some news from town last night," McMillan said without any greeting.

"You mean Abilene?" asked Stovepipe. He had looked around and hadn't seen any sign of Yancey, so he supposed the gambler had already ridden out, heading back where he came from.

"That's right. You two are eager to prove yourselves, right?"

"That's right, boss," Wilbur said. "We want you to see you can trust us and got no reason to worry about us. We owe you a lot, the way your boys got Sam out of jail like that."

McMillan rubbed his goatee with the fingertips of his left hand and scowled. "Well, I've got a job for the two of you," he said. "Take care of it, and you'll be members of this gang just like everybody else."

Stovepipe nodded and said, "Just say the word, and consider it done."

"Good." An ugly grin stretched across McMillan's rawboned face. "I want you to ride back into Abilene and kill a man. A damned troublemaker named Smoke Jensen."

Chapter 18

Smoke knew there was no point in going back by the boardinghouse where George Hoffman lived. The freight clerk might have returned home, unaware of the ambush that had taken place behind him. He would have heard the shots—everybody in Abilene who was awake must have heard all that commotion—but he might not think they were connected to him. Even though Abilene had settled down some, the town was still rambunctious enough that the sound of guns going off wasn't too uncommon.

Or Hoffman might have gone somewhere else, bound on some errand about which Smoke knew nothing. In that case, he was gone and Smoke had no way of picking up his trail.

Either way, Smoke's job of scouting was over for the night. Once Marshal McCormick was satisfied with his story, or at least said that he was, and the undertaker had come to pick up the body of the dead bushwhacker, Smoke headed for the hotel. He was a young, vital hombre, still in the early part of the prime of life, and a long, active day like this one didn't exactly wear him out. Even so, it would feel good to stretch out and get some rest.

He didn't fall asleep immediately, however. Instead, he looked up at the darkened ceiling for a while and thought about Sally, wondering how she was doing and how things were going back on the Sugarloaf. He really hadn't been gone long, but it already seemed like forever since he'd seen her and held her. They had spent time apart before, of course, but it was always a bit of an adjustment.

Smoke took a deep breath and put all that out of his mind. Missing his wife was fine, but cattle had been stolen, innocent folks were dead, and somebody in Abilene wanted to kill him.

His attention needed to be on those things, not pining after Sally.

With that squared away in his thoughts, he quickly went to sleep and slumbered soundly to awake refreshed the next morning.

The hotel didn't have a dining room, but the clerk recommended a café in the next block run by a Chinese man and his family. Smoke walked over there, had breakfast consisting of biscuits and gravy and a thick slab of ham, and washed the excellent food down with several cups of strong black coffee.

He was lingering over a final cup of that brew and pondering his next move when the door of the café opened and a large, brawny figure strode in. Rudolph "Red" Winters stopped just inside the door and looked around the room, his shaggy white brows drawn down in a frown. Smoke had a hunch that Winters was looking for him, and sure enough, when the railroad superintendent's gaze fell on him, Winters stalked across the room toward him.

"Morning, Winters," Smoke drawled as the big man came to a stop beside the table with its blue-checkered cloth. "If you've come to join me for breakfast, you're a mite late, but sit down anyway while I finish my coffee if you're of a mind to."

"I didn't come for breakfast and I don't need to sit," snapped Winters. "I heard that somebody tried to blow holes in you last night."

"A couple of somebodies," Smoke corrected. "And one of them didn't survive the attempt."

Winters jerked his head in a nod. "I know. I went by Martin Rhome's place and took a look at the body. Rhome's the undertaker."

Smoke was genuinely puzzled by Winters's statement. "Why would you do that?"

"You're so blasted determined somebody connected with the railroad is involved with those holdups that I wanted to prove you're wrong."

Winters stopped and didn't go on. Smoke studied the man intently for a moment, then said, "You figured the dead man would be somebody you'd never seen before. But you were wrong, weren't you?"

Winters didn't say anything, just stood there glaring.

Smoke gestured toward the empty chair on the other side of the table. "Why don't you sit down and talk to me? Clearly, you've got something to say."

Winters made a little growling sound, but he yanked the chair out and sat.

"The dead man's name was Jeff Carlin," Winters said as he leaned forward and scowled. "He worked for the railroad for a while as a brakeman. He's not your inside man, though. You can damned well be sure of that. Carlin was fired for being drunk on the job eight months ago, and damned good riddance as far as I'm concerned."

"That was before the holdups started," Smoke said.

"Well before."

"What's he been doing since then?"

Winters shook his head. "I'm not sure. I don't keep tabs on former employees, especially ones we had to give the boot to. I heard rumors that he might have been mixed up in some shady deals, but there's nothing I can tell you for sure."

"He might have a grudge against the railroad for being fired, though," mused Smoke. "That would make it easy to recruit him into a gang that was going to be stopping trains and rustling cattle from them."

"That's what I thought as soon as I recognized him."

"Do you recall if he had any particular friends on the line when he was a brakeman?"

"Not that I know of. He was a surly cuss most of the time." Winters put his hands flat on the table. "I just didn't want you to get the wrong idea in case you found out he used to work for the railroad."

"So you came and told me yourself."

"I figure it never hurts for a man to put his cards on the table. That has to happen sooner or later."

Winters seemed legitimately upset that one of the bushwhackers had turned out to be a former railroad employee. The news came as no real surprise to Smoke. But it didn't actually change anything, either. The fact that some of the men in the gang he was after had worked for the railroad at one time just made sense. Railroad workers were usually tough hombres.

"I appreciate you coming to talk to me, Winters. You didn't have to."

"Rather you heard about it from me and not somebody else with an ax to grind against the railroad. Plus I just don't want you going around stirring up any more trouble than you have to," the older man said. "I'd still rather you went home and left this business to the proper authorities."

Smoke shook his head. "I can't do that, especially after last night."

"Because you got shot at? Because you've got a personal grudge to settle now?"

"Because the fact that somebody went to the trouble to ambush me means that I'm on the right trail," Smoke said. "They wouldn't have done that unless they were worried that I'm going to uncover something."

Winters glared again. "So you still think somebody on the railroad is mixed up in this."

"It makes sense, don't you think?

Smoke didn't say anything about his conversation with Clark Durham or the fact that he'd been following George Hoffman when he was bushwhacked. He didn't see any point in driving a wedge between Winters and Durham. That might make the station manager less likely to cooperate with him in the future.

The legs of Winters's chair scraped loudly on the floor as he pushed it back and stood up. "You're going to keep poking at things, aren't you?" Winters's voice was loud enough to make some of the customers at the other tables glance around at him to see what was going on.

"I'm going to keep trying to get the answers I need," said Smoke. He didn't want to start another fight with Winters, but he wasn't going to lie, either. "I expect that'll stir up more trouble before I'm done, yes."

"Then whatever happens will be on your own head."

"That sounds like a threat," Smoke said coolly.

"No, just telling you that whoever tried to kill you will more than likely try again."

"I reckon I'd already figured that out," Smoke said. He smiled and added, "Could be that's just what I want."

* * *

"Smoke Jensen," Stovepipe repeated slowly. He reached up and stroked his chin with his fingertips as if he were deep in thought. "I reckon I've heard that name somewhere before, but I can't place it right offhand."

There wasn't much truth to that statement, except for the part about having heard Smoke Jensen's name before. Stovepipe reckoned that most folks west of the Mississippi had heard the name. A few years earlier, Jensen had wiped out a whole town of outlaws up in Idaho. During that time, he had garnered quite a reputation for himself as an outlaw and gunfighter. Some people claimed he was as bad as the varmints he had gone after.

Then Jensen had dropped out of sight for a while, and when he resurfaced, it had been as a successful rancher in Colorado, a married man who evidently was trying to leave his violent past behind him.

Unfortunately for him, however, trouble seemed to have a way of finding Smoke Jensen. He had clashed with a would-be railroad and mining tycoon and once again tangled with a small army of outlaws and gunwolves. He had been mixed up in another ruckus involving the U.S. Army and some renegade Indians, and there was no telling what else.

Yeah, Stovepipe had heard plenty of stories about Smoke Jensen . . . enough to know that he didn't want to tangle with the man.

"He's in Abilene causing trouble," Jester McMillan went on. "He's poking into some things that are none of his business, and the man we all work for wants him out of the way." An ugly grin appeared on McMillan's face. "So I figured the two of you are just the pair to get rid of him. Unless you have some objection to killing a man . . ."

"We never objected all those other times," said Wilbur, still playing the part of a hardened outlaw.

"Yeah, but we kind of didn't have a choice about it," Stovepipe added.

"I don't reckon you have much choice about this, either," McMillan said with an unmistakable edge of menace creeping into his voice.

"The thing of it is, we just got out of Abilene by the skin of our teeth. Remember, that fat marshal threw me in the hoosegow and charged me with murder. I ain't sure it'd be a good idea for us to go back this soon. Be better if things had a chance to cool off some first."

"Yeah, well, *the thing of it is*," McMillan said with a sneer, "I don't give a damn what's better for you two. I care about this gang and what the man who gives the orders wants. If you want to ride with us, you'll do as you're told. And if you don't want to ride with us . . ."

McMillan's voice trailed off meaningfully. He had already made it perfectly clear that nobody left the gang alive.

Stovepipe managed a hollow chuckle and said, "Well, if you put it that way, I reckon we'd be plumb happy to go back to Abilene and kill this Jensen fella for you, Jester."

"I figured you'd see it my way."

"Can we at least wait until tonight so we don't have to go waltzin' back in there in broad daylight?"

McMillan thought about it for a second and then shrugged. "Yeah, that's fine. We don't want to be unreasonable about this. Just don't get any ideas about sneaking off. We'll be keeping a close eye on you today, and Clete and a couple of the other boys will be going with you tonight. If you try any kind of double cross, the two of you will be the first to die."

"No double cross," said Wilbur. "You can count on us, Jester."

"We'll see." McMillan nodded toward the cook fire

where Blind Ezra was serving breakfast. "Go get yourselves some coffee and something to eat."

"Thanks, boss," said Stovepipe.

He and Wilbur turned and ambled away. Behind them, McMillan went back into the soddy.

"What the hell do we do now?" Wilbur asked under his breath.

"Get some breakfast, like Jester said," Stovepipe replied. "We'll talk about this later."

"I've heard about Smoke Jensen. He sounds like a ring-tailed roarer."

"Yeah, I've got a hunch he's the sort of fella who's mighty hard to kill."

Ranger showed up while Stovepipe and Wilbur were still eating breakfast. The big dog licked his chops so much and looked so pathetic as he stared at Stovepipe that the range detective wound up feeding him several bites of biscuit.

"He's probably wolfed down a couple of rabbits already this mornin'," Wilbur pointed out.

"Maybe so, but a little more grub won't hurt him."

Tom Church and Jonas Page walked up. Church said, "Jester told us to stay close to you fellas today. You ain't figurin' on tryin' to run off, are you?"

"Not us," Wilbur said.

"Jester's got a little job for us tonight," added Stovepipe.

"Yeah, we know," Page said. "He didn't tell us the details, but he said that Tom and me would be ridin' with you, as well as Clete. But it's up to you two to take care of the chore, whatever it is."

"He didn't explain what it was, though?"

"Not to us. Clete probably knows. He's Jester's *segundo*."

Stovepipe nodded. He wasn't surprised that McMillan was sending men to accompany him and Wilbur to Abilene and see that they carried out their assignment.

The question was whether the two of them would get a chance to talk to Smoke Jensen alone before they were supposed to kill him.

After they had finished eating, Stovepipe said, "Reckon we'll go check on our horses."

"We'll come with you," Page said.

"No need." Stovepipe pointed to the corral at the edge of camp. "That's the only place we're goin'. We'll be in plain sight the whole time. Of course, you're welcome to come along if you want."

The two outlaws looked at each other and shrugged. Church said, "Go ahead. But don't try nothin'. I like you boys, but you ain't part of the gang yet. Don't forget that."

"We won't," Stovepipe said. "You can count on that." He and Wilbur turned toward the corral, and he added, "Come on, Ranger."

The dog bounded ahead eagerly, not knowing where they were going, but obviously happy to be part of things, whatever they were.

"This is goin' to be mighty tricky," Stovepipe said, quietly enough that only Wilbur could hear him. "We got to find a way to talk to Jensen and let him know what's goin' on."

"If we can make it look like we killed him, that'll get us in solid with this bunch," Wilbur replied. "Then we can find out more about who's behind it and what their plans are."

"That's just what I was thinkin'."

"We don't know for sure that Jensen will play along with us, though."

"He must be after the same thing we are," mused Stovepipe. "He wants to find out who's behind the trouble and break up the gang. That's why the fella in the hood wants him dead. He must think that Jensen's hot on his trail." Stovepipe nodded. "He'll play along with us, all right. I'd bet a hat on it. But only if we can fill him in on who we are and what we're doin'."

They reached the corral, and seeing them, the Appaloosa and the dun came over, tossed their heads, and waited to have their noses scratched. Stovepipe and Wilbur visited with their mounts for a few minutes while Ranger nosed around sniffing things. They couldn't really make plans for how they would proceed when they returned to Abilene that night; they would have to wait and see how the situation developed, and then play the hand they were dealt.

One thing was for sure: Smoke Jensen was a mighty dangerous joker in the deck.

Chapter 19

Smoke knew there had been enough witnesses to his conversation with Winters in the café that gossip about it probably had spread all over town. That was one reason he had been so plainspoken about his intention to continue investigating the holdups and rustling. He hadn't kept his voice down, either.

If you want to get some hornets buzzing, it didn't do any good to poke their nest and back off. You had to keep poking.

Smoke started that effort by paying a visit to Clark Durham in the station manager's office.

When Smoke walked in, Durham glanced toward the closed door into the adjoining office.

"Is Winters in there?" Smoke asked quietly.

Durham shook his head. "No, he's gone out to the repair sheds to check on some things. I heard about how the two of you almost got into a fight again this morning. He kept cursing under his breath when he came in."

"We weren't all that close to a ruckus," Smoke said

with a smile. "I wasn't going to allow that to happen. I didn't mind getting under Winters's skin a little, though. And he's the one who tracked me down to the café, not the other way around, so I can't be blamed for that."

Durham leaned back in his chair. "I'm not blaming anyone," he said. "I just wish there wasn't so much trouble, so much anger and hostility in the air." He sighed. "My nerves aren't all that good, you know."

"That tonic not helping yet?"

"I suppose I haven't been using it long enough. I'll continue taking it and hope for the best. Which reminds me . . ."

Durham opened a desk drawer, took out a small brown bottle, and removed the cork from its neck with a tiny *pop!* He took a drink from it, made a face, and replaced the cork.

"It was time for my morning dose," he explained as he put the bottle back in the drawer.

"Hope it helps."

Durham laced together his fingers, white from chalking arrival and departure times on the blackboards in his and Winters's offices, and said, "What can I do for you this morning, Mr. Jensen?"

"I'd like to talk to your freight clerks."

"All of them? Or just George Hoffman?"

"All of them," Smoke answered without hesitation. "It might be a tip-off if I questioned just Hoffman. I don't want him to know that we suspect him more than any of the others."

Durham nodded and said, "That makes sense. Did you follow him last night like you planned?"

"That's what I was doing when two fellas decided to take some potshots at me."

Durham pursed his lips. "Yes, I heard about that. I should have asked you about it as soon as you came in.

According to the stories I was told, however, you weren't injured."

"That's right. One of the bushwhackers wound up dead, though. A man named Jeff Carlin."

Durham's eyes widened in recognition of the name. "He used to work for the railroad!"

"Yeah, I know. That's what Winters hunted me up to tell me a little while ago. He wanted me to hear it from him and make sure I knew Carlin hadn't worked for the railroad in eight months or so."

"Yes, it's been at least that long since he was dismissed from his job as a brakeman. I never knew him that well, you understand. I deal mostly with the men who work here in the station and the repair yard, not the ones who belong to the actual train crews. They report directly to Rudolph. Of course, I see them around quite often."

"You never happened to see Carlin with George Hoffman, did you?" Smoke wanted to know.

Durham frowned in thought and hesitated for a long moment before finally shaking his head. "No, not that I recall—" He stopped short, then went on, "Wait a minute. I don't remember ever seeing the two of them together, but there's something . . . Yes, that's it! When Hoffman applied for the freight clerk position, he mentioned that Carlin had told him he ought to try to get a job here. I asked him if they were friends—because at that point, being friends with Jeff Carlin wouldn't have been that much of a recommendation, you understand—but Hoffman said they were merely acquaintances. They played cards together now and then, he said. But he claimed he hadn't seen Carlin in a while, which at that point was probably true."

"Maybe so, but the two of them did know each other."

"Definitely." Durham nodded. "But I might not have

ever remembered that if you hadn't reminded me of it, Mr. Jensen. Do you think it's important?"

"Might be, might not be. More than likely, Carlin was acquainted with lots of people here in Abilene. Everybody he ever said howdy to can't be part of the gang."

"I suppose not . . . but with George Hoffman already under suspicion, it doesn't exactly help his case, does it?"

"No," Smoke admitted. "It sure doesn't." He got to his feet. "If you don't mind me talking to those men . . . ?"

"Not at all." Durham stood up, as well. "I'll come with you and make sure they understand they're to speak freely with you. I'm confident that the others will. But if Hoffman actually is tied in with those outlaws . . ."

"He'll lie through his hat," Smoke said. "The trick'll be to catch him in it." He grinned. "The lie, not the hat."

By that afternoon, Smoke knew a lot more about how the railroad freight business worked than he ever figured he would. He had talked to each of the clerks separately, and they had all been very cooperative, including George Hoffman. They answered all his questions fully and without hedging—including whether or not anyone had ever approached them wanting information about the shipments of cattle that had been stolen right out of the livestock cars.

They were smart men; they had to be in order to keep up with all the details of their job. They quickly figured out what Smoke was implying, and they resented it. To a man, they insisted that they hadn't passed along such information to anybody.

George Hoffman was just as prickly as the other men when Smoke pressed him on that point. If he was acting, Smoke sure couldn't tell it. All his reactions seemed perfectly genuine.

That didn't necessarily mean anything, Smoke reminded himself. It was possible Hoffman really was that skilled an actor.

Smoke used Durham's office for questioning the clerks. He had just finished with the last of them when Durham hurried in.

"I asked one of the porters to let me know when Rudolph was on his way back from the repair sheds," Durham said. "He's coming now. I expected him back before this, so we were fortunate to have as long as we did."

"I'll get out of your hair, then," Smoke said as he headed for the door.

Durham caught his arm. "Wait a moment. He'll probably go into his office first, and once he's closed the door, you can leave without him seeing you."

"I'm not afraid of him, you know."

The station manager gave Smoke a weak smile. "I'm sure you're not, but I'm just trying to keep the peace, Mr. Jensen. My nerves, you know . . ."

Smoke didn't know how bad Durham's nerves actually were; the man might just want an excuse to keep swigging that so-called tonic. But either way, Durham had been helpful and Smoke wanted to cooperate with him.

"Sure, I'll wait."

Durham looked relieved.

A moment later, they heard the door of Winters's office open and then slam shut, followed by heavy footsteps and then the sound of desk drawers being opened. Durham nodded to Smoke, who went to the door and paused there.

"One or more of those freight clerks might say something to Winters about me being here," he said.

"I can deal with that," Durham assured him. "If you're not right in front of him where he can lay eyes on you, Rudolph can control his temper . . . I think."

"Good luck," Smoke muttered as he went out.

He crossed the lobby and walked out onto Abilene's main street. He had come to a dead end, he mused as he headed back toward the hotel. Or maybe not a dead end, exactly. More like a long, arid stretch of badlands he had to cross before he reached his destination. He could continue his journey, but it wouldn't be pleasant for a while.

He would follow George Hoffman again that night, he decided as he brushed idly at something on his arm. And maybe tonight, Hoffman would lead him somewhere he could pick up the trail of the outlaws.

The gang's hideout was far enough from Abilene that Stovepipe and Wilbur, along with Clete, Church, and Page, started for town well before sundown. Like most outlaws, they were accustomed to traveling without drawing attention to themselves, so they avoided the roads and cut across country, riding through gullies and along creek beds, obscuring their trail as much as possible in case anyone tried to follow them, unlikely though that seemed to be.

Such caution probably wasn't necessary, but it became habit in men who followed the owlhoot trail. Sometime it might help keep them alive for a day longer.

The riders paced themselves so that the sun had sunk below the horizon behind them, leaving an arch of fading reddish gold in the western sky, by the time the lights of Abilene appeared in the distance ahead of them.

Even though Clete hadn't ordered a halt, Stovepipe reined in, which prompted the others to stop as well.

"What are you doing?" asked Clete.

"We ain't goin' on into town until it's good an' dark," Stovepipe said with a nod toward the settlement. "I want the best chance we can get of not bein' spotted by that

lawman or his deputies, or anybody else who might recognize us."

Clete looked a little annoyed, but he shrugged and said,
"I don't reckon it matters all that much when you get the
job done, as long as you get it done. But Jester expects
Jensen to be dead sometime tonight. You've got that much
leeway, no more."

"That'll be fine," said Stovepipe. "When it's full dark,
Wilbur and me ought to be able to slip into town without
bein' seen."

"I just hope we can get back out again," muttered Wilbur.

"You have any idea where we can find Jensen?" Stovepipe asked.

Clete thumbed his hat back and said, "Yancey told
Jester that last night he was following a freight clerk who
works at the depot. The boss had two of the boys who
were in town try to gun him, but they botched the job.
Jensen killed one of them."

"He's a dangerous man," Wilbur said. "I've heard a
heap about him."

"Are you sayin' you can't handle him?"

"That ain't what we're sayin' at all," Stovepipe said.
"Just that it's liable to take some plannin', and we'll need
to be careful. So don't be surprised if it takes a little while
to get things taken care of."

"As long as Jensen's a corpse by the time the sun
comes up in the morning."

Stovepipe and Wilbur nodded in understanding.

"That clerk lives in a boardinghouse," Clete went on.
He told the range detectives how to find the place, then
said, "Jensen will probably pick up his trail there, like he
did last night, so that would be a good place for the two of
you to get on *his* trail."

"This clerk fella, is he part of the gang like Jensen thinks?"

"There's no need for you to worry about that. Just get rid of Jensen. Jester and the boss will handle any thinking that needs to be done."

"Fair enough," allowed Stovepipe. He hipped around in the saddle and looked at the sky. The lingering glow from the sunset was almost gone. He turned to the front again and said, "Come on, Walt. It ought to be dark enough by the time we get to town that nobody'll spot us."

"I sure hope you know what you're doin', Sam," Wilbur muttered as they nudged their mounts into motion.

"So do I, pard. So do I."

Smoke anticipated that if George Hoffman went out tonight, the young man would return to the saloon called the Fandango. But that might not be the case, so that evening he was back in the thickening shadows underneath the cottonwood trees not far from the boarding-house.

Earlier in the day, he had paid a visit to Pinky Ford at Dr. Metzger's house and filled the young cowboy in on what he'd been doing.

"You've been in a fight and somebody bushwhacked you?" Pinky's eyes went wide as he asked the question. "Dang it, Mr. Jensen, you need me watchin' your back! I'm feelin' good enough to get back on my feet—"

Smoke raised a hand to stop him. "The doctor's not going to go along with that, and we both know it, Pinky."

"You're gonna track down those rustlers and rain hell on 'em before I ever get outta this blasted bed," Pinky said with a sigh. "It just ain't fair."

"If things were different, I'd be proud to have you giving me a hand," Smoke assured him. "But for the time being, all you can do is keep on letting those bullet holes heal up."

"I suppose you're right. But you need to be mighty careful, Mr. Jensen. Those varmints wouldn't have tried to ventilate you if you weren't closin' in on 'em."

"That's what I thought. Maybe tonight I'll be lucky and get a little farther along on the trail."

After Smoke had been waiting and watching the boardinghouse for a while, his quarry emerged, just as on the previous night. Hoffman whistled a tune again as he walked toward the saloon. He didn't have the attitude of a guilty man, thought Smoke, but again, that didn't mean anything.

The hair on the back of Smoke's neck suddenly stuck up as he slipped through the shadows. That was his instinct for trouble kicking in, he knew. Although it wasn't just instinct. He could have sensed something—a sound, a smell—something so faint that it hadn't registered on his conscious mind, but he'd been aware of it anyway.

He slowed, listened intently, and after a couple of seconds heard the tiny scuff of boot leather on the ground somewhere behind him.

He was being followed, just as he was following George Hoffman.

Or maybe not. Other people could be abroad in the night who had nothing to do with him or Hoffman. But somebody working for the gang had spotted him trailing the clerk the night before, and it was likely they had done so again. This might even be the same hombre, the one who had gotten away after putting a bullet through Jeff Carlin's brain to make sure he wouldn't talk.

Smoke stepped up onto the boardwalk, moved along it for a few feet, and then eased into the darkened alcove of a doorway to a store closed for the night. The old mountain man called Preacher had taught him to move without making a sound. He had done it so smoothly that to whoever was following him, it would be as if he had vanished in the blink of an eye.

It didn't take long for the tactic to be rewarded. Smoke heard cautious footsteps coming toward him on the planks of the boardwalk. Silently, he slid his Colt from its holster and rested his thumb on the hammer. He was ready when the man moved past him, nothing much more than a deeper patch of darkness slipping through the shadows.

That was enough for Smoke. He stepped out, looped his left arm around the man's neck from behind, and jerked him to a stop. The barrel of the gun in Smoke's hand prodded hard into the man's back. He drew back the Colt's hammer with an ominous metallic ratcheting.

"Don't try anything, friend, or I'll blow your spine in two," he ordered in a low, dangerous tone.

A second later, he felt the cold, hard ring of a gun muzzle press against the back of his neck, and a deep, quiet voice drawled, "Reckon I could say the same to you, old son."

Chapter 20

It was a trick Stovepipe and Wilbur had worked before: one of them let himself get caught, then the other one moved in and got the drop on the man they were after.

This situation was very different in one respect, however: they weren't looking to arrest Smoke Jensen. They just wanted to talk to him, figure out a way to work with him.

And the other difference was . . . this time they were dealing with Smoke Jensen.

Stovepipe had pretty good reflexes, but Smoke moved so fast it seemed supernatural. The fact that Stovepipe didn't actually want to hurt him probably made the range detective hesitate for a shaved instant of time, too.

That was enough for Smoke to twist away from the gun, chop down at Wilbur's head with his own weapon, and whirl around to thrust out his leg and sweep Stovepipe's feet out from under him. Stovepipe yelped in surprise as he went down on his back, landing hard on the boardwalk.

He smelled gun oil and knew that if there had been any light to see by, he would be staring down the barrel of Smoke's Colt.

"Don't shoot, dang it!" he rasped once he got his breath back. "We're on your side, Jensen."

"Stalking me in the dark like that doesn't seem much like being on my side," Smoke said, his voice as quiet as Stovepipe's.

"We didn't have no choice in the matter. That gang sent us here to kill you."

"That's not making me trust you more."

"Listen. My partner and I are range detectives. We're workin' our way into the gang to bust it up, but they gave us the job of killin' you to prove ourselves."

"That's a pretty far-fetched story."

"Can't help that. It's the truth."

Based on everything he had heard about Smoke Jensen, Stovepipe didn't believe the man would kill him in cold blood. Even so, the air was thick with tension and imminent danger.

After a moment, Smoke asked, "What's your name?"

"As far as those outlaws know, I'm a Texas owlhoot called Sam Jones. But my real moniker is Stovepipe Stewart. My partner there is Wilbur Coleman, alias Walt Smith."

Again a few seconds of silence ticked past before Smoke said, "Your ma named you Stovepipe?"

Even under the circumstances, Stovepipe had to chuckle. "Well, no, that ain't what's wrote down in the family Bible. The name got hung on me when I was just a youngster but already grown up to be tall and on the skinny side. Been usin' it so long I sort of disremember what my real front handle is. I might could figure it out if it's really that important."

Smoke had been hunkered on his heels next to Stovepipe. Now he stood up. Stovepipe thought he heard the whisper of steel on leather and figured that was Smoke holstering that iron.

"Your friend's starting to come around," he said. "You'd better see to him. I tried not to wallop him too hard, but there wasn't enough time to get too fancy."

Stovepipe sat up, pouched his own iron, then pulled himself onto hands and knees and crawled over next to Wilbur, who was indeed shifting around and making little noises as consciousness returned to him. Stovepipe slapped him lightly on the cheek and said, "Are you all right there, Wilbur?"

"I will be if you'll quit hittin' me," Wilbur replied. Stovepipe helped him sit up. "What happened to Jensen?"

"I'm right here, Coleman," Smoke said from the thick shadows inside the alcove.

"If he knows my real name, I reckon you must've told him who we are?" That question was directed at Stovepipe.

"Seein' as how he'd knocked you out and had a six-gun stuck in my face, it seemed like a good time to put our cards on the table."

Wilbur grunted. "Too bad we couldn't have done it before I got buffaloed like that. On the other hand, our little trick worked, didn't it?"

"Only sort of."

"Is anybody from the gang watching you two?" asked Smoke.

"I don't rightly know," Stovepipe replied. Clete, Church, and Page had stayed outside Abilene—or at least they had said they were going to—but Stovepipe couldn't know for sure that was what they'd done.

"Well, there could be somebody watching me," said Smoke, "so if we're going to palaver, maybe we'd better find some place quiet and private to do it. I might be able to break into this store—"

"Wait a second and let me take a look at that lock." Stovepipe stood up, clasped wrists with Wilbur, and pulled his fellow range detective to his feet. He took a small folding knife from his pocket, opened it, fiddled with the door for a moment, and then felt the lock snap back. Being able to open doors like that was a handy skill for a detective to have.

They stepped into the store's front room, and Wilbur immediately exclaimed, "Damn it! We're surrounded."

It was true. Half a dozen shadowy figures stood inside the room, dimly illuminated by light that filtered in through the front window.`

"Don't worry," Stovepipe told him. "This here's a ladies' dress shop, and those are dressmaker's dummies."

"Are you sure?"

"Pretty sure. They ain't moved since we came in here, and they're a mite more shapely than any gun-wolves I ever laid eyes on."

"Oh. Well, that's a relief, I guess."

A trace of impatience was in Smoke's voice as he said, "Nobody's going to disturb us here. Start at the beginning and tell me the whole story."

"I reckon I can do that," Stovepipe said, "but I'll turn it around and ask you to do the same when I'm done."

Smoke was quiet for a moment, probably considering what Stovepipe had said, then he responded, "You've got a deal. Go ahead."

For the next quarter of an hour, Stovepipe explained how he and Wilbur had been sent to Abilene by their boss at the Cattlemen's Protective Association, how they had set up the fake "shoot-out" that had landed Stovepipe in jail on murder charges, and how the gang had approached

Wilbur with an offer to help him escape if the two of them wanted to throw in with the bunch.

Wilbur added details to his part of the story, telling Smoke how the gambler called Yancey had approached him and then taken him to meet the hooded man who seemed to be the true boss of the gang.

"You didn't get a look at his face?" asked Smoke.

"Not a bit," Wilbur said. "Well, other than his eyes. They were sort of a muddy brown, I'd say. Hard to say for sure because the pool hall where we were talkin' wasn't lit up very much."

"How was he dressed?"

Wilbur shook his head. "Couldn't say, except that he had on a long duster. That covered up his other clothes. He was definitely tryin' to keep me from bein' able to tell who he was."

"Was there anything else unusual about him?"

"Well, he was fiddlin' with some dominoes. There were several tables in the back of the room where fellas could play dominoes or forty-two or moon. I think he'd been shooting pool before I got there. I could tell he'd been chalkin' a cue. But there's nothing special about any of those things. Plenty of men shoot pool and play dominoes."

"You're right about that," Smoke said. "What happened after you got to the gang's hideout?"

Stovepipe resumed the story, bringing the narrative up to the point where Wilbur had acted as the bait to draw Smoke into the open.

"They're expectin' us to kill you tonight," he concluded. "Seems to me that fella in the hood must be mighty worried you're gonna figure out somethin' that'll blow the whole business wide open."

Smoke chuckled. "I agree, but I wish I knew what that something was."

"All right, you said you'd tell us your side of the story," Stovepipe reminded him.

"I suppose I might as well trust you. If you're lying about being detectives, that's a mighty complicated yarn you've come up with."

"It's the truth," said Wilbur.

"I believe you," Smoke said, "and I like to think I'm a decent judge of character. All right, here's what brought me here and what I've been doing."

Smoke's story didn't take as long to tell as Stovepipe and Wilbur's had, and when he was finished, Stovepipe accepted every word of it as true. Despite the time Smoke had spent as a wanted man, mostly on phony charges drummed up by his enemies, he had a reputation for being honest, a straight shooter in more ways than one.

Besides, Smoke had no reason to lie about anything he had said.

"So Marshal McCormick was in on the whole thing with you," Smoke went on. "I'll give him credit for being a good actor. He told me about that jailbreak, and he seemed genuinely upset about it."

"Well, he got walloped pretty good," said Stovepipe.

"By you," Wilbur added.

Stovepipe's bony shoulders rose and fell in a shrug. "Better than gettin' shot, I reckon."

"No argument there," said Smoke. "Now that we've put all our cards on the table, what's next?"

"We ain't quite figured that out yet."

"Well . . . you said those outlaws are expecting me to die tonight." Smoke paused. "So maybe it would be a good idea if I died."

Smoke was hidden in the shadows half a block away from the Fandango when George Hoffman came out of the saloon a couple of hours later and started toward the boardinghouse where he lived. Smoke gave the young clerk a good lead and then fell in behind him.

Hoffman seemed a bit unsteady on his feet tonight, as if he'd had a little too much to drink. He wasn't falling down drunk. At least, Smoke hoped that he wasn't. If Hoffman passed out and didn't make it back to the boardinghouse, that could ruin the plan he had worked out with the two range detectives.

He was still convinced they had told him the truth about who they were and what they were doing in Abilene. If they had been lying and double-crossed him, he would deal with that problem when it occurred.

But he hoped it wouldn't, because he had felt an instinctive liking for both men.

He would hate to have to shoot them.

Smoke slowed down under the cottonwood trees. Up ahead, Hoffman opened the gate in the picket fence in front of the boardinghouse and went through it. He hadn't reached the porch when Stovepipe and Wilbur stepped out of the shadows twenty feet from Smoke.

"Smoke Jensen!" Stovepipe shouted.

Then he and Wilbur opened fire.

Smoke hauled his Colt from its holster as gun thunder rolled through the street and gouts of orange muzzle flame ripped the darkness apart. Halfway up the walk at the boardinghouse, Hoffman whirled around, staggered a little, and watched with open mouth as shots blasted back and forth a short distance down the street.

Stovepipe and Wilbur were too close for a couple of experienced gunhands such as themselves to miss. Smoke had managed to raise his gun and trigger a couple of rounds, but the bullets smacked into the dirt well in front of the men apparently ambushing him.

Then Smoke reeled back, stumbled from side to side,

and jerked as more shots hammered out. He groaned, bent double, and crumpled in a heap.

The gunfire stopped, but echoes still rolled through the evening air over Abilene. Stovepipe and Wilbur turned and raced through the shadows, jamming their guns back into leather as they ran. Their horses were close by. They vaulted into the saddles, and as the echoes of the shots finally began to die away, the pounding hoofbeats of galloping horses replaced them.

George Hoffman stood there in front of the boardinghouse, turning his head back and forth as he glanced from the fleeing bushwhackers to the fallen body in the street. He looked totally dumbfounded.

Behind him, the boardinghouse's front door opened cautiously, and the landlady called in a quavering voice, "Who's out there? What's all that shooting about?"

Hoffman gulped as he recovered his senses. The violence he had just witnessed seemed to have shocked the drunkenness out of him. He turned and said, "It . . . it's me, Mrs. Anderson. George Hoffman. And I just saw a man murdered!"

He took a step toward the street, but the landlady cried, "George Hoffman, you stay right where you are! Don't you go out there, or you might get shot, too!"

Mere moments later, a large, bulky figure hurried along the street. Marshal Ben McCormick stopped next to Smoke's fallen form and looked around, menacingly sweeping the shotgun in his hands from side to side. Evidently satisfied that the bushwhackers were gone, he dropped to a knee beside Smoke and leaned closer to examine him.

Then he looked up, spotted the crowd gathering in the boardinghouse's front yard, and shouted, "You there! Hoffman! Go fetch Doc Metzger. This man's hit bad. I don't think he's going to make it, but we'll give Doc a chance at him."

Hoffman gulped again, opened the gate, and trotted toward the main street.

He returned a few minutes later, riding on the buckboard driven by Dr. Metzger. Blankets were piled in the back because the doctor sometimes used the vehicle to transport patients. Metzger brought the vehicle to a halt, hopped down from the seat, and joined McCormick next to Smoke's body. Hoffman went back to join his fellow boarders assembled in the yard, buzzing with interest over the shooting. Several of them asked Hoffman to describe exactly what he had witnessed.

After Metzger had examined Smoke, he took the shotgun from McCormick and held it while the marshal picked up the wounded man and placed him gently in the back of the buckboard. In the light from the stars and a newly risen moon, the dark stains on the front of Smoke's shirt were visible.

"What do you think, Doc?" McCormick asked loudly as he stepped back. "Will he make it?"

"I'll do my best, but realistically speaking, a man shot through the body that many times has no chance," Metzger replied.

Both men climbed on the wagon seat. Metzger turned the buckboard and drove away.

Smoke didn't move or open his eyes until the doctor tapped him on the shoulder and said, "It's all right now, Mr. Jensen. The curtains are closed in this room and no one can see in."

Smoke sat up.

He was on a table in one of Metzger's examining rooms. Metzger stood on one side of the table while Marshal

McCormick was on the other. Pinky Ford, leaning on a cane, sat on a chair against the wall with Theresa Harrell, the doctor's nurse, beside him.

Smoke looked down at his shirt, which was soaked from the little bags of chicken blood he had concealed inside it. He had ruptured those bags when he fell, pretending to be shot.

"You did a good job of setting this up in a hurry, Marshal, once those Texans and I talked to you," Smoke said.

McCormick grunted. "That fella Stovepipe is so blasted likable that it's hard not to go along with whatever he asks . . . even if the last time I did that, it got me a punch in the jaw!"

He lifted a hand to the bruise that was still evident and rubbed it gingerly.

"Yeah, he told me about that," said Smoke. "According to him, it was punch you or let that owlhoot shoot you."

"That's about the size of it. So I reckon that was one time I was glad to get hit."

"Were you injured during the, ah, performance, Mr. Jensen?" asked the doctor.

"Nope, I'm fine. At least, I will be once I change shirts. This chicken blood is a mite sticky and uncomfortable."

"I brought you one of mine," said McCormick. "It'll be a little big, but at least the shoulders will fit you. I didn't figure anybody else around here would have one you could borrow that would be closer to the right size."

"And you can take my Colt, too," said Pinky. "You'll have to carry it with the butt forward, like a cross-draw rig."

Smoke nodded. "I'm used to carrying a second gun that way. I appreciate the loan of it, Pinky. I'd get my extra gun rig from my warbag, but it's at the hotel and I can't risk going back there."

"I'm happy to oblige. But I'd be happier if you'd let me come along with you." Pinky held up a hand, palm out. "I know, I know, I ain't healed up enough yet. I won't argue with you, but I sure wish I was gonna get a crack at those no-good sons o—"

He stopped short with an embarrassed glance at Miss Harrell.

"What about horses?" Smoke asked the marshal.

"I've got two good ones saddled and ready for you. I know you'd rather have your own mounts, but if they were to disappear, that might give away the fact that you're not really shot to pieces. Somebody here in town is working with the gang; I don't have any doubt of that now."

"I'm sure the horses will be fine, Marshal. I trust your judgment." Smoke looked around the room. "I appreciate all you folks pitching in to help on such short notice." He smiled. "Some people might say the whole plan is loco."

"Not if it helps you track down those rustlers," McCormick said. "And speaking of that . . ."

Smoke nodded. "Yeah, I'd better get moving. I have a rough idea where I'm headed, but I don't want Stovepipe and Wilbur to get too far ahead of me."

Chapter 21

Stovepipe and Wilbur reached the rendezvous point west of Abilene where Clete, Page, and Church were waiting. In the moonlight, Stovepipe saw lather flecking the flanks of the outlaws' horses. That trio had been riding hard, too, and Stovepipe could make a good guess where.

"You just got back here from Abilene your own selves," he said in an accusing tone. "Did you think Walt and me couldn't do the job?"

"Take it easy, Jones," Clete said. "Jester told us to stick close enough to you that we could lend a hand if you needed it. The most important thing was for Smoke Jensen to die, not your delicate little feelings."

"Well, he's dead," said Wilbur. "We put enough lead in him to sink a riverboat."

"Anybody follow you?"

"Nope, we got clean away before anybody knew what'd happened," Stovepipe said. "We stopped a couple of times to listen and didn't hear anybody behind us."

"That's good. They must not have known which way you went. That was another reason we stayed close by, so we could help you get away if need be. Jester didn't want you boys getting captured."

Stovepipe grunted. "Because we know where the hideout is, you mean. If it looked like we were gonna get caught, McMillan's orders were to kill us to keep us from talkin'."

Church said, "Don't worry about it, Sam. Jensen's dead, and you didn't get caught. Didn't even come close."

"Yeah, things couldn't work out better than that, could they?" Page added.

"I reckon if you want to look at it like that . . ."

"What other way is there to look at it?" asked Clete. He lifted his horse's reins. "Come on, let's head back."

"Does this mean we're full-fledged members of the gang now?" Wilbur asked as the five men filed in alongside each other and rode west. "We did what McMillan wanted. We got rid of a problem that nobody else had been able to handle so far."

"The final decision's up to Jester." Clete shrugged. "It seems to me like you fellas have proven yourselves, though."

"I hope so," said Stovepipe. "We ain't used to jumpin' through hoops for anybody."

They rode on through the night. To pass the time, Church and Page started cracking jokes and recounting exploits they'd had in the past, most of them lewd and frequently unbelievable. Wilbur joined in, spinning some yarns about adventures he and Stovepipe had had down in Texas. Most of those stories were complete fiction, although some of them were based on heavily embellished facts. In reality, he and Stovepipe had been on the other side of those clashes between lawmen and owlhoots.

All five men seemed considerably relaxed by the time

they reached the hideout in the early hours of the morning. The sky along the eastern horizon had begun to lighten with just the faintest gray tinge of approaching dawn. The camp seemed to be asleep except for the sentry who passed them in and Blind Ezra, who was already up preparing biscuits for breakfast. Stovepipe smelled coffee, too.

Jester McMillan wasn't asleep, though. He must have been waiting for them, because as soon as they rode in, he swept aside the blanket hanging over his soddy's doorway and strode out to meet them.

"What happened?" he asked sharply. "Is Jensen dead?"

"He's dead," Stovepipe said.

McMillan said in a cold voice, "I wasn't asking you, Jones. You might have reason to lie about it. What do you say, Clete?"

"I reckon he's dead, all right," Clete replied with a nod. "Or next thing to it."

"What in blazes do you mean by that?"

"Reckon we could get out of these saddles, Jester?" Clete asked instead of answering directly.

McMillan jerked a hand in assent.

The five men swung down, and Clete said, "We were close enough to see these two Texans go after Jensen like you wanted. They hit him at least half a dozen times, and the front of his shirt was soaked with blood. Nobody can take that many bullets and live."

"What happened after that? The undertaker come for him?"

Clete shook his head. "No, that fat marshal showed up and sent for the doctor. They loaded Jensen into a buckboard and took him back to the sawbones' office."

"So he could still be alive!" McMillan didn't sound pleased about that.

"Even if he is, it won't be for much longer. He had enough lead in him to, uh, sink a riverboat."

Stovepipe and Wilbur glanced at each other in the gray light. Clete was just repeating what Wilbur had said earlier, but McMillan didn't know that. If he accepted the story, it didn't matter where the line that sold it came from.

During the hectic, hurried discussion Stovepipe, Wilbur, and Smoke had had with Marshal McCormick after slipping through Abilene's back alleys to the lawman's office and luckily finding him there, they had considered bringing in the undertaker and making it appear that Smoke was dead immediately following the fake shoot-out.

But McCormick had suggested recruiting Dr. Metzger instead, saying that the physician was smarter and more likely to be able to handle his part of the charade without giving anything away. The three outsiders had deferred to McCormick's judgment, since he knew the people involved much better.

That meant Smoke would appear to still be alive when he was taken to the doctor's office, but between the things McCormick and Metzger said loudly enough for the crowd to overhear and spread the gossip through Abilene, and the fake blood soaking Smoke's shirt, they hoped to create the impression that Smoke was badly wounded and not long for this earth.

That the plan had worked was confirmed as Clete went on, "Even if Jensen is still alive now, and I seriously doubt that he is, he won't last the day, Jester. And it doesn't really matter if he's dead yet. He's shot to pieces and can't pose any more of a threat to us."

"I'd rather he was six feet under," said McMillan as he scowled darkly. Then he shrugged and went on, "But I suppose you're right. The main thing was to eliminate Jensen as a danger to our plans." He looked at Stovepipe and Wilbur. "And you two succeeded at that."

"Does that mean we're good enough to join the gang?" Stovepipe asked coolly.

McMillan hesitated a tense heartbeat longer, then said, "Consider yourselves part of the bunch."

"You won't be sorry," Stovepipe said, while hoping that McMillan would indeed be sorry he had ever trusted these two hombres from Texas.

Pinky Ford's holster wasn't attached to his shell belt, so all Smoke had to do was turn it around and run the belt through the holster the opposite way from the usual. That allowed him to position the rig for a cross-draw. If Smoke needed to get both guns talking at the same time, all he had to do was twist his left hand around and palm the gun out that way. He'd had plenty of practice with both methods. It felt good having two irons on his hips again. Sort of balanced things out.

McCormick had brought the two horses to the back of the Metzger place. Wearing the dark blue shirt the marshal had loaned him and a black hat tugged down low over his face, Smoke blended into the darkness as he drifted through the shadows, mounted up, and rode away slowly, leading the extra saddle horse. He kept to the alleys as he worked his way out of town and didn't nudge the horse under him to a faster pace until they were clear of the settlement.

Then he headed for the spot about a mile west of town where Stovepipe and Wilbur were supposed to rendezvous with the outlaws who had come with them to Abilene. Stovepipe had told him the landmark to look for—a grove of trees standing alone in a broad open stretch.

Because of all that open ground, Smoke had to rein in

when he was still a quarter of a mile away. He knew he was looking at the right place. He hoped that he wasn't too late; the plan called for Stovepipe and Wilbur to take their time meeting up with the others, so Smoke would have a chance to get out here and trail them.

In case that didn't happen, the range detectives had told Smoke how to locate the gang's hideout. It wasn't easy to find, though, and it would be better if they were able to lead him right to it.

Of course, he would have to be careful. They didn't want the other men to realize they were being followed. But Smoke was pretty good at being stealthy when he needed to be. All those years spent with Preacher had taught him that much—among many other things.

As he sat there, waiting out the agreed time, he watched the trees in the distance. Even though the moon wasn't very big tonight, the light it cast, along with the silvery glow from millions of stars, was enough to leave the prairie awash with luminance. It was a pretty scene, and Smoke might have appreciated it more if he hadn't been trying to track down a vicious gang of thieves and killers.

He had been sitting there maybe ten minutes when he spotted five riders moving out of the trees and heading west at a steady, ground-eating pace.

To a man with Smoke's keen eyesight, it might as well have been broad daylight out here. He was able to follow the riders without much trouble, hanging well back so that he wasn't likely to be spotted even if any of the outlaws looked around to check their back-trail.

Eventually, after quite a few hours, the riders came to the bluff with the narrow passage through it that Stovepipe had described to Smoke. From this distance, Smoke couldn't see the notched opening itself, so to him it appeared the five men simply disappeared into the bluff's face. He reined in and smiled.

It was his job now to figure out a way to observe the outlaw camp without being discovered, while Stovepipe and Wilbur continued gathering information. The rustled cattle weren't being held here, they had told him. The gang had another sanctuary somewhere else, and that had to be where the cattle were.

Finding it was the next step.

Dawn was at least an hour away. While it was still dark, Smoke circled a mile to the north and then turned west. When he judged that he had gone far enough, he swung south again and began working his way back in a slightly easterly direction.

He found himself in a range of rugged hills. No roads ran through here; the terrain was too rough for wagons. It wasn't good farming country, either, and the hills were so rocky that there wasn't really enough prime graze for cattle, either. Most of Kansas was suitable for farming or ranching or both, but pockets like this existed, small, isolated areas of badlands that weren't much good for anything.

Except outlaw hideouts.

Smoke's progress was slow and careful. He didn't want to ride right into the rustlers' camp without expecting it. He became even more cautious when a faint whiff of wood smoke drifted to his nose. Somebody had a campfire up ahead, and Smoke couldn't think of anyone else who would be out here except the men he wanted to locate.

After a while he dismounted, left the two horses tied to a scrubby bush, and went ahead on foot. By the time the eastern sky had begun to turn gray, Smoke was stretched out on his belly at the top of a hill with his hat off as he peered through a gap in the low, thick brush.

Below him lay a narrow valley with several soddies, a corral, and a campfire blazing brightly as a bald old man got a pot of coffee boiling. Stovepipe and Wilbur stood in front of one of the soddies, talking to a man with a dark goatee. One of the outlaws who had accompanied them to Abilene was there, as well. The other two men who had been in the group Smoke followed left after a few minutes, walking off and taking all the horses with them to the corral.

Stovepipe and Wilbur continued talking to the two outlaws. The one who'd come back from Abilene with them nodded his head and turned away. The bearded man swung around and headed for the soddy from which he had emerged. Smoke saw Stovepipe look around, and he wondered if the lanky range detective was asking himself if Smoke was out here somewhere, keeping an eye on things. . . .

That was when a woman came out of the soddy and walked toward them.

"What are you doing up?" McMillan asked Lena. He sneered. "Kind of early for you, isn't it?"

"I heard voices and thought maybe the men you sent to Abilene were back."

"And what business is that of yours?"

She stopped and faced him squarely. "I like to know what's going on."

"If you need to know something, I'll tell you," McMillan snapped. "You know what your job here is."

Stovepipe and Wilbur had been about to head for the campfire to see if they could get cups of coffee from Blind Ezra. McMillan had told them he would talk to them again later. Everything seemed to be going according to plan.

But hearing how McMillan talked to Lena rubbed Stovepipe the wrong way. The way Stovepipe saw it, a man didn't treat animals or women mean.

But pure meanness seemed to be the biggest part of Jester McMillan's personality.

Lena looked past McMillan and said, "Would you two boys like some breakfast? You're welcome to join us."

"I never said that," McMillan snapped.

"Well, you're not the one fixing breakfast, are you?" She smiled at Stovepipe and Wilbur and added, "How about it?"

Wilbur had already been casting some warning glances toward Stovepipe, knowing full well that the way McMillan treated Lena bothered his partner. "Maybe we should just go get some coffee and grub from Blind Ezra—" Wilbur began.

"Why, we'd be plumb pleased to join you, ma'am," Stovepipe interrupted his partner as he took off his hat and held it politely in front of him. "We're sure obliged to you for the invitation, aren't we, Wilbur?"

"Yeah, mighty obliged," Wilbur said. Stovepipe could tell he tried not to sound too grudging about the agreement.

McMillan was still standing there glaring, but when Lena gave him a defiant look, he shrugged and turned away dismissively, as if declaring that the matter wasn't worth fighting over. Stovepipe knew that getting farther on McMillan's bad side probably wasn't the best way to proceed, but after taking the plunge and accepting Lena's invitation to breakfast, he wasn't going to back out now.

McMillan went into the soddy first. Lena stepped through the doorway next, and Stovepipe and Wilbur followed her. Stovepipe hissed at Wilbur to take his hat off. The redhead did so.

Lena motioned for the guests to take seats at the table.

McMillan was already sitting down. Stovepipe sat opposite him, Wilbur to his right. Stovepipe and McMillan locked eyes across the table in the flickering light from a single lantern. Stovepipe kept his face expressionless. He knew he could push McMillan only so far and didn't want to risk the progress he and Wilbur had already made on the case.

Lena went to the stove and busied herself preparing breakfast. She brought cups of coffee over to the men and soon had platters of flapjacks and bacon in front of them as well.

The food seemed to take a little of the edge off McMillan's anger, so after a while Stovepipe risked a question.

"What do you have in mind for us to do next, boss?"

"The two of you, or the whole bunch?"

Stovepipe shrugged. "Whatever you want."

McMillan didn't answer for a moment. Then he said, "I do the thinking around here, understand?"

"Sure," Stovepipe said easily, even though he knew that wasn't true. McMillan took orders just like the rest of the gang, only his came from that hooded hombre Wilbur had seen in Abilene. But if McMillan wanted to act like he was actually in charge, Stovepipe wasn't going to argue with him.

Again, McMillan hesitated as if he were reluctant to answer Stovepipe's question, but when he spoke, Stovepipe heard self-satisfaction in his tone. McMillan wanted to give the impression that he had come up with what he was about to say, and Stovepipe was more than willing to let him do so.

"There's going to be a train loaded with cattle headed for Abilene in a couple of days," he said. "We're going to stop it over west of Great Bend and take those cows off it."

"Wait a minute," Stovepipe said, looking like he had

never heard of such a thing before. "You're gonna rustle cattle right off the train?"

"That's right." McMillan actually smiled slightly. "I thought it was the most loco idea I'd ever heard, but it's working. And the payoff is going to be mighty big."

McMillan had just admitted that he wasn't the mastermind behind the holdups, but he didn't seem to realize that and Stovepipe wasn't going to point it out to him, now that he was in a better mood.

"Most of those shipping herds are pool arrangements," McMillan went on. "You can't find that many cows in one place unless you hit the big roundups, and with so many ranch crews around those, the odds would be too heavy against you. But on a train, there's not really anybody to stop you, especially if some of the boys raise enough hell with the passengers while the rest of us are unloading the stock cars."

"How in blazes do you get the critters off the train without loadin' chutes and ramps?"

"We have a wagon we built special for that with high sides and a top that swings back and down to form a ramp," McMillan explained. "It takes a while to run the cattle through it a couple at a time, but that gets them off the train without hurting them."

"Yeah, I can see where that might work," mused Stovepipe. "Takes a mighty smart fella to come up with somethin' like that."

"Yeah, it does."

And that wasn't Jester McMillan, Stovepipe thought again.

"So Sam and me get to come along on this job?" asked Wilbur.

"We went to the trouble of getting you out of jail. We might as well get some use out of you."

"And I sure do appreciate the hand you fellas gave me, boss," Stovepipe said.

"We won't let you down," promised Wilbur. "I reckon we've showed that already by gettin' rid of Smoke Jensen."

"Jensen should have stayed home. Now he'll wind up buried in Abilene."

McMillan stayed in a good mood—for him—during the rest of the meal. Then he told Stovepipe and Wilbur to get some rest since they'd had a long night in the saddle.

"I'll be telling everybody about the next job tonight," he added. "Keep it to yourselves until then."

"Sure thing, boss," said Stovepipe.

As they left the soddy, Stovepipe paused, pulled a red bandanna from his pocket, and took off his hat to wipe his face with it.

"Gettin' warm already," he commented to Wilbur, who nodded knowingly.

They had no way of knowing if Smoke was watching the camp right now, but if he was, that move with the bandanna was the signal they had uncovered some information that needed to be passed along. They couldn't meet during the day, but if Smoke had gotten the message, he would try to rendezvous with the range detectives somewhere near the camp that night.

If Smoke didn't contact them, well, something had gone awry and Stovepipe and Wilbur would deal with that when the time came.

Their bedrolls were in the same spot they had been a couple of nights earlier, next to McMillan's soddy. The miles and the long hours without sleep were catching up to them, so it would feel good to stretch out.

They hadn't done that yet when Ranger came bounding up from wherever he had been. The big dog was excited to see them, bouncing around enthusiastically as Stovepipe scratched his ears.

Stovepipe was still busy with that when somebody said, "Can I talk to you for a minute, Jones?"

He looked up and saw Lena standing there. Stovepipe glanced at Wilbur, who wore a worried frown on his face. Talking to Lena while they were right next to McMillan's soddy like this might not be a good idea.

But his nature wouldn't let him refuse the request, so he nodded and said, "Sure, Miss Lena. What can I do for you?"

Chapter 22

"Jester's gone back to bed with a bottle," Lena said in a low voice. "He'll laze around most of the day now. I just wanted to warn you. . . . Don't trust him."

"But, ma'am, he finally seems to be warmin' up to us a mite. He said we was full-fledged members of the gang now and took us into his confidence about what he's plannin'."

She shook her head. "That doesn't have to mean anything. He could just be trying to get you to let your guard down." Her breasts rose and fell as she took a deep breath. "Look, I don't know for certain that he's planning to double-cross you somewhere along the way. But he might be, so I'm just telling you to be careful, that's all."

"I reckon we're already in the habit of doin' that," Stovepipe assured her.

A faint smile curved Lena's lips. "You've heard the old story about the scorpion and the frog trying to get across the river?"

"Where the scorpion stings the frog because it's just his nature and they both drown?" Stovepipe nodded. "Yeah, I've heard that one."

"Well, Jester McMillan's nature is pretty close to the scorpion's."

"We'll bear that in mind. And we ain't hop-frogs, are we, Walt?"

"Nope," Wilbur said. His hand dropped to the butt of the gun on his hip. "We have stingers, too."

As she turned back to the soddy Lena didn't look any less worried than she had when she'd approached them.

"You trust her?" asked Wilbur when she was gone.

Stovepipe dropped a hand to Ranger's head again and did some more ear scratching. "A little," he allowed. "But the only two folks I really trust right now are you . . . and our pard I hope is up in the hills watchin' over us."

Smoke wondered who the dark-haired woman was and what she had said to the range detectives. Given what he had observed, she was probably Jester McMillan's woman, but she seemed friendly toward Stovepipe, too.

Once the Texans had stretched out on their bedrolls to get some sleep, Smoke eased back down the opposite side of the hill. He put his hat on and sat there thinking for a long time.

He had seen several members of the outlaw band lounging near the corral and guarding the horses. Out here in the middle of nowhere, being set a-foot would be a mighty bad thing, especially for lawbreakers who never knew when they would have to make a fast getaway. Nothing could be allowed to stampede that remuda.

So meeting with Stovepipe and Wilbur anywhere near the corral was out. Too many owlhoots around. It would be better to try for a rendezvous somewhere on the other side of the camp. Smoke wondered if Stovepipe's train of thought would follow the same track as his.

He had seen that signal with the red bandanna. Stovepipe had something to tell him, and Smoke wanted to hear it . . . even if it meant running some risks.

He returned to the spot where he had left the horses, loosened the cinch on the one that was saddled, and made sure both animals could reach some graze. There was no water here, but he had crossed a creek not too far back and would go there later to let the horses drink.

In the meantime, since Stovepipe and Wilbur were getting some shut-eye, he would do the same. He propped his back against a little hump of ground, stretched his legs out in front of him, tilted his hat down over his eyes, and dozed off quickly.

That was another thing he had learned from Preacher— to grab some sleep whenever and wherever he could.

The same frontiersman's instincts that allowed Smoke to slumber so easily also woke him up when several hours had passed. It was close to midday now. Smoke stole back up the hill to the point where he had observed the camp earlier.

More of the outlaws were moving around now than there had been early that morning, but the place still had a sleepy, tranquil air about it. Stovepipe and Wilbur were no longer in their bedrolls. Smoke looked around the hideout until he spotted them sitting on some crates in front of one of the other soddies, talking to two members of the gang. One of the outlaws was whittling while the other smoked a pipe. Stovepipe and Wilbur appeared to be having a friendly conversation with them.

Which wasn't surprising, because the range detectives

were trying to fit in and not do anything that might make the outlaws suspect they weren't what they seemed to be.

Given the circumstances under which he had left Abilene, Smoke hadn't had the chance to pack any supplies, but he'd discovered earlier that Marshal McCormick had slipped some jerky into the saddlebags when he'd gotten the horses ready. Smoke had brought a couple of strips of it with him when he went back up the hill. He lay there now, gnawing on the tough strips, as the afternoon dragged past.

Late in the day, the goateed man who seemed to be the boss of this outlaw band called everyone together. He talked for a while, making a few emphatic gestures as he spoke, and then some of the men asked questions.

Smoke would have given a lot to be able to listen in on that discussion, but there wasn't any way to do that without running too great a risk of being caught.

If he was able to meet with Stovepipe and Wilbur later on, they would pass along what he needed to know.

When the meeting broke up, the two range detectives strolled toward the end of camp opposite from the corral. The big, rangy, mostly black and brown dog seemed to have attached itself to Stovepipe.

As they went along, Stovepipe pulled out that red bandanna again and blew his nose in it this time. The sight of the bandanna itself was enough to tell Smoke that Stovepipe was trying to get his attention.

When they reached the edge of camp, Stovepipe picked up a stick and seemed to be trying to teach the dog how to fetch it. He threw the stick out a short distance and motioned for the dog to go after it.

The dog just looked up at him, clearly baffled.

Stovepipe went and got the stick and brought it back. He showed it to the dog and talked earnestly to him, then threw it again.

The dog stayed where he was, sitting there and looking up expectantly at Stovepipe as his tail thumped the ground. Stovepipe shook his head in obvious exasperation and fetched the stick again himself. He talked to Wilbur for a second, then drew back his arm and flung the stick a third time.

This time it sailed farther than before, landing in a clump of rocks and brush well beyond the edge of camp.

The dog leaned against Stovepipe's leg, but made no move to retrieve the stick. Smoke saw Wilbur laughing at his friend's frustrated expression.

Once again, Stovepipe went to fetch the stick. He had to root around in the brush quite a bit to find it, and after a minute or so, he straightened and threw his hands in the air in defeat. He pulled out the bandanna and mopped his brow with it, then stuffed it in his pocket and marched back to rejoin the clearly amused Wilbur and the clearly baffled dog. The three of them walked back across the camp.

As they went, Smoke thought about what he had just watched. The way Stovepipe kept signaling with the bandanna had to mean something, and Smoke nodded slowly to himself as he figured out what it was.

Nothing else of significance happened in the outlaw camp the rest of the afternoon and on into the evening. The men tended to the horses, ate supper, played cards, drank, and generally just passed the time until it was late enough for everybody to settle down except for the guards on duty.

Earlier, after watching the charade with the dog and the stick, Smoke had taken the horses to the creek for water, filled up his canteen, and gnawed some more jerky.

Then he returned to his post in the brush atop the hill to keep an eye on things in the camp.

This had been a long day and Smoke's patience was wearing thin, but these latest developments might pay important dividends. It couldn't get dark soon enough to suit him. When it finally did, he made his move, slipping through the gathering shadows closer to the outlaw hideout.

Many times he had heard Preacher talk about sneaking into Blackfoot camps at night, back in the days when the old mountain man had carried on a long, bloody war with that tribe. Preacher had been able to get into those camps, slit the throats of half a dozen sleeping warriors, and get back out without any of the Blackfeet knowing he had been there.

Until the next morning when they discovered the bodies of their slain friends and knew that the phantom called the Ghost Killer had struck again. It was no wonder that Blackfoot mothers terrorized their unruly children with threats of the Ghost Killer getting them if they didn't behave. Not that Preacher ever would have hurt a youngster, or a woman, for that matter. The Blackfeet didn't know that.

Smoke had never been called upon to achieve that level of stealth and wasn't sure he could. Nobody was better than Preacher. But he could move through the night in almost complete silence and did so now, never rushing, but not wasting time in his smooth, efficient movements.

He had studied the landscape and planned out his route before it got dark, so he knew where he was going. He dropped to hands and knees as he approached the clump of rocks and brush where Stovepipe had tossed the stick several hours earlier.

When he was even closer, he stretched out on his belly

and crawled. As long as he didn't run into a snake he would be all right, and he figured most snakes would move off if they sensed a human getting close to them.

He reached the brush and penetrated it, feeling his way along in what was almost utter blackness. Trusting his instincts to guide him, he headed for the area where Stovepipe had been that afternoon.

After several minutes, he heard a faint crinkle of paper as his fingers brushed against something. He explored by touch and found that a rock was lying on top of a sheet of paper. Making as little noise as possible, he eased the paper out from under the rock, folded it a couple of times, and stuck it under his shirt.

Then he began retracing the path that had brought him here, leaving the area just as quietly and carefully as he had come.

It took Smoke a quarter of an hour to reach a spot far enough away from the outlaw camp that he trusted himself to stand up and move faster through the darkness. In another quarter of an hour, he was back where he had left the horses. He untied them and led them away, putting even more distance between himself and the hideout before he mounted and rode deeper into the hills.

He wanted to find a good place where it would be safe to read the note that Stovepipe had left hidden for him in the brush.

That didn't take long. When he was confident he had put enough distance between himself and the camp, and there were hills in between to block the view, he reined in, fished a lucifer from his pocket, and snapped the match to life with his thumbnail. With his other hand, he took the paper from under his shirt and unfolded it.

In the wavering light from the lucifer, he quickly scanned the words printed on the paper with a pencil.

Gang plans to hold up train west of Great Bend sometime in the next couple of days. Will steal shipping herd loaded on train. Don't know which train, but Stovepipe and I will be with them. Still don't know where stock rustled before being held. Will try to keep anybody else from being hurt, but could use some help if you can manage it. Coleman.

That was all, just half a dozen hastily printed lines. Reading them, Smoke realized that Wilbur must have written the note while Stovepipe was messing with that dog, figuring nobody would be watching him while his partner was making such a production of trying to get the dog to fetch.

Then Wilbur had slipped the note to Stovepipe, who had hidden it in the brush while pretending to hunt for the stick. It was a slick job of communicating in plain sight of the camp.

Smoke put the message away again and pinched out the lucifer's flame. He took off his hat and scrubbed a hand over his face as he thought about his next move. He didn't have enough information, but he had a pretty good idea where he could find out what he needed to know.

He had a pretty good idea about some other things, too, but time would tell about those.

He turned the horses east and headed back to Abilene.

It was long after midnight by the time Smoke reached the town. Even the saloons were closed at this hour. A couple of dogs on opposite sides of town barked at each other, but they sounded like it was so late that their hearts weren't really in it. The desultory *woof-woof* that came from one of them sounded more bored than alarmed.

Smoke knew his way around the back alleys by now. He found himself behind Dr. Allan Metzger's house, where he dismounted and went to the rear door. The house was dark, and he couldn't be sure that Metzger was here and not out on a late call somewhere. He knocked anyway, softly but insistently enough to wake anyone inside.

After a few minutes, the door opened slightly and a wary voice asked, "Who's out there?"

"It's Smoke Jensen, Doctor," Smoke replied, having recognized Metzger's voice.

The door opened wider. The house was still dark, but enough starlight penetrated into the doorway for Smoke to see the revolver in Metzger's hand.

"You won't need that six-gun," Smoke said.

Metzger looked a little embarrassed. He wore a night-shirt, so there was no place to put the gun, but he held it down at his side as he said, "No, of course not. I wasn't expecting to see you again this soon, Mr. Jensen. You're not injured and in need of medical assistance, I hope?"

"No, I'm fine. I'm just looking for some information."

"Come in. I'll light a lamp and we can talk."

Smoke shook his head. "That's not necessary. Just tell me where Red Winters lives."

"Rudolph Winters?" Metzger sounded surprised. "I heard that you and he, ah, had a fight the other day."

"That's true."

"What's he done now?" Metzger caught his breath. "Is he the one who's behind everything that's happened?"

"I can't talk about that just yet," said Smoke. "But I do need to palaver with Winters."

"He has a house not far from the railroad station. . . ." The doctor told Smoke how to find the place.

"Much obliged to you, Doctor. How's Pinky doing?"

"Better every day. And more impatient to be up and doing things, too. If he knows you're in town again, he may insist on joining you this time, and I'm not sure I can prevent him from doing so."

"Well, keep this visit to yourself, then, Doctor. I don't plan to advertise that I'm back in Abilene. In fact, it might be a pretty bad thing if certain folks got wind of it."

"Well, I'm certainly baffled by all this," said Metzger, "but whatever you have in mind, I wish you the best of luck, Mr. Jensen."

"Thanks," said Smoke. "I'm liable to need it."

Chapter 23

Smoke scratched a match into flame, held it to the wick of the lamp on the bedside table, and eared back the hammer of the Colt in his hand.

The combination of light and sound penetrated Rudolph Winters's sleep and made the railroad superintendent's eyes fly open. He started to bolt up out of sleep, but stopped short as he found himself staring down the barrel of Smoke's gun.

"Jensen!" he exclaimed. His face turned red with rage. "So you've come to finish me off, have you?"

Then realization sunk in on his sleep-fogged brain and caused the shaggy white brows to draw down in a confused frown.

"Wait a minute," said Winters. "I heard you were dead, or next thing to it!"

"Sometimes things get a mite exaggerated," Smoke drawled. "Take it easy, Winters. I'm not here to hurt you." As if to demonstrate that, Smoke lowered the Colt's hammer and slipped the gun back into its holster. "Actually, I need your help."

Winters sneered. "Does that mean you don't think I'm working with those damn outlaws anymore?"

"I know you're not."

Smoke's calm statement made Winters frown again. "Is that because you know who it is?"

"Let's say I have a pretty good idea."

"Then tell me who, blast it!"

Smoke shook his head. "Not yet. I don't have any actual proof, and right now, it's more important to stop what the gang is planning."

Without Smoke's gun staring him in the face, Winters felt emboldened enough to sit up in bed. "Are they going to hold up another train?"

"That's right. There's another train with a big shipment of cattle headed this way from the west, but I don't know exactly when. They figure on stopping it and rustling the stock right out of the cars, just like they did before."

Winters continued frowning as he studied Smoke's face in the lamplight. He didn't say anything for a long moment, but then he said, "I still don't understand exactly what's going on here, but why don't I get up and make some coffee, and you can explain things a little better."

"That sounds like a good idea," Smoke agreed.

Dr. Metzger had told him that Winters lived alone, so Smoke had gone to the house and slipped into the kitchen through the unlocked back door. From there, Winters's snoring had led him to the bedroom.

Winters pulled on a pair of pants to go with his nightshirt, and they both went into the kitchen. Winters motioned Smoke into a chair at the table while he stirred up the fire in the stove and then got a pot of coffee on to boil.

"As close as it is to morning, might as well plan on

staying up," Winters said. "You want some breakfast, Jensen?"

"All I've had in the past day is a few strips of jerky, so that sounds mighty welcome."

"While I'm rustling up the grub, why don't you tell me what's going on here?"

For the next ten minutes or so, Smoke did exactly that, starting with the ruse carried out by Stovepipe Stewart and Wilbur Coleman to infiltrate the gang of rustlers and killers.

"I'm not surprised the Cattlemen's Association wants to get to the bottom of these outrages," Winters commented from the stove. "You'd think they could have let me in on what they were doing, though."

"I don't reckon anybody from Abilene knew about Stewart and Coleman except Marshal McCormick, at least not starting out."

Smoke went on to describe how Stovepipe and Wilbur had used the phony shoot-out to reveal themselves and their plan to him, and how they had then recruited Dr. Metzger to put over the charade that Smoke was badly wounded and on the verge of death.

"I followed them to the gang's hideout, and they managed to let me know about the plan to hold up another train."

Winters turned toward him. "If you know where the hideout is, why not put together a posse, go out there, and round up the whole bunch?"

"Because it's not the whole bunch. They're holding the cattle they stole before somewhere else. If we can catch them in the act of robbing another train, we can force them to reveal where that is, and then we can recover all those cattle and save some ranches that might otherwise go under."

Smoke had thought a lot about it while on his way

back to Abilene. He was convinced that was Stovepipe's plan even though there hadn't been room in the note they had passed to him to explain it all. It made sense to him, too. The most important things were preventing any more killings and getting all those rustled cows back.

"I know the train they're talking about," Winters said as he set plates of fried eggs, ham, and biscuits on the table. "It'll be coming through Great Bend an hour before dawn, day after tomorrow. Or rather, tomorrow, now that I think about it, since it's almost morning. If they're going to stop it west of there, it'll probably be somewhere between Larned and Great Bend. Not much out there in that part of the country."

It wasn't surprising that Winters, being a bachelor, was a halfway decent cook. Smoke dug into the food and enjoyed it, especially washed down with hot black coffee. Between bites, he said, "I want to be on that train when they stop it."

Nodding, Winters said, "You can do that. You'll have to take a westbound today, get off in Dodge City, and then pick up the eastbound when it comes through tonight."

"Is there time to do that?"

"There's time," said Winters. "Not much to spare, but enough. And I can guarantee you'll make it by sending a few wires up the line."

"I'd really appreciate that," Smoke said.

Winters chuckled and said, "Maybe you will, maybe you won't. Hear me out, Jensen. I'll help you, but not without a price."

"What sort of price?" Smoke asked with a wary look on his face.

"I'm coming with you," Winters said.

Smoke couldn't help but look surprised. "I'm not sure that's a good idea," he said.

"I am," Winters replied with a firm nod. "Listen, if any

obstacles come up, I can smooth them over. I am the superintendent of this line, after all." He thumped a clenched fist on the table. "And I'm damned sick and tired of those outlaws getting away with what they're doing. If you're worried about me not being able to take care of myself, remember I bossed plenty of tough crews in my time and knocked sense into plenty of stubborn heads."

"This job is liable to involve gunplay," Smoke pointed out. "It's not the same thing."

"I can handle a gun. I'm better with a rifle than a handgun, but I've used both. We had a few scraps with the Indians when we were getting the line this far west."

Smoke knew that was true. And his own ruckus with Winters had proven that while the man might be getting older, he was still rugged, possessed plenty of vitality, and didn't have an ounce of back-up in him.

"I can't let anybody else know that I'm in Abilene and not wounded," Smoke said. "Can you get us on a westbound train without giving that away?"

Instead of answering directly, Winters stood up and went to the window. He pushed the curtain back and looked out. "We've still got a little time before it gets light," he said. "I'll throw some clothes on. Our best bet would be to ride west to the next water stop. We can get on the train there. I'll need to rent a horse—"

"I have an extra horse if you have a saddle," Smoke broke in.

Winters chuckled. "Matter of fact, I do. Give me a few minutes to get dressed and we'll make tracks out of here."

After the meeting of the entire gang where Jester McMillan explained about the next train holdup, the outlaws had gone back to their usual evening activities. Stovepipe and Wilbur got up a game of forty-two with Tom Church and

Jonas Page, playing on a blanket spread on the ground. Ranger sat beside Stovepipe and watched the dominoes being played as if he knew what was going on.

As they played, Wilbur said, "When I had my powwow with the big boss back in Abilene, he was messing around with some dominoes. You fellas ever meet him?"

"You mean Jester ain't the big boss?" Church asked in apparent innocence.

Page looked around. Stovepipe figured he was making sure none of the other outlaws were close enough to overhear what he was about to say.

"You know better than that, Tom. Jester's a lot of things, but bein' smart enough to put together a whole deal like this ain't one of 'em."

Church laughed quietly and said, "Yeah, I know. To answer your question, Walt, naw, we ain't ever seen nor talked to the big auger. We know that he sends word out here by that gambler Yancey or other messengers and tells Jester what to do. But I, for one, ain't curious about him."

"I've always figured that bein' too curious about anything is bad for a fella's health," added Page.

"That's the truth," Stovepipe agreed. "I don't care who's pullin' the strings as long as a good payoff is waitin' at the end."

"It'll be a good one, all right. It's a seller's market, and we got the goods that folks are hungry to buy," Page said.

"Yeah, hungry," Church said with a grin.

It sounded to Stovepipe like that meant something, but he wasn't sure what it was. For now, he was willing to let it go, figuring he would find out more about that part of the mastermind's plan later.

"Jester said that some of us would unload those cattle and drive 'em off, and the rest would loot the express car and gather up all the valuables from the passengers. When will he say who does what?"

"Probably not until right before the job," Page said. "Anyway, it don't really matter, does it? We just do what we're told."

"It don't matter to me," Wilbur said. "I'll go along with whatever he wants."

As long as it didn't involve killing innocent people. Stovepipe knew that was how Wilbur felt, because he felt the same. He planned to find some way to break up this robbery and capture the outlaws with the least loss of life possible. Once they were in custody and facing the threat of a hangman's rope for the gang's previous crimes, somebody was bound to crack and reveal the location of the other hideout, the one where the rustled stock was being kept.

For now, there was nothing to do but wait. They passed the time by playing the game with Church and Page and passing around a bottle of whiskey.

Finally, Stovepipe tossed a double-six next to the three dominoes already in the center of the blanket and said, "I'll take this trick." He swept all four dominoes in front of him and added them to the others lined up there. "And that sets you boys again. Should've passed, Tom, instead of biddin' thirty-two with no better dominoes than that."

Church cursed and then said, "You Texans are just too blasted good at this game. You throw down your dominoes a couple of times and suddenly the hand's over while I'm still tryin' to get caught up on what's happenin'."

Page tilted the bottle up and swallowed the last few drops from it. He wiped the back of the other hand across his mouth, belched, and said, "Yeah, I think I'm done, unless you want to put the dominoes away and break out a deck of cards. Poker's a real game."

"Fine by me," Wilbur said. Stovepipe scratched Ranger's ears and tried not to chuckle. Wilbur was good at poker, and he knew his way around a deck himself.

Wilbur went on, "Why don't we make it interestin'? A dollar to open and no limit?"

Church whistled. "You figure we're made of money, Walt?"

"Well, we're all gonna be rich when the payoff comes, right?"

"He's got a point there," Page said. "All right, let's get started."

Stovepipe and Wilbur proceeded to clean out their two companions. By the time they had done that, it was late enough that many of the men were calling it a night.

Church felt the same way. He threw down his latest losing hand and declared, "That's it. I'm done. I ain't gonna write any more IOUs."

"That's all right, Tom," said Wilbur. "I won't charge you interest on them."

Church snorted. Page said, "I'm out, too. It was an enjoyable evenin', I reckon, but we paid a big enough price for it."

"We'll do it again some other time," Stovepipe said.

"Sure."

The blanket belonged to Church. He picked it up, and he and Page disappeared into the soddy they shared. Stovepipe stretched, unlimbering some of the kinks in his back from sitting on the ground for so long, then he and Wilbur and Ranger strolled toward the area beside McMillan's soddy where their bedrolls waited.

They took off their hats, boots, and gun belts and stretched out on their blankets. Ranger lay down beside Stovepipe and rested his head on his front paws.

"Sure would be nice if we could talk to our old pard again," Wilbur said.

Stovepipe knew he was talking about Smoke Jensen. "Yeah, but more than likely that hombre's a long way from here right now. We'll probably see him again one of these days. I'd even bet a hat on it."

"I suppose so."

They didn't really know that much more now than they had when they passed the note to Smoke, mused Stovepipe. Of course, they could only assume that Smoke had gotten the message and acted upon it. And even if that were the case, they had no way of knowing exactly how Smoke would respond.

Stovepipe knew what he would do if he were in Smoke's place, though. He would be on that eastbound train full of cattle when the outlaws stopped it. . . .

A soft footstep nearby made him reach for the coiled shell belt and holstered Colt beside him. Ranger lifted his head but didn't growl, indicating that whoever was nearby was probably friendly. Stovepipe's hand had just closed around the revolver's walnut grips anyway when a voice that was little more than a whisper said, "Sam? Are you there?"

He recognized the voice immediately—Lena Cooley. He took note of a change, too. She had called him "Sam" this time, when every time she had spoken to him before she addressed him as "Jones."

Whether that meant anything or not, Stovepipe didn't know. But he figured he was going to find out.

He sat up and said, equally quietly, "Right here, ma'am."

He knew Wilbur was still awake, but the redhead didn't show any signs of it. He just continued his slow, regular breathing as if he were asleep. Whatever was going on, he was content to let Stovepipe handle it.

"Can I talk to you for a few minutes?" asked Lena.

Stovepipe let go of the Colt, even though he was a little reluctant to do so, just out of habit, and pushed himself to his feet.

"I reckon so," he said. "But does Jester know you're out here?"

"I don't have to get permission from Jester McMillan for everything I do," she replied with an annoyed edge in her tone. "I talk to whoever I want to."

"Well, I reckon that's your right," said Stovepipe, although he knew McMillan might not see it that way. "What can I do for you?"

"Let's walk a little way up the hill."

The feeling of wariness was strong in Stovepipe, but he said, "Sure," and turned to fall in step beside Lena as she walked away from the soddy. He heard the faint brush of the long skirt she wore as it swung around her hips and legs.

"Don't worry about Jester," she said after a moment. "He's sound asleep."

"You know that for a fact, do you?"

"I know how he's been after every other time we've . . . Never mind. Just take my word for it."

"Sure," Stovepipe said again, not needing to hear any details.

Lena must have judged that they were far enough away from the camp. She stopped and turned to him. The silvery light from the moon and stars touched her face.

"I wanted to warn you to be careful tomorrow night."

"You mean when we hold up that train? I don't reckon it'll be too bad. Jester and the others have done it before, haven't they?"

"Several times," Lena confirmed.

"And they never ran into any real trouble, did they?"

"Sometimes the men on the train put up a fight." In the faint light, he saw her shoulders rise and fall. "Last time one of the men was killed by a lucky shot from a passenger. But usually the resistance doesn't amount to much."

"That's always good to hear."

"It's not the men on the train I'm warning you about," Lena continued with a trace of impatience. "It's Jester."

Stovepipe took a deep breath and let that sink in before saying, "You reckon he plans on double-crossin' us? Maybe gunnin' down me and Walt durin' the holdup when we won't be expectin' it?"

"I'm not saying I *know* that's what he plans to do. But I don't have any doubt he's capable of doing something like that. He doesn't feel like he needs the two of you. The only reason he let you join the gang was because the big boss in Abilene told him to."

"And because we got rid of that troublesome fella Jensen for him," Stovepipe reminded her.

"I'm sure Jester appreciates that. It doesn't mean he won't turn on you if he thinks that's the better course for him."

"Well, we'll be careful," Stovepipe assured her. "We always are. It's sort of a habit for hombres like us who've heard the owl hoot on a heap of lonely trails."

"I'm sure that's true," Lena said dryly. "I'm just telling you not to trust Jester, that's all. With everything wrapping up like it is, he'll be wanting to tie up all the loose ends."

Stovepipe tried to keep his voice calm despite the surprise that went through him. "What do you mean, everything wrappin' up?"

"Tomorrow is the last time they're hitting a stock train. With the cattle Jester plans to steal, they'll have as big a herd as they can handle on the drive north."

"Headin' north with all that rustled stock, are they?"

Lena muttered something under her breath, maybe a curse, then said, "I shouldn't have said anything about that. But yes, this is the last job, and then Jester and the others will be heading for the goldfields up in Dakota Territory."

The whole thing burst like a bombshell in Stovepipe's brain, but he still sounded like he was only idly curious as he said, "Goldfields, eh?"

"That's right. With thousands of miners pouring in and settlements springing up all over the Black Hills, that much beef on the hoof will be worth a fortune. A lot more than most of those prospectors will ever see in the gold they find, if they manage to find any."

Stovepipe nodded slowly. He knew Lena was right. McMillan could sell those cattle to beef-hungry miners for much, much more than their normal value in the stockyards at Kansas City and Chicago. It was an audacious plan, but one that could pay off handsomely.

And as Church and Page had indicated, Jester McMillan wasn't smart enough to have come up with it by himself. Someone in Abilene had done that, brought in McMillan, and organized the whole thing.

There were still questions to be answered, so while Lena seemed to be in a talkative mood for some reason, he probed, "You say we ain't comin' back here after the holdup?"

"That's right. Everybody's going to Little Jerusalem." She paused, then added bitterly, "Everybody except me."

Once again, Stovepipe had to contain his excitement as important information fell into his lap. He didn't know what or where Little Jerusalem was, although the name was vaguely familiar to him. Instead of asking about that, he said, "What do you mean everybody but you?"

"Jester's done with me. He told me so tonight. When he and the rest of you ride out tomorrow, I'm supposed to gather what I want, take the wagon, and go back to Abilene." She laughed, but the sound had no genuine humor in it, only bleak acceptance. "He said I should consider myself lucky he was just sending me back to the house where I came from, instead of throwing me to the wolves tomorrow for a celebration before the gang rides out. That's what I halfway expected him to do."

"Good thing he didn't," muttered Stovepipe. "Don't reckon I'd have been willin' to stand for that."

"You would have had to. That or get yourself killed."

"We may be outlaws, ma'am, but there are some lines we don't aim to cross."

Lena put a hand on his arm. "That's a nice thing to say, Sam. And a nice thing for me to hear . . . even if it might not be true."

Then, for what was hardly the first time tonight, she surprised him.

She took hold of both of his arms, came up on her toes, and pressed her mouth to his in a passionate, urgent kiss.

That lasted less than a minute when Jester McMillan's angry voice yelled, "Get the hell outta my way, Smith, or I'll gun you, too!"

Lena gasped and stepped back. Stovepipe turned and saw an enraged McMillan stomping up the slope toward them, gun in hand.

Chapter 24

Stovepipe had left his gun down beside his bedroll. That was uncharacteristically careless of him, but he hadn't expected to need it while he was talking to Lena.

Maybe that was a good thing. If he'd been armed, McMillan might have started blazing away at him already.

Stovepipe glanced past the outlaw and saw Wilbur hurrying up the hill. Wilbur had a gun in his hand, too. Stovepipe knew his partner; if it looked like McMillan was going to open fire, Wilbur would blast him down from behind.

That would cause their plan to fall apart, more than likely, but Wilbur wouldn't stand by and watch his old friend be killed.

Stovepipe hoped Wilbur wouldn't get trigger-happy. They might still be able to salvage this situation.

"Get away from her, you damn saddle tramp!" McMillan bellowed. "I oughta blow holes in you, Jones!"

"Jester, this wasn't Sam's idea—" Lena began.

"Shut up! You're nothing but a damn slut! I don't want to hear a word from you."

McMillan was only about ten feet away now. Point blank range for a man who was good with a gun. He wouldn't miss if he started triggering.

Lena stepped forward and put herself directly between Stovepipe and McMillan. Stovepipe's jaw tightened. He'd never cottoned to the idea of hiding behind anybody, especially a woman.

He put a hand on Lena's shoulder to move her out of the way, but she twisted out of his grip and still managed to stay between him and McMillan.

"You have to listen to me, Jester," she said. "I think you owe me that much."

"Owe you?" McMillan's face twisted in a sneer. Stovepipe saw the expression pretty clearly, since his eyes had adjusted to the darkness. "I don't owe you a damn thing. I paid you to come out here with me, just like the whore you are!"

Lena's back stiffened. Her hands clenched into fists at her sides.

"Maybe that's what I am," she said. "So why should you be upset that I turned to somebody else when you threw me aside? You told me you were through with me, Jester! You know what that means."

She gestured toward the camp, where several of the outlaws had emerged from their soddies and were gathering to see what all the commotion was about.

"I would have been fair game for anybody who wanted to take me!" Lena went on. "For the whole bunch, if that's what they wanted. Unless . . . I found somebody to look out for me."

She glanced back at Stovepipe. The light was too dim for him to be able to read the expression in her eyes, but he sensed that she was pleading for him to play along with her.

"I thought maybe Jones would want to take up with me. I was the one who approached him, Jester. You don't have any reason to be mad at him."

That was true, as far as it went. He had only come out here to talk to Lena because she'd asked him to. She hadn't said anything about him declaring her to be his woman, though.

Maybe she just hadn't gotten around to it yet.

Still sneering, McMillan said, "How about it, Jones? Is that the way it was?"

"I reckon so," Stovepipe said slowly, because he sensed that was what Lena wanted.

McMillan grunted. "Just because I'm done with her, that doesn't mean I want the likes of you getting my leavings. I told her to go back to Abilene where she came from."

"I just got scared—"

McMillan interrupted her again. "We've got more important things to do than fight over some trail town tramp! We're riding out tomorrow for the biggest job yet, and we're not going to need you around." He jammed his gun back in its holster. "You're stupid, Lena. Pure stupid. Going around trying to stir up trouble for no good reason." He threw back his head and brayed a raucous laugh. "You want her, Jones, you can have her! But not for very long, because you're riding out tomorrow with the rest of us."

"That's right, boss, I sure am," said Stovepipe, glad that maybe this trouble could be headed off before it erupted into something that could ruin all of his and Wilbur's plans.

McMillan snorted in disgust, turned, and stalked back toward his soddy, brushing past Wilbur as he did so. The small crowd of outlaws began to disperse, now that the show was over and there hadn't even been any blood spilled.

Lena looked at Stovepipe again. "You could come back to Abilene with me."

"I don't reckon that's the hand I have to play, ma'am. I've thrown in with Jester and the rest of the boys, and I can't turn my back on that."

"We could slip out together tonight. . . . The others wouldn't know until it was too late. . . ."

Her voice was low, barely more than a breath.

"We'd never make it," Stovepipe told her. "We all know too much. The guards'd gun us down. I'm sure Jester's ordered 'em to shoot anybody who tries to leave before the whole bunch pulls out tomorrow."

"Fine," she said in an icy tone. "I thought you liked me."

"I like you just fine, Miss Lena, but we're too close to the payoff to go changin' things around now. I won't let anybody bother you before we go, though, if that's what's worryin' you."

"I'm not worried," she snapped. "Anybody tries anything with me, he'll be sorry." She turned and yelled down into the camp. "All of you hear that? Lay a hand on me and I'll cut your gizzard out!"

She went back down the hill, quivering with rage.

Wilbur had holstered his Colt when McMillan left. He walked up to join Stovepipe and said quietly, "That was a close call. I hate to say it, but Miss Lena seems a mite loco."

"She's not loco," said Stovepipe as he slowly shook his head. "She's just been through a lot of trouble in her life. I wish I could do somethin' to help her out." His voice took on a flinty edge as he went on, "But we've got a job to do, and I don't plan to let anything get in the way of that now."

Red Winters might have been riding a desk most of the time in recent years, but that didn't mean he had forgotten how to sit a saddle. As he and Smoke rode through the graying light, he said, "It feels mighty good to get back out here on the trail, Jensen. Pushing papers around is no life for a man like me."

"Why do you do it, then?" Smoke asked.

Winters's brawny shoulders rose and fell. "The railroad offered me more money, and I knew good and well that if I turned the job down, they'd just give it to somebody who wouldn't handle it as well as I could. Railroading's in my blood. I couldn't let the line down."

"But you regret it sometimes?"

"It's not like pushing rails through new country, that's for damn sure. But hell, it's been almost ten years since they drove the Golden Spike at Promontory Point. The days of the railroad spreading out all across the country are over. There won't be any more big jobs like that."

"They're still expanding the routes up north and putting in spur lines in plenty of places," Smoke pointed out.

Winters shook his head. "It's not the same. For a while there, every mile of track we laid made history. By the time we were finished, the country was never going to be the same. Now . . . now it's just a business, blast it! I still love railroading, but it's a business, plain and simple, not an adventure." He grunted. "So maybe now you understand why I was bound and determined to fight rustlers with you."

"I'm glad to have you siding me, Winters. The odds are going to be against us."

"With those two range detectives on our side, it'll be, what, four against a couple dozen or more?"

Smoke smiled in the dawn light. "I've faced worse odds, I reckon. I wouldn't be surprised if Stovepipe and Wilbur have, too."

The bulk of a water tank rising on four sturdy wooden legs beside the tracks they were following appeared ahead of them. The sight of it made Smoke realize that dawn was upon them. He glanced over his shoulder and could tell the sun was just about to peek over the eastern horizon.

Winters, who wore a brown tweed suit but no vest or cravat, fished a turnip watch out of his pocket and flipped it open to check the time.

"The westbound will be coming through here in about an hour," he said. "We can board it and take it almost all the way to the Colorado border before we'll meet that cattle train heading the other way. I don't know exactly where that'll be, but I can figure it out once I get to a telegraph key and send some wires. It'll be best to switch over to the eastbound as far up the line as we can. That way we'll be sure to be aboard before those outlaws hold it up."

"Are you going to warn the train crew on the eastbound?" asked Smoke.

Winters's expression was grim as he said, "I don't have any choice. I know those men. I won't allow them to go right ahead into danger without letting them know what they're getting into. They need to be prepared for trouble."

"As long as they can keep it to themselves. The gang could have spies planted on board, and we don't want to tip them off that we're on to the plan."

"The railroad owes it to the passengers to protect them, too." Winters grimaced. "But I see why we can't say anything to them. It might well cause a panic, and that would warn the outlaws for sure that we're waiting for them, if any are on board."

"I'm glad you understand that," said Smoke. "I don't want innocent folks getting hurt any more than you do. When we make our move, we'll have to hit that bunch hard and fast. That's the best chance we'll have of stopping that holdup without a lot of danger to the passengers."

With that settled, the two men rode on to the water stop, which consisted of the tank beside the tracks, a small, shed-like building where a telegrapher was on duty, and about fifty yards away a ramshackle saloon where cowboys or other folks who had to meet the train for some reason could get a drink while they were waiting. A few horses drowsed in a corral next to the saloon.

This early in the morning, the saloon was closed and the telegrapher was sleeping in his chair with his head pillowed on his crossed arms as they rested on the desk.

"Hopkins!" Red Winters blared as he and Smoke stepped into the office.

The young man bolted upright. The green visor on his head was askew, and a line of drool ran from one corner of his mouth. He straightened himself up quickly, pawed at his face with one hand, and blinked bleary eyed at the two newcomers.

"Mr. Winters!" he said. "What are you doing here?" He looked past Smoke and Winters through the open door. "What time is it?"

"Time for you to move aside so I can send some wires," Winters said as he moved forward and his bulky form filled up more of the small room.

"You, uh, you don't work for Western Union, sir."

"I know that, but I can still send just as well as I could when I was shinnying up poles back east. My fist's as good as ever. And I expect your boss back in Abilene wouldn't like it if I complained to him about your lack of cooperation."

"I . . . I want to cooperate, sir," the telegrapher said. "If you promise I won't get in trouble—"

"Out of that chair, son, or I promise you *will* be in trouble—with me!"

Hopkins scrambled to his feet and moved back so that Winters could sit down and reach for the telegraph key.

The young man looked at Smoke in confusion. Smoke just smiled reassuringly.

Winters hunched over the key. His index finger moved almost too fast to follow as he tapped out a message. Smoke had some knowledge of Morse code, but Winters was sending so fast that he couldn't make out any of the words, only an occasional letter.

The operator on the other end must have been able to understand the message, though, because when Winters stopped sending, the sounder began to click a response almost right away. A pad of paper and a pencil lay on the desk. Winters snatched up the pencil and began writing on the top sheet of paper as he translated the sounds into letters forming words.

That back-and-forth continued for several minutes. Winters paused, consulted a printed chart also lying on the desk, and resumed sending. Smoke figured that was a list of telegraph offices and the signals used to identify them.

Winters looked like he was enjoying himself. When he finally finished and pushed his chair back, he smiled and said, "All right, I have the information we need to know."

"Including when the westbound from Abilene will get here?" Smoke asked.

"That's right. In fact, it's a little ahead of schedule and ought to be along before much longer."

As if it had been waiting for Winters's cue, the plaintive whistle of a steam locomotive sounded in the distance and came clearly through the open doorway.

Winters stood up and nodded to Hopkins. "We're obliged to you for the use of your key, son."

"That . . . that's all right," Hopkins said. "Mr. Winters, I'm not sure I've ever heard anybody send as fast as you just did. I could barely follow it."

"Old habits are hard to forget," Winters said with a dismissive wave of his hand. "It felt good to be back on a telegraph key."

Smoke and Winters went outside and peered along the steel rails to the east. The plume of smoke from the big Baldwin locomotive's diamond-shaped stack was barely visible, but it drew steadily closer and soon they could see the locomotive itself with its pointed cowcatcher leading the way. The rails vibrated and the rumble of the engine got louder and louder.

With a squeal of brakes, the train slowed as it approached the water stop. The engineer applied a sure hand to the throttle and brake, bringing the locomotive to a stop in perfect position for a brakeman to swing around the long metal spout and fill the engine's boiler.

While that was going on, Smoke and Winters went to the cab, where Winters called up, "Hello, Harry!"

The engineer looked down from the window on his side of the cab and exclaimed, "Red! I mean, Mr. Winters. What are you doin' here?"

"Hitching a ride," replied Winters, "and we've known

each for too long for you to be calling me Mister when we're out here on the rails." He looked at Smoke and went on, "Jensen, meet Harry Sullivan, one of the best damn railroad engineers on the line. That little monkey with coal dust all over his face is his fireman, Wendall Ferguson. Goes by Windy."

Smoke nodded and raised his voice over the engine's rumble to say, "I'm glad to meet you boys. Obliged to you for the ride."

The grimy-faced fireman said, "You wouldn't be *Smoke* Jensen, would you?"

"That's generally what I go by."

Ferguson practically hopped up and down with excitement. "By grab, Harry, we're gonna have a famous gunfighter on our train!"

Winters made patting motions with his hands and said, "Take it easy, Windy. Jensen and I are gonna ride up here in the cab if that's all right. We don't want anybody else to know we're on board."

"Better tell Jack Purdy," Sullivan advised. "He'll get his nose outta joint if you don't, and then he'll make our lives miserable for the next few runs."

"Purdy's the conductor," Winters explained to Smoke. "We can trust him. He's been with the railroad almost as long as I have."

"I'll trust your judgment on things like that," said Smoke.

Sullivan beckoned to them. "Come on up. It'll be a mite crowded, but I reckon we can stand it if you fellas can."

"I'll go tell Jack what's goin' on," Ferguson volunteered. He hopped down from the cab, as nimble as the monkey that Winters had called him.

A few minutes later, with the engine's boiler full again

and Ferguson having returned from his conversation with the conductor in the caboose, Sullivan eased the throttle forward and a little shiver went through the train as its drivers engaged. The wheels turned and the huge conveyance moved slowly forward and gradually began to pick up speed.

The train went faster and faster until it vanished in the distance to the west.

Chapter 25

Sometime before dawn, while Ranger was stretched out beside Stovepipe, the big dog suddenly lifted his head and growled loudly enough to rouse the range detective from slumber. Stovepipe was wide awake instantly, a skill he had developed out of a long habit of staying alive.

He said, "Shhh," quietly to Ranger as he propped himself on his left elbow. His right hand already gripped the Colt without him being aware of having drawn it from the holster. He had done that in the split-second between sleep and wakefulness.

The sky had not yet begun to lighten. There was a good reason folks said it was darkest before the dawn. The moon was down, and only the glitter of starlight illuminated the camp. Clouds had drifted in during the night, obscuring some of those stars and thickening the gloom even more, so Stovepipe couldn't see ten feet in front of his face.

He heard horses approaching the camp, though. Two or three, he judged. The newcomers rode in and went to

Jester McMillan's soddy. Stovepipe heard the faint rumble of McMillan's harsh voice. Another man answered.

Wilbur was awake, too, his slumber as easily disturbed as Stovepipe's had been. He eased over beside his partner and breathed, "I think that's Yancey's voice. What's he doin' here again?"

"Dunno," replied Stovepipe, equally quietly. The gambler who had first approached Wilbur back in Abilene was the chief courier used to deliver messages from the big boss to McMillan. He supposed it made sense for Yancey to be here the night before the gang set off on its biggest and final job, bringing last-minute instructions from the hooded mastermind.

But whether it made sense or not, Yancey's unexpected arrival put a frown on Stovepipe's face in the darkness and made an icy sensation trickle down his spine. His instincts told him that Yancey being here wasn't a good thing.

But there was nothing he could do about it. He and Wilbur were too close to the end to throw away everything they had accomplished so far.

"I don't like this," Wilbur whispered, indicating that warning bells were going off in his mind, too.

"Nope," Stovepipe agreed. Ranger growled again, prompting Stovepipe to chuckle. "Another country heard from."

He looked up and checked the stars he could see. Not that long until morning, he judged. Given that, it wasn't very likely that he would go back to sleep.

He didn't, and neither did Wilbur. As soon as they heard Blind Ezra stirring around, they got up, pulled on their boots, and went in search of some coffee.

A light burned in McMillan's soddy, Stovepipe noted. The yellow glow seeped out around the edges of the blanket hung in the door opening.

They were the first to arrive at the fire Ezra had kindled, but that wasn't the case for very long. More of the outlaws stumbled up demanding coffee. Ezra cursed them and told them to hold their damn horses.

As the men talked among themselves, Stovepipe sensed a growing feeling of excitement in the air. They were breaking camp today, moving on to a big job that would lead ultimately to a big payoff. For men such as these, who lived from day to day, from spree to spree, from one violent outrage to another, the momentary pleasures their share of the loot would bring them were all that mattered.

The fire got bigger and spread its light over the outlaws as they gathered. Stovepipe noticed a couple of men he hadn't seen in the hideout before. They were talking in friendly fashion with Tom Church, Jonas Page, and the others, so they had to be accepted members of the gang. They were the ones who had arrived from Abilene with Yancey a short time earlier, Stovepipe decided.

Why had the big boss sent three men out here this morning, instead of just Yancey? Were they the last of the gang who had still been in Abilene? If they were all moving on north, driving the huge herd of rustled cattle to the goldfields in Dakota Territory, more than likely the whole bunch would be needed for an undertaking like that.

The boss was closing things down. Would he show up, too, leaving Abilene behind?

Stovepipe had a hunch that was possible, and he was going to be very interested to see if the hunch was right.

The coffee was ready. Ezra poured the stuff in outstretched cups and men sighed in satisfaction as they drank the hot, strong brew. Stovepipe and Wilbur drifted back to the outer edges of the gathering to enjoy their coffee, and that's where they were when Lena Cooley appeared at Stovepipe's side.

"Have you changed your mind?" she asked Stovepipe quietly.

"About what?" he said, although he had a pretty good idea what she was talking about.

"Coming back to Abilene with me."

Stovepipe shook his head. Whether the regret in his voice was genuine, even he couldn't have said as he replied, "I can't do it. We've already taken cards. We got to play out the hand."

For a moment, Lena didn't say anything. Then she told him, "I'm sorry you feel that way."

"So am I, ma'am." Stovepipe paused, then went on, "I know I don't have any right to ask it, but there's a favor you can do for me, and I'd be mighty obliged if you see fit to do it."

"What's that?" Lena asked with a wary edge in her voice.

Stovepipe reached down to scratch Ranger's ears. The dog had followed them over to the fire.

"When you load up the wagon and head back to Abilene, can you take this big fella with you? We'll be ridin' hard today, and he wouldn't be able to keep up. I don't want him abandoned to make his own way out here in the middle o' nowhere."

"What am I going to do with him?" said Lena. "I'll have to go back to what I was doing before to make a living. I can't be stuck with some big stupid dog."

"You don't have to make a pet of him. But maybe he could find a home with somebody else in town, or at least have more of a chance of scroungin' a meal here and there."

Lena blew out her breath in an exasperated sigh. "All right," she said. "I don't know why I'm agreeing to it, but I'll take him with me."

"Like I said, I'm mighty obliged to you. I've gotten right fond of the big galoot in the time we've been here."

"Is that dog the only thing you've gotten fond of?"

"Well . . . no, ma'am, he ain't. And I don't want to see any harm come to anybody else, either. But like I said—"

"I know," she broke in. "You've got to play out the hand."

The sun was up, peeking in and out of the thick white clouds that floated above the prairie, by the time the outlaws were ready to ride out. Lena had avoided McMillan as she packed her belongings and some supplies into the buckboard parked beside the corral. When she was done, she found Stovepipe and Wilbur and told them, "I'm heading out."

No one had bothered her as she prepared to leave. Stovepipe supposed word had gotten around camp that she was under his protection now, and none of the men wanted to test that.

Also, it was likely they were thinking more about the loot that was waiting for them at the end of the cattle drive, rather than the momentary pleasure they might have gotten from Lena. There would be plenty of fancy women for them to consort with once their pockets were heavy with gold coins.

Ranger was sitting nearby. Stovepipe called him over, rubbed his ears, and told him, "You're gonna go with Miss Lena, you understand? You're goin' back to Abilene and maybe you'll find some nice family there to live with. You and me can't be pards no more."

Ranger just looked up at him and whined softly.

"Dadgum it, don't make this any harder than it already is." Stovepipe sighed. "Come on. We'll walk over to the wagon together."

Ranger fell in alongside him as he walked to the buckboard. Wilbur followed and held out some rope.

"I fixed this halter for him," Wilbur said. "If you can get him to jump up there, you can tie him to the buckboard so he can't run off."

Stovepipe nodded. "That's a good idea. Come on, Ranger, hop on up here." He patted the seat.

"I didn't say he could ride beside me. . . ." Lena began. Then she shook her head and went on, "Oh, all right. I suppose it doesn't matter."

"Come on, Ranger," Stovepipe said again.

The big dog sat down and got a stubborn look on his face.

Stovepipe gritted his teeth. He took hold of the buckboard's frame and stepped up onto the driver's box himself. He sat down and once again patted the seat. "Get your carcass up here, doggone it," he urged.

This time, Ranger jumped easily onto the box, clambered onto the seat, and planted his rear end there, looking pleased with himself.

Stovepipe slipped the halter around his neck and tied the other end to the brake lever. "You're gonna stay here," he told Ranger. "You're goin' with Miss Lena. It'll all be fine. I'll see you again one o' these days."

"That ain't very likely," said Wilbur.

"Oh, I don't know about that. Stranger things have happened, I reckon. If nothin' else, he might be waitin' for me up yonder at the Pearly Gates, happen I make it that far when I cross the divide. I've always figured heaven's big enough for some critters, too."

"I don't know about critters, but I wouldn't count on the likes of us bein' welcome up there." Wilbur shrugged. "But like the song says, further along we'll know more about it."

Stovepipe scratched Ranger's ears some more, let the

dog lean against him for a minute, then cleared his throat, gave Ranger a last pat on the head, and climbed down. Ranger looked at him and whined, then started to get off the seat.

Stovepipe put out a hand to stop him. "No, you stay there," he said. He looked at Lena. "If you're ready, you'd best get a move on."

"I'm ready," she said. Wilbur stepped forward to help her as she climbed up onto the buckboard's seat, but she ignored him and pulled herself up without assistance. Then she looked at Stovepipe and said, "Goodbye, Sam."

"Goodbye, Lena," he said, leaving off the "Miss" this time.

"If you're ever in Abilene, look me up," she told him with a mocking smile. Then she slapped the reins against the backs of the two horses hitched to the buckboard.

Ranger looked back at Sam and Wilbur as the vehicle rolled away, but Lena didn't.

Stovepipe sighed. Wilbur said, "Wasn't nothin' else you could do for either of them, pard. At least this way they've both got a chance."

"I know you're right," Stovepipe said, nodding slowly. "That don't make it any easier, but at least I know it." He clapped a hand on Wilbur's shoulder. "Come on. We got work to do."

A short time later, with Jester McMillan shouting orders, the outlaws mounted up and rode out, leaving the camp behind them. One of the men drove the specially built wagon they used for unloading the rustled cattle.

Stovepipe took note of the fact that Yancey came with them. The gambler rode at the head of the group with McMillan.

As for whether the hooded mastermind from Abilene would join them, too, only time would tell about that.

* * *

Late that afternoon, Smoke and Red Winters were waiting at a small flag stop not far from the Colorado border. The tiny settlement didn't have an actual railroad station, just a flat-roofed, open-sided shed where passengers could wait out of the weather, and next to it a building not much bigger than an outhouse where a telegrapher was on duty part of the time.

The flag was already up on the pole next to the tracks. It would signal the eastbound train's engineer to stop, but in this case it wasn't really necessary. One of the telegraph messages Winters had sent that morning had arranged for the train to make an unscheduled halt here to take on two special passengers.

Both men looked up as they heard a locomotive's whistle in the distance. Out on this open prairie, sound traveled a long way. So did the sight of the smoke rising from the engine. Smoke and Winters watched it as it came closer, all the way to the settlement.

When the long train had eased to a stop, the conductor swung down from the caboose and trotted up the tracks toward them. Smoke heard a lot of bawling from the dozens of cattle cars. The blue-uniformed man came up to Smoke and Winters and nodded.

"Hello, Red," he said. "I got word to expect you."

"Good to see you, Verne," Winters said as he shook hands with the conductor. To Smoke, he added, "This is Verne Flynn, Jensen. Verne, meet Smoke Jensen."

Flynn shook hands with Smoke, too. "I've heard plenty about you, Mr. Jensen," he said. "It's a pleasure to have you on my train."

"You may not think so before this business is over with, Mr. Flynn. We're obliged to you for your cooperation."

Flynn looked shrewdly at Winters and asked, "What exactly am I cooperating in, Red? And make it quick, if you don't mind me being blunt about it. We've got a schedule to keep, you know." He chuckled. "I've got a hard-nosed superintendent who insists on it."

It didn't take long for Winters to fill the conductor in on what they were dealing with. As Winters had warned Smoke, Flynn reacted badly to the news.

"Absolutely not," he stated flatly. "I'm not going to allow the passengers to be endangered that way. This train can sit right here, and to hell with the schedule."

"We're not going to let the passengers get hurt," said Winters. "Jensen and I will be ready, and we have men inside the gang working with us, too."

"When bullets start flying around, you can't guarantee where they're going to land," insisted Flynn. "It's just too risky, Red."

"I could order you to cooperate with us, Verne," Winters pointed out.

"And I could quit, too. I will if you force my hand."

A new voice asked, "What's all this palaverin'?"

Smoke looked around to see the burly engineer stalking toward them. The man's florid face had an impatient expression on it. He was probably worried about the schedule, too.

"Red's lost his mind, Ward," Flynn said. "He wants us to drive right into a pack of rustlers and killers."

"That's not exactly how it's going to be," Winters began. He repeated the story to the engineer, who he introduced to Smoke as Ward Powell.

When Winters was finished, Powell turned to Flynn and said, "Break out the pistols and rifles from the locker in the caboose, Vernc. If we arm ourselves and the brakemen and tell the men in the express car what's going on, that'll be almost a dozen guns to take on those damn train robbers."

"Plus two men with the gang," Winters put in. "I'm not saying the odds won't be against us, but we'll have the element of surprise on our side, too. I think we stand a good chance of wiping out half the gang before they know what's going on."

Flynn still looked doubtful. "At the very least," he said, "we should warn the passengers and give them a chance to get off before they reach their destinations. The railroad could give them tickets on a later train."

Winters frowned in thought. Smoke's mind was working rapidly, too. He suggested, "Why not tell them that there's trouble on the line up ahead? You could say the tracks are being repaired and you don't know how long it's going to take. They wouldn't have any way of knowing it's not true. You can say that this train is going ahead with the cattle and the other freight, but the passengers have to get off and wait for a later train, so they won't be stuck sitting in the middle of nowhere."

Winters rubbed his chin and said, "That might work. What do you think, Verne?"

"It's a pretty flimsy story," the conductor responded brusquely. "But, as you point out, Mr. Jensen, the passengers won't know it's a lie. Some of them will be upset at the delay, but as long as it doesn't cost them anything except some time, they're not going to complain about it too much. And although they won't know it, they'll be out of danger."

"Sounds like a good idea to me," said Ward Powell, the engineer. "Now, can we get goin', so we won't be too late getting into Dodge City?"

Winters nodded. "Head on back to the engine, Ward.

Verne, break out those guns like Ward suggested. We'll arm the crew once the passengers are all off."

"Some of them may refuse," Flynn said.

"That'll be their decision. I want to look out for the passengers as much as you do, but one way or another, it's time we put a stop to this thieving and bring those damned rustlers to justice!"

Chapter 26

The clouds thickened as the day went on, changing from fluffy white mounds to gloomy gray slabs that filled up the sky. As a result, once the sun went down a thick, almost impenetrable darkness settled over the plains.

That didn't seem to bother Jester McMillan. Evidently he knew where he was going and kept the gang of outlaws moving steadily. Nobody wandered off, since it was easy to keep track of the other riders by the sound of their horses' hooves. That many riders made quite a racket.

Eventually, far into the night, McMillan called a halt. "We've reached the tracks," he told the other man. "We'll follow them until we get to the spot where we're going to stop that train. We'll let the horses rest for a spell first. Ezra, get a fire going and brew up some coffee."

"Ain't you worried about somebody seein' the flames?" asked Blind Ezra.

McMillan laughed. "There's nobody around for miles, and even if somebody saw the fire, they'd just think it belonged to some pilgrim passing through these parts."

That made sense, Stovepipe supposed. And a cup of coffee sounded like a good idea. The wind that had brought in the clouds had turned a mite chilly after dark.

After the short break, Ezra threw dirt on the fire to put it out and the men mounted up again. With McMillan and Yancey in the lead, the outlaws rode west, following the railroad tracks.

Stovepipe's eyes were pretty good, but even so, he didn't see anything out of the ordinary about the place where McMillan called another halt hours later. The time had to be well after midnight by now. McMillan ordered, "All right, get that brush piled up here."

The outlaws had brought large bundles of cut brush with them from the hideout. McMillan hadn't explained the reason for that, but Stovepipe figured it was because finding enough fuel to build a suitable fire on the tracks might be difficult where the holdup was to take place. In every robbery in the past, the gang had built such a blaze to stop the train.

The men got busy piling brush on the tracks. McMillan took out his pocket watch and lit a match to check the time.

"We've got almost an hour before the train gets here. Clete, you'll be in charge of getting the cattle unloaded, just like before. You want the usual men with you?"

"Yeah, we know what we're doin'," replied Clete. "No point in changing things up now, on the last job."

Stovepipe asked McMillan, "Where do you want Walt and me, boss?"

"You're with me. You'll be part of the group making sure the passengers don't put up a fight and looting what we can from them."

"How about the express car?"

"Nothing worth going after this time," McMillan said

curtly. "But that's all right. The cattle are our real objective."

McMillan's answer was delivered definitively and without hesitation. Stovepipe found that mighty interesting. The only way McMillan could have known that the express car wasn't carrying anything valuable on this run was if someone on the inside had told him. That was just more confirmation that someone connected to the railroad was working with the outlaws.

The horses were split into two groups and taken out a hundred yards away from the tracks, so they would be out of the light from the fire. Once the train had stopped, the gang would swoop in from both directions.

Stovepipe looked at the brush pile and said, "What if the engineer don't stop? I reckon most locomotives could just barrel right through that."

"He won't know what's burning," answered McMillan with a trace of impatience in his voice. "For all he'll know, there could be logs or railroad ties piled behind the flames. He'll have to stop just to make sure he's not going to hit something that would derail the train. We know what we're doing here, Jones."

"Fine by me, I was just wonderin'."

"Just do as you're told."

Stovepipe didn't say anything else. He was glad that this assignment would soon be over. Jester McMillan rubbed him the wrong way, and he was just itching to do something about it.

When everything was set up for the robbery, two men were left by the tracks to light the fire while the others withdrew to wait for the train's arrival. Stovepipe and Wilbur were in McMillan's bunch, south of the tracks. They were all mounted and ready to ride.

Stovepipe had caught a moment alone with Wilbur earlier, and they had swiftly worked out a plan. They would hang back when the others attacked the train so they could launch a strike of their own from the rear. If everything had gone like it was supposed to, Smoke Jensen would be on the train and might have some help with him. They could catch McMillan and the other outlaws in a crossfire, and with any luck would do a lot of damage before the gang knew what was going on.

But before that could happen, the train had to arrive. Stovepipe wasn't the nervous sort, but he was ready for this business to be over.

"Everybody listen up," McMillan said. "Yancey's got something to tell you."

The gambler edged his horse ahead of the others and turned to face the outlaws. "Smoke Jensen's on that train," he said bluntly. "He thinks he's set a trap for us, but it's really the other way around. Be ready for a bigger fight than usual, because there's no way of knowing how many men Jensen has with him."

Stovepipe was thunderstruck. Beside him, Wilbur stiffened in his saddle, obviously just as surprised by this unexpected development.

McMillan said, "When you open fire on the passenger cars, don't hold back. Pour as much lead in there as you can. I want Jensen dead, like he was supposed to be a couple of nights ago."

"But that can't be right," Tom Church said. "Sam and Walt gunned Jensen down! Clete saw it happen."

"What Clete saw was a trick," McMillan said coldly. "Jensen's alive and was never hurt. That means we've got a couple of spies in the gang."

The other men were drawing their horses away from Stovepipe and Wilbur. They hadn't known the truth until now, but it hadn't taken much for them to grasp that they'd been double-crossed—and that it wasn't going to be healthy to be around the two Texans.

Stovepipe wasn't going to give up that easily. He said, "Damn it, I don't know what's goin' on here, boss, but I do know we gunned Jensen just like we were supposed to. If he's still alive, it's a plumb miracle—"

"There's the train!" exclaimed one of the men as he pointed along the tracks to the west, where the locomotive's headlight had come into view, glowing like a giant eye in the thick darkness.

"Grab those two!" McMillan yelled. "No shooting yet!"

Stovepipe jerked his horse around and jabbed his boot heels in the animal's flanks. The Appaloosa leaped away from the group.

Wilbur was spinning his mount as well, trying to make a run for it.

One of the outlaws jumped his horse in from the side. It rammed shoulders with Stovepipe's horse and staggered the Appaloosa.

At the same time, another man closed in from the other direction and left his saddle in a flying tackle. He crashed into Stovepipe and drove him out of the saddle. Stovepipe was able to jerk his feet from the stirrups so he wouldn't get dragged if the horse bolted, but that was all he had time to do. Then he slammed into the ground with the outlaw's weight on top of him.

A gun roared somewhere close by. McMillan had ordered his men not to fire, but Wilbur wasn't constrained by that. He twisted in the saddle and triggered the Colt in his hand as he swept it from side to side.

The man on top of Stovepipe heaved himself up and raised a fist, getting ready to bring it down into Stovepipe's face. Before the blow could fall, Wilbur leaped his horse close and lashed downward with the gun in his hand. It landed with a dull thud on the outlaw's head and knocked him cold.

Stovepipe shoved the unconscious owlhoot off him and pushed up from the ground to grab the hand that Wilbur stretched out toward him. With a heave from Wilbur and a powerful thrust of his own legs, Stovepipe swung up onto the dun's back behind his friend.

A hundred yards away, flames suddenly erupted skyward as the outlaws fired the brush pile on the tracks.

"Kill them!" shrieked McMillan. "Kill them!"

Wilbur's dun was a big, sturdy mount, more than capable of carrying double and running hard, at least for a short time. Wilbur bent forward over the horse's neck. Stovepipe tried to make himself a smaller target, too, although that wasn't easy with his tall, lanky frame. He pulled his Colt from its holster and threw several shots behind them as they fled into the darkness. He didn't figure he'd hit anything, but the flying lead might make some of the outlaws duck.

Looked like it was going to be up to Smoke Jensen to stop the robbery now, Stovepipe thought as Colts bloomed red behind them and the leaping flames on the railroad track threw a garish glow over the prairie.

Smoke and Red Winters rode in the locomotive's cab with Ward Powell and his fireman, Burt Denton. A couple of Winchesters leaned in a corner of the partially enclosed cab, handy for grabbing when Powell and Denton needed them.

That was bound to be soon, thought Smoke. He had halfway expected the outlaws to hit them before now.

Powell leaned out the window on the right side of the

cab, as he would normally be doing so he could watch the track in front of them. The train's headlight lanced along the steel rails for a good distance. Powell had throttled back so that the train slowed down when darkness fell; a good engineer gauged the speed so that he would be able to stop if an obstacle appeared without warning.

Smoke was on the other side of the cab, watching out that window. He and Powell must have seen the burst of flames at the same instant, because the engineer was already reaching for the brake when Smoke called, "Fire ahead!"

Metal shrieked against metal as the brakes took hold. Smoke, Winters, and Powell had discussed trying to break through whatever kind of barricade the outlaws had put together, but they had decided against it.

For one thing, they couldn't tell how sturdy the barrier might be. They didn't want to do anything that might cause the train to derail.

For another, this would be their best chance to destroy the gang. They wanted the gang to attack the train so they could fight back.

So Smoke braced himself with one hand against the window frame as the locomotive lurched and slowed under his feet. Winters and the two members of the train crew had their feet planted solidly, too.

Smoke saw bright pinpricks of light from both sides of the tracks. Those were muzzle flashes from the outlaws' guns as the gang closed in. Smoke filled both hands with his Colts and started firing, triggering each gun in turn. Left, right, left, right, the revolvers roared and bucked against his palms. The sharp tang of gunsmoke mixed with the smell of burning coal from the locomotive's firebox.

In the dark like this, Smoke couldn't tell if the bullets he spread across the prairie were doing any good. To his left, in the opening at the rear of the cab, Red Winters stood with his rifle braced against his shoulder. Flame spurted in an almost continuous stream from the weapon's muzzle as Winters cranked off round after round as fast as he could work the Winchester's lever.

Burt Denton, the fireman, had dropped his shovel and grabbed one of the leaning rifles. He opened fire at the attackers on the north side of the tracks.

"Looks like a bunch of 'em!" he yelled over his shoulder.

"Help Burt!" Smoke told Winters as he pouched one of his irons. With swift, automatic movements, he thumbed fresh cartridges into the cylinder of the Colt he still held. Smoke had reloaded in the midst of battle so many times in his life that he didn't have to think about what he was doing. He could perform the task faster than most men, too, so fast that it would be difficult for a normal eye to follow what he was doing.

When he had a full wheel in one of the Colts, he switched to the other. While he was reloading that gun, he heard bullets whining off the steel of the locomotive cab. A lot of lead was in the air, and it was singing a deadly song.

Smoke knew that tune well and ignored it. A second later, both guns were fully loaded again and he went back to making gun music of his own.

From the corner of his eye, he saw that the engine was getting closer and closer to the blaze on the tracks, even as the massive metal behemoth slowed steadily. When the locomotive finally shuddered to a halt, less than ten feet separated the prow of its cowcatcher from the leaping flames.

The light from the fire spread out across the plains, and in its uncertain glare, Smoke caught glimpses of riders dashing back and forth. They wore long dusters and had bandannas pulled up over the lower halves of their faces. With the guns in their hands, they loosed a torrent of lead at the train, targeting the passenger cars for the most part.

What they didn't know was that those cars were largely empty, the passengers having been left at stops back to the west to await a later train. The only people still riding this train were Smoke, Winters, the two express agents, and members of the train crew. Several brakemen armed with rifles were posted at various places along the train. They opened fire at the outlaws, as did the conductor, Verne Flynn, from the caboose.

It was a lot hotter fight than the outlaws must have been expecting, thought Smoke as he emptied his Colts for the second time.

He wondered fleetingly where Stovepipe and Wilbur were and hoped the range detectives were staying out of the direct line of fire.

As what sounded like a small-scale war erupted behind them, Wilbur hauled back on the reins and slowed the dun. Stovepipe looked over his shoulder, searching for muzzle flashes coming their direction. He didn't see any.

"Looks like all the shootin's aimed the other way now," he told Wilbur. "I reckon McMillan wants them cows more than he wants us dead."

"We'd better circle back and see if we can give Jensen a hand," Wilbur suggested.

"That's just what I was thinkin'."

As Wilbur wheeled the dun, Stovepipe caught a glimpse of movement not far away. Even on this overcast

night, he could make out the black and white form of his
Appaloosa trotting across the prairie. The horse had followed them when Wilbur lit a shuck away from the gang.

Stovepipe gave a piercing whistle, which made Wilbur
wince. "Warn a fella next time you're about to let off a
steam whistle in his ear," the redhead complained.

Stovepipe grinned and said, "There's my Appy." While
Wilbur was still stopped, he slid down from the saddle
and trotted toward the Appaloosa.

The horse came to meet him. Stovepipe rubbed the animal's nose, then took hold of the dangling reins and
swung up into the saddle.

"Let's go," he called to Wilbur.

Side by side, guns in hands, the two range detectives
galloped back toward the battle taking place along the
railroad tracks.

Chapter 27

Although the locomotive cab was a good place to fort up because its steel walls would stop most slugs, Smoke knew he couldn't stay there. The outlaws were too spread out. He needed to be able to move around and take the fight to them.

With both Colts reloaded again, he jumped down to the roadbed on the south side of the tracks and ran beside the tender toward the rear of the train. A man on horseback suddenly loomed on his right and cursed as he spotted Smoke.

Anybody on a horse ought to be fair game, thought Smoke, but he hesitated because he didn't know where Stovepipe and Wilbur were. He didn't want to ventilate one of them.

Then the rider threw a shot at him, the bullet spanging off the tender behind him. That cleared things up sufficiently, and a split second later Smoke's right-hand gun roared. The slug punched into the horseman's chest and flung him backward out of the saddle.

Hoofbeats pounded to Smoke's left. Lead sizzled through the air beside his ear as he twisted in that direction. The left-hand Colt spoke this time, splitting the darkness with the tongue of orange flame that licked from its muzzle. The outlaw cried out, sagged over his mount's neck, and then slid off to land in an ungainly heap on the ground.

Smoke moved on to the next car, which was one of the empty passenger cars. An idea occurred to him. He holstered both guns and reached up to take hold of the grab irons on the side of the car, next to its front platform. The powerful muscles under his shirt bunched as he hauled himself upward.

In a matter of seconds, Smoke reached the car's roof. He rolled onto it and came up on one knee. Steel whispered on leather as he drew both guns. When he stood up, he could look along the train and see the riders on both sides as they fired at the cars. In the backwash from their muzzle flashes, he made out the dusters and masks that hid their identities but not their evil intentions.

Smoke strode along the top of the railroad car, bullets scything from both guns as he delivered powder-smoke justice from above, almost like divine retribution. He reached the end of the car and dropped to a knee again as he holstered one of the Colts and used that hand to reach for fresh cartridges.

Before he could reload, something crashed against his head with stunning force and knocked him sprawling to the side. He felt himself sliding across the roof of the railroad car toward the edge, but couldn't stop himself, and then he was falling, falling. . . .

He didn't feel the roadbed come up and smash against his body.

* * *

Stovepipe and Wilbur were on the side of the train where the group of outlaws led by Jester McMillan were attacking the passenger cars. They drove in, opening fire when they were close enough. Muzzle flame spurted from windows in some of the cars, so there was still a chance they could catch the attackers in a crossfire as they had intended.

With all the commotion going on and so much lead flying through the air already, the outlaws didn't notice they were under attack from the rear until a minute or so had passed. In that time, Stovepipe and Wilbur had downed several of them.

But then McMillan yelled, "Behind us!" and several horsemen wheeled around to open fire at the range detectives. Stovepipe and Wilbur threw slugs back at them as Stovepipe called to his partner, "Split up!"

They veered away from each other and continued fighting. Stovepipe didn't stop pulling the trigger until his Colt's hammer fell on an empty chamber. Knowing he wouldn't have a chance to reload before he was blown out of the saddle, he jammed the gun back in its holster and reined the Appaloosa around hard. They darted away from the light, back into the shadows beyond the glare cast by the fire still blazing on the railroad tracks.

When he stopped hearing the whine of bullets searching for him in the dark, Stovepipe hauled back on the reins and brought the Appaloosa to a stop. The horse was accustomed to the sound of gunfire and the smell of powder smoke, so it stood calmly while Stovepipe reloaded.

He needed to get to the train, Stovepipe told himself. If he could do that, he might be able to join forces with Smoke Jensen and whoever Smoke had gotten to help him. He figured Wilbur would have the same idea, so he hoped to see his partner again once he made it to the train.

With the Colt gripped tightly in his hand, Stovepipe dug his heels into the Appaloosa's flanks and charged back into the fray. As men on horseback moved to cut him off, his gun roared and orange muzzle flame split the night once more.

Stovepipe blasted his way through the line of outlaws, and as he came alongside the stopped train, he spotted a man lying facedown on the roadbed next to one of the passenger cars. He dropped out of the saddle and swatted the Appaloosa's rump with his hat, sending the horse galloping out of the line of fire. As bullets thudded against the side of the car above his head, Stovepipe ran in a crouch to the fallen man and dropped to a knee beside him.

Stovepipe's instincts had been right again, he saw when he gripped the man's shoulder and rolled him onto his back. He was Smoke Jensen, and the splash of blood on his head showed that he had been wounded. Stovepipe didn't know whether Smoke was still alive or not, but he didn't have time to check. He holstered his own empty gun and snatched the two revolvers that Smoke had hung on to despite being shot.

He didn't know how many rounds were in each gun, but he lifted them and blazed away, emptying the Colts. That caused the outlaws to pull back and gave Stovepipe time to drop the guns and grab Smoke under the arms. He lifted the dead weight.

Stovepipe might look scrawny, but he packed tremendous strength in his wiry frame. He flung Smoke's senseless form over his shoulder and hurried to the platform at the closest end of the car. He dumped Smoke onto it and clambered up after him, then kicked the door open and dragged Smoke into the car.

Bullets had shattered the windows on both sides of the

car. Stovepipe flattened his back against the wall next to the door and reloaded his Colt as more bullets passed through the car. When the gun's chambers were full again, he swung back out onto the platform and snapped two shots at the riders on the north side of the tracks, then twisted and triggered twice at the outlaws to the south. He had to dive back through the open door as a storm of lead flew at him.

Smoke was stirring as consciousness returned to him. That was a good sign, thought Stovepipe, because it meant he was alive, anyway. Smoke groaned, lifted his bloody head, and shook it as if trying to clear cobwebs from his brain. That must have hurt like the devil, because Smoke gasped and winced.

"Take it easy, Jensen," Stovepipe told him, raising his voice to be heard over the gun thunder still rolling outside the train. "You're all right now."

Stovepipe could see a bloody welt on the side of Smoke's head. Crimson had stained his fair hair. But it appeared that the bullet had barely nicked him, hitting just hard enough to knock him senseless for a few minutes. Smoke would have a headache for a while, but likely no lasting damage had been done.

"Stewart," Smoke said. "What . . ."

"That bunch is still attackin' the train," Stovepipe explained. He realized as he spoke that the gunfire from outside was tapering off. "But it sounds like the fightin' is gonna be over pretty soon."

Whether that was a good thing or a bad one was yet to be determined.

It didn't take long to settle that question. Stovepipe heard a swift rataplan of hoofbeats outside and tensed, ready to go into action again, but then heard a familiar voice shouting, "Stovepipe! Stovepipe, where are you?"

Stovepipe stepped out and called, "Wilbur! Over here!"

Wilbur rode up on the dun a moment later. Enough light spilled through the shot-out windows of the train car for Stovepipe to see his partner. Wilbur looked to be unharmed.

"Stovepipe, are you all right?" Wilbur asked as he reined in.

"Yeah, I'm fine. How about you?"

"All that flyin' lead missed me somehow. Have you seen Jensen?"

"He's inside," Stovepipe answered as he leaned his head toward the open door. "He got creased on the *cabeza*, but I reckon he ain't hurt bad." Stovepipe realized he didn't hear any more gunfire. "What's happened? Is the fight over?"

Wilbur had grinned at being reunited with his trail partner, but that expression disappeared and a frown replaced it.

"Those damn outlaws unloaded the cattle and got away with the whole bunch! Some of them covered the ones drivin' the critters. They're gone!"

Stovepipe heaved a sigh. They had tried, but they hadn't had enough men to stop the holdup from being successful.

However, quite a few owlhoot bodies littered the ground, prompting Stovepipe to say, "We made 'em pay a hefty price, anyway."

"That ain't enough," Wilbur said bitterly. "They still got away with all that rustled stock."

"Yeah, but we know where they're headed with it."

"What's that?" asked a new voice. Smoke Jensen appeared in the doorway, grasping the edge of it with one hand while the other reached out to take hold of Stovepipe's shoulder. "You know where they're going?"

"That's right," said Stovepipe. "I'll bet a hat they plan on takin' those cattle to the same place they've been holdin' the other stock they rustled. They're headed for somewhere called Little Jerusalem."

Several hours later, Smoke held a council of war next to the locomotive with Stovepipe, Wilbur, Red Winters, Verne Flynn, Burt Denton, and Giff Connelly, one of the express agents.

Smoke had retrieved his guns and had a bandage tied around his head. It had stopped the bleeding and helped a little with the throbbing inside his skull.

Winters was wounded, as well. His left leg was bandaged where a bullet had bitten a chunk of meat out of his thigh, but he was still able to get around without hobbling too much. Burt Denton's left arm was in a sling. Patching up the injuries from the battle had taken quite a while.

Flynn and Connelly weren't hurt, and neither were the two range detectives. But Ward Powell, the engineer, was stretched out on the floor of the first passenger car with a blanket over him, victim of a bullet that had drilled his heart as perfectly as if a marksman had taken aim at a target painted on his chest. Bad luck had guided the bullet, but Powell was just as dead as if it had been directed by a human eye.

Beside the engineer was another blanket-shrouded figure, this one belonging to the other express agent, who had been shot in the head. One of the brakemen was badly wounded and might not make it.

Seven of the outlaws still lay sprawled on the prairie where they had fallen. Among them were two men Stovepipe and Wilbur identified as Tom Church and Jonas Page.

"I ain't sayin' they didn't have it comin'," Stovepipe had said as he looked down at the corpses. "They were part of the bunch and had innocent blood on their hands, same as the others."

"But they weren't bad sorts, for all that," Wilbur added. Stovepipe sighed and nodded in agreement.

They hadn't found any sign of Jester McMillan, Yancey, or Clete. Those three ringleaders had gotten away with the others and the rustled cattle.

Now, Smoke looked at the grim-faced men around him and asked, "Red, you're sure you can find this Little Jerusalem place?"

Winters nodded. "Yeah, I've been there before. When we were building the railroad line across Kansas, I went out a few times with the buffalo hunters, just so I'd know what that part of the job was like. On one of those trips, while we were following a herd of those shaggy critters, we rode as far as Little Jerusalem. It's an area of badlands the likes of which you wouldn't expect to find out here on the prairie. You'll be riding along, and then suddenly you find yourself in the middle of all these chalk spires and bluffs and canyons. Because of their color, some of them look like giant teeth sticking up, ready to bite you and grind you down to nothing." Winters grunted. "It's an ugly land. An angry land."

"But a good place to hide a big herd of stolen cattle," Smoke said.

"Yeah, there's enough graze. There are no springs or creeks inside the badlands, but the Smoky Hill River runs along the northern edge of them. The rustlers can let the cattle drink there, then run them back up inside the canyons. The best thing about the place, from those owl-hoots' point of view, is that there's no reason for anybody to come around. Nobody is likely to stumble over them."

"Well, if you can guide us there, we're going to do more than stumble over them," said Smoke. "How far is it from here?"

"Twenty miles, I'd say."

Smoke nodded. "If we ride all day, we can get there tonight."

"We can switch out mounts and keep movin' at a pretty fast pace," Stovepipe put in. "Wilbur and I managed to round up most of the horses those dead outlaws were ridin'. With the horses we already had, that'll give us enough spares."

Verne Flynn said, "But there'll only be six of us. We'll still be outnumbered three or four to one."

"I'm not ordering you to come along, Verne," Winters said.

The conductor glared at him. "I'm not backing out, Red, you know that. I was just stating a fact."

"We'll be outnumbered, all right," Smoke agreed. "But they probably won't be expecting us to follow them."

"Having the element of surprise on our side didn't stop them from killing several of us and running off with those cattle."

Stovepipe said, "Things should've worked out better than they did. It didn't help that McMillan knew Wilbur and me weren't who we claimed to be, or that Smoke was still alive and would be waitin' for 'em."

Smoke frowned in thought and scraped a thumbnail along his jawline. "You think that gambler Yancey brought that news from Abilene?"

"I don't see how else McMillan could've known."

Smoke nodded and said, "Well, we've suspected all along that the real boss behind this scheme was back in Abilene. That's just more evidence of it."

Winters snorted and said, "I'm just glad you don't still figure it's me anymore."

Smoke smiled. "No, I reckon I know better than that now, Red."

Flynn said to Denton, "Are you sure you can get the train on in to Great Bend all right even though you're wounded? It really goes against the grain for me to leave it."

Denton nodded. "I can manage. I'll get one of the brakies to fill in as fireman while I'm at the controls. We'll get the train in, don't worry about that, Verne." He swallowed hard. "That's what Ward would have wanted."

"Yeah, he sure would have," Winters agreed. He clapped a hand on the shoulder of Denton's noninjured arm. "I'm obliged to you, Burt. The whole line is."

"Just get the skunks who did this," said Denton. "That's all the thanks I want."

"We damn sure will," Winters vowed.

The eastern sky was splashed with red and gold from the approach of dawn by the time the six men were mounted up and ready to ride, trailing the spare horses on lead ropes behind them. Winters and Smoke were in front, leading the way. Stovepipe, Wilbur, Flynn, and Connelly followed them in a loose group. They were all well-armed and had plenty of ammunition, having scavenged it from the outlaws who had been slain.

Those bodies had been placed in one of the other passenger cars to be turned over to the law. Smoke would have been fine with leaving them for the buzzards, but he supposed it was best to let the authorities deal with them. For one thing, there might be rewards posted on some of them, and that money could go to the families of Ward Powell and the express agent who had been killed in the fighting.

The riders were a quarter of a mile north of the tracks, following the trail left by the stolen cattle and heading in the direction of Little Jerusalem, when the locomotive's whistle sounded behind them. They looked back and saw the train rolling slowly along the steel rails, building up speed. Burt Denton blew the whistle again, as if he was saying farewell.

It wasn't long before the train was gone and the riders were all out of sight, and the scene of the bloody battle was as lonely and desolate as ever.

Chapter 28

The riders kept up a good pace all day, just as Smoke intended. He hoped Red Winters actually did know where he was leading them, because the gently rolling plains were mostly featureless, and even with the trail of the rustled herd to follow, it would be easy to get lost out here once the railroad tracks were out of sight.

The men rode in silence for the most part as the miles fell behind them. They stopped only to rest and water the horses and switch saddles onto fresh mounts, then gnawed jerky and swigged from canteens while they were riding.

An air of grim determination rode with them. They were going to deliver hot lead justice and finish this today.

The fact that they were outnumbered didn't matter. Smoke had faced long odds before, as had Stovepipe and Wilbur.

Late in the afternoon, when the sun had dipped almost to the western horizon, Smoke said to Winters, "We ought to be coming in sight of this place soon, shouldn't we?"

Winters shook his head and said, "You won't see Little Jerusalem until the ground drops out from under you and you're in the badlands before you know it."

"Then you can't be sure we're going the right way."

Winters rasped fingertips over the white stubble on his jaws. "We're going the right way," he declared confidently. "These parts look familiar to me."

"All this country looks the same," said Smoke as he gestured toward the prairie around them.

"I know, but my gut tells me we're headed in the right direction, and if I've learned one thing from working on the railroad, it's to trust my gut."

Smoke grunted. "I reckon we don't have any choice but to trust your gut, too."

The sun dropped below the horizon and a short time later the light began to fade. Smoke's nerves stretched taut. Winters had said that Little Jerusalem was twenty miles from where they had left the railroad, and Smoke estimated they had covered that much distance today by pushing hard and swapping horses.

Then with no warning, just as Winters had said, suddenly the badlands were spread before them. The prairie dropped steeply between chalk bluffs and mesas that jutted up eighty or ninety feet so that their tops were roughly level with the surrounding plains. That was why they couldn't be seen from a distance. Grass grew in the canyons between those heights.

Smoke and Winters reined in sharply. The others stopped behind them. Stovepipe and Wilbur eased their mounts up alongside Smoke. Stovepipe said, "There it is, all right. And it looks like it stretches for a good distance east, west, and north. How do we go about findin' them rustled cattle?"

"If those rustlers are here," said Wilbur, "they'll have to eat. Blind Ezra will have a cook fire goin'. If we can't spot it once night falls, we ought to be able to follow the smell of the smoke from it."

Smoke nodded and said, "That's right. We'll wait here until it's dark, then do some scouting. If we stay back a ways from the rim, nobody in there should be able to spot us."

It was a rudimentary plan, but that allowed for flexibility and the others agreed to it. The six men drew back a couple of hundred yards from the southern edge of the badlands and picketed the horses. Then they squatted on their heels and made a sparse supper of jerky and water. Coffee would have been good, but they didn't want to risk a fire.

When it was dark enough, Smoke said, "Stovepipe, why don't you come with me? The rest of you can wait here while we try to locate the rustlers' camp. When we find it, one of us will come back to fetch you while the other keeps an eye on that bunch."

"That sounds like it'll work," Stovepipe agreed. "Are we goin' on foot?"

Smoke chuckled. "I've been a cattleman long enough that I hate to go anywhere on foot, but that'll be the quietest way for us to move around, I suppose."

"I feel the same way. Can't be helped, I reckon."

Red Winters said, "Are you sure you're up to that, Jensen? You were shot less than twenty-four hours ago."

"It was just a scratch," Smoke insisted. "My head still hurts, but not enough to worry about."

His tone made it clear that he wasn't going to be talked out of going on this scouting expedition, so the others didn't even try. Smoke and Stovepipe carried their Winchesters with them and headed into the badlands.

Smoke knew it would take quite a while to cover the area on foot, but he was hoping they wouldn't have to search all through Little Jerusalem before finding the outlaws' hideout. The two of them stopped from time to time to let their senses work, listening for anything that might lead them to their quarry and sniffing the air for wood smoke from a cooking fire.

After a while, Stovepipe stopped short and put out a hand to touch Smoke lightly on the arm and bring him to a halt as well.

"I smell somethin'," whispered Stovepipe, "but it ain't a cookin' fire."

"I do too," Smoke replied, equally quietly. "That's the smell of burning hide." Realization dawned on him. "They're working over the brands on those cattle."

"Slappin' road brands on the ones they just drove in a little while ago," said Stovepipe. "We know they're fixin' to head the whole bunch north. They've probably already put new brands on the ones they wide-looped before."

"We ought to be able to follow that smell all the way to their camp."

That proved to be trickier than it sounded. The night breezes were fickle, blowing this way and that, so from time to time Smoke and Stovepipe lost the scent they were following. They always picked it up again, but each time the smell of burning hide and hair had faded more. The rustlers had carried on with their branding after darkness fell, but more than likely they were finished by now and the two searchers were smelling the last vestiges of the distinctive scent.

There were no clouds tonight, which meant the sky was awash with starlight. Even though the moon hadn't risen yet, Smoke and Stovepipe had no trouble seeing where they were going.

They were slipping along the base of a bluff with the slope rising to their right when Smoke caught a flash of movement from the corner of his eye. He looked up at the top of the bluff and realized a man was standing there, training a rifle on them. Silvery reflections from the stars winked on the weapon's barrel.

Smoke's first instinct was to pull iron and try to beat the man to the shot. The rifleman had to be a sentry posted by the outlaws. A gun blast would alert McMillan and the others that trouble was nearby, but it couldn't be helped.

Smoke had just cleared leather, though, when the man above them yelped, pitched forward, and lost his rifle as he tumbled out of control down the slope.

A large, dark shape darted after him, and as the man came to a stop, the animal closed in, snapping and snarling.

Smoke and Stovepipe dashed forward, hoping to silence the guard before he could raise any alarm. The animal that had knocked the man down backed off as Smoke rushed in. The gun in his hand rose and fell. He had reversed it so that the Colt's butt slammed against the guard's head and knocked him cold.

"What in blazes?" breathed Stovepipe. "Ranger?"

Smoke saw now that the animal was a big, dark-colored dog. It bounded up to Stovepipe, not threatening at all now unless one counted the potential danger of being licked to death. Stovepipe dropped to a knee and petted the dog.

"What in the sam hill are you doin' here? I sent you back to Abilene with Lena."

"And I didn't go," said a new voice from up the slope.

Smoke still had his gun in his hand, but it was ready to fire now, if need be. That didn't seem to be the case. He could tell the figure making its way down toward them wore a dress, and the voice that had spoken was female.

Stovepipe stood up and went to meet her as she reached the bottom of the ridge. The dog trailed eagerly behind him. She came up to him and hugged him. Stovepipe wrapped his arms around her in return.

"I had a pretty good idea where this place was from hearing Jester talk about it," Smoke heard her explain to Stovepipe. "I thought maybe I could find it. I figured that one way or another, sooner or later, you'd show up here to recover the stolen cattle that were already being held here."

"You were right about that, but dadgum it, I was hopin' you'd be safe in Abilene a long time before now."

"Blame that fool dog of yours. He kept running off and trying to follow you. After a while I got the idea that I ought to do the same thing."

Ranger looked up at Stovepipe and whined.

Stovepipe laughed softly and hugged the woman again, then turned to Smoke.

"Jensen, this here is Miss Lena Cooley," he said.

With his head bandaged like it was, Smoke wasn't wearing a hat he could tip, but he nodded politely and said, "Pleasure to meet you, ma'am. Stovepipe told me a little about you."

"I'm sure whatever he said was true, even the ugly parts."

Stovepipe cleared his throat. "There ain't no need to go into that."

"I agree," said Smoke. "And he's right that it's not safe in these parts for a lady right now."

"Then it's a good thing I'm no lady. And it's really a good thing that Ranger and I came along in time to keep that guard from raising a ruckus and alerting Jester and the others."

"Speakin' of which, we'd best tend to that hombre."

Stovepipe went to the unconscious guard, bound his hands behind him, and gagged the man with his own bandanna. That would hold him for a while.

"I got here before Jester and the others," Lena went on. "I know where their camp is."

"Can you take us there?" asked Smoke.

"I'm pretty sure I can find it."

"That'll save us some time. We're obliged to you for your help, Miss Cooley."

Stovepipe said, "Well, I wish you'd just light a shuck outta here and let us tend to those varmints."

"It's a little late for that," Lena argued. "Come on. I'll show you where they are."

The starlight was bright enough for Smoke to see the frown on Stovepipe's face, but the range detective didn't waste any more time or breath trying to persuade Lena otherwise. *He probably knows her well enough to realize it wouldn't do any good*, Smoke mused.

He had learned that same lesson about Sally a long time ago.

A quarter of an hour later, the three of them, along with Ranger, were crouched in a clump of boulders on top of a small rise overlooking a broad canyon between two rugged chalk ridges. The canyon was half a mile wide at its northern end, and a short distance beyond that, the Smoky Hill River was a silver thread in the starlight.

As it ran south, toward the vantage point where Smoke, Stovepipe, Lena, and Ranger were hidden, the ridges angled in so that the canyon narrowed down to no more than fifty yards in width. The rocky slopes at the southern end formed a natural barrier to keep in the large herd of cattle bedded down in the canyon.

On the other side of the herd, which was a dark, shapeless mass in the shadows, several small fires glowed. That was the outlaw camp, where they had been putting road brands on the most recent arrivals earlier in the day.

"You know," Stovepipe whispered to Smoke, "the way them ridges funnel in, if them cows were to stampede they wouldn't have no place to go except right over those cold-blooded killers."

"The same thing occurred to me," said Smoke. "And the damage they'd do would go a long way toward evening up the odds."

"That's just what I was thinkin'." Stovepipe turned to the woman. "Lena, you go back and find Wilbur and the other fellas who came with us. Smoke and me'll wait here."

"You know right where they are," said Lena. "It'll be faster if you go and get them. I might get lost."

"I don't reckon you—"

"And I know what you're doing," she went on. "You're just trying to get me out of the way. You think the others will leave me behind, especially that partner of yours. Walt will know what you have in mind."

"Wilbur's his name, if you want to get right down to it. Wilbur Coleman."

"I suppose you're not Sam Jones, either. What was it Mr. Jensen called you? Smokestack?"

"Stovepipe. Last name is Stewart."

"Who are you, really? What are you?"

"We, uh, work for the Cattlemen's Protective Association. We're what they call range detectives, I reckon."

Lena shook her head. "Well, you sure fooled me. I believed the two of you were Texas outlaws, like you claimed to be." She paused. "But I'm glad I was wrong."

"Why don't I go get the others?" Smoke suggested. "The two of you can keep an eye on the camp while I'm gone. When I get back with the others, we'll see if we can get those cows to running so they'll do some of our work for us."

"All right," Stovepipe said. "I reckon that's the best we can do."

"Don't worry," Lena said. "Ranger and I will be glad to keep you company."

Smoke had a hunch that's what Stovepipe was worried about.

Chapter 29

Stovepipe sat on a rock slab with Lena on one side of him and Ranger on the other. The night was quiet and peaceful. Several hundred yards away, a few men were still stirring around in the outlaw camp, their silhouettes moving between the watchers and the fires that were dying down for the night.

"This is one of the nicest times I've ever spent," Lena murmured.

"Sittin' on a rock and keepin' an eye on a bunch of owlhoots?"

She laughed softly. "I guess that tells you what sort of life I've had, doesn't it?"

"Well, I still wish you'd gone on back to Abilene like I told you . . . but I got to admit, I'm enjoyin' sittin' here with you, too."

After a few moments of companionable silence, Lena asked, "What are you going to do when this is all over?"

"I reckon me and Wilbur will head on back down to Austin. We work outta the Association office there. I'm sure by the time we get back, the Colonel will have some other chore for us to tend to."

"That's your boss, the Colonel?"

"Yep. Good man to work for."

"And what's Austin like?"

"Oh, it's plumb pretty," said Stovepipe. "It's right on the Colorado River, and there are some nice hills just west o' town. They built it to be the capital, you know, back when Texas was still a republic."

"I'll bet they have some saloons there, don't they?"

He chuckled. "That they do."

"I could probably get work in one of them."

"You mean . . ."

"I mean, I'm a pretty good dealer when it comes to cards. It's not exactly what you'd call respectable work, but it's better than some things."

"Sounds like you plan to maybe drift down that way."

She leaned her head against his shoulder and said, "It's a pretty thing to think about, isn't it?"

Before he could say anything in response, the swift drumming of hoofbeats somewhere nearby made both of them jerk upright. Stovepipe's arm around her shoulders pressed her down. He knelt beside her so that both of them weren't easy to see among the rocks. He put his other hand on Ranger to keep the dog under control.

A rider raced past them no more than fifty feet away, heading for the outlaw camp. As Stovepipe and Lena watched, he went down the hill with a clatter of rocks and gravel from his horse's hooves, then circled around the herd and started yelling as he reached the fires.

"What's going on?" Lena asked.

"Don't know for sure," replied Stovepipe, "but I've got a hunch he's another guard, and he must've found that fella we knocked out and tied up."

They started to stand, but then more hoofbeats sounded

and Stovepipe pulled Lena down again. A second rider galloped past on his way to the outlaw camp.

"I'll bet that's the hombre his own self," Stovepipe whispered. "Blast it! Smoke ain't had time to round up the rest of our bunch and get back here yet."

A lot of shouting was going on now as men rushed around the fires. Stovepipe heard somebody yelling something about getting the cattle moving.

Lena heard that, too, and exclaimed, "That's Jester giving orders. They're going to search for whoever attacked that guard."

"Yeah," Stovepipe agreed grimly, "and they're liable to find us if we don't do somethin' about it. That means we won't have a better chance to stop 'em than right now." He put his hands on Lena's shoulders and turned her to face him. "You stay here and get down amongst these rocks. They'll give you enough cover that you oughta be safe."

"What are you going to do?"

"No time to wait for Smoke to get back. I got to stampede that herd *now*!"

With that, he leaned forward, planted a kiss on her lips for a second, and then let go of her and turned to run toward the herd as fast as his long legs would carry him. Ranger leaped along beside him.

Stovepipe didn't look back to see if Lena was doing what he'd told her. He was almost afraid to.

Instead, he yanked his hat off his head, waved it in the air, pulled his gun with his other hand to begin firing, and at the same time let out a scream that sounded just like a cougar.

Smoke was actually closer at the moment than Stovepipe knew. He and Wilbur, along with Red Winters, Verne

Flynn, and Giff Connelly, were on foot, but each leading a horse as they approached the canyon in which the rustlers had concealed the stolen cattle. Wilbur had brought Stovepipe's Appaloosa with him as well as his dun. With what was coming up, the men would need to be mounted, but they had left the extra horses picketed where they were.

So when Smoke heard the shouting and shooting, he didn't hesitate. With all that racket going on, there was no longer any need for stealth.

From here on out, gun thunder would erupt over Little Jerusalem.

"Mount up!" Smoke called to his companions. "Let's go! Get the cattle running and hit those rustlers hard!"

They all leaped into their saddles. In the heat of impending battle, even the wounded Red Winters was surprisingly spry. The horses lunged forward as Smoke and the others urged them on.

Smoke had warned them that the slope down into the canyon was rather steep. He and Wilbur were expert horsemen, but that wasn't the case for Winters, Flynn, and Connelly, all of whom were railroad men, not range riders. Those three had to slow slightly to keep their horses under control as they started down the slope. Smoke and Wilbur pulled ahead a little.

Smoke spotted Stovepipe on foot, waving his hat and yelling and shooting as he ran back and forth near the herd. The big dog, Ranger, darted in and nipped at the heels of some of the cattle, doing his part to spook them and start them running. The dark mass was already milling around, and as usually happened, once the cattle reached their breaking point, they tipped over that point in a hurry.

Stampede!

It was a terrifying cry to anyone who'd spent much

time around cattle. Some of the outlaws were probably yelling it at the top of their lungs right now as the herd thundered toward them. Smoke and Wilbur added their gunfire to the shots Stovepipe was triggering. They yipped and yelped, as well. The rumble of hooves welled up and overwhelmed the racket the men were making.

"Stovepipe!" Wilbur called. "Over here!"

Stovepipe had spotted them already. He ran to meet his trail partner as Wilbur veered the dun toward him. The Appaloosa was right with him. Stovepipe reached up, grabbed the horn, and swung his long-limbed form into the saddle while the horse was still moving.

The three railroaders had caught up by now. Together, the six men rode hard behind the herd as the cattle pounded northward toward the river. They swept over the camp like a black tide, obliterating fires, bedrolls, and some of the outlaws. The gang's horses, which had been picketed beyond the camp, had broken free and bolted in sheer terror as the stampede surged toward them, leaving the outlaws on foot.

Some of the men had been able to race out of the way, and as they spotted Smoke and the others, they opened fire. Muzzle flashes lit up the night.

"Spread out!" Smoke called to the others. "Ride them down!"

A whirlwind of spurting flame and flying lead filled the canyon. Smoke put the reins in his teeth and guided his mount with his knees as he filled both hands with his guns. The Colts roared and bucked as he fired right and left, and with each shot, a bullet slammed another rustler into eternity. Stovepipe and Wilbur were almost as accurate in their withering volleys, and the three railroad men pitched in as much as they could.

As Stovepipe galloped past one of the outlaws he had just drilled, the wounded man heaved himself up on his knees and started to lift his gun to take aim at the range detective's back.

Before he could pull the trigger, Ranger hit him from behind at full speed, driving him forward on his face. The big dog's fangs found the outlaw's throat and clamped down hard, making the man's legs flail wildly in his death spasms.

Wilbur's horse went down suddenly, throwing the red-head forward, out of the saddle. Wilbur hit hard and rolled. When he came to a stop, he didn't move.

Seeing that, Stovepipe knew his partner was stunned—or worse. He threw himself off the Appaloosa and ran to Wilbur's side, dropping to one knee.

"Wilbur!"

A gun crashed somewhere nearby. Stovepipe felt the hot breath of the slug as it passed his cheek. He jerked his head up and saw Jester McMillan coming toward them, his hate-filled face twisted in grotesque lines. The gun in McMillan's hand blasted again. Stovepipe went over backward as the bullet tore through his upper left arm.

But his right arm still worked fine as he lifted the Colt in that hand and thumbed off two swift rounds. The shots caught McMillan in the belly, folding him over like a jackknife. He dropped his gun and fell hard, ramming his face into the ground. He didn't move again.

Smoke spotted one of the outlaws trying to scurry away rather than staying to put up a fight. He holstered his gun, sent his horse after the man, and left the saddle in a diving tackle that brought the fleeing man down. He might as well have tackled a wildcat, he discovered an instant later, because the outlaw fought with an almost maniacal fury.

He was no match for Smoke Jensen, though. Smoke shrugged off the wild punches the man threw at him and slammed a right and left into his face that knocked all the fight out of him. Smoke got to his feet, grabbed hold of the man's shirt front, and hauled him upright, as well. With a shove, he sent the man stumbling toward Stovepipe, Wilbur, and Red Winters.

Wilbur was on his feet now, shaking his head groggily from the effects of his fall. The shooting had stopped, and Verne Flynn and Giff Connelly were holding their guns on the few members of the gang who had survived the wild melee.

"Who's that you caught, Jensen?" Winters called. Then the starlight revealed the bloody features of Smoke's captive and Winters exclaimed in sheer astonishment, "Durham!"

"That's right," Smoke said. "Clark Durham was the boss of the whole thing. I figured that out a couple of days ago when Wilbur told me about his meeting with that hombre in the hood." Smoke caught hold of Durham's right wrist and lifted that hand. "He didn't get white stains on his fingers from playing pool. He got them from writing on those chalkboards in his office and yours, Red! When he grabbed my arm the other day and left chalk on my sleeve, I remembered what Wilbur had said and it all made sense. Durham was going to cut and run for the goldfields with the rest of the bunch."

"He won't make it there now," said Winters as his shaggy white brows drew down in a grim scowl. "He'll hang, instead, for his part in all those killings!"

Smoke thought about his friend Wallace Dixon, who had met his death at the hands of Durham's gang, and nodded in agreement. That was exactly the fate Clark Durham had coming to him, all right.

"Stovepipe, you're bleeding!"

That was Lena Cooley's voice. With the fighting over, she had left the rocks and come down to see what had happened. Stovepipe grinned as he turned to watch her hurrying toward him. His left sleeve was stained darkly with blood.

"It ain't nothin' to worry about," he assured her as he put his good arm around her and drew her close. "Bullet went straight through and just knocked a chunk o' meat outta my arm. It'll be fine. I still got one good arm."

He proved that by hugging her even tighter, then the whining beside his leg made him look down at Ranger and tell the dog, "You're just gonna have to wait your turn, old son!"

They reached the railroad the next afternoon with five prisoners, including Clark Durham. They had buried the outlaws who had been killed in the fighting.

The men caught in the path of the stampede were a different story. The cattle hadn't left enough of them to bury.

Smoke and his companions found a train waiting on the tracks as a posse unloaded horses and prepared to mount up. Sheriff Ben McCormick, looking enormous on a tall, sturdy horse, rode out to meet them and greeted them by saying to Winters, "We were just about to head up to Little Jerusalem to look for you, Red!"

"A little out of your jurisdiction, aren't you, Big Ben?" asked Winters.

"Yeah, I suppose, but I wasn't going to let that stop me. I see you've already rounded up what's left of that gang of train robbers and rustlers, though." McCormick stared. "By the Lord Harry, that's Clark Durham!"

"That's right," Winters said. "Hate to say it, but he was part of the whole thing." Winters snorted. "Part of! He was the boss of the whole damn business!"

McCormick nodded and said, "This'll take some sorting out, I think. In the meantime, here's somebody else who wouldn't be left behind, Jensen."

Smoke grinned at the young cowboy who rode up to join them. "Pinky, I'll bet Dr. Metzger didn't tell you it was all right for you to come along on this little jaunt!"

"No, but he wasn't gonna stop me," said Pinky Ford, who looked considerably healthier than he had the last time Smoke saw him. "But as it turned out, all I did was ride on the train. Haven't been on a horse until just now. It feels pretty good."

"You'll have plenty of riding to do," Smoke assured him. "I need to put together a crew to round up all those stolen cattle from the badlands and drive them back to Abilene. Some of the spreads back home need the money from them to make it this year." Smoke thumbed his hat back and grinned. "I figure you're going to help me ram-rod that drive."

"You bet I will!" Pinky responded with an eager grin of his own.

Stovepipe, whose bandaged left arm was in a sling rigged from his and Wilbur's bandannas, turned to Lena, who had driven the buckboard back from Little Jerusalem. Ranger was sitting on the driver's seat beside her.

"You still figure on payin' a visit to Austin?" asked Stovepipe.

"After hearing you describe the place, it sounds pretty appealing," she said. "Especially if I have some friends there."

"Oh, you'll have two friends, at least. Won't she, Wilbur?"

"Sure," Wilbur said. "You and that mutt." Then he laughed. "I'm just joshin', Miss Lena. I can think of several saloons in Austin that'd sure be brightened up by havin' you around."

"And somebody's got to look after Ranger," added Stovepipe. "Wilbur and me are out on the trail workin' for the Colonel most of the time, so he'll need some place to stay, if you're up to havin' him around."

"I think I can manage to take care of a dog," Lena said with a smile. "But I'm not sure he'll ever really be happy without you around, too, Stovepipe. He's gotten pretty attached to you." She rubbed Ranger's ears. "He's not the only one."

Smoke hadn't been deliberately eavesdropping, but he'd overheard enough of the conversation for it to put a smile on his face. He nudged his horse into motion toward the railroad tracks, eager to get started on the work that waited for him.

And knowing that one day soon, the scent of danger and gunsmoke would once again beckon to him.

Turn the page for an explosive preview!

JOHNSTONE COUNTRY. THE ULTIMATE KILLING GROUND.

There are a million ways to die in the Black Hills of Dakota Territory—but only one way to make it out alive if your name is Buchanon: with guns blazing . . .

THE HILLS HAVE EYES

The Buchanons are no strangers to hard times—or making hard choices. After losing a hefty number of livestock to a killer grizzly, Hunter Buchanon is forced to sell a dozen broncs down in Denver for some badly needed cash. Everything goes smoothly—until he's ambushed on the way home. The culprits are a murderous bunch of prairie rat outlaws, as dangerous as any Buchanon has ever tangled with. But Hunter is hell-bent on getting his money back. Even if means pursuing the thieves into Dakota Territory—where even deadlier dangers await . . .

Meanwhile, Angus Buchanon has agreed to guide three former Confederate bounty hunters into the Black Hills, on the trail of six cutthroats who robbed a saloon and killed two men in Deadwood. This motley trio of hunters are as cutthroat as the cutthroats they're after. And it doesn't take long for Angus to realize they mean to slaughter him as well at the end of the trail . . .

One family of ranchers. Two groups of cold-hearted murderers. So many ways to die.

National Bestselling Authors
William W. Johnstone
and J.A. Johnstone

THE WHIP HAND
A Hunter Buchanon Black Hills Western

On sale now, wherever Pinnacle Books are sold.

Live Free. Read Hard.
www.williamjohnstone.net
Visit us at www.kensingtonbooks.com

Chapter 1

Hunter Buchanon whipped his hand to the big LeMat revolver jutting from the holster around which the shell belt was coiled on the ground beside him.

In a half-second the big revolver was out of its holster and Hunter heard the hammer click back before he even knew what his thumb was doing. Lightning quick action honed by time and experience including four bloody years during which he fought for the Confederacy in the War of Northern Aggression.

He didn't know what had prompted his instinctive action until he sat half up from his saddle and peered across the red-glowing coals of the dying campfire to see Bobby Lee sitting nearby, peering down the slope into the southern darkness beyond, the coyote's tail curled tightly, ears pricked. Hunter's pet coyote gave another half-moan, half-growl like the one Hunter had heard in his sleep and shifted his weight from one foot to the other.

Hunter sat up slowly. "What is it, Bobby?"

A startled gasp sounded beside Hunter, and in the corner of his left eye he saw his wife Annabelle sit up quickly, grabbing her own hogleg from its holster and clicking the hammer back. Umber light from the fire danced in her thick, red hair. "What is it?" she whispered.

"Don't rightly know," Hunter said tightly, quietly. "But something's put a burr in Bobby's bonnet."

Down the slope behind Hunter, Annabelle, and Bobby Lee, their twelve horses whickered uneasily, drawing on their picket lines.

"Something's got the horses' blood up, too," Annabelle remarked, glancing over her shoulder at the fidgety mounts.

"Stay with the horses, honey," Hunter said, tossing his bedroll aside then rising, donning his Stetson, and stepping into his boots. As he grabbed his Henry repeating rifle, Annabelle said, "You be careful. We might have horse thieves on our hands, Hunter."

"Don't I know it." Hunter jacked a round into the Henry's action, then strode around the nearly dead fire, brushing fingers across the top of the coyote's head and starting down the hill to the south. "Come on, Bobby."

The coyote didn't need to be told twice. If there was one place for Bobby Lee, that was by the side of the big, blond man who'd adopted him when his mother had been killed by a rancher several years ago. Hunter moved slowly down the forested slope in the half-darkness, one hand around the Henry's receiver so starlight didn't reflect off the brass and give him away.

Bobby Lee ran ahead, scouting for any human polecats after the ten horses Hunter and Annabelle were herding from their ranch near Tigerville deep in the Black Hills to a ranch outside of Denver. Hunter and Annabelle had caught the wild mustangs in the Hills near their ranch, and Annabelle had sat on the fence of the breaking corral, Bobby Lee near her feet, watching as Hunter had broken each wild-eyed bronc in turn.

Gentled them, rather. Hunter didn't believe in breaking a horse's spirit. He just wanted to turn them into "plug ponies," good ranch mounts that answered to the slightest tug on the reins or a squeeze of a rider's knees, and could turn on a dime, which was often necessary when working cattle, especially dangerous mavericks.

Hunter and Annabelle needed the money from the horse sale to help make up for the loss of several head of cattle to a rogue grizzly the previous summer. Times were hard on the ranch due to drought and low stock prices, and they were afraid they'd lose the Box Bar B without the money from the horses. They were getting two hundred dollars a head, because they were prime mounts—Hunter had a reputation as one of the best horse gentlers on the northern frontier—and that money would go far toward helping them keep the ranch.

Hunter wanted desperately to keep the Box Bar B not only for himself and Annabelle, but for Hunter's aged, one-armed father, Angus, and the boy Hunter and Annabelle had adopted—Nathan Jones, who after his doxie mother had died had ridden with would-be rustlers, including the boy's scoundrel father, whom Hunter had killed.

The boy was nothing like his father. He was good and hard-working, and he needed a good home.

Hunter moved off down the slope but stopped when Bobby Lee suddenly took off running and swinging left toward some rocks and a cedar thicket, growling. The coyote disappeared in the trees and brush and then started barking angrily. A man cursed and then there were three rocketing gun reports followed by Bobby's mewling howl.

"Damn coyote!" the man's voice called out.

"Bobby!" Hunter said and took off running in the direction in which Bobby Lee had disappeared.

"They know we're here now so be careful!" another man called out sharply.

Running footsteps sounded ahead of Hunter.

He stopped and dropped to a knee when a moving shadow appeared ahead of him and slightly down the slope. Starlight glinted off a rifle barrel and off the running man's cream Stetson.

"Hold it right there, you son of a bitch!" Hunter bellowed, pressing his cheek to the Henry's stock.

The man stopped suddenly and swung his rifle toward Hunter.

The Henry spoke once, twice, three times. The man grunted and flew backward, dropping his rifle and striking the ground with another grunt and a thud.

"Harvey!" the other man yelled from beyond the rocks and cedars.

Harvey yelled in a screeching voice filled with pain, "I'm a dead man, Buck! Buchanon got me, the rebel devil. He's over here. Get him for me!"

Hunter stepped behind a pine, peered out around it, and jacked another round into the Henry's action. He waited, pricking his ears, listening for the approach of Buck. Seconds passed. Then a minute. Then two minutes.

A figure appeared on the right side of the rocks and cedars, moving slowly, one step at a time. Buck held a carbine across his chest. Hunter lined up the Henry's sights on the man and was about to squeeze the trigger when something ran up behind the man and leaped onto his back. Buck screamed as he fell forward, Bobby Lee growling fiercely and tearing into the back of the man's neck.

Hunter smiled. Buck screamed as he tried in vain to fight off the fiercely protective Bobby Lee. Buck swung around suddenly and cursed loudly as he flung Bobby

Lee off him. The coyote struck the ground with a yelp and rolled.

"You mangy cur!" Buck bellowed, drawing a pistol and aiming at Bobby.

Hunter's Henry spoke twice, flames lapping from the barrel.

Buck groaned and lay over on his back. "Ah, hell," he said, and died.

"Good work, Bob," Hunter said, walking toward where the coyote was climbing to his feet. Hunter dropped to a knee, placed his hand on Bobby Lee's back. "You all right?"

The coyote shook himself as if in an affirmative reply.

"All right," Hunter said, straightening. "Let's go check on—"

The shrill whinny of horses cut through the silence that had fallen over the night after Hunter had shot Buck.

"Annabelle!" Hunter yelled, swinging around to retrace his route back to the camp. "Come on, Bobby! There must be more of these scoundrels!"

The coyote mewled and took off running ahead of Hunter.

Only a minute after Hunter and Bobby had left the camp, the horses stirred more vigorously behind where Annabelle sat on a log near the cold fire, her Winchester carbine resting across her denim-clad thighs. She'd just risen from the log and started to walk toward the string of prize mounts when a man's voice called from the darkness down the hill behind the horses.

"Come here, purty li'l red-headed gal!" The voice was pitched with jeering, brash mockery.

Annabelle froze, stared into the darkness. Anger rose in her.

Again, the man's voice caromed quietly out of the darkness: "Come here, purty li'l red-headed gal!" The man chuckled.

Several of the horses lifted their heads and gave shrill whinnies.

The flame of anger burned more brightly in Annabelle, her heart quickening, her gloved hands tightening around the carbine she held high across her chest. She knew she shouldn't do it, but she couldn't stop herself. She moved slowly forward. Ahead and to her left, thirty feet away, the horses were whickering and shifting, pulling at the ropes securing them to the picket line.

Annabelle jacked a round into the carbine's action and moved toward the horses. She patted the blaze on the snout of a handsome black, said, "Easy, fellas. Easy. I got this."

She stepped around the horses and down the slope and stopped behind a broad-boled pine.

Again, the man's infuriating voice came from down the slope beyond her. "Come here, purty li'l red-haired gal. Come find me!"

Annabelle swallowed tightly, said quietly, mostly to herself: "All right—if you're sure about this, bucko . . ."

She continued forward, taking one step at a time. She had no spurs on her boots. Hunter's horses were so well-trained they didn't require them. She made virtually no sound as she continued down the slope, weaving between the columnar pines and firs silhouetted against the night's darkness relieved only by starlight.

"Come on, purty li'l red-headed gal," came the jeering voice again. "Wanna show ya somethin'."

"Oh, you do, do you?" Annabelle muttered beneath her breath. "Wonder what that could be."

She headed in the direction from which the voice had come, practically directly ahead of her now, maybe thirty, forty feet down the slope. That she was being lured into a trap, there could be no question. Hunter had always told her that her red-headed anger would get the best of her one day. Maybe he'd been right.

On the other hand, the open mockery in the voice of the man trying to lure her into the trap could not be denied. She imagined shooting him, and the thought stretched her rich, red lips back from her perfect, white teeth in a savage smile.

She took one step, then another . . . another . . . pausing briefly behind trees, edging cautious looks around them, knowing that she could see the lap of flames from a gun barrel at any second.

"That's it," came the man's voice again. "Just a bit closer, honey. That's it. Keep comin', purty li'l red-headed gal."

"All right," Annabelle said, tightly, loudly enough for the man to hear her now. "But you're gonna regret it, you son of a b—"

She'd smelled the rancid odor of unwashed man and raw whiskey two seconds before she heard the pine needle crunch of a stealthy tread behind her. She froze as a man's body pressed against her from behind. Just as the man started to wrap his arm around her, intending to close his hand over her mouth, Annabelle ducked and swung around, swinging the carbine, as well—and rammed the butt into her would-be assailant's solar plexus.

The man gave a great exhalation of whiskey-soaked breath, and folded.

Annabelle turned further and rammed her right knee into the man's face. She felt the wetness of blood on her knee from the man's exploding nose. He gave a wheezy, *"Mercy!"* as he fell straight back against the ground and lay moaning and writhing.

Knowing she was about to have lead sent her way,

Annabelle threw herself to her left and rolled. Sure enough, the rifle of the man on the slope below thundered once, twice, three times, the bullets caroming through the air where Annabelle had been a second before. The man whom she'd taken to the proverbial woodshed howled, apparently having taken one of the bullets meant for her.

Annabelle rolled onto her belly and aimed the carbine straight out before her. She'd seen the flash of the second man's rifle, and she aimed toward them now, sending three quick shots their way. The second shooter howled. Annabelle heard the heavy thud as he struck the ground.

"*Gallblastit!*" he cried. "You like to shot my dang ear off, you wicked, red-haired bitch!"

"What happened to 'purty li'l red-haired gal'?" Annabelle spat out as she shoved to her feet and righted her Stetson.

She heard the second shooter thrashing around down the slope, jostling the branches of an evergreen shrub. He gave another cry, and then Annabelle could hear him running in a shambling fashion downhill.

"Oh, you're running away from the 'purty li'l red-haired gal,' now, tough guy?"

Anna strode after him, following the sounds of his shambling retreat.

She pushed through the shrubs and saw his shadow moving downhill, holding a hand to his right ear, groaning. He'd left his rifle up where Anna had shot him. "Turn around or take it in the back, tough guy," she said, following him, taking long, purposeful strides.

"You're crazy!" the man cried, casting a fearful glance behind him. "What'd you do to H.J.?"

"What I started, you finished."

"He's my cousin!"

"*Was* your cousin."

He gave another sobbing cry as he continued running

so awkwardly that Anna, walking, steadily gained on him as she held the carbine down low against her right leg.

"You're just a bitch is what you are!"

"You were after our horses, I take it?"

The man only sobbed again.

"How'd you get on our trail?"

"Seen you passin' wide around Lusk," the man said, breathless, grunting. "We was huntin' antelope on the ridge."

"Market hunters?"

"Fer a woodcuttin' crew."

"Ah. You figured you'd make more money selling my and my husband's horses. At least you have a good eye for horse flesh."

The man gained the bottom of the ridge. He stopped and turned to see Anna moving within twenty feet of him, gaining on him steadily—a tall, slender, well-put-together young lady outfitted in men's trail gear, though, judging by all her curves in all the right places, she was all woman. He gave another wail, sunlight glinting in his wide, terrified eyes, then swung around and ran into the creek, the water splashing like quicksilver up around his knees.

He'd likely never been stalked by a woman before. Especially no "purty li'l red-headed gal."

Anna followed the coward into the creek. "What's your name?"

"Oh, go to hell!"

"What's your name?"

He shot another silver-eyed gaze back over his shoulder. "Wally. Leave me be. I'm in major pain here!"

Now that Anna was closing on him, she could see the man was tall and slender, mid- to late-twenties, with long, stringy hair brushing his shoulders while the top of his head was bald. He had small, mean eyes and now as he turned to face her, he lowered his bloody right hand to the pistol bristling on his right hip.

"You stop there, now," he warned, stretching his lips back from his teeth in pain. "You stop there. I'm done. Finished. You go on back to your camp!"

Anna stopped ten feet away from him. She rested the Winchester on her shoulder. "You know what happens to rustlers in these parts—don't you, Wally?"

He thrust his left arm and index finger out at her. "N-now, you ain't gonna hang me. You done blowed my ear off!" Wally slid the old Smith & Wesson from its holster and held it straight down against his right leg. "Besides, you're a woman. Women don't behave like that!"

He clicked the Smithy's hammer back.

"You're right—we don't behave like that. Not even we 'purty li'l red-headed gals'!" Anna racked a fresh round into the carbine's action, raised the rifle to her shoulder, and grinned coldly. "Why waste the hemp on vermin like you, Wally?"

Wally's little eyes grew wide in terror as he jerked his pistol up. "Don't you—!"

"We just shoot 'em!" Anna said.

And shot him.

Wally flew back into the creek with a splash. He went under and bobbed to the surface, arms and legs spread wide. Slowly, the current carried him downstream.

Anna heard running footsteps and a man's raking breaths behind her. She swung around, bringing the carbine up again, ready to shoot, but held fire when she saw the big, broad-shouldered man in the gray Stetson, buckskin tunic, and denims running toward her, the coyote running just ahead.

"Anna!" Hunter yelled. "Are you all right, honey?"

He and Bobby stopped at the edge of the stream. Both their gazes caught on the man bobbing downstream, and Hunter shuttled his incredulous gaze back to his wife. Raking deep breaths, he hooked a thumb over his shoul-

der. "Saw the other man up the hill. Dead as a post."
Hunter Buchanon planted his fists on his hips and
scowled his reproof at his young wife. "I told you to stay
at the camp!"

Anna strode back out of the stream. She stopped before her husband, who was a whole head taller than she.
"We purty li'l red-headed gals just need us a little blood-
letting once in a while. Sort of like bleeding the sap off a
tree."

She grinned, rose up on her toes to kiss Hunter's lips
then ticked the brim of his hat with her right index finger
and started walking back toward the camp and the horses.
"Come on, Bobby Lee," she said. "I'll race ya!"

Chapter 2

The next day, late in the afternoon, Hunter had a strange sense of foreboding as he rode into the Arapaho Creek headquarters.

He stopped his horse just inside the wooden portal in the overhead crossbar of which the Arapaho Creek brand—A/C—had been burned. He curvetted his fine grullo stallion, Nasty Pete, and took a quick study of the place.

The house sat off to the right and just ahead of him—a large, two-and-a-half story stone-and-log affair. A large, fieldstone hearth ran up the lodge's near wall shaded by a large, dusty cottonwood, its leaves flashing silver in the breeze blowing in from the bastion of the Rocky Mountain Front Range rising in the west. A couple of log barns and a stable as well as a windmill and blacksmith shop sat ahead on Hunter's left, beyond a large corral.

The wooden blades of the windmill creaked in the wind, and that hot, dry, vagrant breeze kicked up finely churned dirt and horse apples in the yard just ahead of him; they made a mini, short-lived tornado out of them. The breeze brought to Hunter's nostrils the pungent tang of sage and horse manure.

Likely impressive at one time, the place had a time-worn look. Brush grew up around the house and most of the outbuildings. Rusted tin wash tubs hung from nails in the front wall of the bunkhouse. Also, there were few men working around the headquarters. Hunter spotted only four. Only one was actually working. A big, burly man in a leather apron, likely the blacksmith, was greasing the axle of a dilapidated supply wagon, the A/C brand painted on both sides badly faded.

One man sat on the corral fence to Hunter's left, rolling a sharpened matchstick from one corner of his mouth to the other with a desultory air. Two others sat outside the bunkhouse between the stable and the windmill, strad-dling a bench and playing two-handed poker.

Of course, most of the hands could be out on the range, tending the herds, but Hunter had spied few cattle after he, Annabelle, and the ten horses they would sell here, had ridden onto Navajo Creek graze roughly twenty miles north of Denver, near a little town called Javelina. The graze itself was sparse. It was a motley looking coun-try under a broad, blue bowl of sky from which the sun hammered down relentlessly.

It was all bunch grass and sage, a few cedars here and there peppering low, chalky buttes and meandering, dry arroyos. It was, indeed, a big, broad, open country with damn few trees, the First Front of the Rocky Mountains cropping up in the west, some of the highest peaks show-ing the ermine of the previous winter's snow. This dry, dun brown country lay in grim contrast to those high, for-midable ridges that bespoke deep, lush pine forests and roaring creeks and rivers.

What also appeared odd was that three of the four men

Hunter could see appeared old. Late fifties to mid-sixties. Only the man sitting with his boot heels hooked over a corral slat to Hunter's left appeared under forty. He regarded Hunter blandly from beneath the weathered, funneled bridge of his once-cream Stetson that was now, after enduring much sun, wind, rain, and hail of this harsh country—a washed-out yellow.

The man slid his gaze from Hunter to the main house and said, tonelessly, "Looks like the hosses are here, boss."

Hunter followed the man's gaze toward where an old man with thin gray, curly hair and a long, gray tangle of beard stood on the house's front porch. He had to be somewhere in his late-sixties—hard-earned years, judging by the man's slump and general air of fragility.

He appeared to be carrying a great weight and was damned weary of it. He wore wash-worn, broadcloth trousers, a thin cream longhandle top, and suspenders. He squinted at Hunter, his bony features long and drawn. He looked as though he might have just woken from a nap.

"Hunter Buchanon?" the man called raspily.

"Rufus Scanlon?" Hunter countered.

The man dipped his chin, his long beard brushing his flat, bony chest.

"We have the horses up on the ridge," Hunter said, hooking a thumb to indicate the low, pine-peppered ridge behind him. "I rode down to see if you were ready for 'em."

He glanced into the corral where only three horses stood still as stone save switching their tails at flies, hangheaded, regarding the newcomer dubiously.

The man beckoned broadly with a thin arm; his lips spread an eager smile, giving sudden life to the otherwise lifeless tangle of beard. "Bring 'em on down!"

Hunter glanced around the yard once more. He was

selling his prized horses for two hundred apiece. He had a hard time reconciling such a price with such a humble looking headquarters. He hoped he and Anna hadn't ridden all this way for nothing.

"All right, then," he said.

He neck-reined Nasty Pete around and galloped back out through the portal. He followed the trail across Navajo Creek and up to the crest of the ridge where Anna was holding the horses in scattered pines. They stood spread out, calmly grazing, Anna sitting her calico mare, Ruthie, among them.

When they'd stopped here on the ridge, Bobby Lee had disappeared. Likely sensing they'd come to the end of the trail, the coyote had lit out on a rabbit or gopher hunt. Seeing Hunter, Anna booted the mare over to him, frowning incredulously beneath the brim of her dark green Stetson, its horsehair thong drawn up securely beneath her chin. The Rocky Mountain sun glinted fetchingly in her deep red hair.

"What is it?" she asked, the mare nuzzling Nasty Pete with teasing affection.

"What's what?"

"I know that look. What's wrong?"

Hunter shrugged and leaned forward against his saddle horn. "Not sure. Humble place, the Navajo Creek. Doesn't look like the kind of outfit that can afford these hosses. I told Scanlon in my letter that this was a cash deal only. That's two thousand dollars. Just a might skeptical that old man down there has two thousand dollars laying around, lonely an' in need of a home." The big ex-Confederate gave his wife a pointed look. "I'll guaran-damn-tee you, though, I'm not goin' home without the cash he agreed to pay or without the horses he agreed to buy if he can't buy 'em!"

"You should've had him put cash down."

"Yeah, well, I've never had to do that before."

"That's because you've always known the men you were selling to."

Hunter sighed and raked a thumb through a two-day growth of blond beard stubble. "I gotta admit I ain't the shrewdest businessman."

"No, you're not. You're a simple, honest ex-rebel from Georgia." Anna sidled Ruthie up next to Nasty Pete, thumbed Hunter's hat up on his forehead, and kissed him. "And that's why this Yankee girl loves you. Not sure I could've fallen in love with a shrewd businessman. My father was one of those."

Hunter smiled.

Annabelle frowned with sudden concern. "You don't think he might try to take them from us, do you? The horses."

Hunter shook his head. "Doesn't seem the type. Besides, not enough men around, and those who are, all but one, don't look like they could raise a hogleg. Nah, he's probably one of those tight Yankees who let his place go to pot because he was too cheap to hire the men to keep it up. He probably has a mattress stuffed with money somewhere in that old house. He's likely ready to spend some of that cash on horses, maybe try to build up his own remuda. Hope so, anyways." Hunter glanced around, again seeing no sign of a herd. "Looks like he might be out of the cattle business."

Anna straightened in her saddle. "Let's go see. With any luck, we'll be in Javelina by sundown, flush as railroad magnates and sitting down to a big surrounding of steak and beans!"

"Mrs. Buchanon, you are indeed a lady after my own heart."

"Oh, I think you've known for a while now that you have that, dear heart." Anna narrowed an eye at him and hooked her mouth in a crooked smile, jade eyes shimmering in the late afternoon light. "Lock, stock, and barrel!" She started to rein her calico around, saying, "Let's go drive these broomtails down to—"

Hunter touched her arm. "Hold on."

She turned back to him, frowning. "What is it?"

"Whatever happens down there." He gave her a commanding look and jerked his chin to indicate the humble headquarters at the base of the ridge. "Don't go off half-cocked like you did last night."

"Oh, I went off fully cocked last night, dear heart."

"Anna!"

But she'd already reined away from him and was working Ruthie around to the far side of the herd.

Hunter stared after her, shaking his head in frustration. But wasn't it his own damn fault—letting himself tumble for a fiery Yankee girl, a redhead spawned and reared by the equally stubborn and warrior-like Yankee Black Hills Rancher, Graham Ludlow, who'd become Hunter's blood enemy when the man had tried to keep his prized daughter from marrying into the Confederate Buchanon family?

In fact, the two families had nearly destroyed each other in the feud that had followed.

But after the smoke and dust had cleared, Hunter had found himself with the prize he'd lost two brothers, and nearly his father, old Angus, in winning. Annabelle's father had been ruined, his ranch, nearly reduced to ashes, now defunct. All for Hunter had so unnecessarily nearly been lost. Hunter had to admit, as he watched Anna now, expertly working the mustangs, that she'd been worth it.

If anything had, she had . . .

He chuckled wryly. "You romantic fool, Buchanon."

He rode out and joined his young wife in gathering the herd and hazing them on down the trail, across the creek, and into the Navajo Creek headquarters, where the man who'd been sitting on the corral fence stood holding the gate wide. When Hunter and Anna had all the horses inside the corral, obscured by a heavy cloud of roiling, sunlit dust, Rufus Scanlon strode over from the main lodge, grinning again inside the tangle of beard.

He wore a corduroy jacket over his underwear top—a concession to having guests, especially one of the female variety, Hunter silently opined—and rested his bony arms on the top corral slat, inspecting his new remuda.

"Nice, nice," he said, blinking against the dust. "Say that brown and white pinto looks to have some Spanish blood. Look at the fire in his eyes!"

Hunter and Anna sat their horses behind him.

"Most of these do," Hunter said, surveying the fine-looking remuda, all ten stallions stomping around, skirmishing, nosing the air, getting the lay of the new land. A lineback dun tried to mount a steel-dust with a long, black snout and black tail and nearly got into a fight for his trouble. Others gazed off into the distance, wild-eyed, wanting to be free once more. "Some very old bloodlines in this string. Old Spanish an' Injun blood. You'll have some good breeders here, Mister Scanlon. Get you a coupla fine mares, an' you'll have one hell of a remuda."

"Were they hard to break?"

"Oh, they're not broke," Hunter said with a dry chuckle. "Do they look broke to you? Nah, their spirits are intact. But you try to throw a saddle on any of the ten, an' they'll give you no trouble. Now, when you try to mount . . ."

"That's when you'll have trouble," Anna cut in. "They'll test any one of your riders"—she grinned beautifully, gazing at the herd fondly and with a sadness at the thought of parting with them—"just to make sure they're man enough."

"Or woman enough?"

Hunter turned to see a young woman striding over from the main house—a well setup brunette in a white blouse and long, black wool skirt and riding boots. She took long, lunging strides, chin in the air, a glowing smile on her classically beautiful face.

Her hair hung messily down about her shoulders, blowing back in the wind, strands catching at the corners of her mouth. She was olive-skinned, likely betraying some Spanish blood of her own, and there was a wild clarity and untethered delight in her eyes as brown as a mountain stream late in the day—as late as the day was getting now, in fact.

"Or, yeah," Anna said uncertainly, cutting a territorial glance at Hunter whom she'd no doubt spied eyeing the newcomer with keen male interest, "woman enough. Even gentled, they'll throw you for sure if they sense you're afraid of them." She glanced at Scanlon who stood packing a pipe he'd produced from the breast pocket of his worn corduroy jacket. "Who's this, Mr. Scanlon? The lady of the house?"

Scanlon merely chuckled as though at a private joke, eyes slitted, as he fired a match to life on his thumbnail and touched the flame to the pipe bowl.

"Lucinda Scanlon," said the young lady, somewhere in her early twenties, Hunter judged while trying not to scrutinize her too closely, knowing he was under his wife's watchful eye. She extended a hand to Anna. "The lady of the house and the whole damn range!" Chuckling, she added, "Pleased to meet you . . . Mrs. Buchanon, I assume?"

"Annabelle," Anna said, returning the young lady's shake, regarding her dubiously, as though a wildcat—tame or untamed, was yet to be determined—had so unexpectedly entered the conversation.

"Annabelle, of course," said Lucinda Scanlon, casting Anna a broad, warm smile before turning to Hunter whom she also offered a firm handshake and welcoming smile. Her eyes were not only as brown as a mountain creek but as deep as any lake up high in the Rockies, Hunter found himself noting. "And you're Mr. Buchanon."

"Hunter." He felt a sudden restriction in his throat at this sudden newcomer's obvious charms and forthright, refined, open, and friendly manner. Appearing so suddenly out of nowhere here at this humble, going-to-seed headquarters, she was definitely a diamond in the rough. A bluebird in a flock of crows.

"Indeed, Hunter. I enjoyed your letters describing the remuda."

"Well, uh," Hunter said, hiking a shoulder in chagrin. "Anna helped me with it. I can ride all day, but I ain't . . . *haven't* . . . exactly perfected my sentences." He chuckled self-consciously. "Letters but not always my sentences."

Annabelle cut him a sharp look as though silently throwing a loop over his head and reining him in. He realized he'd removed his hat and quickly donned it.

Scanlon saw the interplay and laughed.

Visit our website at
KensingtonBooks.com
to sign up for our newsletters, read
more from your favorite authors, see
books by series, view reading group
guides, and more!

Become a Part of Our
Between the Chapters Book Club
Community and Join the Conversation

Betweenthechapters.net